Perfume River Nights

Perfume River Nights

A Novel

by

Michael P. Maurer

NORTH STAR PRESS OF ST. CLOUD, INC.
St. Cloud, Minnesota

Quotation from *The Hero With A Thousand Faces* by Joseph Campbell, copyright © 2008; used with permission of Joseph Campbell Foundation (jcf.org).

ISBN: 978-1-68201-021-1

Printed in the United States of America.

First edition: May 2016

Published by
North Star Press of St. Cloud, Inc.
P.O. Box 451
St. Cloud, MN 56302

www.northstarpress.com

All royalties from sales of this book are dedicated to the Vietnam Veterans Memorial Fund.

For those unable to tell their stories.

Where we had thought to slay another,
we shall slay ourselves.

Joseph Campbell
The Hero With A Thousand Faces

1

In the predawn at Pope Air Force Base next to Fort Bragg, North Carolina, Rhymes helped Singer pack his M16, strap on his parachutes, and hang his kit bag with his combat field equipment. Nearby, the other men of Charlie Company's fourth platoon were getting ready for the parachute assault that would involve more than six hundred paratroopers from the 82nd Airborne Division.

Rhymes circled Singer, tugging at the gear, white teeth gleaming from his coal-black face. "Looks good." Rhymes came around to face him. "You okay, Singer?"

"Yeah," Singer said, even though he wasn't sure. He was still getting used to everything, including his name. They all had their nicknames, carryovers from past units or their Nam days. While he hadn't been to Vietnam yet like most of them, he felt a measure of acceptance and was pleased when everyone started calling him by a unit name. Singer. That's how Jimmy thought of himself now.

"It's just like jump school," Rhymes said. "Just remember to drop your kit bag before you hit the ground."

Singer patted his kit bag. "Got it."

"I'm right behind you. Don't worry."

"I'm not, except I never jumped with equipment before. The rifle pack's awkward."

"We're going to bust some Cherries today," Shooter said. He slapped Singer's helmet as he moved past, striding as though he wasn't carrying any gear, showing the slight catch in his left leg that was always there.

Rhymes waited until Shooter was some distance away. "Just get out of the plane. After that it won't matter. We'll probably get separated on the jump, but you know the rally point, right?"

"Right."

"Stick with me."

"Airborne." Singer's affirmation was softer than he intended.

"All the way."

They assembled at the order of Sergeant Edwards, the acting platoon leader, and shuffled up the ramp of a plane more than halfway back in a long line of C-130s, feeling the airstream of idling engines. The ramp raised slowly, shutting out the growing dawn and dampening the engine noise as it clamped shut and locked in place. Even before they lifted off, Rhymes took a book from inside his shirt, caught the bookmark in his left hand, and held the open pages up near his face.

Climbing, the plane lurched. Singer's nervous stomach rose in his throat and he clenched his teeth and swallowed down his fear. He touched the pack that encased his M16. His other hand clutched his reserve parachute, which he hoped he wouldn't need. He tried to steady his breathing, not think about what was coming.

His kit bag rested heavily on his lap. His main parachute pushed against his back as he sat on a fold-down jump seat along the plane's wall, tightly packed with the rest of the men of fourth platoon. The droning noise of the C-130's four wing-mounted prop engines filled the fuselage, making it difficult to hear, so most of them stayed silent.

The ninety-minute flight to their Florida drop zone allowed plenty of time to worry. Besides being his first combat equipment jump, it would be Singer's first combat field exercise. He checked his watch and was surprised how little time had passed since he last looked. With some difficulty, he leaned forward and looked up and down the plane. Bear's head was slumped to the side, his eyes closed. His snoring competed with the engine noise. His large black hands hung relaxed atop his kit bag, long fingers dangling like huge worms. Beside him, Red sat with his freckles and choirboy face, placid-looking. His lips were pursed as though he might be humming. Singer had seen him sitting perfectly still, cross-legged on his bunk, hands cupped in his lap repeating the same tone again and again. Ghost, the guy with caramel skin and features that reminded Singer of a mouse, sat dwarfed by Bear, his head bowed and small hands folded as if in prayer.

Singer sat back and kneaded his hands, pulling at each finger. On his left, Trip held the blade of a small knife in rough hands scarred by past labors, working at his fingernails, the tip of his tongue protruding from the corner of his mouth. On his right, Rhymes turned a page and pressed his face inches from the text. Singer studied his watch again, tapping on the dial.

The butterflies were there as they'd been each jump before, maybe a little worse. He was new to the unit, to these guys, and he wanted to show them they could count on him. Mostly, he didn't want to fuck up. Once more he thought about the details of the briefing and what he needed to do once he was on the ground. He knew the others would be watching, judging him.

Just a few weeks before, two months after his eighteenth birthday, he'd finished jump school, drew his orders, and reported to Fort Bragg. His high school days in Minnesota and life before already seemed far in the distance. His brother's indictment of his enlistment and the war were almost forgotten, along with his mother's distress at his not going to college. Times he chased through the woods below the house with his dog, Duke, seemed a lifetime ago. Abandoning Duke had been harder than he expected, but the ache had faded. Only leaving his girlfriend, Susan, was still recent and raw. Once she stopped crying, she promised she would wait. Right now, this was more important. His ex-girlfriend, Kathy, was the one person who understood his desire to be a paratrooper and his need to prove himself in combat. She'd even cheered him on, telling him how good he'd look coming home a hero. He never remembered why they broke up.

He slipped his hand inside his harness straps and touched the jump wings sown to his fatigues just above the left pocket. After he graduated from jump school at Fort Benning, Georgia, he had them sewn on all his fatigues. A paratrooper's badge. You had to volunteer to be a paratrooper and he believed that created a bond stronger than in other units. He turned his head to see the patch on his left shoulder, running his fingers over it, feeling the stitching. Airborne above double "A"s for All-American. The insignia of the 82nd Airborne Division. He was one of them now. Like his father had been. His father, he was sure, would be proud of him, if he were still alive.

Trip looked up at Singer, gave a tight-lipped smile, and shook his head.

Across the aisle from Singer some men dozed, their heads bobbing. Others gazed at the ceiling and the cables that ran the length of the plane. Would he ever be able to relax enough that he could sleep en route to a jump? He doubted it. Shooter smiled, perhaps knowing what he was thinking. Or it might have been a growl. Shooter touched his reserve and rolled his head back, mouth open in a laugh that Singer couldn't hear. A joke he didn't understand. Near Shooter, Stick, another new guy who reported the same day as he had, sat looking pale, shifting in his seat.

At the end of the line was Sergeant Milner, the acting platoon sergeant who Rhymes had told him to avoid and who Bear had said to just ignore. Though that was hard to do with the man's voice like a faulty siren, somewhere between a scream and a wail. The first time Singer heard it, he figured it could set dogs to howling. Bear said the man was a clerk who got sent to the infantry after an administrative fuck-up. What kind of screw-up could send an overweight staff sergeant to the infantry? Rhymes was kinder in saying Sergeant Milner transferred in to advance a stagnant career. Both agreed the man was dangerous. Sergeant Milner looked alone even in a line of men. His black face shiny with sweat. His eyes blinking. White strobes.

"Ten minutes!" Sergeant Edwards yelled.

"Ten minutes," men repeated.

Rhymes closed his book and shoved it down inside his shirt. Trip folded his knife and slid it into his pocket. One long nasal groan came from Bear, then his snoring stopped. Men lifted their heads and brought their feet square under them. A few rubbed their eyes and some checked their helmet straps. Singer touched his reserve with both hands, then his kit bag and rifle pack. He just had to follow Trip out. Rhymes would be right behind. Spanish words, a litany in Ghost's voice, grew in volume and then went silent.

Every face was turned to the back, where Sergeant Edwards stood between the still-closed doors. His feet were braced, making him look taller than he was. His eyes showed a hardness Singer hadn't noticed at the barracks or parade ground. Another sergeant, white and taller, stood behind him, closer to the right-hand door.

When Rhymes's feet shifted, Singer leaned, pushing against his load.

"Not yet," Rhymes said. Then he grinned. He looked like he was having fun.

Singer settled back, swallowed, and grit his teeth together hard. He hadn't been sick on any training jump and he wasn't starting now.

"Stand up," Sergeant Edwards yelled while raising his hands in the "stand-up" command.

"Stand up," men repeated.

The lines rose on both sides of the plane and faced back toward the doors. Singer struggled to his feet, wedged between Trip and Rhymes.

"Just a few more of these," Trip said, then looked at Singer and laughed.

Behind him, Singer could feel Rhymes's reserve and the pressure of the line of men each pushing against the next, but there was nowhere to go until the doors opened. Events and the men behind him would carry him forward despite the weakness in his stomach and the knot growing in his throat.

"Hookup," Sergeant Edwards yelled, pumping his fist with a hooked finger above it.

"Hookup," Singer said in one voice with the men around him, snapping his static line that would deploy his chute to the cable overhead. On command, he checked his static line and the parachute and the lines on Trip's back as Rhymes inspected his. Shouts of "okay" rolled forward from the back of the line.

The engine pitch changed, the roar softening as the plane throttled back to a slower jump speed. The decent to the 800-foot jump height was nearly imperceptible. Still, Singer felt it and his stomach went with it. The low-altitude jump meant less time suspended from a chute exposed to enemy fire. It also meant little time to react if anything went wrong. Singer touched his free hand to his reserve chute, said a silent prayer.

Air rushed through the cabin with the opening of the doors, filling the world with a roar that made it hard to even think. A red light glowed beside each door. Blue filled the newly opened space, but in the absence of clouds or a horizon it was a constant blue with no hint of speed or even of movement. Sergeant Edwards, as jumpmaster, and the Safety at the other door leaned out into the slipstream to check to see the rear was clear.

Singer squinted at the rush of air that would come and tugged a finger in his chin strap. The line of men tightened, pushing harder at Singer's back. He shuffled his feet to hold his balance. He wished he could turn and see Rhymes's reassuring smile.

The line shuffled forward, Singer swept up in the tide, not even sure his feet were moving. The door light was green. He hadn't seen the light change or the first man go, though he was sure he had been watching.

"Go! Go! Go!" Sergeant Edwards was yelling.

One man disappeared, then another. And another. Trip was gone. He saw the open door, let go of his static line, expansive blue, blur of the horizon, his mouth too tight to allow a smile, barely slapped his fingers against the fuselage before he was swept away in a powerful blast of air, tumbling.

"One thousand, two thousand, three thousand . . ." Singer began the count as soon as he was out the door, measuring time, waiting for his static line to deploy his chute and the chute to catch. If his main chute failed to deploy, he would have a second, maybe two, to cut it away and deploy his reserve. At "four thousand" his main chute was out, ballooned, and caught air. It ripped him violently upward by his harness as though some giant hand was trying to tear him from the sky. Singer quickly looked up. Only after he saw the full, intact canopy did he relax and smile. But jumping from so low, there was no time to enjoy the scene or the sense of floating.

There was no gunfire, only the drone of planes still passing through and then away from the landing zone. He swiveled his head, thinking to find Rhymes or Trip or anyone he knew, but in the sea of white canopies around him it was impossible to identify anyone.

The ground was close and rushing toward him. He saw a blur of activity of men gathering chutes and equipment, running in all directions from the tree-rimmed field. He let out a breath and set his eyes to the horizon to prepare. He could feel the ground coming more than see it. At the last second he remembered to release his kit bag. It dropped, pulling heavily when it hit the end of its line. Then the line went slack as the ground and kit bag met. Singer quickly grabbed his downwind risers, pulling down strong, dumping air. He hit hard and rolled even before he thought to keep his legs together and curl his body. His left side and shoulder slammed into the ground. He was dragged a short way on his back before he could slap the releases and cut loose his chute, and it was whipped away in the strong breeze.

He was down. It wasn't pretty, but there was nothing broken. He stood up, grinning. For a moment he couldn't help but stand there and take in the scene of planes and chutes, men coming into the drop zone under white canopies. It was an impressive sight beyond any jump school scene, one that until now he had only imagined.

In the distant treeline he made out fourth platoon's rallying point and men already running in that direction. Still no ground fire from enemy forces, played by another Fort Bragg unit. Apparently they were going to let them get on the ground and organized before the action started. After he hurried out of his harness, he put on his gear from his kit bag, grabbed his M16, and was off running. He ran hard, his rifle in both hands and carried high across his chest, swinging back and forth with each step. It felt almost effortless.

Something slapped his back. He stumbled forward, nearly losing his balance.

"Good shit. Huh?"

Bear ran beside him. In his hands his M16 looked like a toy.

"Great. That was cool, jumping with my rifle and—"

"New guys." Bear gave a deep booming laugh like thunder. "This is just a game, man. Pretend shit. Just wait." He clasped Singer's shoulder. "Just wait."

Bear slowed to a walk. Singer slowed beside him, held back by Bear's hand. "No need to hurry. It's just playacting." Bear's face tightened and he spoke through nearly closed lips, "I done the real thing, and it ain't nothing like this."

"Get moving, soldiers!" That grating voice. "Get moving!"

Singer started jogging before looking back to see Sergeant Milner catching up to Bear, who was still strolling casually.

"Shiiit, Sarge," Bear said, drawing out "shit" like a groan. "I'm going home soon."

"You and most of the unit, but you ain't home yet. So move it."

"When you go home, Sarge?" Bear asked as he started to jog.

"Move it, goddamn it!"

Bear snorted. "Man, I'll be home before this exercise is over, while you just going to the Nam."

Singer stretched his legs, gaining speed, leaving Bear loping and laughing behind him. He looked down at the wings on his chest and pushed harder, his grin widening with each stride. His pack and web gear bounced, and he rowed the air with his M16. When he reached the trees where the guys were gathered, he eased up as though crossing a finish line.

The sky was clear of chutes, the drop zone growing quiet with the last C-130 barely visible. A few soldiers still ran from the drop zone while others were chasing down and gathering the last of the chutes. Bear looked to be the last coming their way, taking his time, Sergeant Milner snapping at his heels.

"Still alive, Singer?" Shooter pointed deeper into the forest. "Your man's over there."

Singer walked past trees the size of pillars with deep green foliage that seemed too full for January, though he knew nothing of Florida and its vegetation. Tall grass grew under the trees and in scattered openings bathed in intense sunlight. He was already sweating. The men were spread around in a loose perimeter. Some knelt, while others stood against trees catching their breath. Only Stick, his face bent down over his rifle, holding tight to a tree, looked serious about the exercise. Most of the others, Nam vets, seemed to have attitudes like Bear's.

Singer found Rhymes standing next to a tree, his M79 hanging in his right hand, pointed at the ground. To his right, Trip stood, weight heavy on one leg, leaning on his M16, the stock butt on the ground, his hand atop the front sight like it was a cane. Further right, Ghost sat his back to a tree, his M16 across his outstretched legs, hands resting on the ground. His head leaned back, mouth slightly agape, eyelids all but closed.

Singer jogged the last few steps and knelt down in a space between Rhymes and Trip, looking out into a sea of massive tree trunks. After checking his flash suppressor, his magazine loaded with blanks, he aimed out at imaginary targets.

"Good you could join us," Trip said.

"I got distracted by all the planes and chutes. I've never seen anything like it."

"In the 1st Cavalry we would have left you."

"That's what I've heard." Bear sauntered up, carrying his rifle one-handed.

"What?" Trip turned and tilted back his head.

"That the Cav left guys. All show and no go."

"Better than the Puking Buzzards any day," Trip said, looking at Bear's 101st Airborne patch on his right shoulder.

"We never left guys behind, not even guys like you."

"Shit, the Cav went places no one else would go."

"Airmobile still ain't airborne."

"Ever hear of the Ia Drang?"

"Heard the Cav got their ass kicked there. Almost sent us to save you."

"Fuck you."

Rhymes rose and moved to step between them.

But Bear opened his mouth and let out a laugh that had his chest and arms shaking.

Boom! Boom! Boom! Three sharp explosions sounded from a couple hundred yards ahead. Trip dropped to the ground, his rifle in both hands. Rhymes spun toward the sound. Singer went flat.

Bear only laughed, shorter, sharper than before. "It's just part of the game to make things more real. Man, you all take this stuff so serious. Don't matter no more, we all going home. Well, except Singer and the fat ex-clerk."

Then Bear shuffled over toward Ghost, who hadn't opened his eyes.

"It okay." Rhymes said to Singer. "Take that better cover over there. Always take the best cover you can find. Relax. There's no prize or penalty today."

Singer shifted to the tree on Rhymes's left. "I heard the second platoon's lieutenant yelling at them all week. He sounded like it was serious."

"Lieutenant Creely. He's just worried about his career. He wants to make captain, have his own company. Good exercise, good performance report, faster rank. He's trying to impress the general, his future father-in-law."

"Really? The general's daughter? We should be wired, then."

"That kind of pressure is hard to live with. Be thankful you're not in his platoon. Nothing in this for us. Just a few days camping and playing war games most of us have seen enough of. Couple days of snakes and Cs and we'll be back at the barrack again with hot showers and grub. Just take it easy. Remember, it's a game. Be a while before you see the real thing."

The real thing. Singer nodded.

A strong breeze that wound through the trees and cooled the back of Singer's neck carried Sergeant Edwards's voice as he briefed the squad leaders.

". . . if you or any of your men are killed, report to the company CP and stay there throughout the remainder of the exercise. Most of your men have been to Nam and are just waiting to go home. Still, I expect a good effort from everyone. Sergeant Royce, Sergeant Prascanni, look after your new guys. See that they learn this. It'll help keep them alive when they're sent to Nam. Okay. Let's go."

"Okay. Let's go." Sergeant Milner said, but it sounded uncertain, a poor impersonation of command.

Sergeant Royce approached his squad with his bull-legged swagger. He looked sober today. He stopped in front of them and stood there silent too long, as though he'd forgotten what he was going to say. Singer waited, imagining there was a bottle in his pack.

"Rhymes, keep an eye on Singer," Sergeant Royce said.

It looked like he intended to say more but then he caught sight of a sleeping form.

"Ghost. Goddamn it, Ghost! Get up, for Christ's sake, and look like a soldier. Try not to fuck up today. Move out behind second squad."

He turned to Bear. "See he doesn't sleep again."

Bear shrugged. "We're lucky when he shows up."

Ghost climbed slowly to his feet, extending his full five-and-a-half-foot height. "Fuck this. Why after surviving Nam do I still have to play these fucking games?"

No one offered any answer. Sergeant Royce ignored him or didn't hear as he moved away. The squad formed a loose, staggered line within the platoon column. Far ahead, the line started off, moving among the trees.

More explosions boomed much farther off to the right. This time no men went down and Trip barely flinched. "Fuck," someone said, the point of the curse unclear.

"Turn around," Rhymes said. "Let me check your ruck."

Singer turned and felt the pull at his pack.

"Hold still. I'll tie this up so it doesn't rattle." Rhymes slapped Singer's shoulder. "Okay. Just follow me. Keep me in sight, don't lose me. Trip's got your back."

Singer looked and Trip nodded.

Then they were weaving their way deeper into the Florida forest. The others might have hated it. He guessed he could understand that, they having done a year or more of this. Maybe he would end up never wanting to hike or hunt or camp again like many of them. But right now it was a wonderful adventure. Hiking in the Florida wilderness, a rifle in his hands, a group of guys—some almost friends—around him with the common bond of being paratroopers and volunteers. All this, and he was getting almost one hundred dollars a month, plus now another fifty-five dollars in jump pay. There was no other adventure or test like it. No similar bond among men. He would have paid to do it.

"Okay?" Rhymes turned and asked in a near-whisper.

Singer nodded, sure he hadn't hid his smile.

Rhymes had made it, Trip, Bear, Royce, all of them. Why had they all made it through Vietnam while others had not? Could he learn from them what he needed to know?

* * * * *

After four days of playing war, they went back to barracks life. It hadn't gone so badly. Most of them made it and in the end they captured their objective, a mock enemy camp. Ghost was captured, but Bear said he expected that with the man always running off or sleeping. Sergeant Milner and Stick and another guy in the same squad were "killed." Sergeant Edwards wasn't entirely happy about that, except for maybe being rid of Sergeant Milner for most of the game.

Now they were all back at Bragg washing off the Florida mud and stink. Sergeant Milner, Ghost, Stick, and the other "dead" guy had been returned to the unit and were walking around the barracks in their usual routines, none the worse for wear.

"It was my plan to get captured. That camp had cots and real food. I ain't nobody's fool," Ghost said to no one in particular. No one answered.

Men moved about in various stages of transition to civilian clothes and off-duty activities. Slowly, the barrack's bay was emptying out.

"I need a two-man detail before anybody goes."

The voice ripped across Singer's nerves and he grit his teeth until they settled. He heard some groans and catcalls. Ghost streaked past in the opposite direction from the voice and disappeared behind a bank of lockers, any one of which he could easily hide inside—which he had reportedly done on more than one occasion. After waiting a minute, Singer risked crossing the aisle to where there was no sign of Sergeant Milner. He cut though a line of lockers and was brought up short by the flash of what he'd seen.

Taped inside the open door of Sergeant Royce's locker was a photo. A reclining figure, long bare legs spread apart, dark nest at their meeting. Left hand on her thigh, the right cupping a breast, the left breast bare, slightly sagging, a large, dark nipple. The young woman's head was turned to the side, eyelids half closed, parted wet lips. A look of pain or pleasure.

"Nice, huh?"

"Jesus," Singer spun around to find Sergeant Royce behind him.

Sergeant Royce smirked, showing teeth that might have never seen a dentist. "Best fuck east of the Mississippi. When she wraps those legs . . ."

Singer turned away, chancing the main aisle.

Near the door, Shooter, the platoon sentry, sat shirtless on a foot locker, arms and chest showing time spent in the gym, tattoos on each shoulder. One booted foot was propped up on the locker as he paged through a magazine.

Stick was coming down the hall, head rolling on a long neck, fatigues hanging loose on narrow shoulders, slightly bowed, no chest, arms dangling. Face without color even after days in Florida.

"Damn." Shooter turned the magazine sideways. "That bitch is built like a brick shit house."

Shooter looked up at the sound of scraping boots. "Hey, Stick, wait a minute."

When Stick stopped, Shooter flipped the magazine over and held up the photo of a brunette, all breasts, wearing only a gold chainlink belt that dangled down her thigh. "You ever see anything like this?"

Stick looked at his feet.

"I didn't think so." Shooter closed the magazine. "Tough getting killed on your first exercise."

"I'll do better."

"Sure. Is it true your old man is a one-star?"

"Yeah," Stick's eyes brightened and his back straightened. "34th Armor."

"Damn. A fucking general's son. What the hell are you doing here?"

Stick shrugged.

"Tanks? Your dad want you to go armor, too?"

"No."

"A Leg, huh? What'd he think about you being a paratrooper?"

"He said I'd never make it."

"I guess you showed Daddy, huh?"

Stick's mouth widened, without showing teeth.

"Better not tell him you got killed in your first war games."

"He'd probably laugh."

"Fuck him, you're a paratrooper now. He might be a general, but he's still a Leg." Shooter flipped open the magazine. "Singer, Singer where you going?"

Singer kept walking, ignoring the name that Shooter had given him as though he hadn't learned it.

When Singer got back from the supply room, Shooter had left his sentry's post, along with his magazine. Sergeant Royce was gone, too, his locker closed, the photo shut up in the dark though Singer could still see it and Sergeant Royce's bad-toothed grin talking of the prospects. At his bunk he found Trip sitting in jeans, a t-shirt, and bare feet, picking at his cuticles.

"Aren't you going to town?" Singer asked.

"Fayetteville? Have you been there yet? Bunch of angry vets and short-timers getting drunk, looking for the thrill of combat or wondering why they're alive. Some of them looking to die. New guys or crazy guys made crazier with booze wanting to show how tough they are. Easier to die there than in the Nam. I'm too short for that shit. I'll spend my last few months here on base, out of trouble. Maybe shoot a game of pool. You up to a lesson?"

"Maybe later, I got to polish my boots and brass."

"Be careful if you go to town. Don't go alone, that's just asking for trouble." Then Trip slipped on a pair of tennis shoes with no laces and left.

"Good advice."

Until then, Singer hadn't noticed Rhymes lying on his bunk in OD skivvies, an open book lying facedown on his chest, held with one hand, the other up behind his head, a bicep bulging. A small mat of short, curled black hair grew at the center of his chest.

"Trip's right. Better to go with a group. Someone's always looking for a fight, usually backed by friends. Shooter goes most nights, but stay away from him. Bear already left, but he's not a bad choice. He's big enough to be intimidating and doesn't look for trouble even when he drinks. Still, there's a few white boys down there might take issue with you palling with a black and a few bars you wouldn't be safe in, even with Bear at your side."

"I can skip it. I'm not that hard up for entertainment. What you reading?"

Rhymes swung his feet out and sat up, closed the book after a marker was in place.

"Dante's *The Divine Comedy*. Ever read it?"

Singer shook his head. "I'm not much of a reader."

"It's poetry. A classic. Every time I read it I find something new—"

"You've read it more than once?"

"A couple of times. I've got something shorter if you like poetry."

"That's okay."

But Rhymes was already retrieving a book from his locker. He handed the much thinner book to Singer. "James Weldon Johnson. A black poet from Florida, wrote around the turn of the century. His poem 'The Young Warrior' is about a son's request for his mother to pray that he'll fight well. You can keep it for a while if you want."

Singer leafed through a few pages, then handed the book back to Rhymes. "Thanks, but I probably wouldn't read it. . . . What do you think will happen?"

"What do you mean?" Rhymes asked.

"With me. When I reported, Sergeant Edwards said I wouldn't be here long."

"Yeah, most less than two months. You'll come up on a roster for Nam duty. You'll get a leave, a couple weeks, then report to the West Coast, Oakland Army Base, to ship out to Vietnam with other replacements from around the country. After a week of training at Bien Hoa or Cam Ranh Bay, they'll send you to your unit."

"I'll go alone?"

"From here, anyway. You'll meet guys when you report, but you'll all be going to different units."

"I won't know where I'm going?"

"You get orders for either the 173rd Airborne or the 101st, but it'll depend where they are when you get to Nam, and then what unit needs people.

They can change your orders there. You could go anywhere from the delta to the DMZ."

"Shit. Alone, and a new guy again."

"That's how it is for most." Rhymes slapped Dante against his leg in a soft rhythm.

"Your patch, the wing and sword?"

"The Herd. The 173rd Airborne Division."

"Your Nam unit?"

The tapping stopped. Rhymes gripped the book in both hands. "Yeah."

"What was it like?"

"No one can tell you that."

"Was it hard?"

Rhymes looked away.

"I mean, being brave."

When Rhymes turned back toward Singer, something had changed in his face. He squinted though the light wasn't any brighter, and his jaw was set. He spoke slowly, in nearly a monotone.

"The first months are the most dangerous, those and the last one for different reasons. When you get there, find someone whose made it six months, or four at least. Watch them and pay attention. Don't be careless or too cautious. Bravery is somewhere in between."

Singer started to leave, then tuned back.

"Do you regret going?"

"I regret a lot of things. You will, too."

2

S inger leaned against the wall, his ankles crossed, weight on his left leg, talking softly into the phone.

"Hang up!"

"What the—"

A hand pulled him roughly and spun him around. "Hang up now!"

Singer looked at the two military policemen, both about the same height as him, but one was at least twenty pounds heavier, tightly packed. Their faces were taut with similar scowls. Helmets were pulled low just above hard, challenging eyes. The larger of the two brandished a metal pry bar.

"I got to go . . . I don't know . . . I'm sorry, I—"

The smaller MP yanked the receiver from Singer's hand and with his other hand, reached across and slammed the hook down, cutting the connection.

"Hey? What the fuck? I was talking to my girlfriend."

"You just finished," the MP said, hanging up the handset.

"You can't do this."

"Get out of the way or you'll be in handcuffs."

The larger MP pushed Singer aside, wedged the pry bar behind the phone, and tore it from the wall. Torn wires dangled from a dark hole and crumpled plaster drifted to the floor. Outside, the MP tossed the phone onto a tangled pile of black cases, curled cords, and handsets in the back of a military police jeep. Singer tried to follow out the door to search for another phone, but the smaller MP stepped across and put his hand on Singer's chest.

"No one goes out." The MP settled his other hand on his nightstick.

"Just going to the mess."

"No one goes out."

"What the hell's going on?"

The MP merely glared. Two MPs, sidearms, nightsticks, and pry bar were not good odds. Still, Singer set his feet and clamped his teeth so his jaw hurt. They stood this way for a moment, neither moving nor speaking.

The larger MP opened the door, still holding the pry bar. "Anything wrong? Let's go. I want to get this done. The sentry's coming now."

A third MP took up a post outside the door and struck a formal stance as if he planned to stay. After the smaller MP backed out, Singer turned and ran up worn stairs, two at a time, toward the fourth platoon bay.

"Watch where you're going, Singer." Sergeant Royce held a bottle of Jack Daniels aloft, the remaining whiskey sloshing up the sides. He wore cowboy boots, a checkered shirt, and cologne that reminded Singer of animal smells.

"You can't get out. Something's going on."

"Get out of my way. Mama's waiting." Sergeant Royce pushed past and was gone.

The normalcy of the scene at the top of the stairs brought Singer up short. No MPs. No urgency or signs of any crisis. Sergeant Edwards's door was closed as it always was after a day of training. Rhymes said he drank in there each night and Sergeant Royce often joined him, Jack Daniels being both their favorite. Tonight it seemed he would drink alone.

Sergeant Prascanni's rich bass voice floated from the john, filling the hall. It was the same tune Sergeant Prascanni always sang every time he showered. Only Sergeant Prascanni understood the words. "An Italian love song. The one that won my wife," Sergeant Prascanni had said. "No woman can resist it." The melody was smooth, and Singer could sense the sweetness in the phrases. Tonight it made him think of love and his ended call to Susan. His hands curled into tight balls.

Red walked by, a toilet kit in his left hand, a towel around his waist. A ragged hole of scar tissue high on Red's chest made it hard to look him in the face when he was shirtless. He paused in front of Singer.

"Two more months I'll be sitting in Crosley Field watching my man."

"Right," Singer said, trying to concentrate on Red's blue eyes.

"My dad got first-baseline seats for us, right behind the dugout."

"Great."

Red turned back toward the showers, showing the small pink entrance wound so near the base of his neck Singer wondered how it missed his spine.

Singer found Rhymes at his bunk, applying polish with a wet cotton ball to the toe of one of his jump boots in slow, careful motion.

"How's your girl?" Rhymes asked without looking up.

"Don't know. Fucking MP grabbed the phone from me, hung it up."

Rhymes stopped making circles on the boot toe. "MPs? Here in the barracks?"

Trip came up, stood behind him. Then Bear was there.

"Yeah, I was just talking then these two MPs showed up. Tore out the phone. Said no one can leave."

"Maybe Shooter hit an officer again," Bear said.

"He's done with no more rank to lose," Rhymes said.

"His medals protected him before, will again, I'd bet," Bear said.

"How am I going to call?" Singer asked.

"Probably another knifing in town," Trip said. "They'll search lockers for the blade before we can get out of here."

"Hey man, mine's clean," Bear said. "I don't need to carry here. Shooter and some of those other guys I'm not so sure of."

"I don't like being locked in for anything." Trip said.

"Now there's something we agree on," Bear said.

Rhymes laughed first, then Trip grinned, which started Bear laughing. Only Singer didn't understand what was so funny. Maybe he would have to be here longer before he got every joke.

"I'm not so excited about being stuck here with you guys, either," Rhymes said.

"Hell, you never go out anyway, all you do is read like some damn professor. That poetry shit going to fuck your brain. No man reads poetry. No black man, anyway," Bear said.

"When I get home I'll send you a copy of Vilakazi's poems," Rhymes said.

"What?"

"A black African. A Zulu. You can—"

"Listen up!" Sergeant Edwards's gravelly voice boomed through the bay.

"Here it comes," Trip said.

Lockers slammed shut. Men sat up, swung their legs to the floor, or jumped down from top bunks. Everyone drifted into the center aisle. Singer,

Rhymes, Bear, and Trip shifted toward the voice with the others. Sergeant Prascanni had stopped singing and stood in the hallway, wrapped in a towel and dripping water, along with Red and two other men. Nearby, Sergeant Milner paced.

Sergeant Edwards stood framed in the doorway in freshly starched fatigues and polished jump boots, as if he had dressed for the occasion. His black face had the tightness he had as jumpmaster on last month's training jump. His feet were braced as if he were standing on a bouncing plane. He was silent as men pushed closer and an expectant quiet settled over the group.

Behind him, Sergeant Royce rounded the top of the stairs, cowboy boots clomping. "Damn MPs don't understand. I got to—"

"Not now, Sergeant," Sergeant Edwards said, then turned back to the group gathered in the bay.

Sergeant Royce faded back, brought the bottle of Jack to his mouth, tilted it up.

"Okay, everyone listen up. We're on deployment alert as of now." Sergeant Edwards's eyebrows rose, then settled low over his eyes. He didn't speak again until the murmurs died down.

"Most of you know the drill. An info blackout's been ordered. No one goes out. No calls."

"Jesus," Sergeant Royce said. He dropped his empty hand to his crotch and took another drink.

"Load your stateside issue in your duffel and turn it into supply. Keep only combat gear. New gear will be delivered. New weapons are on the way now. Squad leaders, assign details to unload trucks. The move-out order could come at any time. Be ready."

"Is this an exercise?" someone asked. Heads swung toward the questioner, then back toward Sergeant Edwards.

"We won't know 'til the stand-down order comes. 'Til then, treat it like it's not."

"Where we going, Sarge?" Sergeant Prascanni asked.

"Anywhere's good with me," Shooter said.

"Why we getting new weapons?" a voice asked.

"You'll know when I know. Just be ready," Sergeant Edwards said and walked back down the hall toward his room, carrying Sergeant Royce's bottle of Jack.

"Here we go again," Bear said, rubbing his hip. "Been hurting me all week. Must be going somewhere."

"Shrapnel," Rhymes said after Bear walked away.

"What do you think?" Singer asked.

"This can't be serious with most of us so close to going home," Trip said. "Shit, Red, Ghost, Bear, Sergeant Royce . . . we're all out of here in a few weeks. I guess most of the company is done. The only one staying is Shooter. How short are you?" Trip asked, looking at Rhymes.

"We're probably just being timed. The general likely wants to boast about our readiness. Sooner we're ready, sooner we'll be released," Rhymes said.

"Another game," Trip said. "My last with the little time I got left. Maybe I should just pack for home."

Rhymes opened his locker and took out a fatigue shirt, carefully folding it on his bunk. Singer stood and watched as Rhymes started on another, making precise folds, then smoothing each one.

"Better get started," Rhymes said. "Just ask me if you're not sure what to pack or bring."

"Did you ever go anywhere like this before?"

"Detroit last summer."

"Detroit?"

"The riots. This is different, though."

"Like an exercise?"

"More serious. See if they really give us new weapons. Hurry and pack."

With his duffel on the floor, Singer threw his extra pair of boots in first, then rolled up three sets of stateside fatigues and dumped them in the bag.

Sergeant Royce dropped heavily onto his bunk and buried his head in his hands. When he raised his face, he tugged the western boot off his left foot and flung it at his locker, the crash ringing through the room. "Fuck." After the second boot was off and dropped at his feet, he pulled himself up and started emptying his locker, pausing to look at the picture each time he removed an item.

Maybe Singer had been too slow or too obvious being the new guy in the squad, but Sergeant Royce looked over and then, as if remembering, came up and sent him on the equipment detail with Red, who made the mistake of passing by at that wrong moment. Before Singer hit the top of the stairs. Red was into it again.

"He batted .301 last year. Third year in a row over .300. If he can keep this up, you know what it means . . ."

Singer didn't know and didn't care and tuned it out. Instead he worried about where they might be sent, if they were going anywhere. He was waiting to go to Vietnam. It was his destiny. It wasn't possible they would send him somewhere else along with all the others to be some border patrol or monitor some civil strife and he would miss his chance to go to war.

On first floor near the barracks doors, Singer and Red found Stick with three other men Singer didn't know, in a line of about fifteen others he guessed were from the other three platoons. The same MP was at the door while two others were in the street managing a line of duce-and-a-half trucks that stretched out of sight down the street.

The first boxes contained jungle boots, which to Singer was an ominous sign. The signs continued with cartons of jungle fatigues, then flak jackets they lugged up to the fourth platoon's bay and tossed into a growing pile that men dug through with a measured urgency. An elaborate exercise or a serious mission.

The MPs grew more surly, shouting orders, waving flashlight beams in the settling darkness, rushing trucks in and out. Red had run out of Pete Rose statistics to report, and even his optimism about first-baseline seats for the coming season had grown dim, so he climbed the stairs in silence.

By the time Singer carried up the first boxes of C rations, most of the men of fourth platoon were already in jungle fatigues that brought on a shiny uniformity lacking the Combat Infantry Badges and combat unit patches that had marked most men's stateside uniforms. Men stripped of their identities, their histories, though Singer knew they had all survived something he had yet to face. He worried about being ready and quickened his pace.

Halfway up the stairs with two more cartons of Cs, Singer ran into Stick, who had stopped and was resting two cartons on his knee. Stick's shoulders and head were bowed. Singer wondered if he was sleeping.

"Come on, we're almost done," Singer said. "Want me to take one of those?"

Stick didn't answer, but took the weight up in long, spindly arms and climbed ahead, leaving Singer to bring up the rear.

When one of the last trucks backed into position, it revealed a load of new weapons. Singer felt a surge of excitement and fear. Rhymes said new weapons would mean something serious when their own weapons were locked up at supply, just a few paces down the hall. Singer forgot his exhaustion.

Fourth platoon's bay went quiet for a moment then filled with loud chatter when he and Red carried in the first load. After the last truck pulled away and there were no more cases to carry, Singer ran up the steps on tired legs.

The bay light seemed more harsh, men more subdued. The likelihood of any sleep seemed a remote prospect. Many of the men were sitting on bunks or footlockers with M16s disassembled, wiping parts with rags that looked to have been t-shirts a short time ago.

"We should test-fire these," a voice said.

I'm betting we'll get a chance in a few days," Shooter said, while he continued reassembling a new M60 machine gun.

Two bunks down, Jammer, a lanky black man with a grim expression and angry eyes that aged an otherwise boyish figure, held a barrel up, squinting through one eye. "Damn."

Beside Jammer, a man with a smooth complexion and a color that suggested a mixed background, released the operating handle of his M16 and the bolt slammed shut. The man aimed at a light and Singer heard the firing pin click on an empty chamber. "Dead."

"I'm telling you, I won't fight no brothers again." Jammer ran a thin finger down the scar that ran across his cheek. "I'll go to Korea, even back to Nam if I have to, but if that bird's going to Detroit or any other city where there's brothers, I ain't going."

"What makes you think they're going to tell you where they're taking you, much less give you a choice?"

"I'm just saying I ain't doing it again."

Trip was on his bunk, arms behind his head, sleeves rolled up, ankles crossed, staring at the bottom of the top bunk as if he might discern some necessary truth from the pattern of the springs. A rucksack, web gear, and rifle lay next to his feet.

Rhymes met Singer before he reached his bunk. "Sorry for the long detail. I was just coming to get you."

"It's okay," Singer said, rubbing his left bicep.

"I set boots and fatigues at your bunk. If they're the wrong sizes, trade them out from the piles. I'll draw your rifle and start cleaning it while you change. Then you can finish up while I take your duffle to supply."

"Thanks."

"I remember what it's like to be new to a unit. Besides, if you aren't ready it reflects on me."

* * * * *

When Singer woke, for a moment he thought it was daylight and he was somewhere else. He'd dreamt they'd gone already, parachuting in, and he'd been heroic on the first day of fighting saving half the platoon, winning medals and accolades requiring a visit to the oval office. The white lights overhead belied the appearance of the dawn that was just a faint glow in the windows. He found his gear stacked beside his bed where he'd left it and the residue of night clinging in his mouth. Hushed voices came from more than one location.

Singer washed and shaved next to a couple others he didn't know, both in their fatigues, like him not able to risk a shower until the alert was over. The piles of surplus equipment and the cases and boxes still clogged the center aisle. He understood the ache in his arms and the stiffness in his thighs.

A formation was called and Singer thought, *Here we go*, until Sergeant Edwards said to leave their gear. They were marched over to the mess, the formation shadowed by MPs as if they were all some kind of prisoners. At the smell of food, Singer recalled they'd had no dinner except for the Cs they opened in the middle of the night. Singer had barely settled down with his tray of cold eggs and nearly raw bacon before they were ordered back into formation and led back to the bay.

Despite their hurried return, once back at the bay they waited, the air growing warm and confining, sour with the lack of showers and the emotions of the night. Men checked rucks and gear and wiped down weapons or sharpened knifes, none of which needed doing. Some men lay on the bunks looking reflective or remorseful. Red sat cross-legged and closed his eyes and hummed. Singer tried to rest, but after just a few minutes was up and moving around.

He found Rhymes reading Dante still, his M79 beside him, his right hand resting on it as he held the book in his left hand. The M79 was an ugly weapon with its short, big barrel and stubby stock. It was a single-shot weapon that required the shooter to open the breech, remove the fired shell casing and insert a new round, then close the breach before they could fire one round again. It was a damning feature. Even the fastest shooters Singer watched in AIT seemed slow. A lot could happen while a man reloaded again and again and was defenseless in those moments. In woods—or more likely, jungles—in close quarters it seemed they would be even less functional, dangerous for the shooter. He'd decided in AIT he'd never carry one, even if it meant refusing an order. Thankfully he'd been assigned an M16. Maybe Rhymes viewed the weapon differently or had been ordered to carry it and was unwilling to fight about it.

Even after he pulled over a footlocker and sat down next to Rhymes's bunk, Rhymes seemed reluctant to visit.

"It's a good part," Rhymes eventually said, returning immediately to the book.

"What do you think?"

It was a minute before Rhymes stopped, inserted a bookmark, and set down the book.

"Have you read the papers the last week?"

"No, I guess not."

"Nam. Communist attacks on most the province capitals, Hue, Da Nang, Pleiku, Dak To, Long Binh, Bien Hoa, even Saigon."

"So you think we're going there?"

"Looks like it."

"But Trip says you're all too short to send anywhere."

"The army's probably got a different view. Sixty days left is enough. A couple of guys from the third platoon who had something like fifty days left got moved to a company that isn't on alert. The word is anyone with sixty days will have to go."

"But you guys were already there?"

"I guess it doesn't matter."

"I heard guys saying they wouldn't go."

"It's just talk. We'll all go. We're all still soldiers. Paratroopers. We have our pride, in ourselves if not the unit."

"Will we parachute in?"

A smile started on Rhymes's face then quickly faded. "No. In the Nam it's all helicopters. Jumping days are over 'til we get back."

"Are you scared?"

Rhymes turned away for just a moment. His face bore the same countenance when he looked back, but Singer felt he'd asked something he shouldn't have.

"You can't think about it. Push it from your mind. You just believe you'll be all right. Trust in God to protect you."

Rhymes pulled his M79 closer and picked up Dante.

"Yeah."

When Rhymes didn't say anymore, Singer got up, pushed the footlocker back, and moved on. As he walked away he thought of the first time he'd seen Rhymes's wounds. It was in the shower sometime that first week. The memory of his embarrassment at being caught looking still brought a flush to his face. Rhymes had turned and Singer hadn't been quick enough to look away. Rhymes touched the mark on his right buttock and then his left, as if to verify it had gone through. The right cheek had a circle of white flesh drawn tight at the edges, stark against Rhymes's dark skin. The left side was a large and shapeless form of holes and knotted cords that looked like it must still hurt.

"My head was down, but I guess my ass was in the air," Rhymes had said. "Maybe my ass is just too big to hide."

Then he finished washing off the soap, shut the water off, and walked out, hiding the wounds under a towel.

Singer paused now between bunks, uncertain. Trip was sleeping, or at least had his eyes closed and didn't open them. But Bear was sitting on his footlocker, a fatigue jacket on his lap, a needle almost hidden between his fingers. He pushed it through from underneath, then pulled at it twice before getting it and yanking it through, the thread trailing behind it.

Bear looked up at Singer watching.

"I'm putting on my combat patch. I ain't going anywhere looking like no Cherry. No offense, man."

Bear smiled and Singer laughed.

"Don't blame you. I wouldn't either, if I weren't one," Singer said.

"My fingers weren't made for this." He held out both hands that looked like baseball mitts.

"Shit, let me do it. I've sewed before."

"Sit down, then. I got it started, but it took forever."

Singer took the jungle shirt and the needle and had one side done before either of them spoke. Bear dragged over another empty footlocker and sat watching while flexing his fingers that had held the needle.

"Rhymes says you got medals like Shooter," Singer said, pausing the needle.

The laugh came deep from Bear's belly. "Nothing like Shooter's. Hell, there was nothing brave about what I did. Went out to get a guy. The guy was screaming and nobody doing nothing. What could I do? If I had to listen to that guy scream one more minute, I would've killed myself. So I went and got the guy, told him if he'd shut up I'd bring him in. If not . . . well, they gave me a Bronze Star for it, which made me laugh."

"It sounds brave."

"Shooter, he has a couple of Silvers Stars. I don't know what else. Three Purple Hearts and he wants to go back. But they're stalling him. Brave or crazy. I don't know. I don't like the guy, and he scares me a little, but if you're in a firefight, it's guys like him you want around you."

Singer shifted the jacket, pulled the needle and thread through again. "You want to go back?"

"Hell, no. I ain't crazy like Shooter. I want to go home, see my mama, hang with the guys, chase pussy." He laughed, shallow from his throat. "Man, I'm finished with that stuff. Once was enough for me."

Singer handed Bear the shirt and Bear took his off and put it on. "That looks better. One more?"

"Sure."

"Singer?" Sergeant Royce's voice.

"Yeah."

Sergeant Royce walked over, slow, heavy steps, and held out a white envelope in a trembling hand. His eyes were puffy and bloodshot.

"Hey, Sarge," Bear said. "Whiskey ain't helping?"

Sergeant Royce shoved the envelope at Singer, then dropped his hand to his side. Singer held it, reading the name, Jimmy Miller, above the unit address, as if it were new to him. It bore his brother's initials and return address.

"It's you, isn't it?" Sergeant Royce asked.

"Yeah, it's me."

Jimmy Miller wasn't the name anyone used. Maybe Sergeant Edwards had referred to him by it at their first meeting, but that same day Shooter had dubbed him Singer, and then out of deference to Shooter or for their own reasons they all took it up. By the end of week even Sergeant Edwards called him Singer, his old identity forgotten.

"Why mail now?" Singer asked.

"Came over last night with everything else. After we leave they have to forward it." Sergeant Royce looked one way then walked off in the other direction.

"A love letter?" Bear asked.

"No." Singer looked at the two pages of notebook paper with precise, tight script. He settled on the first sheet, his eyes scanning down the page. Before he reached the bottom he tore the sheets in pieces, then crumbled them into a ball and shoved them in his pocket.

"Bad news?"

"No, just bullshit. Someone thinks I ruined my life and wants to lecture me. You got that other patch you want sewed on?"

* * * * *

The call came suddenly, almost unexpectedly after so much waiting. Singer was nearly dozing, his mind wandering through past events, drifting so he could barely recall what he'd been thinking a moment before. Such were the volume and urgency of Sergeant Edwards's first words that he sprang alert and was sitting up, aware of the rush of movement around him within those first few seconds.

"Let's go. Downstairs now! Full gear and weapons. We're moving out. Don't leave anything. We're not coming back."

Before Singer had all his gear on, Rhymes was there, web gear, rucksack, and M79 in hand. "Ready?"

"Yeah. I think so."

A blur of bodies rushed down the aisle. Singer saw rucks and rifles and faces that were difficult to read. He hurried beside Rhymes almost at a run, ignoring Sergeant Milner near the doorway, his squealing voice imploring them to go faster, and descended to the growing formation. Crowded into duce-and-a-half trucks with MP escorts, they sped across the base the short distance to adjacent Pope Air Force Base. Along the route soldiers stopped and watched the convoy pass, some pointing and saying something to the men beside them.

It might have been possible to still believe it was an exercise, even as they assembled on the air base tarmac in a formation larger than Singer had ever seen. Thousands of men in combat gear with banners waving was an impressive sight. If it was a show, it was a good one. The waiting line of C-141s with open doors and crews standing by could all be part of it. Singer imagined that some men, Sergeant Royce, Ghost, and even Trip still clung to that hope. Maybe everyone did except Shooter and him. Shooter definitely wanted to go. Singer went back and forth about it. Anxious to go now, and then wanting to wait until later when he might be more ready. Though Rhymes had told him you could never be ready.

Any doubts that this was real were lost when Air Force One landed and taxied up, and stopping near the group. The president descended the steps to a cluster of the top brass and other officials gathered at the bottom. Before ascending a flag-adorned stage, the president inspected the ranks, walking past Singer and led by a general wearing a helmet with a single star.

It was only Singer's military training and his guess at the consequences that kept him from turning to Rhymes and Trip, who were on either side of him, and saying, "Holy shit. The president. Close enough to touch. Did you see that?"

The president took the podium at the center of the platform, a crowd of dignitaries and security behind him. He was a big man whose face by nature seemed to hold some sadness, or maybe it was the weight of office, or the things he knew but couldn't share. Everyone had come, it seemed, to see them off, except the people they would really want to see before they left.

The day was overcast, but bright rather than dreary. It was warm enough, comfortable for a February day. The president's voice carried well in the still air. Singer tried to listen carefully, but his mind wandered to imaginings of what might lie ahead. Afterward, the only phrase he could recall the president saying was: "I can't tell you where you're going, but it's going to be hot in a few days." For some reason, this stuck with him.

Later, as they filed to the plane, Bear said, "The man can't tell us where the fuck we're going like it's some big secret. Shit, probably been in half the papers. You can bet Charlie knows we're coming."

It caused a few men around him, those who'd been to Nam before, to nod while pursing their lips. Sergeant Royce got on the plane looking pale and dry-lipped. He looked around as if wishing there was a stewardess so he could get a drink. Ghost showed up and took his place in line, though Bear had given even odds he wouldn't. Red had popped some gum and was chewing vigorously, forsaking any talk of his hero on the occasion of this day.

"It makes no sense. All of us so short," Trip said, moving toward a seat.

"Two months can be forever," Bear said.

"They could extend us once we're there," Rhymes said.

"Goddamn it, they can't do that," Trip said, but Singer could hear the uncertainty in his voice.

Singer suspected they could and imagined they all knew it, but no one took up the argument. He stored his equipment as he saw Rhymes do and then settled in beside him.

"Well," Rhymes said before pulling out a book. "You aren't going alone."

Singer kept quiet, not knowing how to say he was sorry that they had to go again, but happy he was going over with men he knew and liked, men who had survived and could show him how. Or how to tell of his guilt for his happiness at his good fortune that came at their expense, knowing it would mean little to any of them.

Words rose softly from a few rows ahead, gaining volume as the men nearby went silent. It was the first time Singer had heard Sergeant Prascanni sing the tune outside the shower. Today he sang slower, softer, giving the Italian words a mournful quality. Singer thought of lost love, though he had little experience in such things. Then the jet engines roared to life, and the song was lost or Sergeant Prascanni simply stopped singing.

Singer felt the rush of racing down the runway. The wheels lost contact with the earth, and he was pushed back in his seat with the force of the steep climb, Italian words of love replaying in his mind.

Sometime in the night he awoke thinking he heard crying, but then thought it might just be the engine noise combined with Bear's snoring. A soft whimpering within the engine drone. A quirk of C-141s or someone's uncontained despair?

Could it really be that bad?

3

February 19, 1968
Vietnam

Singer and the rest of the fourth platoon moved west from the Americal Division's base at Chu Lai where their C-141 from Fort Bragg had landed just two days before. They walked slowly in a staggered line across the grassy plain toward green mountains that loomed ahead.

Only a few hours earlier they had sat in low bleachers amid a sea of tents, listening to an Americal staff sergeant, a trim black man in a baseball hat and pressed fatigues, with a Combat Infantryman's Badge above the left pocket but no paratrooper wings, who paced back and forth in front of the bleachers as he talked. His voice boomed, trailed off, and boomed again as he emphasized each point. The scene was more like a stateside training center than a combat zone.

"You men will forego usual in-country training," the Americal sergeant said. "You will move north in a few days. Meantime, you'll patrol here with Americal Division guides." The sergeant stopped pacing and stood still near the center of the group.

"A Leg's going to show us around," Trip said.

Shooter looked to Sergeant Edwards, who raised no objection.

"Our guys know this area. You don't," the Americal sergeant said. "I know you all have been here before. You've done this. You know it." The sergeant paused and looked across the group as if measuring his words. "Most of it will be the same. We'll do this patrol together then you'll go north on your own."

Singer watched the sergeant closely, trying to weigh and retain everything he said. Rhymes had said these first few weeks would be the most dangerous for a new guy. Next to him, Rhymes kneaded his hands and pushed the cuticles back on each finger. Trip had his elbows on his knees and his head

31

bowed as if looking at the ground below the bleachers. Sweat beaded on his face. Bear leaned back, sprawling across the seat. Occasionally his eyes closed, opening again before he started snoring. Sergeant Royce looked off toward the mountains, or maybe it was the airfield and the flight path he was searching out. Stick sat on a lower bench next to Sergeant Prascanni, leaning toward the speaker. A few seats over, Shooter drew his knife across his arm then examined the hairless patch. If the talk was long, Shooter would have his entire arm shaved.

The Americal sergeant took a step closer and continued, nearly shouting the first word. "Here it's mostly Viet Cong. You'll find NVA up north where you're going."

Singer waited, expecting more exact information, but the sergeant never explained where exactly they were going though he talked as though he knew.

"Some booby traps will be new to you." Then the Americal sergeant, with the aid of a buck sergeant, spent the next fifteen minutes demonstrating various booby traps. At the end of the demonstration the Americal sergeant introduced his assistant as the one who would accompany them on the patrol. He was a small blond kid with freckles and dark eyes, whose fatigues were neither clean nor pressed. That was the end of in-country training.

"That's it?" Singer asked.

"What more do you want?" Rhymes asked.

"I don't know. Just seems like there should be more?"

"You got everything you need," Rhymes said, looking at Singer's M16.

They walked from the training site along white-rock-lined paths, past gardens and neatly lettered signs. The low sandbag walls around tents and the occasional bunker were the only indications this was something other than a stateside camp. They locked and loaded before they left the front gate, which held a sign proclaiming the camp HOME OF THE AMERICAL DIVISION. Outside the gate, a group of Vietnamese women and children stood, some carrying buckets of Cokes, others with baskets of bananas or pineapples. A few held bundles of folded laundry that looked mostly like army fatigues. Beyond them was a sea of ramshackle shelters of cardboard and tin. Singer stared. These were the first Vietnamese he'd seen.

"How do you tell the good ones from the bad?" Singer asked.

"If they shoot at you, they're bad." Bear's laugh rumbled from somewhere low in his big frame.

"Fuck, they let the VC hang out at the camp gate," Trip said.

"Half of them working in the camp are probably VC," Bear said.

"You think we'd be smarter," Rhymes said.

"Helping the people, brother. Helping the people," Bear said.

Kids trailed beside the patrol, holding out cans, the same red labels as home. "Coke, Coke. One dollar. You want?"

Some held out empty hands. "GIs numba one. Give me dollar."

"Get the fuck out of here, you little pissants," someone yelled.

"Fuck, give me the boonies," Trip said.

After fifty yards, the last kid gave up and the patrol was alone. Well beyond the camp they left the dust of the dirt road, crossing onto a grassy plain, moving toward the rice fields to the west. Eventually they reached them and climbed up on the banks, moving in single file across an expansive checkerboard of dikes and green, unlike any green Singer had ever seen.

The sun beat down on the treeless plain and Singer's shadow became a small oval at his feet. His body protested with streams of sweat. Heat rose up from the paddies in oppressive currents. The smell of decay hung in the air. Other smells drifted to him that he couldn't identify, but he imagined they were familiar to all the second-tour guys.

While they were crossing the expanse of paddies, Rhymes asked from behind, "You okay?"

"Great," Singer said, immediately feeling bad for the enthusiasm in his answer. He turned and looked at Rhymes, thinking he should say more, but then could think of nothing that wouldn't sound stupid.

It was all new to him and held the excitement of discovery. He had never seen rice paddies before and thought he would always remember the green even though he wasn't sure how to describe it. An artist would know the color. The mountains, the mosaic of greens and browns, were beautifully offset by the expanse of blue sky. The string of men leading them across the paddies, helmets bobbing, rifles sticking out to the sides, presented an image of adventure. He knew of danger that the dikes and brush-lines held, as well as the mountains beyond. At least, he'd been told of it in obscure terms. But without the real reference of experience, the prospect of danger didn't diminish the excitement of it all. More likely, it added to it. He scanned the dikes that paralleled the one they walked on, wondering how many enemy soldiers could be hiding just on the other side of the dike ready to jump up, AKs blazing. He imagined charging toward it, firing his rifle, and felt a rush through his entire body.

After they left the paddies, they moved into a small village of scattered bamboo huts. A young girl came toward them, following a water buffalo, holding a rope tied to a ring in the buffalo's nose. In her right hand she held a switch, with which she hit the buffalo's rump. She took little notice of Singer or the other soldiers of the fourth platoon, as though patrols were a common thing. Chickens pecked at the ground, unbothered by the soldiers until Jammer ran up and kicked one and they all scattered, squawking as they fled.

Ahead, a white-haired man with a wrinkled, leathery face couched in front of the first hut, his legs like sticks, chopping wood with a short, odd-shaped knife. The old man looked up without breaking the rhythm of his strokes. Singer watched the man add more sticks to a growing pile, wondering if he might be the enemy. The platoon spread out through the village, the soldiers splitting up into groups of twos and threes, each heading for a different hut. The village and movement confused Singer and he stood there uncertain what to do.

"Singer!" Bear was heading toward a hut by himself.

Singer looked back at Rhymes, who had been behind him, but Rhymes had already headed in the opposite direction with Red. The old man at the first hut was standing, his knife lying on the ground. A solder stood in front of him, his M16 pointed at his chest, while a second soldier pointed his M16 into the doorway of the hut and leaned in cautiously. Singer ran to catch up to Bear.

"Get out here!" Bear yelled into the dark doorway, sweeping the blackness with his rifle. "Out now!" He stepped back slowly, keeping his rifle pointed into the hut.

Singer brought his rifle up, feeling the touch of the trigger and pangs of fear that dampened his eagerness. A man shuffled out, head down, eyes on the ground, gnarled, weathered hands at his side. A woman, at least as old, followed behind him on unsteady legs. The couple stood together in front of the hut, leaning against each other as though holding each other up. The old woman was shaking. She glanced at Bear and then Singer and then to the old man, perhaps looking for some reassurance. The old man kept his eyes lowered as though studying the ground.

"Watch 'em," Bear said, disappearing into the hut.

The voice that came from Bear and the heartlessness in his eyes were different from the man Singer knew at Fort Bragg. This Bear frightened him.

The old couple tottered before him. What kind of threat were they? Were these the VC the Americal Division sergeant talked about? How could anyone this old be dangerous? Still, he kept his weapon pointed at them, more afraid of what he might be expected to do than of the old couple. Singer ran a dry tongue across dry lips. He glanced quickly over his shoulder toward the other huts but there were no soldiers nearby, no one to help him. The old man and woman hadn't moved. What was taking Bear so long? Would he look weak if he called to Bear?

The old woman continued to look around with darting eyes as though thinking about running if she were younger. The old man shuffled his feet then raised his face and caught her eye just briefly, then they both looked away. Singer saw it. A look of conspirators. Singer raised his rifle so it pointed at their chests.

"Don't move!"

The couple didn't move except for the old woman's shaking. But their looks seemed a tired defiance. He feared they saw his weakness and tried to hide it with a determined face. In his peripheral vision he watched the dark opening of the hut, willing Bear to reappear.

The old man's feet moved again, maybe setting himself for a break. Singer waved his rifle and tried to warn the man with his eyes of what he'd do, though unconvinced himself.

Damn. Should he shoot him if he ran or made a move forward? What if they made a break in opposite directions?

What would everyone think if on his first patrol he let an old couple run away? He didn't want to shoot them, but he couldn't be seen as scared or weak, a liability to the group. Not everyone had a weapon one could see. Wasn't that what the Americal Division sergeant had said?

He'd shoot them. He would, if that was what he had to do. Resigning himself to this brought a different fear. He swiped the sweat from his eyes and tried not to let his rifle shake. Finally Bear emerged, ducking to pass through the doorway, rescuing Singer as much as the old couple. Singer lowered his rifle and gasped for breath as if he'd just made it to the surface from some great depth.

Bear stormed past without a word. The foray inside the hut had not softened Bear's eyes or the tightness in his face.

Singer wiped his trigger-hand across his belly and followed at a distance, keeping his questions to himself. What ghosts had the return to Vietnam awakened in Bear and the others? What fears and angers had been raised that none of them would speak of? He thought himself different, maybe even above some of it. But he couldn't escape the thought that he was looking at himself in a time to come.

The faces of the old couple stayed with him even after they left the village, as did the fear of what he might have done and the fear of how easily he had resigned himself to it. In the end he shot no one and no shots had been fired in the village, but the damage left in the wake of their visit was impossible to gauge.

The sun now was past the middle of the sky and it was much hotter than when they started. The men's fatigues were dark with sweat. They moved west, well beyond the village, into tall brush and then towering trees. The shade offered a surprising coolness, and Singer could feel the wetness on his back with a slight chill. They moved on a well-worn trail packed hard by lifetimes of travel, under a canopy of trees that shut out the sun. The slope was gradual at first and then grew steeper, forcing the men to lean into the climb. Singer's pack grew heavier as they climbed and the hours passed. The excitement he had felt crossing the rice paddies had faded long ago, left behind in the village with the old couple. Now he only felt the weariness in his legs and the weight on his back. The trees ended abruptly, as did the trail, and the sun exposed a ground that looked tortured and dead. Trees sheared off with splayed ends, leaning at odd angles. Ground torn and rolled over on itself. Holes of red-brown earth.

They continued to climb more gradually beyond the shattered earth and then across a saddle of low grass that clutched at their tired feet. The mountain fell off steeply to their right, into a cascade of boulders worn smooth by water that ran during the wet season, finally pooling in the paddies in the valley. Singer moved, tiredly waiting for a break. His weapon, which had been held high at the start of the day, hung lower from heavy arms, mirroring the others.

Singer watched men move through the saddle below him and saw it happen. Sergeant Prascanni stumbled and fell forward, hitting hard, his rifle and right arm trapped strangely under his body and his left arm sprawled out beside him. Oddly, he never reached out to break his fall. Everyone behind Sergeant Prascanni began to stop in accordion-like fashion, though the point kept moving unaware.

Two, maybe three seconds later, the sound arrived, a single bang so distant and diffused it was hard to recognize it for what it was. Weak echoes between mountains masked its source.

"Sniper," Trip yelled, and was already down.

"Medic! Medic!" someone yelled. Then another joined him in the call.

Men went to the ground, though some like Singer were slow to get down, confused by the distance, time delay, and the muffling of the shot. Sergeant Prascanni made no move to crawl or rise. The fingers of his visible left hand were still.

With a medic bag in his right hand, Doc Randall ran past Singer in a half crouch, dropping down beside Sergeant Prascanni. Sergeant Edwards's voice, strong and even, without panic, ordered a medevac, though Singer could hear the urgency just short of pleading.

While they waited, an eerie quiet descended over the mountain. There was only the one shot. With the time between Sergeant Prascanni falling and the shot, it seemed unreal. Singer had seen that same thing duck hunting on big water. A flock of birds, barely visible, would fly over a distant marshy point and some of them would tumble silently from the sky. He would see the splashes before the sounds of the shots reached him. It had been interesting then, even entertaining.

The men lay where they fell, looking off at the distant hills or watching the treeline below them. Singer glanced at Rhymes, just behind him downslope, staring off at the mountains and turning his head back and forth, his M79 pointing more up than out.

"Shouldn't we fire?" Singer asked.

"No way to tell where he is. Could be on any of these mountains. More than a mile away, judging by the delay," Rhymes said.

"We just lie here?"

"He'll shoot again. Watch for a muzzle flash."

They lay there waiting for the next shot, watching for a target. Singer could hear Ghost praying a Spanish litany, which stood out against the silence on the mountainside. A petition for salvation or a requiem for the sergeant, Singer wasn't sure. Singer thought of Sergeant Prascanni talking of the magic of the Italian song that gave his wife no chance.

Singer heard the bird before he saw it. *Whump, whump, whump.* It broke over the trees below and to his left, climbing, swinging hard toward the swale where a man stood both arms raised, setting low with its nose pointed downhill, grass swirling and flattening in the rotor's wash. The right-door gunner aimed his gun at the closest hillside, which loomed above their heads. The pilot held the ship there, light on the skids, looking ready to go.

Four men, Shooter and Doc Randall in the lead, broke toward the chopper before the skids had settled, each holding a corner of a poncho bearing Sergeant Prascanni. The poncho sagged with the weight, the center almost dragging. Singer watched for signs of life, wondering if Sergeant Prascanni was still alive. There was no movement he could see.

The gunner frantically waved the men forward. The chopper's right front window shattered. The chopper tail swayed and the bird lifted slightly. The pilot raised his head, apparently unharmed, and the bird steadied. The sound of the shot, when it came, was covered by the rotor noise and the sound of guns some men fired, but no one yelled to ID the target. Singer watched and waited on Rhymes's word, though Trip fired at the mountains despite the distance.

The crew chief was there pulling at the poncho as the four men pushed Sergeant Prascanni onto the chopper, then sprinted away. Singer could see the crew chief return toward his gun, the gunner screaming, and the motionless form on the poncho. The Huey's engine revved and the ship lifted sharply, slipping forward. Both door gunners opened up, firing their M60s, and Singer watched the tracers disappearing into the mountainsides, wondering if it would pin the sniper down, if not kill him.

The right-door gunner's foot exploded in a spray of color, and he stopped firing. Seconds later, Singer was sure he heard the faint echo of the shot amongst the guns and engine noise. The sound of the engine changed as if the bird was struggling, and Singer wondered if it was hit. The chopper continued gaining air, then fell slightly and pitched right and struggled east at altitude. Singer lay in the grass listening for the *whump, whump*, while in his mind hearing Sergeant Prascanni's love song fade away. Then the guns went silent, the chopper was gone, and everything was quiet.

Across the valley on the hillside a black cloud rose, and then another and another until the hill was covered in black smoke. Artillerymen at the Americal base were firing their big guns. The sounds of the exploding artillery rounds drifted to Singer first as individual booms, then quickly grew to a continuous roar. The men got up and moved forward as the rounds were still exploding.

Just that morning, Singer had heard Sergeant Prascanni announce, "Fifty-nine days and a wake-up."

Despite trying, Singer suddenly couldn't repeat one line of the Italian words or even hum the melody. This bothered him somehow more than the knowledge that one of them was gone.

4

March–April 1968
Vietnam

The truck jolted forward and started a slow acceleration. Singer grabbed the sideboard, jostling against the men beside him. Children scattered when the truck lurched into motion, though some ran along beside it. In less than a hundred yards, they were stopped again. The truck behind them braked too hard and skidded, stopping just a couple feet behind the men who sat at the rear, their legs dangling over the edge.

"Fucker," someone said.

A rifle was raised and pointed. The driver leaned away and held up his hand, as if that might stop a bullet.

Singer strained to look down the road and see the lead truck in the convoy to gain some clue as to their erratic progress up Highway One.

"This is bullshit," Trip said. "In the Cav we'd have gone in choppers and be there already. At this rate it'll take three days to get there."

"You're in a big hurry to get to the fighting," Bear said.

"We're sitting ducks on this fucking road."

"Better keep an eye out, then, instead of whining about your choppers. You ain't in the Cav no more."

Bear looked out beyond the line of Vietnamese moving down the road in the opposite direction, surveying the fields that stretched toward mountains too distant to be a threat.

"That's for damn sure," Trip said. "I wonder if the 82nd has anything besides trucks."

The trucks rolled forward, gaining speed, and dust rose up along the convoy. In the procession at the side of the road, people carrying loads on yokes, bicycles, and carts covered their mouths and moved without pause in what seemed an endless line plodding south. A woman stooped with age and the weight she carried bent lower in a coughing fit then set down her load and squatted, twisted fingers holding the yoke vertical like a cane. It made Singer wonder if she'd get up. A white-haired man with eyes hidden amongst wrinkles balanced on wobbly legs and peed to no one's obvious concern, then shuffled onward, on a trek that looked to be his last. Children ran along dangerously close to the big truck's tires before turning back to continue moving south, while other children joined the chase.

"Where are they going?" Singer asked.

"Away from the fighting," Rhymes said.

"They aren't bringing much."

"That's all they have or all they can carry."

Singer couldn't see the end the procession or where it might begin. "Is it bad in Hue?"

"It might be over before we get there," Rhymes said.

Singer secretly hoped it wasn't so he could see some part of it. *Some real fighting.* He hid his smile at the thought. Even though he'd heard Sergeant Prascanni was dead, it didn't seem like it except that he was gone. There hadn't really been a fight. And the way Sergeant Prascanni went down, with no sound at first and far enough away so Singer couldn't see the blood or the wound, made it seem as if he had just fallen. Though certainly the sniper's bullet, which Rhymes said was a large caliber, would have done massive damage. Singer hadn't even had a chance to fire his rifle, which was what he was waiting for.

No one spoke of Sergeant Prascanni's death. Certainly no one said anything about how it made them feel. Something, though, had changed, subtly. Mostly it was just that things were subdued, more quiet, as though no one knew what to say or were thinking of their own vulnerability, resolving to hold their breath through their remaining days. It wasn't outright anger, but the men seemed more irritable. Rhymes was the steadiest and least unchanged by it. Bear and Trip were at each other more. Just small things, grating and poking, always stopping just short of something ugly. Red, perhaps in deference to the mood, had given up promoting Rose as MVP, which left him mostly silent. Sergeant Royce seemed withdrawn, preoccupied with something. He gazed at in the distance no matter where they were. Shooter went on lugging the big gun and sharpening his knife. Stick, who Singer had heard saying, "It wasn't fair," seemed sullen and downcast.

It was a long stretch before the truck stopped again, though they'd never built up much speed. With the line stalled, the dust settled except for that stirred by the hundreds of feet moving past. The children were there again, all but climbing on the trucks, hands out, some silently pleading with eyes that were difficult to resist. Others offered English platitudes of GI being number one or petitions for a dollar. Singer dug out a can of Cs, crackers with a condiment, and tossed it to the side so the smaller kids might have a chance. Then he watched them scramble on the ground, fighting for possession before rising and rushing back beside the truck, arms outstretched again. The scene reminded Singer of times as a boy when he had fed ducks at a local park, the ducks crowding around in a tight group, quacking loudly, stretching their necks, begging for food, and pushing at each other for the best position. They would all scramble, fighting madly over the pieces of bread he threw. Singer lobbed another can and watched the children dive for it.

"Don't give them Cs," Trip said.

"The kids are hungry. Go ahead," Rhymes said.

"They'll use the cans for booby traps. I seen it." Trip said.

"They'll find things even without our help," Rhymes said.

Bear leaned over the side and dropped a candy bar into a boy's open hands, then looked at Trip.

"I ain't sharing mine when you guys are hungry," Trip said.

"Didn't expect you to," Bear said.

The truck crept forward, settling into an even but slow speed. Smells were stirred up with the dust, and Singer swiped at his nose in a gesture that held no hope of removing such pervasive odors. The swish of water he ran around his mouth did nothing to eliminate the grit that still clung to his tongue and teeth. Maybe it was the smells and grit that really had Trip wishing for choppers. They passed a group of kids trailing a woman pushing a bicycle with bundles and pots tied to it. Two small girls paused and turned, wide-eyed, holding hands, dirty smiles spread on their faces. Singer smiled back, thinking the girls' grins were just for him.

"Cute, huh?" Singer said.

"Yeah, cute," Bear said without conviction.

"Their faces, smiles," Singer said.

"You won't think they're so cute when one of them throws a grenade at you or you trip a booby trap made from a C-rat you gave them."

Singer was quiet a moment, feeling the heat in his cheeks.

"But you threw—"

"A candy bar to fuck with Cav boy."

"You think they're VC?"

Bear leaned closer fixed a stare on Singer. "Where are their fathers?"

"What?"

"See any men all morning, other than the ones older than my grandpa?"

Singer studied the procession. When it dawned on him that all day he'd seen only women, children, and old men, he turned to Bear with a question on his lips.

"One army or another," Bear said. "You won't ever see the men. Some are out right now setting booby traps or hiding weapons."

"Shit," Singer said.

"Jesus Christ, you new guys are all alike, slower than an inbred mule." Trip edged closer. "I hope you live long enough to learn something."

"What can we do?" Singer asked.

"That's the big question. Now the man's starting to understand. You don't know who's who and you can't just kill them all," said Bear.

"There's an idea!" Trip said, pointing his rifle back and forth as though spraying the line with gunfire. "Let God sort them out."

The truck lurched, bringing an end to the conversation—or maybe it was over already. Singer looked at Trip and then at Bear, uncertain if he knew them. They were both starting to sound like Shooter. Is that what was destined to happen to all of them if they stayed long enough? He had his ideals and understood right and wrong. He'd never be like them. He wanted to push away, to get out and walk, but he was stuck there between them, pinned against the sideboards.

Smoke billowed from the vertical exhaust with a sudden acceleration that had Singer grabbing at the sideboard with his left hand. He rode in quiet, thinking about where they were going, where events would take them, and what it might mean for each of them. He tried not to think about Sergeant Prascanni, but he could still see him falling, thinking he had only tripped, never seeing the impact of the shot, nor any blood, and not understanding until seconds later when he heard the far-off shot and Trip had yelled, "Sniper." Would all his understanding of this time be like that? Delayed seconds or even years until some realization cracked from the distance across his consciousness, bringing clarity to earlier events?

Occasionally he could hear one of the other men on the truck talking, though the words were swallowed by the noise of the convoy. The light was already fading when they turned off the main road onto a dirt trail that angled west. After a short, bone-shaking distance, they stopped in the shadow of a sea of bunkers, tents, radio antennas, and equipment piles. They were on the southern edge of a low, expansive hill. Rice paddies stretched out below them, dark in the shadow of western mountains. The last bit of light rose up from behind the mountain peaks, shooting up into the sky in a brilliant display that was not without some beauty.

The men dismounted slowly on unsteady legs, and the trucks moved off toward the security of the base behind them. The base was new or had expanded in recent days beyond old perimeters, as there were no bunkers or wire where the men stood. They were the new southern perimeter. They spread out by fire teams, dug shallow fighting holes in the last of the day's light, and set out trip flares and claymores before eating cold Cs. Darkness settled in over the men with the quiet uneasiness of night in a combat zone. The men sat together at each position, staring into the shadows before beginning the first guard rotation.

"Put out the cigarette, you stupid fuck," someone down the line yelled. "Christ, you want to get us all killed?"

In the southwest, near the mountains, red tracers originated out of the blackness in the low sky and raced toward the ground in a continuous stream. Green tracers in short, broken streams rose from the ground toward the spot where the red tracers began. There was no sound, only the streaks of crimson and emerald intermingling on a dark canvas. Singer was transfixed by the beauty of the lines of bright red and green racing back and forth with the backdrop of the ghostly mountains, their shapes standing out even against the murky sky. He wondered who might be dying, thankful to be watching from a distance. Then he saw Sergeant Prascanni tripping and going down, not moving, but the deadly tracer light show remained beautiful.

That night Singer dreamed of watching fireworks, sitting on the lakeshore, the blossoms of colors exploding over the lake. In his dream it was a hot, sticky night, the kind typical of the Fourth of July. Susan was next to him, and he had his arm around her. He could smell the lingering scent of shampoo in her hair when she leaned her head on him and the smell of her sweat in the hot night, which he found pleasant and made him think of lying together sweating and exhausted. Then he woke to the gloomy view of rice paddies and distant mountains and he felt tired, despite the sleep.

Throughout the following days they filled sandbags and strung concertina wire, working shirtless and sweating in the hot sun. Occasionally in those first few days, when the wind was right, Singer heard sounds from the north of what could have been gunfire and explosions but were too muted to say with certainty.

"Hue," Rhymes said.

"I thought we were going there."

"Soon enough."

Singer lost track of the days. His arms hurt from digging and throwing sandbags to build bunkers, each large enough to hold a squad if everyone crowded in. Maybe this was how they made each unit pay their dues before they let them fight. If Bear was bothered by Ghost's daytime absences, he didn't let on, and seemed content that he showed up each evening and was still there at dawn. Singer wondered though if Bear trusted him enough to let him pull nighttime guard alone. It became sort of an obsession for Singer, or a diversion to the mindless work and oppressive heat, to discover how Ghost slipped away each day unnoticed. But even though he tried to watch, he never saw Ghost leave. At some point he'd realize he hadn't seen him and would look around, unable to find him. He never did see him lift a single sandbag or touch a strand of wire.

Sergeant Milner regularly appeared and stood up on the hill surveying the work, sometimes yelling out an order that everyone seemed mostly to ignore. During each break Rhymes sat with a book, and only sometimes put it down when Singer talked to him.

"You brought all those with?" Singer asked, seeing the pile beside Rhymes's ruck.

"What's life without a good book?"

This made Singer quietly confused by something he never considered before, that life might be empty, or at least incomplete, without a story to read. He had never found this to be true, but Rhymes said it with the conviction of someone who firmly believed it.

The days of labor were beginning to take on a dull routine, and the irritation of boredom started to grow around the edges. Some days Singer found himself even sitting down near Red, who had regained his enthusiasm for citing statistics and telling memorable games play by play. Singer even asked a few baseball questions, a game he cared nothing about at all, but Red seemed pleased. It killed the time and temporarily displaced Singer's anxiety over their lack of action.

Even the old guys were showing signs of stress over being stuck in the work of firebase expansion, something any laborer could do.

"This is fucking nuts. They brought us over here again for this shit. Sending us back was just political bullshit." Trip threw down a wirecutter and his gloves and walked away.

It was Rhymes who eventually retrieved him. They walked back down the hill side by side and Trip went back to work as if nothing had happened. Rhymes never did say what he told Trip to get him to return. When Singer asked, Rhymes merely said. "This is not a good place to get crosswise with the brass, or anyone else for that matter."

Sergeant Royce just ignored the whole episode, and luckily Sergeant Milner wasn't there and likely never heard or, as Bear said, he would have probably loved to nail Cav boy with an Article 15 and hang his ass. Sergeant Edwards probably heard, or that was at least what they figured, but he understood such things and might have even thought the same as Trip, though he could never say it.

Things reached a peak—or the bottom, depending on the view—when in the middle of the day Shooter opened up with the M60 from the top of one of the completed bunkers, sending a trail of red tracers out into the empty paddies. The gunfire sent everybody diving for the ground. When the sound of the machine gun stopped, Singer could hear Shooter laughing, a high-pitched, crazy wail with a rhythm similar to gunfire. Some men cursed. A few laughed, as well, after looking around and then standing up.

"That fucker is one crazy white guy," Bear said.

Rhymes shook his head and went back to work, ignoring Shooter and the commotion. Sergeant Milner stormed down, ranting about undisciplined fire and endangering men.

Shooter spun around with the M60, so that Sergeant Milner ducked. "Got to get more ammo, Sarge." He left Sergeant Milner alone, talking to himself.

Singer saw Sergeant Edwards watching from up the slope, and he seemed to smile. Later he saw him talking to Shooter, though, they both stood relaxed and it looked to be a friendly conversation. It was understandable. Singer wanted to fire his weapon, too, and perhaps if Shooter had told him of his plan he would have stood beside him with his M16 and run through a clip or two. Though he saw that Rhymes didn't like it and probably would have chewed him out, which would have upset him, so maybe it was better he hadn't known.

After Shooter's episode there were a few more eventless patrols into the paddies below them, likely more to remind them of their real role as infantrymen than to actually look for the enemy. At least it gave Singer a chance to feel like a soldier and to embrace the illusion that he was really doing something.

On one of the patrols, they were working a brush-line at a field edge. Singer was taking it slow, then held up to check for what he thought might have been a trip wire but was just a vine. Sergeant Edwards must have come forward to check with Sergeant Royce because Singer heard him as he was down on one knee checking.

"Why do you have Singer on point again?" Sergeant Edwards asked.

"He wants to," Sergeant Royce said.

"Rotate your point man, Sergeant."

So Singer got pulled off point right then. Afterward, even though he asked, it was only occasionally that he was allowed, which meant some of the second tour guys had to take a turn. Whether he did it because it was the most dangerous and thus the most exciting position or by doing it he might spare Rhymes and Trip, he wasn't quite sure.

The patrols were a small relief in the days that mostly involved shoveling and the piling of sandbags. In the end, they had a perimeter with a bunker line and triple coils of wire strung and staked to the front. When the perimeter was done and the men had comfortable positions to defend, they moved on. Despite the relative safety of their new perimeter, Singer was relieved at the news.

Trucks carried them the short distance north into the city of Hue. The first sign of the fighting that had taken place came even before they reached the city. They crossed an engineer's floating bridge installed across a small river beside concrete-and-metal wreckage of the former bridges. A contingent of gaunt Marines with fifty-caliber guns were in place as guards.

"Where is this?" Shooter asked from the front of the truck.

"An Cuu Bridge, Phu Cam Canal," a Marine said. "Hue's open now. You Cherries on the tourist plan?"

"Fuck, you're the Cherry. Every man here is a second-tour man," Shooter said. "What took you guys so long to kick a few farmers out of town? They're always sending us in to mop up stuff you guys can't finish. Talk to me after you've done two tours. Fucking jarheads."

They were already over the bridge, well beyond the Marines, and Singer doubted that they heard. But he kind of liked being included as a vet in Shooter's boast even if it wasn't true.

The signs of destruction grew as they moved farther toward the city center, where Rhymes said the Perfume River and Citadel were. What the hell the Citadel was, Singer had no idea, but he figured better to wait and see rather than ask and sound like he didn't know anything.

"Jesus," Singer said, seeing all the bombed-out buildings and bullet-pock-marked walls. The scenes resembled images in his high school history books, though Vietnam fighting wasn't in any of those books. They had never even discussed the war. He covered his mouth and nose at the pervasive smell, which reminded him of the stench around small lakes in the spring that had frozen out and whose shores were lined with piles of rotting fish. The source of the smell wasn't evident, and he tried not to imagine the scenes of dead or where the corpses might lie.

"They say the Marines saved Hue," Rhymes said.

"It looks like they destroyed it," Trip said.

"Never seen nothing like this," Bear said. "They bombed the hell out of this place."

On a main street called Hùng Vương, Ghost crossed himself and started on some Spanish homily with the cadence of a prayer as they passed a huge rubble pile that might have been a church. Parts of benches, maybe pews, protruded from piles of stone, and within the debris was a pointed structure that could have been a steeple that still held two arms of what looked to have been a cross.

A few Vietnamese were bent over, straining to move bricks or look under collapsed concrete walls at what must have been homes. A woman squatted beside a half-wall, face buried in her hands while her body convulsed in inaudible sobs. But mostly, the streets were empty, though they passed an ARVN patrol whose faces offered nothing but exhaustion. There were no children playing on the streets or sidewalks. None rushed out to run beside the trucks begging for treats. Singer saw one child looking out from a first-floor window, a frightened face pressed against the iron grate across the opening. A few people here and there stood in undamaged doorways and shopfronts, looking nervous and afraid to venture out. A woman pulled two young children closer to her side, keeping her arm wrapped tightly around them, and stepped deeper into the shadows. Not the hero's welcome Singer envisioned.

"Where is everybody?" Singer asked.

"We saw some of them on the road when we came up from Chu Lai. Most probably left weeks ago at Tet, when the fighting started. The Americal guys said it was bad here," Rhymes said.

"It looks quiet now, almost like a ghost town."

"Don't let that fool you. A few weeks ago you would have had to fight to come up this road and it might have taken days to make a hundred yards, with half of you dying."

"Jesus. That must have been something. We were stuck filling sandbags while that was going on."

"It was probably mostly over. In Chu Lai they were all talking about Hue, said the NVA held the town for weeks and didn't run even when the Marines came in."

"What happened?"

"After almost a month of fighting, most the NVA left. It must have been some heavy shit if it took the Marines so long to take back the town. Be thankful we didn't get here a month ago."

"Damn!" Singer said, regretting that he hadn't gotten in on the fight and wondering when they would get their chance. Still, it was puzzling how they could drive up this road unmolested and that none of the remaining residents showed gratitude. No one applauded their arrival. No flowers were thrown to them. No women rushed up to hug and kiss them. He didn't feel much like part of the liberating army.

On the north end of Hùng Vương, near a compound signed MACV, which hadn't entirely escaped the damage, they dismounted the trucks, which immediately turned around to retrace the route with just the drivers and a man riding shotgun on each. An APC blocked the compound entrance and guards with M16s looked on with disinterest.

The Perfume River lay ahead, a wide span cutting east and west, appearing to bisect the city. Hùng Vương went straight, the road rising on to a metal-span bridge that clearly wasn't right. The first section dropped toward the water, as did a length from the other side, and part was simply missing.

"Guess we got to swim," Bear said.

They formed up in platoons and moved off on separate assignments. The fourth moved north the short distance to the river, then went west on Lê Lợi Street, paralleling the waterway.

Before they started walking in a staggered double column, Rhymes slid up next to Singer.

"You have a round chambered?" Rhymes asked.

Singer opened the bolt just enough to see the brass. "Yup."

"Keep your safety on, but stay alert. Don't get careless."

"Isn't it supposed to be secure?"

"It doesn't look secure. You never know who stayed behind."

They pushed down Lê Lợi past the blackened hull of a burnt-out truck, its tires burned away. Past blocks and bricks, tree limbs and torn sheets of corrugated metal scattered in the street. The Perfume River on their right was wide and muddy, with a fast flow that carried debris of tree limbs and boards easterly. No boats plied the waters.

"What's that?" Singer asked, pointing at the huge walls across the river.

"The Citadel," Rhymes said. "The walled city of the emperor. Built 900 years ago."

"You were here before?"

"I read about it."

"Looks like a fortress."

"It is or was."

"Your man there knows everything," Bear said.

"Shut up and watch our flanks," Sergeant Royce said.

Even with towering walls broken and breached, giving some clue to their thickness, and shattered towers that would have been fighting positions, it still looked impressive and a tough obstacle to take. The challenge of fighting in Hue was beginning to form in Singer's mind and he worried it was where they'd stay.

The odor of death lingered even in the air beside the river, but he'd already become used to it and no longer felt the need to cover his nose or suppress a gag now and then. They were on foot, moving through what truly looked like a war zone, away from the tedium of bunker construction that offered to save no one except the nameless men who might come to occupy them in the months ahead. Here there was hope of heroic acts and of actually saving people, though, from the look of things, for many they were already too late.

On their left they passed the shell of a two-story building with bullet-scarred walls and dark, distorted window shapes blown out by gunfire. A yellow flag with three red horizontal bars across the center flew from a pole in the litter-ridden courtyard, a smaller version of the one that hung above the Citadel on a pole that still stood atop the center tower. The flags hung limp in the heat, lifting half-heartedly at a sporadic breeze.

During the patrol down Lê Lợi Street the only people they saw were four ancient Vietnamese men bearing a box that surely was a coffin, trailed by a woman and two girls of almost the woman's height. They passed almost soundlessly, except for footsteps and soft sobs. Singer stopped and watched them pass until Rhymes prodded him to get going.

Near what seemed the west edge of the city, a tall concrete tower loomed on a small island connected to each shore by an unbroken trestle that stood starkly vacant. A thread across the water, connecting things, though Singer couldn't say what. The tower stood dominant and undamaged, a contrast to the scenes of rubble, and Singer wondered how it had been spared. In the far distance were the indigo forms of mountains that made Trip stutter-step before he looked away, making Singer wonder what he saw.

Once they closed the distance to the island, Singer saw the railroad tracks leading across the bridge. A mounted quad-50, which Singer marveled at, unable to imagine the firepower, sat nearby. The Marine in it waved as fourth platoon turned to follow the tracks single file, north onto the bridge. At first it seemed they were going to cross the river on the walkway that ran beside the tracks to the fortress that extended the entire way until the massive wall bore north to parallel the rail line. But instead they dropped off beside the tower onto the island. There they found two unoccupied concrete, one-story houses which still contained the meager furnishings of the former occupants, who had likely fled the fighting. Sergeant Edwards set up a command post in the westernmost house while Singer and the others were assigned defensive positions around the island perimeter.

At night, the men of the fourth platoon lay in shallow holes around the island's edge. Singer gazed into the blackness, straining to see the far riverbank, but somewhere over the water the blackness merged, swallowing distant shapes and forms. The night air was calm and held the daytime heat. It was quiet enough that Singer could hear the current slide and bubble against the island's banks, only the sound giving a hint of the river's eastward flow in the darkness. The mosquitos that had swarmed at twilight, forcing Singer to roll down his sleeves and apply bug dope that was little deterrent, had largely gone quiet.

"Where does it go?" Singer had asked before the last light gave out.

"The South China Sea. About six miles," Rhymes said.

"And the mountains?"

"They look closer than they are. They extend into Laos about thirty miles as a crow flies, I would guess. A short helicopter ride, but a long march."

Maybe Trip, when he flinched at the sight of the mountains, was seeing Laos or imagining what they would have to go through to get there. Did he know something the rest didn't?

Beside Singer was Rhymes's sleeping form, so hard to discern in the blackness that he kept looking toward it every few minutes, resisting the urge to reach out for reassurance. He tried to concentrate, listening for the soft stroke of a paddle, the stir of a swimmer, or the movement of grass which swimmers might make pulling themselves from the water, imaging himself on a deer stand listening for a footstep or scrape of a branch. The stillness was so complete Singer wondered if he could hear at all. His mind wanted to drift. He turned his head slightly, scanning the nothingness, struggling to avoid being hypnotized by it.

He tried not to think about the fear he felt sometimes. Tonight was one of those times when he felt it, the hole in his gut and the dryness in his mouth. Perhaps it was the new position, trapped on a small river island. Or maybe it was the images of the damaged town and Citadel, weeping women digging in rubble, and the coffin he couldn't push from his mind. If only a breeze would come up it might chase away the smell of death, if not the images.

He lifted his hand from his M16, pushed his arm out his sleeve until his watch was visible, then held it close to his face trying to make out the time. Only ten minutes had passed since he last checked. He was certain it had been an hour. In the dark stillness it was easy to believe he was alone. The last survivor on the planet. Was the form beside him real?

"Wake me if you hear anything," Rhymes had told him. He thought of waking him, telling him he had heard something. Then they could sit up together and he wouldn't feel alone or afraid. It was just the strangeness of everything and not knowing what to expect. He couldn't let it get to him.

He tried to think of mornings in a duck blind, sitting in the darkness with a gun in his lap waiting for dawn and the first sound of wings. He hadn't been scared then, but this was so different. He gazed into the blackness, determined to see the river bank and anchor himself. If he could see the river bank maybe the aloneness, the feeling of floating, would fall away. But his vision gave out only a few yards in front of him.

That night passed into another, and the days into a week. The monotony of nighttime guard challenged Singer's ability to stay alert. Daytime patrols provided more images of destruction and grief, their repetitiveness already threatening to harden him. But the fear and uncertainty had lessened with each night, though his anxiousness for what he imagined they were there for grew.

On one of their patrols, Singer got two ducklings, just weeks old, from a woman they encountered with at least fifty jammed into a basket, a yellow, peeping mass. She let him hold one and it sat there in his hand, turning its small yellow head to examine him with one eye, then peeping in acknowledgement or petition. It sat while he stroked its back with two fingers, the touch of down and the small heartbeats soothing so that he had to keep it.

"You can't eat those. They're too damn small," Bear said.

Quickly he made a deal and left with two ducklings peering from his pocket as he continued the patrol.

"Jesus," Trip said. "Get a dog if you want a pet."

Back at the island, Rhymes helped Singer pick seeds and catch bugs to feed them. The ducklings ate easily from their hands and took to waiting for the next morsel. They ventured into the river, slipping from the bank and looking near panic, peeping frantically, before climbing out two meters downstream. They took to following Singer around, which was a problem when they had formations, which Sergeant Milner liked to call often. But the problem was solved when on the third day they disappeared. "Maybe the river or some animal," Rhymes said. Singer suspected Trip was involved in their demise, though he denied it.

The evening the ducklings disappeared brought some excitement, at least for Singer, with the announcement that it was their last night and tomorrow they would move. The news had little effect on Rhymes, who clung to the comfort of his reading whenever he could. If he marked off each day as one closer to leaving, he kept it to himself, unlike Trip who announced it maybe to assure himself rather than for the public display. Like Bear and a few others, Trip seemed content with the island duty and the relative peacefulness of post-Tet Hue. Trip muttered to himself at the news, and then he and Bear shared a glance, perhaps each unhappy that they shared a common thought.

The blanket of clouds brought an early nightfall that didn't dampen Singer's spirits. He settled down in his island foxhole that had nearly become a familiar home, entertaining scenes of battles and heroic rescues of grateful villagers that played out absent of any fear. Tonight he had no doubts. Rhymes had already lain down after abandoning his book, well beyond the point Singer thought it might be possible to read.

* * * * *

With a start, Singer woke bolting upright, frightened. He groped for his weapon and pushed the poncho liner off his shoulder. His fatigues clung to his body in a wet clamminess and his heart pounded like he was in a sprint. He looked about, trying to chase his confusion and determine what had scared him.

"You all right?" Rhymes asked.

"Yeah."

But he still didn't have his bearings. The first rays of dawn reflected off the river though the island trees, and the concrete tower threw long shadows over them. The blackness was gone, replaced by browns, grays, and the green of the distant riverbank.

He remembered being woken by gunfire in the night and Rhymes touching his arm and whispering, "Don't fire. Don't give our position away." Then Rhymes put a grenade in his hand, the pin still in. "Use this if you hear them. Let the handle fly before you throw it." They lay side-by-side, listening, but nothing else happened and eventually Singer fell back asleep.

Now, in the dawn, Singer studied the riverbank and its marsh grasses for a long time, as though trying to memorize it for a test. He took a drink of warm, stale water from his canteen, trying to wash the night from his mouth and his mind.

When they gathered in the courtyard near the houses, Shooter sauntered up to Trip. Shooter's pants were wet up to his knees and his boots were leaking water.

"Way to light them up, Ace," Shooter said. "The Marines found a body in the reeds and a sampan a half-klick further down. Three rounds in the chest. One burst and you ripped him. Impressive when you couldn't see your hand in front of your face."

"I heard the rhythm, had to be paddle strokes. Counted. Measured," Trip said.

"Yeah, but one blind burst and you nail the guy. I underestimated you. A young gook, too. Good shooting." Shooter shook Trip's hand.

"I won't have that shit. The man had no weapon," Sergeant Milner said. "He was a civilian. I won't—"

"His weapon's on the bottom of the river. Be my guest recovering it," Trip said.

"I won't allow indiscriminate fire."

"I'm going home. I ain't getting zapped by some dink." Trip brought his M16 up across his chest.

"You need some fire discipline, soldier."

"A kill's a kill, Sarge. One dead gook's as good as another. Weapon or no weapon, they all go in the same column," Shooter said. "One more for our side."

"Without a threat, we don't shoot."

"What do you call a nighttime probe? Next time I hear something I'll let you take care of it," Trip said.

"You'll follow the rules or else."

Bear stepped in next to Sergeant Milner. "The man was Viet Cong. No fisherman's out in the middle of the night like that. Drag the river, I bet you find an AK. Hell, I'd have shot him, too. Lighten up, Sarge, this is the Nam. There are no rules."

Sergeant Milner slid away from the arm Bear tried to lay on his shoulder and went back to the house that had become the platoon CP, Bear's laugh following him.

"I'm going home," Trip said. "That guy better not get in my way."

Late that morning they left the island as they arrived, single file over the trestle with the same number as they'd brought. Two Marines beside the quad-50 watched them leave, giving them a thumbs up. When they arrived at a field where the river ran south along the expanse of grass and sinkholes, a few with cattails that to Singer looked the same as those at home, the rest of the company was there waiting in three bunches with the command group forming a fourth side. White birds with long legs, but necks shorter than a blue heron, lifted from the field in twos and threes, circled and resettled. Some rode the backs of buffalo, white passengers atop massive black ships.

At a familiar sound, Singer searched the southern skies and never looked away as a line of specks grew into Hueys that settled down before them, idling without urgency.

"Finally, fucking helicopters," Trip said. "Wonder where they got these."

In the first group, Singer raced for the assigned bird and settled on the floor with the others, who were talking nonchalantly. Singer guessed it was nothing new to them and maybe at some point would be the same for him. But now he felt the thrill of having just climbed onto an amusement park ride and looked from one open door to the other waiting for lift off, not caring if the others saw his grin.

The Huey's blades chopped the air, the engine pounded above his head, and the air streamed through the cabin while the ground sped by below them. Singer saw the river, a grass field, pockmarked hills with trees that hid the ground, but hardly any human structures or signs of habitation. At times he could see another of the Hueys flying beside them, men seated, legs hanging from the door just above the skids, the helmeted gunner swiveling his head, peering at the ground, both hands set on his weapon.

They crossed the river, heading west toward a sea of rising green peaks stretching toward the horizon. To the south the river split, and they headed toward the westward branch before circling a dominant peak with bunkers, artillery pieces, tents, and bare earth that marked a more permanent army encampment.

Singer leaned over to ask Rhymes what firebase this was, but Rhymes either didn't know or didn't hear him, as he didn't respond. No one paid much attention to their arrival, as if it were a common thing. They stood around waiting for the last group. Below the firebase, the river meandered through a mottled green landscape that looked almost tranquil. A single-lane dirt road ran between the river and the mountain, climbing from the east, running past the base of the mountain winding south, then north, then disappearing behind the next mountain.

After a brief wait in which Captain Powers, Charlie Company's commanding officer, probably conferred with the firebase commander, they left the firebase on foot heading northwest. They descended easily, then crossed open ground in the blaze of sunlight before finding shade under an increasingly thick canopy at the start of a difficult climb. After a few hours of seemingly endless ups and downs, they flopped to the ground on a side slope. Singer's legs felt like they were still climbing, his body like he was in a steam cooker. He set his helmet in his lap, making his head dizzy with the lightness.

"Keep drinking water," Rhymes said "Just a little at a time. Stay alert. This is where the NVA live."

Singer looked around him and put his helmet back on.

"We should have stayed in Hue," Bear said from downslope.

"Fuck, we should have stayed home," Trip said.

"I could maybe grow to like you," Bear said.

"Now you're scaring me," Trip said.

Even Rhymes smiled. Bear might have let go with one of his raucous laughs had they been back in Hue or even on a firebase, but here he merely showed large teeth and creases beside widened eyes.

At times Singer heard the *whack* of a machete, dull, reverberating blows, and he saw Trip cringe and swing his weapon from side to side as though expecting an attack. A long time later, as Singer climbed through sharp stumps of bamboo, where he was careful not to fall, fearing he'd impale himself, he began to understand why Bear and some of others disliked the mountains. Only one day and he already hated the darkness. He could climb hills all day in sunlight—or at least he believed he could, though he had never climbed mountains before nor experienced such heat. There were enemies here besides the NVA that could bring a man down. Still, he was hopeful to find them, though the thought waned with his fatigue and recovered itself after he rested.

He knew things had become more serious since Rhymes didn't dig out a book during breaks but held onto his M79. Besides this, and Bear's withheld laughter and Trip's flinching at each sound, Red had gone silent again, appearing to withdraw inside himself. Ghost looked restless and spooked, bouncing around like a nervous colt while others sat and rested. If he prayed, he did it silently.

Top was often there beside the column as they climbed, watching, as if studying each man, taking some measure. Then he'd come climbing past, acting stronger and younger than all of them though Rhymes said he'd fought in Korea and had heard he'd turned down a field command.

The first days in the mountains were spent patrolling, sometimes as a company but usually as platoons, searching for an enemy that seemed either absent or unwilling to be found. In the evenings they dug in on some mountaintop in a defensive perimeter, waiting and listening for the enemy, staring into the darkness, alone with their thoughts. They went out on ambushes and listening posts that brought Singer a new sense of the night and a different anxiousness. In the morning they moved on to new country, new mountains and new valleys that looked the same as those they left.

Sweat streamed down Singer's face and soaked his fatigues. Dirt clung to his skin and clothes, weariness grew in his bones, and he wondered if the others felt it, too. Trip counted days, claiming fewer than forty-seven, as Singer guessed everyone was doing except him and maybe Stick. With too many days left to consider, Singer let the days pass untallied.

In late afternoon one day, Singer sat on a rocky edge, his feet hanging over the side, looking over the treetops of the valley they had worked through the past week without finding anything or taking any casualties. With Rhymes and Trip slated for a listening post, he was sharing the night position with Bear, who sat cross-legged next to the shallow fighting hole they had given up on digging any deeper. Bear was heating water over a heat tab in an old C-ration can for instant coffee. His M16 lay beside him, on top of a bandolier of magazines. He had his shirt off and his muscular, hairless chest shone in the sunlight, still glistening with sweat. It had been a tough climb. Sometimes the men above had had to help the men below scramble ahead, holding out their hands or extending an M16 to pull men up the steep slope. Once on top, Singer found a commanding view that almost made the day's long climb worth it. The NVA, if they had ever used it, weren't here now and left no signs of earlier occupancy.

They had reached the summit late in the afternoon and held up for the day, stopping earlier than usual. It was a rare break that Singer hoped would give his aching body some relief. He relaxed when he didn't draw an ambush or LP assignment and could spend the night on the perimeter. With some luck, fourth platoon had drawn a rocky open side of the mountaintop with a steep drop that made it an unlikely approach. That and the days without contact had Singer feeling complacent, letting go of some of the vigilance Rhymes constantly reminded him to maintain.

Below him, a mosaic of shadows played through the treetops. Black holes amid the green gave a hint of the jungle floor far below. The sky was a deepening blue with soft, loose swirls of clouds stretching out over the mountains. A line of distant choppers moved silently across the horizon. The soft murmur of the voices of men in other positions drifted to Singer, the evening so tranquil he almost forgot where he was. He touched his M16 to hold to reality. Drifting away would be dangerous.

He took his helmet off, again lightheaded without the weight, and then removed his shirt. Singer's hands and arms were a dark brown, in sharp contrast to his starkly white torso. His ribs had begun to show so that each one was defined and easily counted. Though leaner, he'd grown tougher with the days of mountain patrols and the climbs—even like the one he'd just made—were more bearable. Still, the fatigue that came with the long days of battling the terrain and too little sleep was always there.

A few days earlier the first mail from the States had finally caught up with them and he remained cheered by it and the promise of more. That day they'd stopped early on a grassy plateau that seemed to hold few perils and waited for a scheduled resupply. A large, red mail bag came in on the bird that brought in Cs and water. Men clambered toward the bag, leaving the food and water piled for the moment. It was a bright moment in which even the dourest seemed encouraged. Field discipline broke down, with only a small contingent of men staying on the perimeter, but no one said anything. Shooter was one of those who stayed in position, perhaps knowing his name wouldn't be called. Men crowded around Sergeant Milner, who held the red bag. Singer saw expectation in faces that he imagined mirrored his own.

The bag included a letter for Sergeant Prascanni, and Sergeant Milner called his name before realizing his mistake. They all stood quietly and awkwardly for a beat before Sergeant Milner hurriedly called another name.

Singer walked away with a letter and box of cookies from Susan, a letter from Kathy, and one from his mom. His brother hadn't written since Singer asked his mom to tell his brother to stop preaching at him. His mom's letter was filled with mundane small-town gossip and news about food she was baking. He smiled at Kathy's inappropriate humor about Susan and her sexual comments meant to cheer him up. The cookies were hard as rocks, but no one refused and the box was quickly empty. After reading Susan's letter twice, he put it in his helmet liner. He shredded and buried the other letters and box wrapping so as to leave nothing for the enemy.

Rhymes received a few books from his father, which had him as excited as Singer had ever seen him. The cache included two more books of poetry and a Steinbeck novel, *Of Mice and Men*. When Rhymes said he'd have to bury some and hope to get back to them, Singer offered to carry some if he didn't have to read them. Apparently even Rhymes could only carry so many books along with the bulky and heavy M79 rounds. Trip got one letter, which he said was all he needed. Red got a Cincinnati baseball schedule, which he ran around showing everyone but wouldn't let anyone hold. Singer listened as the last letter was announced and saw Stick melt away, empty-handed and with downcast eyes.

A good letter, Singer already realized, could keep a man going for days, give him something to fight for, and increase his resolve to make it home—as if that needed any help. Now, sitting on the ledge with twilight not far away, Singer removed the envelope from its safe position inside his helmet. He held the powder-blue paper to his nose. The perfume had faded, and the letter now smelled only of sweat. Some of the ink had faded, but it was still mostly readable—at least the important parts where Susan said she was waiting and what they would do when he got back. He held the letter in his lap, looking at the sinking sun and deepening shadows, reluctant to put it away.

"You reading that again?" Bear asked. "You going to wear that letter out."

Singer just smiled, not ready to speak, feeling the heat of the letter.

"That the girl you sending your paychecks to?"

"What need is there for money here?"

"I don't know if I'd ever trust any woman with my money except my mama."

"We're saving for our future."

"Man, that girl's got you by the balls. There's no helping you."

"She's just a friend."

"Fuck just a friend. That kind of perfume, you been giving her something for sure. Don't be carrying that with you, Charlie will follow that smell right to you, kill both our asses."

"I'll tell her to be careful with the smell, that she's making you crazy."

"You be careful with your thing, too." Bear gave a soft chuckle.

After carefully refolding the letter, Singer put it back in the top of his helmet liner. Bear was drinking his instant coffee, for which he begged three extra sugars and two powdered creams. Each time Bear brought the C-rat can to his lips, his bicep bulged above a thick forearm.

"You never talk about a girl," Singer said.

"I'm between girls. Easier right now," Bear said, grinning as if he had a secret.

"You miss that?"

"What? Sweet letters? I smell enough perfume from yours. There'll be plenty girls wanting to see me when I'm back on the block. I might even go see your girl, tell her you miss her since you won't be seeing her any time soon. Thirty-two and a wake-up and I'll be on the street."

"Fuck you," Singer said without anger.

"What are friends for?" Bear asked, spilling his coffee as he laughed. "Thirty-two and a wake-up, then you'll have to do it without Bear."

This was closer to the Bear that Singer had come to know from those first days back at Fort Bragg. The stern, sullen Bear of the first patrol near Chu Lai that had disturbed, if not frightened him, was gone, at least tonight. Maybe Bear was over the shock of being back in Nam or, having survived those first patrols, saw himself surviving and was now counting the days and thinking of being back on the block. In thirty-three days, Bear was going home. Singer wondered sometimes what things would be like and what he would do after all the guys left. So many had little more than a month remaining.

For a while they sat quietly, shadows expanding in the valley far below and the sun settling toward the peaks in Laos. Singer put his shirt back on and then his helmet. Soon it would be time to be serious again. He pulled his M16 across his lap

"Think we'll find them?" Singer asked.

"The NVA?"

"Yeah. Think we'll find them?"

"Fuck. Hope we don't. I seen enough of them. If you want to make it back to that girl, you'll hope so, too."

"It's been quiet. I mean, it just seems like we're doing nothing, you know?"

"Shit, we're burnin' days! Good days. Each day's another day closer to going home. Alive."

"But . . ." Singer hesitated, uncertain if he should say it. "We . . . ah . . . I came to fight. I mean, that's what we're here for, isn't it?"

"Christ, Singer, you're fucking hopeless," Bear said, shaking his head. "Where'd you get them dumb white-ass ideas? This ain't your war. It sure the fuck ain't my war. We should all be home smoking, drinking, and chasing pussy. Instead we're on some fucking godforsaken mountaintop that we fought through jungle to get to and that we'll leave tomorrow."

Bear leaned toward Singer, his eyes drawing tighter and darkening.

"It don't mean a fucking thing to anyone but our mamas and our girl-friends whether we get killed. You think the army gives a shit about you? After enough of us die, some politicians will shake hands and that'll be the end and our deaths won't mean a goddamn thing."

Bear put on his shirt and took up his rifle.

"And afterwards, what do we go home to? I can serve here, but try to find a job or even buy a car with money in my hand and some white guy don't want to let me in the door. Now they shot our man in Memphis. Don't you get it? We're fighting in the wrong place. Where you from, anyway?"

"I'm sorry."

"Fuck, you're a pawn as much as me."

"But you still do it."

"Yeah . . . I still do it."

Bear picked up the C-rat cans he'd used for a cup and a stove and put them back in his ruck, then stood up and walked to the ledge beside Singer, his rifle pointed at the treetops.

"Just stop wishing for it," Bear said. "It's fucking bad luck. Ain't enough men died? Wish for good days, man, at least 'til I'm gone. Thirty-two and a wake-up. Then you can have this fucking white-ass war and all the fighting you want."

The lump in Singer's throat cut off anything he might say. He still believed they were here to do something good. To stop a bad system and save another. He needed to believe that. He was committed to it and all it meant. He was ready. Maybe there were just too many differences in experiences and backgrounds. Things he couldn't understand. Yet Bear was here beside him and Rhymes and Sergeant Edwards. It couldn't all be bad, like Bear said. Was he wrong to want to do what they came here for?

"Get some sleep. I'll take the first watch," Bear said

Singer curled up under a poncho liner away from the ledge, behind the shallow fighting hole. It was barely dark and he hardly felt like sleep now. In addition to Rhymes, he saw Bear as a friend and someone to rely on if things got rough. He still did, but he needed to think about what Bear said. Why did he still fight if he believed that? When had things changed, if he hadn't always thought that way? He finally fell asleep, wondering if Bear believed in it the first time he came here and what had happened to change that.

5

April 17, 1968
Vietnam

It was just another formless mountaintop that would be this night's NDP, an easy climb from a narrow, stream-cut valley they had worked for a few klicks without incident. To Singer, it seemed they were miles from any NVA and had been looking in the wrong place for weeks already. He had just started digging in with little enthusiasm when Sergeant Royce, holding a string of canteens, came up to Trip, who had just gotten out his entrenching tool. Singer stopped digging to listen.

"Send a couple Cherries," Trip said.

"I'm sending you," Sergeant Royce said, his voice rising until it cracked. "What about the hole?"

"You can dig in when you get back. Right now, you and Singer go fill canteens."

"Fucking army." Trip threw down his entrenching tool. "In the Cav choppers brought our waters and Cherries pulled the details."

Singer stepped from the beginning of the hole and came and took the string of empty canteens.

"No sweat, we got it," Singer said, looking at Trip.

With his M16 in his right hand and canteens in his left, he started back toward the stream they'd crossed a short distance back. In truth, he was nearly as irritated as Trip at being sent out after just starting to dig in. There was no trail, just the occasional bootprint or bent twig from their earlier climb. The descent was easy on the gradual slope and Singer focused all his attention on where he stepped and keeping a straight line, confident Trip wasn't far behind him. He wanted to do this fast and get back before it got dark. He would find the stream, fill the canteens, then reverse directions and take a direct course back to the perimeter. It grew darker as he descended. The sun was low behind him and the hill cast a long shadow over the canopy, increasing the dimness in the shallow valley. Fronds bent down toward him, like giant hands threatening to grab him. The canteens jangled softly against each other with each step, despite his efforts to keep them still.

Singer drew up sharply, halted by the sense that something was wrong. The canteens were quiet. The leaves gave no indication of even the slightest breath of air. The sounds of digging that he'd heard behind him as he first started out were swallowed by the distance and the vegetation. Ahead was the whisper of flowing water. Still, something wasn't right. He turned his head to check with Trip, but there were only the trees, a weave of limbs and branches amidst the shadows. His gaze raced up the slope, searching for Trip's form beside a tree trunk, a silhouette camouflaged by brush. Nothing. No human form. Not even the soft pad of steps of Trip catching up. He was utterly alone. A lightness fluttered in his chest and the vertical lines that held the canopy shifted back and forth, threatening to spin. He blinked and felt the sting of sweat. With care not to lose his orientation of the stream and the direction back to the platoon, he turned in a circle, trying to conjure up Trip. There were only shadows and his craving for company.

He was drifting in space, untethered to anything. His mouth was just opening when he caught himself, closing it forcefully, biting down so he wouldn't call out. He saw himself tearing uphill with all his energy until he was in the comfort of the company of the others, but his legs wouldn't move. Beyond the pounding of his heart was the gurgle of water moving over rocks. He was nearly there. If he went back now he would only have to return again through even darker shadows. He had his rifle and could do this if he could just control his fear.

The water was a welcome sight, swirling about rocks, small patches of white foam bubbling up and quickly being carried away. The bottom was a mosaic of stones, tans and browns set in red clay. It would take just a few minutes to fill the canteens and then a few minutes more to return to the guys. He slipped up to the stream edge, nearly distracted by the magic of moving water, but then Singer saw him.

The canteens clunked and rattled when he dropped them on the rocks. He fumbled to bring up his gun.

A few meters down the stream, the man looked up, still holding his hand and something in the water. He lifted his hand to show a canteen encased in dark canvas. Water spilled off the canteen, darkening his sleeve and dribbling back into the stream. He rose slowly from his crouch. His black hair was matted against his head and his face glistened with water as if he'd just washed it. He wore a dark green uniform of a North Vietnamese soldier and had an olive-colored bandolier hung across his chest. He continued to hold the canteen out, as if to offer a drink. His other hand hung loose and empty at his side.

Singer brought his rifle to his shoulder and sighted down the barrel.

A gold tooth sat dully in the man's weak smile. His eyes were dark and soft, like his skin, and grew wider with a silent pleading that Singer clearly heard. Still, he lined the muzzle on the man's chest and felt the smoothness of the trigger on his finger. It would only take a touch. His first kill.

The corners of the man's smile sagged and he took a step back, as though that might make a difference. His head bowed, a greeting or surrender to his fate.

* * * * *

"I'm coming in, I'm coming in," Singer said, hoping none of the new guys would shoot him.

Inside the perimeter he rushed at Trip and threw the canteens at his feet, then shoved him with his free hand.

"Where the hell were you? You're supposed to have my back."

"Why didn't you wait?"

"You prick, you let me go alone."

"When I looked, you were gone. It was more dangerous for both of us to go look for you. You're all right, aren't you?"

"No thanks to you."

"Stop the yelling before you get us all killed," Sergeant Royce said from somewhere in the twilight behind them.

"There's the fucking canteens. I'm not doing that again," Singer said. He kicked the canteens and walked away.

He knew he should warn them, but couldn't. How could he tell them he saw an NVA soldier without having to explain why he never fired? No one would understand, least of all Sergeant Royce or all the other second-tour vets. Rhymes might, but even with him, Singer wasn't sure. None of them would forgive him. They'd all seen too much and become hardened by it all.

He was unsure now what was his bigger crime: not killing the man or not telling anyone.

He just couldn't shoot the guy. Even though the man was an enemy soldier, he was unarmed. At least, there'd been no weapon Singer could see. Who could shoot an unarmed man? It was different than with a deer or duck, where he'd never had a problem. He saw the man's extended arm of offering and the pleading in his eyes. He sighted down the barrel and saw himself. Next time he'd do better. Next time he would shoot.

6

May 4, 1968
Vietnam

Red fox six. This is red fox four. Over." Singer checked the frequency. He had been carrying the radio for almost two weeks now as Sergeant Edwards's RTO, but he still wasn't comfortable with it. He held the handset to his ear and called again, "Red fox six. This is red fox four. Over."

"Red fox six. Over," the company commander's RTO answered.

"Red fox four. Com check. Over."

"Red fox six. Lima Charlie. Over."

"Red fox four. Out." Singer put the handset down on his ruck and turned up the volume just by feel. He didn't dare flash a light and risk revealing his position despite everyone else being away from the platoon CP set up inside the company perimeter. Sergeant Edwards was still up at the company CP for a briefing with Captain Powers after they had moved into the NDP late, feeling their way through the last hour. Sergeant Milner was checking the platoon's section of the perimeter and would likely find something he was unhappy with and try to make someone move. There still wasn't a platoon medic, Doc Randall having left a few weeks before without explanation, some saying to take a unit transfer. Some said he'd had enough and was just gone, though they offered no speculation as to where he went. Shooter said Doc had likely finagled some beach assignment at Nha Trang or Cam Ranh Bay doing health checks on whorehouse girls to keep the rear cadre safe. When Singer first heard this he wondered if there really were such places or if it was just Shooter telling wild tales. It was Rhymes's explanation that Doc's brother, a Marine, had been killed up near the DMZ and Doc left to escort his brother's body home that seemed the most believable.

With Doc gone they were mostly on their own in the event of a medical emergency, which would likely be a bullet or frag wound. Until they got a new platoon medic, the company medic, Doc Odum, was filling in. He was a loose-limbed black guy with an elastic face and demeanor better suited to a comic than a combat medic. Maybe that was why Singer liked him.

Despite staring toward the perimeter, Singer couldn't make out any familiar shape and had to guess at where Rhymes, Trip, Bear, Red, Ghost, and Sergeant Royce were. It had only been nine days, but he hadn't stopped regretting the assignment or wishing he were back in his squad.

"You do a coms check yet?"

Sergeant Milner was more grating in proximity. Another drawback of being the platoon RTO.

"Just did one, Sarge," Singer said.

"Do another and stay near your handset."

"Right, Sarge."

He picked up the handset and held it to his ear, putting it down as soon as Sergeant Milner walked away. Had Sergeant Edwards been there, Sergeant Milner wouldn't have said a thing, but in his absence Sergeant Milner was always trying to exercise authority he would never have, no matter what rank he carried. It came off as the efforts of an insecure man trying too hard. Yet the man seemed oblivious to the men's contempt.

Singer focused on where he imagined the guys were dug in, setting up their guard rotations after already putting out claymores. Rhymes was probably brushing his teeth for the second time, meticulous in their care. Trip probably had his calendar out, marking off a day. Bear was probably complaining to someone about the fucking "white-ass war." Singer shook his head recalling Bear's many tirades, wishing he could listen to one now. Bear complained about the war but he was steady, dependable. You could count on Bear. Red was probably boring someone with a recitation of Pete Rose's statistics for the past two years. Once, after one of Red's passionate orations, Singer had told Red, "You should be Rose's PR man," to which Red beamed as though Singer had paid him some great compliment.

What would happen to them if he wasn't there? What would happen to him without them beside him? He wanted to kick the fucking radio and cursed his luck for the assignment.

It all changed nearly two weeks ago, when Borkman was hit and medevac'd. Borkman, a short, quiet white guy from somewhere in the Midwest, had been Sergeant Edwards's RTO from the beginning. But Singer didn't know Borkman. He doubted anybody did, since, like Singer now as Sergeant Edwards's RTO, Borkman had little contact with the other men. Singer would see Borkman on the trail always walking behind Sergeant Edwards or next to him monitoring the platoon communications, but he never had any occasion to talk with him. He would see Borkman hand Sergeant Edwards the handset and stand patiently next to him, seemingly oblivious of the inviting target they offered. Perhaps Borkman had merely found a way to tune it out to allow himself to function, as Singer was learning. Borkman's short stature emphasized his chunky body and he hardly looked fit enough to be humping jungle trails in the oppressive heat, especially with the added weight of the PRC25. It had to be harder for a fat man, but Singer never heard him protest, even though complaining seemed part of a foot soldier's obligation.

They medevac'd him from a jungle clearing after he was hit in the legs by small-arms fire in a brief gun battle during a platoon patrol. The fight was quickly over and only Borkman was hit. It frustrated Singer that once more he missed out on the action and the chance to fire. It seemed he wasn't doing much except, as Bear said, burning days.

When it happened, Bear was closer and saw it all, though he said he never saw the enemy. Borkman didn't cry out or say a word. He just went down and lay there quietly, bleeding. He didn't talk while Shooter dressed his wounds and Sergeant Edwards called in a medevac. Nor did he say anything while waiting for the helicopter that would carry him to an aid station. Borkman seemed as quietly resolved to his wounds and his fate as he had to carrying the radio.

They removed the radio from Borkman's ruck. Someone threw the ruck and web gear onto the medevac as they slid Borkman onto the floor of the Huey. The helicopter lingered on the ground for only a few seconds, just long enough for them to load Borkman on his last chopper ride. A Cobra chopper circled overhead, ready to suppress any enemy fire. Then the medevac rose and both choppers turned east, heading for the closest aid station.

Singer watched Borkman go as he had Sergeant Prascanni, with the same sense of relief that it wasn't him. The dustoff grew smaller, fading as he imagined his memory of Borkman would, and he wondered in that moment where Borkman was from. It didn't bother him that he didn't know. Maybe that was the beginning of not caring or of his own hardening. How many choppers would he watch come and go before it was all over?

The Huey carrying Borkman was barely out of sight and Singer was still looking at the sky wondering at these things when Sergeant Edwards came over.

"Singer, you're my RTO. Strap the radio on your gear."

Rhymes and Trip were there, and Singer looked to them for help. Didn't they know how important it was for him to stay with them? No one objected before Sergeant Edwards turned away.

"I'll help you strap it on," Rhymes said. "I can take my books back if it's too much weight."

"I've never been an RTO," Singer said.

"Most guys haven't. It's just radio com. You just have to say 'over' or 'out' after everything. It should keep you out of the worst of things, being with Sergeant Edwards."

"Right."

After Rhymes helped Singer rearrange his gear and tie the radio on, showing him the purpose of each dial, he left to rejoin the squad while Singer moved to stand beside Sergeant Edwards.

Recalling it now, he still wasn't sure whether Sergeant Edwards simply grabbed him for RTO because he was the first man he saw or if Sergeant Edwards thought he possessed some qualities that would make him a good RTO, whatever those might be. It didn't matter. What did matter was that in that moment he was separated from the guys and everything changed.

After Borkman was gone, the platoon saddled up again. Singer struggled into his ruck, surprised at its heaviness even though while they strapped it on, Rhymes had said it weighed about twenty-five pounds. When they moved out, he stood quietly beside Sergeant Edwards, his M16 loosely in his left hand, the radio handset in his right, and watched the platoon pass him.

Rhymes, Trip, Bear, Red, Ghost, Sergeant Royce, Shooter, Stick, and the others filed by in a slow, funeral-like possession. It was as though Singer was dead and they were filing past the casket. Singer thought to say something but couldn't find words. Most averted their eyes, or perhaps they were just focusing on the trail ahead. Rhymes nodded slightly and grinned, showing glistening white teeth. His eyes still held some life, unlike so many others which held emptiness or something akin to despair.

"Giving up the infantry for radio work?" Trip asked, but seemed amused, not angry.

Bear looked at the antenna above Singer's head, winked, and raised his weapon in an enormous black hand in what Singer saw as a salute.

Singer watched them go, tight-lipped, steeled against the loss and wondering how he could still have their backs. The PRC25 weighed heavily on Singer, but it was light compared to the ache he felt inside his chest.

It would all be different now. He would travel next to Sergeant Edwards and set up at the platoon CP. There would be no more shared foxholes with the guys, no more promises to take care of each other, no more talk of the world or of plans upon their return. No reminiscing about girlfriends, cars, or parties. Well, there would be, but he just wouldn't be a part of it. Sergeant Edwards would talk with him in the way sergeants talk with their subordinates, giving orders and protocols for each day.

With the radio on his back that first day, Singer watched each man move away until they all passed, then he fell in behind Sergeant Edwards near the end of the platoon, carrying his new burdens quietly as Borkman had. That night, he pulled radio watch inside the perimeter and behind the men, as he had every night since becoming the RTO. In the morning he watched the procession of men depart without really feeling a part of it.

His first week with the radio after Borkman was hit was quiet. They patrolled the jungles southwest of LZ Birmingham, one of a number of mountaintop firebases the brigade had built along the dirt road that wound through the mountains toward Laos. South of the river the slopes were less steep, but the climbs were difficult with the radio pushing him down. There were no signs of the men who shot Borkman or of any larger force from which they'd come. Singer handled the platoon communications uncertainly but well enough that no one complained or corrected him. Sergeant Edwards gave him orders and direction in a businesslike though not unfriendly manner, but there were no personal conversations to fill the empty hours.

Each day Singer had watched his squad come and go on patrols and ambushes, feeling a sense of separation and a new kind of anxiety. He listened to radio coms as a new mother listens to a newborn breathe, seeking reassurance they were alive. He watched the guys working, eating, and visiting from a distance, tied to his radio and new position.

Occasionally when Sergeant Edwards or, rarely, Sergeant Milner covered the radio, Singer walked over and visited his old squad. There was a new awkwardness Singer couldn't understand or explain. The guys teased him good-naturedly about his "new gravy job," as though he had sought it out and used it to escape.

"Keep it up and you'll be a fucking general soon," Trip said, then walked away.

It was clear that things were different. He didn't walk point anymore or go out on ambushes. The bond that had existed was broken, or at least bent. He was off the team.

This morning when the gunfire came, thinking his squad had the point, he started forward on a run and made two steps before being brought up short.

"Stop! Where you going?" Sergeant Edwards said, already down on one knee.

"It's my squad."

"Your job is here now."

Singer returned, but kept looking toward the gunfire. Sergeant Edwards took the handset and called in the contact to the company CP, which was two platoons back in the company column.

"Medic!" someone yelled, but Singer couldn't identify the voice.

Singer shifted his body on the ground while continuing to watch the front.

"Who is it?" Singer asked, even though he understood Sergeant Edwards couldn't know.

The call for the medic passed back quickly and then Doc Odum was there, panting like a smoker. "How much farther?"

"Maybe fifty meters," Sergeant Edwards said.

"Take my rifle," Singer said, holding it out to Doc.

"It will only get in my way. If I'm holding a rifle I'm not doing my job."

Then Doc was up and running, all arms and legs, just a medical bag in his hands.

"I could go help," Singer said.

"Goddamn it, Singer, just man the radio," Sergeant Edwards said.

The second platoon moved up on the flank and after a short time the gunfire died. Doc was back beside them, blood on his hands and sleeves and a dark stain on his leg, likely where he'd knelt.

"Was it Rhymes?" Singer asked.

"A white guy—" Doc said.

"Trip?"

"I think they said the guy's name was Styler. He was lucky. They're bringing him back now."

"Wasn't Sergeant Royce's squad on point?"

"Don't know about that. Just the name they told me."

"Thanks," Singer said.

"Lucky I still make house calls." Doc sat down and busied himself arranging items in his bag.

"Medevac's on the way," Sergeant Edwards said.

After the medevac left, they moved on without further contact, eventually stopping and digging in for the night.

Now as he sat with the radio after making the sit com check, the gunfire and his fears kept replaying in his mind, as they had all afternoon. Eating at him. Building toward some explosion.

Singer looked up to see Sergeant Edwards emerge from the darkness and settle down next to his ruck. Small amounts of moonlight filtered through the canopy, softening the night, though the moon itself was blocked from view. Sergeant Edwards's face looked weary, showing tight lines Singer hadn't seen before. They were the first crack he'd noticed in Sergeant Edwards's toughness. He wondered what he might have heard at the briefing that had exhausted him and worried his mood.

"Any news on Borkman?" Singer asked.

"No. Don't expect any. It looked like he'd make it."

"I'm sorry."

"There's no place for sorrow here. You don't have any whiskey, do you?"

"No."

"Does Sergeant Royce still have some?"

"I don't think so, Sarge."

"Where's Sergeant Milner?"

"Checking the perimeter."

"Good."

Sergeant Edwards brought bony fingers to his face and pressed them to his eyes before running them along the bump on his crooked nose, which looked to have been broken more than once.

"Tomorrow we have the point again," Sergeant Edwards said.

"The captain seems to favor us that way."

"The captain . . ." Sergeant Edwards said, but didn't finish the thought. He shook his head. "We'll lay up early to pull security for a supply convoy going west."

"Right."

Singer's resolve wavered, but then he recalled his frustration and fear of the morning, which was greater than his fear of telling Sergeant Edwards.

"Things okay?" Sergeant Edwards asked.

"Yeah, things are quiet, Sarge." Singer searched for the right words and his courage. "Can I talk to you about the radio?"

"What about it?"

"Being separated from the guys is killing me. I'd like to go back to my squad."

Sergeant Edwards listened while Singer presented his case.

7

May 5, 1968
0700 Hours
Vietnam

The morning light seeped through the jungle, bringing a soft grayness to the day. The air was damp and cool, comfortable when compared to the heat that would come with midday. Singer stood and stretched, still trying to lose the nighttime kinks from sleeping on the ground. He'd been awake since 0400 hours, when he'd started his last shift.

Sergeant Edwards rose, wide awake, walked a short distance away, stood with his back to Singer and pissed. On his way back, he touched a boot to Sergeant Milner's butt.

"Better get up, Sergeant, and check on your men."

Then he pulled out a map and settled on the ground with his back against his ruck, knees drawn up.

"Anything new?" he asked Singer.

"Nothing. LP reported the same digging sounds they had earlier. Last ambush is back in without incident," Singer said.

It was all business with Sergeant Edwards this morning, though Singer felt a new awkwardness and tension. Their conversation last night ended without Sergeant Edwards offering any answers or promises. In the light of a new morning, Singer wondered if he'd been out of line and said too much when he asked to give up the RTO position and return to his squad.

Singer picked up his M16 and slung a bandolier over his shoulder, thinking Trip would have already marked off and announced another day. Rhymes was maybe trying to read a couple pages before they moved out. Bear was probably sharpening his knife and hoping for the passing of a good day without contact or a casualty while working at his tough guy façade.

Sergeant Milner was sitting up but still had a poncho liner draped across his shoulders, looking like some kind of sleepy black Buddha. It seemed like a fifty-fifty bet whether his eyes would stay open or not.

"Can you cover the radio, Sarge? I got to shit."

"Make it fast," Sergeant Milner said.

Things seemed little different from any other morning when Singer walked down to check on his former squad. Men who'd survived another night were preparing for another day. Everyone was getting short. Well, most everyone. No one, he thought, had more than ninety days left except him and Stick and the lifers who would do their twenty years. Some guys, Trip and Bear for sure and maybe Rhymes, were under thirty days now. They could likely see the end and had started to believe coming back hadn't been so terrible. They would make it and go home. He desperately wanted them to make it, even though he didn't know what he would do after they were gone.

Rhymes pulled the toothbrush from his mouth and spit white foam.

"Hey, what's up?"

"Just came down to say hi."

"Getting the hang of the radio?" Rhymes rinsed, then touched a finger to his teeth and put his toothbrush in his pocket.

"It's not too tough. That was close yesterday."

"Yeah, we just rotated off point ten minutes before. Odd, just a couple guys who ran without much of a fight."

"Too close," Trip said, then reseated a magazine and aimed at the trees. "Twenty-five and a wake-up. Boom. Then you can have this shit."

"How long before you go now?" Singer asked, looking at Rhymes.

"It's bad luck to say. Last tour guys who said too much never made it."

"But you're getting close."

"Thirty-eight days."

"You probably wouldn't trade, huh?"

Rhymes grinned, teeth shining. "I'll give it some real serious thought."

"Where'd you ditch the radio?" Trip asked.

"Sergeant Milner's covering, thinks I'm taking a shit."

"Christ, I wouldn't trust that guy to watch a latrine."

"Any word?" Rhymes asked.

"Convoy security. Just a short move. Should be an easy day. You'll probably get some reading time. Probably routine so close to the firebases, huh? They got to take us in for a few days after this."

"A shower and mail would be good. Maybe some new books." Rhymes picked up his M79, opened the breech and inspected the round, rubbing it on his shirt.

"I got to get back," Singer said.

"See you on the firebase."

Singer checked his watch. With Sergeant Edwards likely up at the company CP already, it probably wasn't wise to go there to see Doc Odum. He'd catch him on the firebase tonight or tomorrow and see what Doc knew. Even if he didn't learn anything he'd at least be entertained by Doc's wit and irreverent antics. Doc might be at the Platoon CP already, waiting for him like many mornings if Sergeant Milner didn't run him off. Still, he could swing by Bear's position on the way back without pissing Sergeant Milner off too much if he didn't stay too long.

". . . a rest, man. I know you love the game, but damn, you tire a man out. Can't you talk about pussy or anything else for a while?"

Red shrunk back from Bear, his cheeks flushed. "I'm just trying to tell you—"

"I'm telling you, enough! Damn, you and Ghost can share positions tonight. You keep a man awake with all that shit. Give me baseball nightmares."

Singer held back, waiting.

Bear hefted his ruck and shook it. "Hey, the 300-day man."

"That's fucking cruel. I'm under 300 already," Singer said.

"I get confused by all those big numbers." Bear chuckled.

"Don't be giving me extra days. I got enough."

"Anything more than a month is still a lifetime. The man let you out?"

"I get ten minutes of exercise every day."

"You should come back and join the gang. We get plenty."

"Not my call. Your patches staying on?"

"Yeah, they're good. That eagle's keeping me safe."

"You need it without me here."

"Man, what's a skinny little white boy like you going to do?"

Singer patted the bandolier on his chest. "I got friends."

"You got friends. Keep your head down and get me a bird in twelve days."

"Keep your ass down, too."

"Tell that to your man Rhymes."

"I will. I'm betting we get beer and mail at the firebase tonight."

"Don't count on anything 'til you're there. I'll have one for you in the world."

"You can buy if we go in. Got to go or Sergeant Milner will be pissed."

"Man, that man was born ornery. Ornery and dumb."

Bear's laugh followed Singer back to the CP, where Sergeant Milner was only mildly upset. Singer tuned him out. Nothing would ruin his good mood. He'd seen the guys and that made it a good day. Their moods seemed lighter, more optimistic. Maybe because they were near the road, just a stone's throw away from Firebase Birmingham with Firebase Bastogne just a few more klicks down the road. They were in their own backyard now. Nearly safe. Maybe, like him, they all saw the prospects of mail, a beer, and maybe even a hot meal with a couple days on the bunker line. Maybe they saw themselves almost home. Burning good days 'til they could leave. Though he saw them as days lost being RTO, where he'd never see or do anything and had to satisfy himself with occasional visits with the guys. Bear was right, though, that he still had a lifetime to do and would be here long after all of them were gone.

". . . radio is your responsibility. If you can't shit without taking so long you better learn to hold it." Sergeant Milner ambled off without saying where he was going.

Sometimes alone wasn't so bad. Singer opened his last can of Cs, not knowing if he had the time to heat it, uncertain how soon before they'd leave. Heat didn't often help the flavor, anyway. Eating it now would leave him with nothing until they got resupplied or went in. The texture was mushy and the flavor something like cardboard, but he finished it and washed the last mouthful down with a couple gulps of Kool-Aid that failed to flush away the metallic aftertaste. The burger he promised himself when he got back would be huge and so rare the juices would soak the bun, with thick slices of onion and tomato, crisp, fresh lettuce, and lots of mayo. The kind he and his buddies had had at the Lake Side Inn, just outside of town, where they killed time in the summer months or when school was too boring to bear. Where they nursed their Cokes and played with their french fries, pretending to still be hungry while ogling the waitresses.

One girl in particular, Patsy, Patrice, or something like that, held the most interest. She was tall and thin with a figure no high school girl should have and straight blonde hair that hung down to the middle of her back. Her eyes danced with a mischievousness that suggested a hint of trouble. She was something to look at and he lusted for her just like his buddies did. At the burger joint, which was the only place he ever saw her, she was friendly and flirtatious, leaning over her elbows on the counter while she talked, exposing her cleavage and bending over to adjust things on the lower shelves, putting her little ass in the air. All of it seemed intentional, done with awareness of its effects on them. She smiled at their staring, youthful agony and they always left her big tips. Life had been good and simple then, when all he had to worry about was girls and cars and burgers. He stored the empty can in his ruck, making sure it didn't rattle, resigning himself to months of Cs and persistent hunger.

After closing up his ruck, he checked the straps, making certain the radio was secure and wouldn't shift while he walked. He checked the chamber of his M16 and the seating of the magazine, then the magazines in his web gear and bandolier. While checking the rounds he was beginning to believe he might never use, he thought about the guys and how they'd ended up together here, reliant on each other, and how this life was so different and separate from their past that they even had their own names which identified each other in this time. Their jungle fatigues were absent labels of their birth, as if it were irrelevant. Only their dog tags would allow this time, should they die, to be connected with their past.

With everything ready, he settled back to wait. The jungle turned into countless shades of green in the growing light, almost beautiful. It seemed like it was taking Sergeant Edwards a long time at the briefing for what was supposed to be an easy mission. He pulled Susan's letter from his helmet, putting it back on lest Sergeant Milner come back and say something about it. The paper was limp, blue gone pale but still a reminder of her eyes. The ink of the address bled in spots across the parchment but the beauty of the flow of her hand across the page was mostly intact. It reminded him of times he sat beside her on the basement sofa while she wrote a paper, the drone of some TV show in the background. Her thin fingers would hold the pen lightly as it floated across the page, leaving blue swirls in its wake. He wanted to lift her hand and kiss it, to kiss each finger. A few weeks ago she touched this paper.

Today he didn't need to read the words. It was enough to hold something she had held, to feel her energy. He tried to hear her voice saying the words he'd memorized from the letter but it faltered, like a radio station gone out of range. It had been so long already since he'd talked with her that he struggled to recall the tone and tempo of her voice, though he knew he'd recognize it. But it irritated him that he couldn't conjure it up now. The MP had slammed the phone hook down, ending the last conversation. They never got to say goodbye.

He had met her in the school hall when, on a rainy day, he helped her pick up books and papers she dropped while fumbling with a wet umbrella. She'd said chivalry was dead. He told her for some it hadn't died. So they started hanging out. They were both seventeen, though he was three months older and a year ahead of her in school. She was finishing her senior year now and would graduate in a month. He wondered how she'd fill her summer without him.

He ran a finger over the swirls of his name, seeing her draw each letter in her meticulous manner, as if crafting a piece of art. Sometimes when he sat beside her as she did homework, something she was more serious about than him, she would start to write his name and keep going until she filled a notebook page. She'd hold the page up to show him, proud of herself as though she'd just solved a difficult chemical formula. He couldn't help but laugh. She'd pretend to pout, eventually giving in to giggles before leaning over and kissing him.

Maybe she was trying to remind him to hold on to his true self. How could she have known?

The days here pushed his old name deeper into the past so that at times he nearly forgot it. Then a letter would arrive holding the familiar script and he'd have to puzzle over the name, trying to remember.

She wrote his name as she always had, unaware he was someone different now. It was something he could never tell her, along with so many other things.

"Singer" was more than a name. It was his identity, marked by this place and the guys around him. An intimacy few would understand. He doubted he would ever think of himself by any other name again.

"Sergeant Edwards back yet?" Sergeant Milner asked, flopping down beside his ruck then proceeding to spread out its contents of socks, boxers, towel, toiletries, notebook, and too many cans of Cs for the last day.

Singer looked around the otherwise empty CP. "Nope. Still at the briefing, I guess."

"No, Sergeant."

"No, Sergeant, it's just you and me here."

"Show some proper military discipline. This is still the army."

"Right, Sergeant."

"Sergeant Edwards may like you, but I don't. You spent too much time talking with the old guys."

"You mean the second-tour guys?"

"Be careful how you act. You're just a Cherry."

"Like you, Sergeant?"

"Insubordination will get you an Article 15. You should remember you're just a private. The army has rank for a reason—"

"Singer."

He turned to see Sergeant Edwards's expectant look and he wasn't sure if he'd missed an order or how long Sergeant Edwards had been listening.

"Call all the squad leaders up here."

Singer stood with his rifle and bandolier in hand, happy to get away from Sergeant Milner.

"And Singer."

"Yeah, Sarge."

"Tell Stick to come to the CP with all his gear."

With his rifle relaxed in one hand and his bandolier slung on his shoulder, Singer wove his way through the trees and vines to the platoon's line to look for the squad leaders and Stick. Why did Sarge want Stick at the CP with all his gear? It was unusual that he'd want to see him at all, much less with all his equipment. It sounded like Stick was going to be sent someplace.

Some of the squad leaders had already gathered around Sergeant Edwards when Singer returned and sat down next to his gear. Sergeant Edwards had the map on his lap, but was sitting quietly, looking tired and old.

Stick ducked under a branch and around a tree, stepping into the platoon CP with his rucksack on, carrying his web gear in his hand. His ruck was open, straps hanging loose. Something clanged inside the pack as he rounded the tree. Then he stopped and stood there with a bewildered expression on his face. His gangly body looked as disordered as his gear, like a teenage body still trying to adjust itself after a growth spurt.

When the equipment jangled, Sergeant Edwards looked up from the map and watched Stick come to a halt.

"Stick, you're my RTO today. Get the radio from Singer and be ready to move out in ten minutes. Singer, get back to your squad."

Without pause, Sergeant Edwards leaned over the map, pointed with a bony finger and talked in quieter tones to the four assembled squad leaders. Sergeant Royce looked between Singer and Sergeant Edwards like he was waiting for an explanation.

It took a second before Singer could move. Despite his request last night, it came now without warning or preamble. He wanted to jump and yell and pump his fist. He was going back with the guys.

Instead, he turned to Stick. "Come on, I'll help you set up your gear and strap it on."

"Thanks," Stick said, glowing as if he'd just won some prize.

While he helped Stick move his pack to the bottom of his ruck frame, he could hear the murmurs of Sergeant Edwards's voice in the background. He fumbled with his straps, hurrying too much as he undid the radio and handed it to Stick, who held it for a moment, seeming to admire it before putting it on his ruck. Singer helped Stick make it tight and showed him how to run straps behind it to keep it off his back. After he explained the dials and the handset, he busied himself readjusting his pack, unable to think of anything else to say.

His discussion with Sergeant Edwards last night about wanting to return to his squad, he knew, brought about the switch. It was what he had asked for, but it felt strange now giving up the radio and handing it to Stick. During the past week he had taken on some ownership of it. He would miss his visits with Doc Odum and the contact with Sergeant Edwards, but being back with the guys, with Rhymes, Trip, Bear, Red, and even Ghost would overshadow any regrets or guilt.

Stick stood and slid into his ruck with the radio, his shoulders less stooped than normal, turning slightly as if examining himself in a mirror.

"Thanks. Really, thanks."

"Right."

Singer picked up and shouldered his ruck, which felt weightless now without the radio. Standing there, he watched Stick looking pleased and grateful, though he knew he hadn't done him any favor. He'd shifted the burden of the extra weight and the danger of the radio to someone else who had no more say in it than he had when it had been thrust on him. It was even more troubling that Stick didn't seem to understand this, but instead seemed happy.

"Fuck it." All he cared about was that he was back with the guys. That meant everything to him.

The jungle seemed less an obstacle as he nearly bounded up to the squad's night positions, where Rhymes and Trip sat with Bear and Red in a loose group. Their web gear was on, weapons in their hands, but rucks still rested on the ground.

"Aren't you a little bunched up?" Singer asked.

Rhymes folded his book shut, his eyes questioning.

"You the new tactics officer?" Trip asked.

"We're moving out. You better get back to the CP," Bear said.

"What the fuck are you doing back here again without the radio?" Trip asked.

Singer dropped his gear on the ground as if to reinforce the fact that he was back and staying. He couldn't suppress his grin. No amount of teasing could upset him. In fact, the teasing just made him happier. It was part of what he missed. All he could think about was how happy he was in this moment and how he cared about these guys like he had never cared about anyone before.

"Shit, Sarge sent me to look after your sorry ass. Said you're worse than a fucking new guy and someone needs to help you." Singer grinned, enjoying pushing the limits with Trip again. Bear laughed from his belly, which started Singer laughing, too.

"Fuck you! The day I need you looking after me is the day I'm really fucked." Trip stood looking indignant, but he was a poor actor.

"You are definitely fucked, then."

"Fucked for sure," Trip said, finally grinning. "Fucked for sure." He started laughing with the others.

Rhymes set his book aside and came over to Singer. At first Singer thought Rhymes was going to hug him, but he merely clasped his shoulder with his free hand.

"Good to have you back." Then he gave his reassuring smile.

Singer felt unsaid promises pass between them that were spoken once on a grassy, windswept hillside, one of those first dark nights when the air was thick with a sense of death and he had grappled with his fear. He'd awakened Rhymes, who listened, but dismissed the noise as just the wind. Then Rhymes talked in his calming voice of how it was normal to be scared, but that they were in this together. They had each other's backs. If they stayed close, they'd both be all right. They had never spoken of it again, but marked and reaffirmed those promise, many times since with a nod and a smile.

"Yeah, I can't tell you how good it is to be back."

"How'd you swing it?" Trip asked.

"Just told him the truth, that you needed me."

"Yeah, we need someone to go in the next tunnel we find," Trip said.

"Don't get too comfortable. Your fucking vacation is over. It's about time you came back to work." Bear grasped the back of Singer's neck in his large hand, squeezing gently and pulling Singer toward him while Singer bent and twisted to get away. "Welcome back," Bear said as he released Singer.

Singer stood rubbing his neck. "Shit, Bear, someday you're going to hurt someone doing that."

"You got soft sitting up at the CP. I'm going have to toughen you up again." Bear shook with laughter as he walked back to his ruck.

Singer picked up his ruck by the top frame and carried it over next to Rhymes. He sat down and rubbed his neck again.

Rhymes had packed up his book and sat examining an M79 round, his weapon open across his pack beside him, the chamber empty. He spun the round slowly, wiping each side, though to Singer it already looked clean.

Singer took out a round from Rhymes's gas mask bag that carried a large share of his supply and held it up, turning it around. "Someday you're going to make somebody a good wife."

Rhymes grabbed it back and wiped it off carefully again. "I'm not letting my stuff get fucked up. Dirt will kill you."

"Dirt will kill you? Shit, I should write that down. I thought it was the gooks."

"You better hope your weapon works when you need it."

"Hey, my weapon's always ready," Singer said, patting his M16.

"I saw a guy get killed when his rifle jammed. Wasn't that dirty."

"Don't worry, that M79 of yours ever locks up on you, I'll be there with this." Singer held up his M16.

Acknowledgement spread on Rhymes's face and Singer felt good his friend believed in him.

"Hey, I saved one of my girl's brownies for you." Singer turned and opened the top of his ruck. "It might be a little old," he said as he dug for the remnants of the last package he'd gotten, a few weeks earlier.

"You saved one all this time?"

"Yeah."

"Thanks. Even old, those brownies are great, but I'll save it 'cause I just brushed my teeth." Rhymes stored the brownie and closed up the gas mask pouch with his cleaned M79 rounds. He picked up his M79 and ran the cloth across the already spotless barrel before slipping in the round and closing the breach.

Sergeant Royce came back from the briefing looking tense, his lips pressed tight and his eyes pinched.

"Singer, quit fucking around with your gear. Fourth platoon has the point. Get your shit together. And the rest of you keep it down. Christ, I could hear you up at the CP. You probably got every gook in the country heading this way. Bear, where's Ghost? Goddamn it."

Bear shrugged as Ghost materialized from some bushes as though he'd been there waiting for his entrance all this time.

"Going with us this morning or staying here by yourself?" Bear asked.

"Jesus, I don't know why we're back here," Ghost said.

At the edge Red hung back, still looking uncertain about saying anything after his rebuke from Bear. When there was time, Singer thought he would ask him some baseball question.

"Ghost, don't be goddamn disappearing again," Sergeant Royce said. "We'll go the farthest down the road. The drag platoon will be dropping off to cover independent sectors close enough to act as reaction forces for each other. We've moving out now."

Everything seemed the same to Singer as he quickly closed up his ruck. It was as though he hadn't been gone at all, and he delighted in the easy transition back. The guys seemed the same except for Sergeant Royce, whose surliness had grown in just over a week. It wasn't much of a welcome back from his squad leader, but he hadn't expected much. Sergeant Royce had become more humorless and short-tempered since they arrived in Nam. Back at Bragg when he was drinking he had been more likable, a happy if somewhat obnoxious drunk. But perhaps it was being back in the Nam with too many days left rather than the lack of drink that had taken away Sergeant Royce's humor.

Rhymes was already standing and strapping on his gas mask bag of rounds. Singer shouldered his ruck and stood beside Rhymes. Being back next to Rhymes and the others had lightened the day far more than being free of the twenty-five-pound radio. He felt like he could easily run, even with his ruck and gear. It would be a good day.

Sergeant Edwards, with Stick bearing the radio near his side, looking proud, moved up past Singer until they were out of sight among the network of trees and fronds. Singer looked away as Stick passed, though Stick looked happier then he'd ever seen him, eyes locked on Sergeant Edwards rather than the ground.

They must be moving up to send off the point, Singer figured. On past days when Singer had the point, Sergeant Edwards always came up, trailing Borkman and offering some words on the day. It was usually something like, "Stick to the high ground," "Watch it today," "Take it slow," or "Stay sharp." Things he already knew, but valued nonetheless. Still, it always felt in some ways like a goodbye. It seemed something Sergeant Edwards felt compelled to do, perhaps knowing the vulnerability of the point and that he might never see the man again. This morning Singer guessed he might have told the point, "Take a good look before you move out on the road. We're close to home, but don't get careless."

The line started moving and they slowly found the spacing and rhythm. Singer fell into his usual place behind Rhymes with Trip at his back, as though he never left. Quickly they moved to the place from where Sergeant

Edwards had sent off the point and now stood with Stick watching them pass, waiting to fall in somewhere to the rear of the platoon. Surprisingly, Top was there too, his fatigues somehow looking crisp and clean like the first day in the field rather than the eighteenth, watching each man move by. Just before they reached them, Top said something and Singer saw Sergeant Edwards turn back toward Top and give a one-word response. Standing near the two sergeants, Stick, his helmet cocked low to one side, looked bright and energized, still flashing the smile he didn't often offer.

"Hey, Top, we going in tonight?" Bear asked.

Sergeant Edwards grimaced.

"I hear you like the field, Bear," Top said.

"Not me, Top. I'm a city boy. I need buildings and concrete. No black man likes camping."

But they were already past and Singer was unsure if Top heard it. They followed the winding path the point was setting over fairly even terrain, moving north toward the intersection with the road. Diffused light found its way through the canopy without offering a hint at the sun's direction, though Singer took heart in it nonetheless.

They moved slowly, able to be careful today, unhurried by off-scene commanders or overzealous lieutenants. Singer placed each foot with care, looking up to catch Rhymes's back before checking each flank.

Rhymes carried his M79 at his side, the large muzzle pointed at the ground. It was a familiar sight that today brought renewed comfort. Singer laughed to himself, thinking about being with Rhymes again. He wasn't sure why it was so funny. Perhaps it was watching Rhymes with his many cleaning rituals again or the things he said, like, "Dirt will kill you," that he didn't mean to be funny, which made them even funnier. Still, nothing seemed to rattle him. He was steady and reliable, without bullshit. When Rhymes said he was going to open a bookshop when his time was done, you could believe it. After all this was over, maybe Singer would look him up and help out at the bookstore, as Rhymes had invited him to do. But Rhymes always said no comics, so he'd have to start reading other things. Up ahead Rhymes paused, looking back as if reading Singer's thoughts.

"You okay?" he asked softly when Singer got close.

"Yeah, great."

Then they hurried ahead, closing the ranks. He watched Rhymes disappear behind a wall of vegetation and reappear like a ship dropping out of sight in a big wave. Each time Rhymes disappeared, Singer's stomach fell and he held his breath, waiting to see Rhymes's back again.

After a short time, Rhymes halted and Singer held his place, as he knew Trip would behind him. They stood in their positions, watching to either side and listening. The sound of rotors far to the east filtered through the leafy cover. After that passed, the jungle was quiet again, without even the voice of any animal or the buzz of any insect. Everyone was waiting.

Singer guessed the point man had hit the open strip next to the road, where chemical spray and Rome Plows had removed the vegetation for maybe fifty yards back to deny the enemy cover close to the road, reducing the chance of ambushes.

"I don't like this." Trip had edged up closer so Singer could hear him.

"Must be at the road," Singer said.

"It's taking too long."

"Maybe they sent a team out to look before we all go out."

"We should stay in the cover. Every time we go up and down that road I feel like a duck trolled across a shooting gallery."

"Here we go."

"We should stay in the cover."

In just a few meters, Singer could see the brightening ahead where the jungle gave way in an abrupt line not found in nature. The flood of light silhouetted Rhymes and the man beyond him. Featureless, shadowy forms were framed in the glow in a way that, in another place, he might have stopped and admired.

At the edge, Singer stopped momentarily and squinted against the stark brightness. The point was already on the road, moving west, with men of the first three squads trailing back toward Singer in a staggered double column. The cheer of the sunlight was inviting, and the scene looked serene if he ignored the weapons each man carried and didn't think of the enemy that might be hidden at the jungle's edge. Singer saw the advantage, as Trip said, of skirting the jungle edge rather than parading down the center of the road. On the edge they would have quick access to cover, and he would still have his consoling sunshine.

"Spread it out more and watch where you step," Trip said at his back.

"Hasn't it been swept for booby traps?" Singer asked.

"I doubt it. We're the first today. If the convoy comes quick we can be in long before dark."

"Yeah, this shouldn't take long."

Singer trailed down the slight grade, over rough ground and low grass until he was on the road, a graded red dirt lane that cut through the walls of jungle on either side.

From the road he eyed the jungle, troubled that it formed a dark green curtain he couldn't see beyond. The closest cover was a long ways off. He preferred to be in the treeline watching the road than on the road watching the treeline. In the daytime darkness of the jungle he often wished for the sunlight, prayed for it. But now, exposed in the sunlight, he wished for the cover of the jungle, or at least the edge of it.

His shadow stretched before him nearly to Rhymes, who settled his foot on a spot he studied with seemingly as much concern about the dust as about booby traps.

Trip scuffed his feet along, almost dragging them. Singer turned to see him run an olive-drab towel across his face.

"Christ, it's hot. We should have stayed under cover."

Singer tasted the grit and heat of the morning, felt it building and reflecting up from the road. His back was clammy and his fatigues blotched with growing pools of sweat. He lifted his canteen and held the warm water in his mouth, swishing it about before swallowing. But he felt the grit again almost immediately.

The jungle looked placid and cool, little different from one meter to the next. Meters and meters of road edge. They'd been over this ground before without results. They'd have to go farther from the firebases than this if they were going to find the enemy. But today was one of those routine things they did regardless of prospect for results. A thousand NVA could be watching them from the jungle and they'd never know it. Their passing, though, was likely unnoticed by anyone and they wouldn't see a single NVA today.

The air was still, the sky blue and cloudless, with little promise of change, like a Midwestern day in the heart of summer. Beyond the point man the road disappeared in a slight right-hand curve. Distant, shadowy mountain peaks marked the horizon and Laos.

He watched the flanks as Rhymes did, but there wasn't much to see. Tangles of trees, brush, and vines disclosed nothing. It was only when a person got close that one could see the breaks where sunlight and a man might pass.

Turning and walking backward for a step, Singer saw Trip, his eyes and rifle pointed at the near side of the jungle, and the entire company trailing down the road. The farthest men looked like miniatures. A cluster of antenna marked the company CP in front of the last platoon. Not far back was Stick across from Sergeant Edwards, striding with the radio, the handset held ready. He turned back quickly before either of them made eye contact.

In little more than a klick they'd lay up in the shaded jungle edge to await the convoy, resting and eating until it passed and they could retire to the FB. Most of the short-time second-tour guys would likely be happy marking an easy field day, moving one more day closer to going home. He and Rhymes would share a position, rest through the heat of the day, eat Rhymes's brownie, drink some Kool-Aid, and visit about their girlfriends and about plans after the war. At the FB they'd clean up, share care packages and mail, and reaffirm their friendships. These were good prospects that already allowed Singer to forget about Stick and the radio.

After a few days' break they'd get serious again and go back out hunting. Singer was still waiting for the first good fight and the chance to prove himself. Nothing had come of the man he'd seen near the stream. No one knew. It was days ago and a long way back in the mountains, and he left it there. The man had surprised him and he had froze. Back home they called it buck fever when someone had a deer in front of him but couldn't for some reason bring himself to shoot. Next time he wouldn't hesitate.

8

May 5, 1968
0817 Hours
Vietnam

The jungle offered no warning. They had walked almost a klick past non-descript forest, sweating and kicking up dust while their shadows grew shorter in the dirt of the road. It was the kind of morning and movement that could easily lull someone into complacency and daydreams, and Singer had to keep bringing himself back to watching the jungle. But there'd been nothing alarming or even unsettling before the first shots came.

Singer dove to the ground at the first cracks of the AKs that came from behind him, from the stretch of road they just walked. An M16 might have fired first, but it was quickly overwhelmed by the sound of AKs and then machine guns. The firing grew rapidly as countless weapons joined the battle, sweeping westerly toward Singer and the fourth platoon like a wildfire carried on a strong headwind.

He wasn't hit even though he'd been a fraction slower diving to the ground than Rhymes, Trip, and Bear, whose reactions seemed still tightly wired from their first Nam tour.

With the shock of the first rounds, he looked back east toward the sound and saw a few men from Charlie Company running the last few meters into the jungle south of the road, then disappearing. After that the road and open ground between the two borders of trees lay empty.

The closest fire to fourth platoon was light and sporadic. But about hundred meters back, the gunfire was heavy and still growing. This looked like the fight he'd been waiting for and his heart raced as he worked on his first magazine, firing three or four shot bursts toward the tree line. He couldn't see any muzzle flashes or targets so he kept his fire low in the jungle edge some fifty meters or more away where the enemy was most likely positioned.

When his first magazine went empty, he jettisoned it and pressed home a full one, doing it quickly but without panic. Then, staying prone, Singer began firing again, measured shots minus any real urgency. It surprised him that he wasn't afraid, more exhilarated than frightened. This was not unlike lying on the range at Fort Bragg firing downrange at distant human silhouettes, with an added rush of a real enemy. Rhymes's M79 boomed near him, and he saw the round explode just short of the tree line. He looked at Rhymes and smiled, feeling the thrill of the engagement, but Rhymes had the M79 action open and was intent on shoving in a new round. A stream of tracer rounds from Shooter's M60 strung out across the distance, disappearing into the jungle and creating a red rope-like line linking the two positions.

Singer pressed the trigger, feeling the rounds rip from his M16 and the exhilaration ripple through his body. He watched Rhymes's next round explode in the trees. They were on it now.

The sounds of battle just down the road grew to a constant roar of gunfire, but they seemed beyond the worst of it and only a few rounds came into their position. As the firing rolled west, incoming rounds kicked up dirt in front of Singer. He heard the *zing* of bullets and ducked instinctively but days late, had the rounds been on target.

He continued firing, still unsure of any targets. At one point he looked to find Trip or Bear, not so much for reassurance as for affirmation of the excitement he was feeling. But both were bent over their weapons, sighted at the jungle. He wanted to tell them this was what he was waiting for, what he'd been talking about, and perhaps affirm their solidarity in the effort as they did in a football huddle.

When the magazine was empty Singer fed another, firing short bursts at the trees, thinking he was being effective. This was good shit. Now he understood what Shooter had said about it being fun. This was more exciting than any of the shows he'd ever seen or anything he'd imagined.

Heavy explosions tore through the ambush site one hundred meters back. At the sound, Singer looked left. First one, then two together, a pause, then a fourth larger than the first three. Singer heard them along with everyone else, but was too far away to feel the concussion. Clouds of smoke and dirt rose up out of the jungle. Rifle and machine gun fire continued unabated, and Singer couldn't imagine what kind of hell the rest of the company was catching. By comparison, it was quiet at fourth platoon's position. The real battle was going on just a few hundred meters down the road, and he wanted to be a part of it. While he was firing and there were occasional incoming rounds, their position was more one of spectator than participant. Back down the road he could hear the battle raging. He drew his legs up and listened for Sergeant Edwards, waiting for an order to move.

On his left he could hear Sergeant Edwards's voice, louder and speaking faster than normal but without alarm. He imagined Stick lying there, the radio on his back, not firing but ready to take back the handset and monitor calls.

"Hang on. We're coming," Sergeant Edwards said. "Red fox four out."

Singer let up on the trigger and looked to the voice. He saw Sergeant Edwards pass the handset back to Stick, grab his M16, and stand up, oblivious to the incoming fire.

"Let's go! The company's in trouble. Drop your rucks. Let's go!"

Men rose quickly and without question, running back toward the heaviest fire. Shooter was the first up and running. Bear was right behind him and then his graceful speed carried him past Shooter, who was running with labored strides carrying the machine gun. Shooter was yelling, cursing his slow legs, Bear for passing him, or the NVA, Singer couldn't tell which. Sergeant Edwards stood with Stick at his side waving the men forward, yelling, "Let's go, Let's go," all the time offering a stationary target.

When Sergeant Royce passed, Sergeant Edwards grabbed his arm and yelled above the explosions and rifle fire so everyone nearby heard.

"The company's pinned down on the south side of the road and caught in a crossfire from the north. We got to hit the north side and break it." Then he let go and waved the others on.

At the first order, Singer pulled the release on his ruck and rolled out of it, struggling for a moment to free his right arm and regain his rifle. Then he was on his feet, running back into the ambush kill zone they passed through moments before. He watched Bear out in front leading the group and admired his athleticism and bravery that seemed at such odds with his tirades about the war. Seeing Bear out front, Singer ran harder, and soon he was passing men and closing on Shooter, who had fallen back in the group.

"Let's get these fuckers," Shooter yelled.

Singer was aware of men running with him, not of their identities, just that other bodies were in motion around him. Initially he didn't think about Rhymes and Trip, who had been beside him as they all started to run. It was all too chaotic and too hurried. Singer just ran toward the gunfire and explosions, not thinking really about the danger, just that everyone else was running, too, and that it was exhilarating.

This was it. Finally, he was doing something important. It didn't matter that, except for a few of the men with him in fourth platoon and Doc Odum, most of the men of the company were nameless faces he knew nothing about. They all wore the same uniform and were fellow paratroopers. He would help save the team.

The roar of the battle grew as he moved toward its center. He could smell it now, that burned powder smell left in the wake of exploded firecrackers and something else, like the pungent smell of burnt hair. Adrenaline fueled his legs and his heart raced with the exertion and excitement. He gripped his M16 with both hands, swinging it from side to side with his running motion, too focused on speed to fire.

He glanced back, trying to locate Rhymes or Trip, but didn't dare pause. Toward the back of the group, Ghost jogged in a jerky motion, his head pulled down tight into his shoulders and one hand atop his helmet, pulling it tight to his head. Sergeant Milner labored just behind him, belly bouncing, helmet tilted back as if he might lose it. At the rear Sergeant Edwards ran, his face dark, eyes lost under the brim of his helmet. Just behind him Stick dashed, open-mouthed, arms and legs flailing, radio bouncing with his strides. But Singer couldn't pick out Rhymes or Trip before turning back to the front to see that he was falling back in the group. He dug in and kicked harder.

An explosion tore the road open just ahead of Bear, sending up a geyser of dirt. A cloud of smoke and dust billowed above the road. Bear and Red stumbled, then caught themselves. Singer saw them disappear into the cloud of dirt. The shockwave washed over him, and he felt the heat change and for a moment he was blind or he'd closed his eyes and there was only the tremendous roar, and he wondered if this was the end.

Still, he saw Shooter go down as if it were in slow motion. Shooter landed awkwardly on his right leg and then his left seemed to catch, as if trussed to the ground. His head and chest rode forward over his extended leg until he was stretched out, floating above the road. His left hand flew up toward his chest and then flailed against the air as he fell forward and crashed into the ground. The big gun slammed against the road and skidded away from him in the dirt. His right hand stretched out toward the gun, fingers flicking the air. His face lifted slightly from the dirt but then fell back as if his head was too heavy to lift. Throughout it all he never uttered a sound, or none that Singer heard, though he might have said something that was smothered by the deafening gunfire.

Singer froze and stood there, unable to look away. Rhymes ran past him and knelt beside Shooter.

"Medic! Medic!" Rhymes yelled.

Others took up the call in the distance. Singer wondered how far away Doc Odum might be and if there was any chance he'd hear them and come. He watched Rhymes roll Shooter over, his arms flopping, exposing his blood-soaked chest.

"Jesus," Singer said. "Is he dead?"

He felt so tired now, as if his own life were seeping into the dirt. The excitement of the game was lost. His legs were weak.

Something slapped his shoulder.

"Let's go, Singer. Come on."

Singer looked to see Trip loping by. Ghost sped past, nearly tripping on Shooter's machine gun, crossing himself repeatedly and mumbling as he ran.

Trip bent beside Rhymes, grabbed two belts of M60 ammo, then picked up the machine gun, leaving his M16, and took off.

"Goddamn it, Singer, come on."

Even though he started jogging, Singer couldn't stop looking back at Shooter, his empty face, the bravado gone, and his blood-soaked fatigue jacket.

"Bring him. Let's go." Sergeant Edwards said, pausing near Shooter, looking around as if seeking people to help, but everyone else was past and Sergeant Milner didn't stop.

Singer slowed, thought about going back to help.

Before he could decide, Rhymes slung his M79 and threw Shooter over his shoulder, running in short, choppy steps that reminded Singer of the Vietnamese woman he seen in Hue bearing a yoke, each end slung with a basket piled high with large, spiky green fruit. Even bearing Shooter, Rhymes was nearly keeping up with Sergeant Edwards and Stick at the rear of the platoon.

Singer started sprinting again, trying to catch Bear and the others or to distance himself from Shooter. How could that happen? Shooter was indestructible and yet he saw him. Saw the blood.

After passing through the explosions' thinning smoke, Singer saw Bear, still in the lead, turn and dive to the roadside, firing even before he hit the ground. Everyone behind him followed suit as if on some hidden cue. With the acrid smell still clinging in his nostrils and the vision of Shooter still in his mind, Singer threw himself to the ground, firing at the trees fifty meters away across open ground and slightly uphill. He'd made it this far and was still alive. They were all lying at the road edge firing now: Bear, Red, Jammer, Sergeant Royce, and the others. Trip had the machine gun working. Only Ghost wasn't firing, but instead covered his head with one arm as though that might save him. Singer slammed the trigger back in a frantic pulse. The pressure of his hand around his rifle while it recoiled in quick succession still brought a tingle that started in his chest and coursed through his body, but something had started to change.

"Charge the trees! Get up! Get up! Charge the trees!"

He had barely fired twenty rounds when the order came. It was Sergeant Edwards's voice screaming from behind them, still somewhere back down the road. Singer never turned to look, but took up the call, "Charge the trees," like many of the others as he jumped to his feet. He saw or sensed the men around him rise and surge forward. It seemed they nearly all stood at once, though he guessed Bear was probably first up and moving. Even Ghost was up and running, perhaps driven more by the rounds impacting around them than by the command to charge. He may have even been firing. Singer could hear him screaming above the gunfire, "Sweet Jesus, save me. Sweet Jesus, save me," as he ran as though the words offered more protection than his rifle. The throaty bark of the M60 assured him Trip was still okay. Where Rhymes was and what he might have done with Shooter Singer wasn't sure and hadn't the luxury to ponder. He could only think of what he had to do to stay alive. Fire and charge. Fire and charge.

The trees loomed, forbidding and inviting; death and salvation. Cover and the waiting enemy. Yet, if he could only make the trees he'd have a chance. The flash of muzzles from amidst the dark foliage made him want to look away. Instead he ran toward them, firing from his hip, sacrificing speed to fire and have some hope.

He looked when he heard a sound like a hurt animal and saw Jammer crumpled in a heap, but he didn't break stride. Nor did anyone else. Jammer would lie alone. Singer knew they had to make the trees or they'd all die in the open. How could it be so far? He dropped a magazine and pushed another in, cursing himself for his clumsiness, expecting to die at any moment.

"Charge the trees," he screamed, encouraged by the screams and rifle fire of the others. He raced toward the muzzle blasts, closing on them, more amazed in each step to find himself alive and empowered by it. "Kill these fuckers." His rifle kicked and his legs ate up ground. He was coming to them. How close the AK fire was to hitting him he didn't know, as he had no awareness of it as he ran through it. He was aware only of the force of his rifle and the growing strength of his strides and the tremendous power he felt that he'd never felt before. He was beating death. Charging into heavy enemy fire, he was still alive. He'd never been so alive. He could run forever, screaming and firing. He would run right through them. Whatever he was feeling now, he wanted to feel forever. "Kill 'em," he screamed again, pressing the trigger much harder than was needed.

It would all end in a few more steps at the trees.

9

May 5, 1968
0851 Hours
Vietnam

Before Singer reached the trees, he saw others slightly ahead on both sides of him tumbling into the treeline, diving or falling wounded. He collapsed into the trees and lay there. The elation of the charge bled away. The weight of what was happening and what they were facing dawned on him. They had charged the north half of the ambush, but even in the face of their assault the enemy fire never ebbed. That was when he heard the screams for help that might have been going on all along. He envisioned the people dying all around him. His imagined glory of war was lost. He lay there briefly, not firing, unable to see through his tears.

"Singer, pull yourself together," Sergeant Royce said.

"Everyone's dying. My friends—"

"More will die if you don't get with it." Sergeant Royce crawled off on his hands and knees the way he'd come, flattening out with each heightened flurry of gunfire, leaving Singer lying in the tree edge alone.

When Singer pulled the trigger, his M16 popped ceaselessly, sending out a stream of bullets, but it brought none of the thrill of just moments before. Singer stopped and wiped the tears, trying to clear his vision. Then he fired again. Around him he could hear the cries of "Medic!" Some were near but others faint and distant, barely discernible within the wail of AK, M16, and machine gun fire and explosions. Even the faintest petitions were raw and painful. It was obvious to Singer that many of them weren't going to make it.

With a new magazine seated, he fired, spraying rounds to the front. The enemy remained invisible, but AK fire was everywhere. He knew he had to fight, to kill the enemy. Survival was in question. The first side that broke would be overwhelmed by the other. His hand shook as he pried another magazine from his web gear and fed it into his M16. Real fear escaped from some dark recess of his mind and settled over him. His stomach fell, his mouth went dry, and he had to piss. But still he fired at the enemy positions.

In the run back down the road and the charge into the trees, he'd lost track of everyone. An M60 still fired, far to his right. He guessed it was Trip and was heartened by it. He figured Sergeant Royce hadn't crawled far and might be the closest M16 firing. Otherwise, he was alone.

Empty magazines and shell casings were strewn about beside him. He'd fallen into a trance-like routine of firing and reloading that brought a new determination. Once he stopped to count his remaining full magazines. Though he was in danger of running out of ammo he kept up the pace, it was his fire keeping the enemy off him and holding off the fear that was a budding thickness in his throat. His rifle shuddered with each burst, and he took comfort from it.

AK-47 and enemy machine gun fire pounded his senses, and he wondered if they would ever stop. Waves of concussions rocked him. Even though the enemy was just meters away, he couldn't see them so he fired at the boom of enemy guns and the rush of heated air that he thought might be muzzle blasts. But still the enemy fire didn't slacken. The whole jungle vibrated until he feared the trees might collapse and bury them all.

"Medic! Medic! Medic!"

The cries persisted. When one voice went silent, another somewhere else took its place. Someone screamed for ammo. Other yelling, perhaps someone shouting directions, was mostly unintelligible within the noise of the battle. But the pleading shrillness of the calls for a medic stood out.

He was still alive and still firing after what already seemed like hours. The little piece of ground he lay on was starting to feel like his own. A place he might hold. Then Sergeant Milner came.

"Sergeant Royce. Sergeant Royce. There is no fire from our positions on the far left," Sergeant Milner yelled, speaking too fast, running the words together while struggling to breathe. "Take Singer and one other man and check it out."

"Singer. Get over here."

Singer crawled right a few meters. Sergeant Milner was sitting, crouched down, his arms extended, supporting his upper body. His body heaved, his mouth agape. It was his eyes that caused Singer's breath to catch in his throat, two large headlights in the dark. Sergeant Royce was lying on the ground, his knees pulled in and upper body raised up on one elbow.

"Red. Get over here." Sergeant Royce yelled.

"Where's Rhymes?" Singer asked.

"Goddamn it. There's no time. Shooter's dead," Sergeant Royce said.

A white hand and then Red's shiny face materialized, pushing past leaves. "Sarge?"

"We're going west." Sergeant Royce pointed. "Red. Go." The man took off.

"Singer. Go. Go."

Singer ran past Red, who had advanced, then crouched and was firing. A few meters past Red, Singer crouched and fired. Sergeant Royce ran up to Red and Red rose and advanced past Singer and went down. Then Sergeant Royce was next to Singer.

"Go. Go."

So, Singer ran west again. It was something like a maneuver they had practiced at Fort Bragg. Never under anything even close to these conditions, though. He ran along the edge of the jungle, across the ambush, trying not to think of the enemy fire. Only by blocking it out was he able to move.

They bunched together about thirty meters away from it. Singer stopped when he saw the body, and Sergeant Royce and Red came up next to him. Even from here he knew who it was, and trembled at the knowledge that it should be him. Before guilt took seed, Sergeant Royce ordered him forward.

"Singer, cover the front."

Without hesitation he was up running toward the crater. Enemy gunfire screamed around him and he was sure they were all shooting at him. He ran harder, thinking his speed might save him. The ghostly face waited for him without recognition, eyes as still as the hands. The radio was caught under Stick's body, its antenna lying along the ground. Maybe Stick had just been too slow.

"Medic! Medic!"

The image cut through him, the details searing into his mind. Stick lay on the right rear edge of the crater with his head downslope back toward the road, as if bullets had bowled him over or the weight of the PRC25 had pulled him backwards despite his forward charge. Or perhaps he had stopped his advance to respond to a call. His left leg hung over the edge, dangling into the crater. His right leg was bent back underneath him as if he had collapsed back on it, so it appeared that he had no leg below the knee. The platoon radio he carried for just less than two hours lay under him, canting his trunk at an angle and making it look like he was trying to roll onto his side. His right arm was sprawled out away from his side, his fingers tight around the radio handset, the cord trailing back under his body. Beside his head his helmet sat upside down, with the picture Stick had once shown him of his parents, his father in an army officer's uniform, his mother a plump, unsmiling woman in an unbecoming print dress, looking out through the helmet liner's webbing. Stick's head was turned to the side, away from the crater. His eyes held a frozen, startled look, as if he'd been surprised. His hair was wet and matted and a thick stream of blood ran across his forehead and down the bridge of his nose, pooling in a dark stain around his head. There was a ghostly pallor to his flesh, more fitting to a wax figure than any human being.

The crumpled form didn't resemble the man Singer talked with that morning, Stick thanking him for the radio as if it were a gift. Without the radio on his back and the handset in his hand, he might not have even recognized the man as Stick.

It should be him lying there. Yet rather than remorse he felt a thrill of being up and running. The exhilaration of so fortuitously dodging death.

He looked away, past Stick, to the hole, hoping to make it, driving his legs despite their weakness.

Motion caught his attention and he almost fired. Hands flailing the sky. A prone form the other side and to the rear of the crater. Black hands, fingers splayed, wet with blood, fluttering above glistening coils that spewed from the gut. Repeatedly the hands pressed against the protruding cords. Sergeant Edwards attempted to raise his head, perhaps in an effort to get up or to look down at his wounds, then appeared to give up, his head falling back heavily. His mouth moved ceaselessly in what Singer imagined to be a prayer, though he'd never thought Sergeant Edwards to be a praying man.

"Medic! Medic!" Singer yelled.

Close enough, he launched himself at the hole. That was when he saw him down in the crater. In that moment's glimpse, Rhymes never blinked, but Singer refused to believe what the fixed stare meant.

"Medic!"

The groan that came with the hard impact left Singer without breath. The world rolled, started to spin, stopped, then righted itself. His M16 was caught under him, biting into his ribs. The ground was hard and gravelly. He gasped for a breath and tasted the dirt along with the sour taste of panic.

Christ, they're all down. This place is a trap.

He tugged his M16 out from under him and checked the muzzle for dirt. When he kicked out to push himself higher his boot touched Rhymes's and he lay still, their boots touching. He wanted to go to him. To at least turn and look, but he was afraid. He already knew.

Without turning, he could see the image of Rhymes lying on his back against the rear wall of the crater, as if he might have leaned back to rest. His eyes were open, staring off at the sky. His lips were parted, not quite a smile. His teeth were clenched, smeared with blood, and a thin finger of blood trickled from the right corner of his mouth, but didn't reach his chin. Blood smeared the right shoulder of his fatigues where Singer saw him hoist and carry Shooter, though he must have laid Shooter down somewhere because Shooter's body wasn't here. His arms were rigid at his side. He made no move to wipe his mouth. His hands were empty, fingers of his right hand loosely curled. His M79, with the action open, lay just beyond his reach.

"Medic! Medic!"

Doc would know what to do.

Stick being down was devastating enough, but he never anticipated the worst. Now he wished he hadn't found them.

He rested his face on the front crater wall, the lip of his helmet digging into the dirt. The smell of ground back home. The mosaic texture of the red clay. He wished he could be anywhere else. But what he'd seen coming to the crater wouldn't leave him.

Bullets cut through the air just above his head and when one hit the crater edge he pulled his head lower and sucked in a breath. Then an explosion took away the air and for a second it was still, until rifle fire filled the world again.

When he ran to the crater he expected Sergeant Royce and Red would quickly follow, crashing in beside him, bringing firepower and company. He needed them. But, minutes later, he was still alone.

He brought this on them. How had he ever thought there was glamor in this? He would die alone beside the others. Proving nothing. Winning nothing.

Still keeping contact with Rhymes's boot, he raised his M16 over his head and fired. Brass rained down until the last round was fired and the chamber locked open.

The running footsteps behind him had to be Sergeant Royce and Red. He waited. This was his first flash of hope since coming to the crater. But first one, then the other went past. He saw Red disappear near where Sergeant Edwards lay.

Christ, they were leaving him alone to hold the crater.

Shortly after the footfalls ended, he heard the tortured whisper, rising out of a moment of slackened fire.

"Kill me. Please kill me. Don't leave . . ."

An explosion drowned out further words. Though the voice was distorted, as if coming from a great underwater depth, he knew it was Sergeant Edwards. The desperation mingled with his own.

"Goddamn you, Doc, where are you?" Singer yelled.

Sergeant Royce and Red said nothing, nor did either of them fire. They might both be helping Sergeant Edwards, but it made no sense at all when the position was so tenuous. Maybe they were dead.

Maybe everyone was gone. He'd be dead, too, lying beside the crater, if he hadn't traded places just a couple of hours ago. Likely he still would be.

His hand searched his web gear but all his grenades were gone, already thrown or lost on the run.

Just the grass, thick blades at the crater edge, and beyond a tangled wall of darker greens was all he saw in the few seconds it took to empty the magazine. With the volume of incoming rounds, muzzle flashes should be obvious, but he didn't see them. He dropped below the lip to reload.

Pressed against the front crater wall, he couldn't see or hear anyone else. Just the crushing noise of gunfire. And the oppressive sense of isolation. No friendly gun fired from a nearby position. He hated them for leaving him to fight alone.

He popped up and held the trigger, firing until the magazine was empty. Before he could duck he heard the *zing* next to his head and felt the rush of air beside his face almost like a slap. There was no pain, but still he touched his face and then examined his hand, seeing only that his fingers shook. Twice he tried before being able to seat a new magazine.

The round had had his name on it. But somehow it missed. He dropped his face against the dirt. To die alone was not what he'd envisioned. He stretched out his leg to touch his foot to the unmoving one behind him.

Between explosions he thought he heard the murmur of a voice, the words indistinguishable. But then he wasn't sure. He wanted to rise up look around to assure himself he wasn't the lone survivor, but that would be madness. Instead he pushed his body tighter to the ground, covering his head with his left hand. The near miss had stripped away his courage.

A faintness rose from his gut until his head felt weightless and drifting. He wasn't sure he could pull his face away from the dirt. The smell of the earth was intoxicating and took him home. Running through the fields as a small boy, he could feel the mud collecting on his feet until his feet grew almost too heavy to lift, and the birds that had settled on the freshly plowed ground rose up only to settle back a bit farther on, teasing and taunting him with their calls.

A sound startled him alert and he lifted his head, then held perfectly still, listening. Within the sound of rifle fire he heard it clearly. He swallowed the panic that rose in his throat.

"Medic!" The word came out a strangled wail.

"Royce? Red?"

Together the three of them might have a chance. What chance was there alone?

The sound was still there. Clearer. Unwavering. As soon as he heard it he knew what it was. Men crawling. Death coming for him.

His mouth was dry with terror and any thought of more screams died in his throat. With the M16 above his head he sprayed the area, jamming the trigger even after the clip was empty.

Still they came, crawling toward him. How many, he couldn't determine.

He had to look, to expose himself to see them. Flock shooting never worked. His father taught him that. You had to focus, pick a target. First one, then another. He could do this. Wasn't it just like hiding in a duck blind, then at the last minute jumping up to take them? Wasn't it just like that?

After checking his magazine and chamber he started to raise his head, slowly lifting his face from the pull of the earth, inching up into the buzz of bullets, hoping to see them first, when the flash of an explosion seared his face. He ducked or was pushed down and the air whooshed above his head. Debris showered the crater.

Almost before the roar faded, the sound returned. A scratching, padding sound from all around, as though big cats were creeping through the grass toward their prey. Relentless. Growing closer.

How long had he been in the crater? A minute? Maybe five. Not more than ten. Already it seemed like forever. Like he had always been here. He knew no other place. Life had started and would end here.

Time and space shifted. He was floating. Everything became surreal. The rifle fire and explosions faded into the background, as though on a separate soundtrack that someone had turned down. Just the sound of enemy soldiers creeping toward him. Isolated and magnified.

He squeezed his rifle in both hands, his hands growing white with the pressure. He clamped his eyes shut just for a second and tried to shut his mind to the sound. Pressing out the fear. When he opened his eyes, the crawling and the fear persisted.

The spirit of the bayonet fighter is to kill. The mantra of his training ran through his mind. He steeled himself against what was to come. *The spirit of the bayonet fighter is to kill. The spirit of the bayonet fighter is to kill . . .*

After a deep breath he started up again, seeing the crater lip far above him, imagining what he would meet beyond it. His teeth cut into his lip. He tasted his blood. He edged his rifle and then his face just enough, firing without aiming. The recoil slapped his shoulder as rounds ripped from the gun.

The crawling never paused.

He fired wildly where he thought he heard the sound, then thought he heard it somewhere else. It was hard to think or see.

"Stop crawling!"

If he could get just a little higher he could see more and make his fire more effective. *Focus, find the target.* Close now, he had to be able see them.

The agony made a few seconds seem like an hour. His throat constricted and he labored to breathe. Streams of tears rolled down his cheeks, mingling with his sweat.

"Doc. Goddamn you. I don't want to die alone."

The explosion rolled him and the ocean roared in his ears. The vegetation towering above the crater blurred. The pain slammed against his skull from the inside out when he moved his head. He rubbed his eyes. Spent brass and empty magazines were scattered beside him. The ocean noise stilled. Crawling took its place. They were still coming for him.

The spirit of the bayonet fighter is to kill. He pulled his left hand back from the handguard of his M16 and shoved the rifle and himself higher, pressing his cheek tight to the stock. He looked down the barrel. Movement. A target. He sighted and pulled the trigger. His rifle exploded in his hands.

The blow of the round dropped him back and his left hand fell from the rifle. He slid off the crater lip.

"I'm hit," he said, without thinking there was no one there to hear it.

There was no pain, though he was sure he'd taken a round. He studied his chest then brought his hand up and searched, but found nothing. Only on his left cheek did he find a cut and a thin trickle of blood, which he wiped away.

When he looked at his rifle for reassurance, what he saw drained away any residue of hope. His rifle took the impact of the round meant for his head. The plastic handguard was smashed, pieces gone, and the gas recycling tube that ran the length of the barrel was severed, the broken ends torn and bent by the bullet's force. What the effect was on his rifle's function he wasn't sure.

He tensed his body against the impact of the next shot, the one that would kill him, his will more damaged than his rifle. He gave no thought to going for Rhymes's M79. Even if he could get to it, he'd be dead before he could load it. In close quarters, fighting alone, he judged its single shot as nearly worthless. It failed to save Rhymes.

The world fell away. He was drifting now. Listening to them coming. Waiting. He was going home. He closed his eyes and laid his head against his broken weapon.

The rapid AK fire just behind his back thundered in his ears as if his head were exploding. He jerked at the first concussion of rounds. His mouth opened in a scream. He knew he was about to die, that the AK-47 was the last worldly sound he would record.

Still, he wanted to turn to face his killer. Or maybe it was an instinct born of hours wing shooting in a duck blind, when the whirl of wings at his back would startle him and he would rise, swing, and fire in one smooth, unconscious motion, sending a bluebill or a late-season mallard plummeting to hit in a geyser of water, where it drifted, dead.

With his M16 in his right hand, he pushed off the crater wall with his left and rolled, pivoting in place, propelling the M16 around in front of him as he spun. From the sound of the AK, the NVA was nearly in the crater, firing. Everything would be decided in a second.

10

Singer's roll was smooth. His one-handed grip of his M16 was strong, the barrel moving in an even arc. He had no thought, no plan. In the terror of believing he was dead, his mind shut down. Some part of him died the instant the AK fired near his back. Yet he was still alive, his move driven by reflex.

The NVA was at the crater's edge. His head tilted, his face down on his AK-47 pointed across the hole at where Sergeant Royce and Red had been. The AK's muzzle flashed and bounced.

He must have caught a glimpse of Singer's movement because he raised his head and turned. His eyes changed with what must have been understanding. He started to shift his fire. The AK's muzzle moved toward Singer, rounds etching their way across the crater.

But the muzzle of Singer's M16 was already crossing the man's face. His only hope hung on a weapon he wasn't sure would work. Singer slapped the trigger hard and held it. He saw the impact high in the man's cheek. The NVA's head jerked back, his expression froze, then his head fell forward. The AK went silent. His left hand hung in the crater just below the barrel of his rifle. The man's helmet tumbled down into the crater, settling at Rhymes's feet. Rhymes offered the same near-smile, unchanged from before.

Though he buried the trigger to deliver a burst of shots, Singer's M16 fired one round and quit. One round was not enough. He had to kill this guy and the others coming with him. He slammed the trigger again, trying to keep his rifle on target, fighting the momentum of his roll. Nothing happened.

"Goddamn it."

He struggled to bring his left hand to the shattered handguard of his M16 and get it back around to finish the man. The ejection port was closed, his rifle armed. Repeatedly he slapped the trigger to no effect, before the extent of the damage to his rifle registered.

The shattered handguard and severed gas tube. The gas from the exploding round that would normally drive the bolt back, ejecting the spent shell and chambering a live round, was escaping through the torn end of the gas recycling tube. Thus, after the shot, the bolt never moved. The rifle was uncocked, the spent round still in the chamber.

He released his trigger grip and worked the bolt. Unless he was quick he would die with his hand on the bolt instead of the trigger. As soon as the bolt closed on a new round he fired directly on the NVA slumped on the crater edge just ahead of Stick's body. The NVA barely quivered with the impact of the round. Again the rifle quit after just one shot. Again he worked the bolt.

"Royce? Red?"

He raised up and turned, risking a glimpse at where the NVA had fired. Red's body, his back wet in blood, slumped on top of Sergeant Edwards. Neither of them moved. There was no sign of Sergeant Royce.

"Goddamn them."

He spun back to the NVA. From the bottom of the hole, he fired again and again as fast as he could work the bolt and pull the trigger. Steady now, just a few feet away, he couldn't miss. He killed the man over and over again, unwilling or unable to stop.

The crawling faded back into the sounds of battle. He held a new resolve free of fear. He would kill them all.

Then the NVA moved. It was impossible, yet he did. Singer shot him again and then again, but still the NVA backed away, though he never lifted his head nor fired his AK that remained caught under him. Singer screamed with rage and fired.

Nearly from the first he realized the dead NVA was being pulled backward by another NVA who must have crawled up with him. He wasn't letting them get away. He counted his last two magazines, loading one.

The gunfire, explosions, even the crawling didn't matter. When he stood, stretched his neck up and raised his head back, he caught a brief glimpse of the second NVA hiding behind the first, inching awkwardly backward and dragging the first man's body by the feet. He raised his gun above his head to fire one shot, then had to lower it to eject the round and chamber another. He fired as fast as his rifle would allow. Still the NVA inched away, affecting his escape using the body of his comrade as a shield.

"Goddamn this rifle."

He ejected the empty magazine.

"Ammo! Ammo!"

He slammed in his last magazine, cursing his limited firepower. Without help, he'd have to crawl out to get ammo and look for Stick's or Red's rifle. With a working rifle he could kill this bastard. Never had he hated anyone more. He pulled the trigger with more force, willing each bullet to strike the man.

Around him the company's battle raged, but Singer gave it no thought. His singular focus was on his lone battle to hold the crater and his efforts to kill the retreating NVA.

When his rifle quit, he heard the firing pin hit against an empty chamber. He slammed it to the ground. Stick's body was the closest, but he was uncertain where Stick's rifle was. He never considered Rhymes's M79, its single shot worse than his broken rifle. He turned toward Red's and Sergeant Edwards's bodies to size up a move to their weapons and ammo and saw him.

Sergeant Royce was sitting behind the bodies with head slightly bowed, his right hand resting on Sergeant Edwards's face.

"Royce! Goddamn it, throw me a rifle!"

Sergeant Royce blinked once and his mouth twisted, but he never turned his head or lifted his hands.

"Royce! Sergeant Royce! Throw me a rifle!"

Slowly Sergeant Royce turned his head and looked at Singer without showing any recognition.

"For Christ's sake, throw me a rifle."

Sluggishly, Sergeant Royce picked up Red's rifle and flung it. Singer had to stretch his arm out of the crater to reach it. With a functioning rifle, he searched for the retreating NVA along the drag path and saw a form nearly lost in the jungle growth. The movement gave the man away. When the M16 ripped off what was almost a full magazine, Singer nearly laughed.

"Try to get away now, fucker."

He grabbed a magazine off Stick's chest and emptied it in the same direction, though he couldn't really see the man or make out any movement.

"I got you, goddamn it. I got you."

Looking at Rhymes was still too hard to bear, so he left him without a glance to stare at the sky alone. He scrambled out of the crater, crawling back to where Sergeant Royce still sat beside the bodies as if there were no incoming at all.

"For Christ's sake, get down," Singer said.

Singer rolled Red's body over to get at his ammo. Sergeant Edwards lay still and without protest as Singer stripped ammo and grenades from his body, too.

"Get down!" Singer said, pulling Sergeant Royce roughly to the ground.

"Help me," Sergeant Royce said.

"Are you hit?"

"I need to get Sergeant Edwards out."

"It's too late."

"He'll be okay," Sergeant Royce insisted.

"He's dead."

"I heard medevacs."

"It's Cobras."

Sergeant Royce cocked his head but didn't let go of Sergeant Edward's arm.

"We'll get him out when we can. Where's your rifle?"

"I saw him kill Red," Sergeant Royce said.

"Are you hit?"

"I thought he would kill me."

Singer found a rifle next to Sergeant Edwards and shoved it into Sergeant Royce's hands.

"Everyone's dead," Sergeant Royce said.

"We'll be dead, too, if you don't start firing."

Singer cut loose a long string of shots.

"They're all dead," Sergeant Royce said.

"I know. You got to fire, Sarge."

Again Singer sprayed across the front. *Let them come,* he thought. He wanted them to come so he could make them pay. After another burst he quickly checked the rear. They wouldn't surprise him again. His terror was gone, replaced by something more primeval and sustaining. Something that felt good.

11

G renade!"
The grenade arched above them, floating out of the vegetation. Singer lost sight of it as he rolled. The explosion came from the crater. The walls of the shell hole and Rhymes took the blast. He fired a burst at where he thought the grenade came from.

"Fire, goddamn it," Singer yelled at Sergeant Royce.

Once more he pulled Sergeant Royce's hand away from Sergeant Edwards and pushed his rifle back at him.

"You can't do anything for him, Sarge. You got to keep shooting."

It was incredible to him that after all the artillery and the Cobras worked with their rockets and miniguns, the NVA where still fighting. The AK fire even surged once the gunships pulled out. Only Sergeant Royce seemed to believe things were over.

The roar came fast, building until it blotted out the gunfire. The first bombs were so close his body shook along with the ground, and he thought the pilot had made a mistake. Still, Singer laughed.

He raised his head before the debris had settled and fired, believing he was driving them into the bombs. And he laughed more. Had it been safe he would have stood and cheered.

The jets made run after run, working farther out on later passes. The escape routes, Singer imagined. "We got you fuckers now," he muttered. As the thunder of the next jet grew overhead, he rolled on his side, tilted his head up and watched a lone fighter streak in low from his right and then get lost below the jungle canopy, followed shortly by the concussions, frightening even with the distance. The jets would end it soon.

Hueys started coming in behind him. The first medevacs. He could hear the pitch of the rotors change as they settled briefly, then raced away. Sergeant Royce was up on one arm looking anxiously toward the road, but Singer didn't turn to look. There was nothing there he wanted to see. Besides, there was no rush. Rhymes, Stick, Sergeant Edwards, and Red were past caring. They would ride one of the last Hueys out.

He spun around and nearly unleashed a volley, scaring himself with how close he'd come to firing.

"Hey, take it easy. It's over," Bear said.

Bear stood there, towering over the scene, his rifle casually at his side, looking unworried by the rounds still being fired. Behind him at a distance Ghost crouched, reminding Singer of a sprinter's set.

"Fuck," Bear said, drawing out the word as though it were a lengthy eulogy. His glance shifted from one body to the next. His eyes narrowed and he shook his head back and forth, looking as though he would say more. Finally he looked down at his own chest, where Singer was staring.

"It ain't my blood. You two okay?"

"Mostly," Singer said.

"We got to get Sergeant Edwards to a medevac," Sergeant Royce said.

"He can wait," Bear said. "There ain't no hurry anymore. We're pushing out to clear the front."

Bear stepped closer, peering into the hole for the first time. The cords in his neck went taut. "Fuck. Rhymes, too."

"I couldn't help him," Singer said. "Doc never came. I don't know where the fuck he is. He promised—"

"Doc's dead. Captain Powers and the whole CP. Top's running the company," Bear said.

A chopper settled on the road and Bear turned his head toward it. Singer watched Sergeant Royce pull Sergeant Edwards's head up on his knees then bend down beside the dead acting platoon leader's ear.

"Fuck! Get your ass up here, man," Bear said, looking at Ghost, who was glancing between the helicopters and Bear.

Ghost crossed himself and began to creep forward as though he were walking through a mine field.

"If you don't hurry up I'm going to fucking shoot you," Bear said. Singer didn't doubt he was serious, for it was the first move Bear made with his weapon.

"Let's finish this," Bear said when Ghost was close.

"I got to stay with Sergeant Edwards," Sergeant Royce said.

"Yeah, you stay with him. We got this," Bear said, bringing his rifle up to the ready.

The three of them, Singer, Bear, and Ghost, pushed forward, walking abreast in a loose line. Sometimes Singer lost sight of Bear, but then he'd hear him fire or yell at Ghost to catch up and he'd adjust his step or shift over. Even as he left it behind, the crater followed him, events playing across his mind.

He fired to rid himself of all of it and to kill any lingering NVA. Bear fired less often, Ghost not all. At least, Singer never heard any fire he took for Ghost's. The last grenade he'd taken from Red and Sergeant Edwards didn't explode. It just rattled through the brush and fell, as ineffective as a rock.

The absence of NVA bodies was disturbing. He was watching, expecting to count them in the tens, but he'd yet to discover one. He wasn't sure what Bear was seeing, or if Ghost even had his eyes open and was seeing anything beyond his own fear.

The brush was thick so it would be tough to see them and Bear was moving too fast to do any kind of search. He should have taken the side where he knew the first one was. But he was sure he'd killed more. Though he hadn't found a body, he'd discovered drag trails and scattered evidence of the carnage: bloody clothes, gauzes, and stains on the ground where men had lain and bled.

The leaf of a low shrub held a splat of blood that smeared when Singer touched it. Looking at the most likely path, he saw another splat a few meters away, slightly smaller than the first. With his rifle ready he scanned the ground ahead for anything that didn't fit. He was sure he could track the man and make the kill, as he had trailed and killed his first buck in a willow swamp when he was only thirteen. While he'd dreamed of that first buck long before he shot it, he wanted this kill more. The blood trail went west, away from Bear and Ghost. To follow it would mean leaving them and heading off on his own. Just then, Bear fired and the decision was made. He hurried to catch up, vowing to come back and make a proper search.

Another jet rocketed overhead. The air shuddered and for a few seconds he was deaf to everything but the plane. It was a long minute before the explosions drifted back to him from the northwest. The pilots were chasing the retreating force. Singer formed a new love for fighter jets and gunships.

The narrow river corridor brought an abrupt break in the jungle vegetation, sharply illuminated by the harsh midday sun. Singer stopped in the shadows, as he was sure Bear would, too. He heard his breath, but the stream was silent. Behind him and far to the east came sporadic gunfire and occasional explosions.

The stream, he was certain, ran east. Some ways on it would join the Perfume River, flowing on to Hue, through the city, and would pass by the island where he watched the darkness just a few months ago when Rhymes, Doc, Stick, Red, and Sergeant Edwards were still alive and Sergeant Royce was still strong and in charge of the squad and he had still believed. Now Hue seemed unreachable.

From the shadows, Singer squinted against the blinding brightness that was almost painful. About thirty feet wide, prominent rocks guarded stagnant pools. Upstream, a leaf lay on the surface, barely moving. Darkness again reclaimed the far bank and vegetation formed a living wall. When the fall rains came, the flow would bury the stones and sweep away any evidence that today had ever existed.

Just downstream, near the edge of the opposite bank, two NVA lay in full sunlight. They were sprawled facedown in a shallow pool, their arms entangled, hands touching. There were no weapons that he could see. Tufts of black hair floated, shiny in the light. One soldier's arm was extended beyond his head, his hand on a rock at the river's edge as though he was trying to pull the two of them into the cover of the jungle. They almost made it.

He fired into the men's backs, watching the dark holes explode and water spray. The bodies rocked slightly and the gentle ripple spread across the stagnant pool and became still again. Something rippled through his body even as his rifle grew quiet and settled there, leaving him feeling heavy and tired. No response came from the jungle that sat like a door to a dark room beyond the river. He knew he had already crossed the river and entered the room.

"Jesus, Singer, they're dead already."

It wasn't until then that he noticed Bear watching him from downstream, standing motionless in the shadows. How could such a big man be so quiet and so hard to see? He was certain, though, that Bear nodded in agreement or acknowledgement of what they both knew before signaling to head back. They turned and worked back over the same ground toward the road. Despite looking hard, Singer found no more NVA to kill.

The light was more diffused at the cut beside the road, less blinding than it had been at the narrower river corridor. Breaking out of the jungle edge, Singer watched the dust kick up from the road in a billowing cloud as another Huey settled in and men came toward it carrying a poncho with one boot sticking out the end and the middle sagging low. Another group stood waiting with a second poncho, less heavily laden. When they moved, it was with downcast faces and plodding steps. The wounded were all gone, as was any urgency.

A couple of piles of gear sat near the road; rucksacks and weapons from dead and wounded along with a smaller pile of captured NVA gear. A soldier walked up and dumped two M16s and a handful of magazines on a pile. Two Cobras circled menacingly, but neither fired.

To Singer's left he saw the crater looking bare and abandoned, no longer valued by either side. The bodies were gone and there was little to indicate what had happened there. He stared at it for a moment, wanted to go to it, but was held back by some internal force he could not name.

Ahead, Bear waited for him, his helmet pushed back on his head, his rifle again one-handed at his side. Together, with Ghost trailing, they walked slowly toward the road, Singer uncertain of what came next.

There was no sign of Sergeant Royce, who he guessed had followed Sergeant Edwards. He doubted he would see him again.

Shooter's body was gone from the roadside where Bear said Ghost saw Rhymes lay him. Perhaps Shooter and Rhymes rode the same bird together back to graves registration, united in a way neither had envisioned. The sprint down the road seemed a lifetime ago.

Loose groups of men milled near the road looking aimless. There didn't seem to be a perimeter anymore, though a few men still worked along the jungle edge as if looking for something they'd lost. Some men already had their rucks on and seemed anxious to leave. Singer looked west up the road to where he'd left his ruck, to where it had all started, when it had still been an exciting game. But the road was empty, all their rucks gone. If Bear noticed, he didn't say anything.

They headed toward where the remnants of fourth platoon were assembling on the west end of the road. So few of them were left. Sergeant Milner had survived and was pacing slowly back and forth, pointing a bouncing finger, counting and recounting the platoon's survivors, looking confused, as though he couldn't understand where everyone was. Or perhaps without Sergeant Edwards's leadership, he was lost as others likely were. Certainly Singer missed him, but there were others he missed more. He saw Trip standing alone, still lugging the M60 he took from Shooter. His relief was swallowed by his emptiness. They caught each other's eyes, but there was no reaction. In Trip's eyes he saw only weariness.

He stood near Bear, neither speaking, and watched men load the last bodies and then the equipment until only those standing and able to walk were left. Ghost had disappeared. Once Ghost talked of lying down among the dead in a plan to be evacuated, and Singer wondered if he had done it.

Back east on the far end of their position, Top was standing next to a stocky man with the bearing of a senior officer, both men looking back to the southeast. Top was pointing, as though explaining where the battle started. Three RTOs huddled nearby, showing radio antennas that a few hours ago would have guaranteed their deaths.

Days before he carried a radio, only that morning ridding himself of it. Stick took it and its fate, thanking him. Only Sergeant Edwards heard his reasons. Who could he explain it to? There was no one to tell he was sorry. Stick was gone, but the image of his ghostly countenance, his fingers wrapped around the handset, stayed with him.

The safety of the firebase was waiting, but he was in no hurry to leave. He looked at where he knew the crater was and then at the ground he had crossed and re-crossed to get there. He thought of Rhymes's tireless half smile and unfocused eyes that would never read a book again, the NVA who nearly killed him, the other who tried to get away, of the blood trails that he wished he'd followed, and the NVA in the stream. His M16 was light in his hands, the trigger waiting. It wasn't finished yet.

Was this what Bear warned him about?

12

The sounds of the chopper that took the stocky senior officer away faded, leaving the battlefield eerily quiet. It was a long time since Singer had heard any gunfire. Even the distant bombing had ceased. Most of the men stood in restless, staggered groups along the road. The shrill chirping of a lizard announced its survival and the return of natural sounds.

"It ain't nothing like you imagined, is it?" Bear asked.

"You think I wanted this?"

"Man, we all want to prove ourselves. It's what fucks us up."

Singer dropped his face and turned away. He felt the big hand on his shoulder.

"It ain't your fault, man. We all been there. Except maybe guys like Shooter who found it just like they thought it would be and loved it. Look what it got him."

Bear shook his head as if dismissing it all. Singer couldn't think of anything to say.

"Maybe now you'll wish for quiet days." Bear took his hand from Singer's shoulder.

That wasn't what he wanted now, but Singer was afraid to tell him.

For a while they stood silent.

Down the road, Singer watched Top move through the company, the RTO nearly running to keep up. Men started forming a staggered double column. Lieutenant Creely, the second platoon leader and ranking officer after the captain, approached Top, and Top waved his hand as if swatting a fly and walked away.

"Why's Top running things?" Singer asked.

When Bear didn't answer, Singer turned to see Bear staring at the jungle, maybe thinking about their charge across the open ground that made Singer feel so alive or about his mama and the house he said he would buy her when he got home.

"Bear, why's Top running the company?"

"Better Top than one of—"

Bang, bang, bang, bang, bang, bang! An AK-47 on full auto. The sound exploded in the silence that had settled over the battlefield.

Men fell to the road around him. For a second Singer heard the echoes of Sergeant Edwards's earlier command: "Charge the tree line!" But everyone else was down and he was aware that he stood alone, offering the most appealing target. Still, he took a step, hesitated, then dove to the ground. With nowhere to go, he threw himself on top of Bear. The road edge depression offered only the illusion of cover.

"I'm hit," Bear said in a low, unexcited voice.

It was silent again after the AK stopped as abruptly as it started. For a moment it seemed as if everyone held their breath, uncertain of what happened and what was next.

"I can't believe some motherfucker shot me." Bear turned his head. "How bad is it?"

"I saw him. But I can't find him now," Singer said.

In the instant before diving atop Bear, when he looked toward the crater, he saw him—the top half of him, anyway. A lone, helmeted NVA in an olive-colored shirt standing at the jungle edge, firing an AK from his shoulder. But Singer lost sight of him while getting down. Now the NVA had disappeared. So near the crater. Rhymes's vacant stare petitioned him. He rose on a knee. Bear pulled at his arm.

"Let someone else. How bad?"

His ears rang with the muzzle blast of an M60 as it opened up from the slope just above him. He buried his head down on Bear's back. A line of red tracers streamed overhead, disappearing into the ground near the crater. It had to be Trip.

No one else fired, perhaps concerned about hitting the two GIs who materialized at the jungle edge. Singer watched the two Americans working toward the crater. Could he run and safely join them with the M60 firing just above his head?

"Damn, tell me what it looks like," Bear said.

Singer turned away from the line of red tracers and the two GIs. Bear's back showed no blood. No hole that he could see or feel.

"My neck," Bear said.

Lifting up to see, Singer pulled Bear's fatigue collar back, expecting the wound to be worse after what he had already seen today. What he saw surprised him.

"Can you move?"

Bear cranked his head around, trying to see his wound or to read the expression on Singer's face.

"Just tell me. You're heavier than you look."

"Can you move your legs?"

Singer felt Bear wiggle beneath him.

"I could walk home if they'd let me."

"Shit, you're a lucky fucker. There's nothing, Bear. No blood. Nothing. Just a small mark. Shit." He stared at the small white spot on Bear's black skin where the bullet had passed through his neck without hitting the spine or any blood vessel. Incredibly, the hard AK bullet had barely torn the flesh. "Damn, you're lucky."

"Guess I'm going home early."

"You'll be back on the street before I'm eating breakfast,"

"Thanks for covering me."

"Hell, you had the best spot. There was nowhere else to go."

Beneath him, Bear's body trembled. At first Singer thought the big man was crying. Then he heard the laugh, even with the noise of machine gun fire.

The tracers still had the shooter pinned. A few others on the slope behind Singer had joined in with M16s. The two men working the treeline were inching in on the spot. The NVA was trapped. Singer shifted off of Bear. He still wanted in on it.

Bear large hand settled on his back.

"Man, ain't you learned nothing today? They'll get him."

Singer looked at Bear's face, the streaks on his dusty cheeks, eyes that showed concern.

"You still think this is your war?"

"You're going home."

"Be careful. You'll become another Shooter."

Singer turned back to not miss the finale.

The two men were almost there. Methodically, one fired into the ground just in front of his feet while the other stood ready to take on any NVA who jumped up. The second man covered while the first reloaded. Trading off, they eased ahead through thigh-high brush to the shot-up ground. The second man fired into the new ground while the first stood braced. Then they repeated the process, moving ever closer. Second-tour guys. They'd done this before. A line of tracers from Trip's machine gun pinned down anyone farther ahead, shifting west as the two men advanced.

Singer raised his head and tightened his grip in expectation.

Just after he started to fire again, the lead man jumped back, continuing to fire while the second American opened up, as well. Then they stopped and waited, rifles ready, staring at the ground. Trip held up on the machine gun. Singer held his breath.

Finally one of the men got down on his stomach, his head and arm disappearing in the ground. The other man stepped closer, pointing his M16 to the same spot. The first man pulled back, rising to his knees, and heaved an NVA from the hole. While his partner stood over the unmoving NVA, his rifle pointed at the man's chest, the first man reached in a second time and hauled out the man's AK-47. With the AK shouldered, he grabbed the NVA's foot and dragged him toward the road.

The NVA's head and body flopped over the uneven ground. It reminded Singer of dragging a deer in from the woods, pulling the carcass through the brush and over downed timber. A trophy he would hang and display from the large oak tree in the yard, where his friends would come to admire it and congratulate him. But there was some sadness mingled with the sense of triumph.

The NVA lay motionless and bloody in the dust of the road where the man dumped him. Singer had to stare a long time before he saw the slightest movement in the man's chest. Though the NVA was still alive, no one moved to help him. The man who dragged him in dug through his pockets while the other still pointed his M16 at the man, as though even near death the NVA might make a break for it and need to be shot again.

The company slowly regained their feet. Most ignored the dying NVA, though a few men moved closer and stood around the man. Singer could see well enough from where he was, as the NVA was dropped just a few feet away, as though they'd known what he'd been wishing. The man's shirt was dark with blood and a thin stream of blood ran from his mouth and down his cheek. His eyes were clouded. It was hard to say what he saw.

Bear insisted on standing and waved off any effort to bandage his neck.

"Get away from me, man," he said when Sergeant Milner tried to examine his wound.

Singer stayed beside him, though they both were out of words. Everyone looked up as the sounds of slapping blades as a Huey grew from the east. It came alone this time, without a Cobra escort.

They crouched below the spinning blades. Bear climbed in unassisted.

"Take care," Singer said loudly to be heard above the rotor noise.

"Be careful, man." Then Bear grinned and slapped the eagle patch on his shoulder.

The wounded NVA was thrown onto the helicopter deck next to Bear, the man he shot. Singer heard the sharp crack when the man's head hit the floor. Bear patted the man's leg.

The Huey rose in a din of a surging engine, revving blades, and a storm of churned-up road dust. The men nearest the chopper turned their faces away, fatigues whipped tight against their bodies by the wind. Squinting, Singer looked into the dust, feeling the sting on his face, and watched Bear disappear. A loneliness settled over him as the chopper receded. Even after he walked back and found Trip, the emptiness remained.

"You can bet there's more of them sitting in holes waiting," Singer said.

"As long as they stay down until we leave, I don't care." Trip felt the barrel of his M60.

"They'll sneak off when we're gone."

"Let the fuckers go."

"We should leave an ambush behind."

"You want to stay?"

"If it means getting the guys who got Rhymes, Stick, and Doc."

"You can never fix it. Be happy we're leaving. We survived."

"Did we?"

Trip didn't reply.

Without any further word, the company began moving down the road toward LZ Birmingham. Men moved and others followed. Progress was plodding, likely more from exhaustion than any special care. Trip swung the big gun at his hip, sweeping it along the jungle. Ghost had shown up and was shuffling along, head down, rifle on his shoulder. There was still no sign of Sergeant Royce, but Sergeant Milner didn't seem worried by his absence. Top paced back and forth along their diminished column.

Twice Singer caught himself in those first meters looking to find Rhymes and Bear, unable to orient himself without their presence.

He couldn't understand things. The day had started with so much promise, but he could no longer recall his elation at returning to his squad. Now there was no squad. So much had gone wrong. Had he kept the radio and stayed with Sergeant Edwards, he wondered if they all might still be alive. Or if he'd just stuck with Rhymes, might he have changed events at the crater, and would Rhymes be beside him now? How had they gotten separated? The charge. Yes, the charge. He had to figure out what happened.

When he stopped and turned he could no longer see the ambush site. He needed to go back and check. He was forgetting something. He'd left something behind.

"Keep moving," Sergeant Milner said, moving past without waiting.

13

Men on the firebase stopped their work or looked up from where they rested and watched Singer and the others pass, as though seeing something strange. Something that scared and fascinated them at the same time. Singer saw the questions on their faces that he had already asked himself many times on the trudging retreat to the firebase. What had happened today? Why had he survived when so many near him died?

After he was assigned to a perimeter bunker with Trip, he went to the aid station and asked about Bear. The medic, a rail-thin, bespectacled guy with sandy hair and a peace medal around his neck, said Bear walked into the aid station alone and waited without question until they evac'd him.

"He was the lightest casualty we saw today. A lucky guy," the medic said. "Barely needed a bandage."

"What about the NVA?"

"What NVA?" The medic wiped his hands on a towel he carried.

"The wounded one that came in on the same bird."

"There was no NVA. I was at the pad waiting. Your friend came in alone."

Leaving the aid station, Singer went searching for his ruck. One of the clerks told him where to look. A mousy-looking guy with oily skin and nervous hands stared at Singer when he showed up, looking shocked before he finally found his voice.

"Shit," the clerk said, his hands momentarily going still. "We thought you were dead."

Singer merely looked at him and the man shifted nervously from one foot to the other, his hands fluttering at his sides, typing on imaginary keys.

"Well, your gear came in KIA," the clerk said, then walked away swiftly. Singer indeed found his ruck in the pile of equipment of those killed and reclaimed it without wondering how it had gotten there or what it meant.

It was at the pile of gear of those killed that Singer saw Sergeant Royce for the first time since they separated at the crater. He watched Sergeant Royce pull worn envelopes from a rucksack and called out to ask him where he'd been. But Sergeant Royce hurried off, clutching the letters.

Next he went to the company area. To hell with dealing with Sergeant Milner. Who was left in the platoon to ask? A freckle-faced kid with carrot-colored hair was sitting outside the tent paging through a journal, his feet up on a couple of stacked ammo crates.

"You with supply?" Singer asked.

"Yeah, why?"

"I need ten more magazines and ammo."

"I can't just give that out. Besides, it looks like you have enough," the clerk said, eyeing Singer's web gear and bandolier.

"You know what happened today?"

"We all heard."

"Then you know you don't want to fuck with me."

"The supply sergeant won't be happy."

"But you'll get to finish your reading without a visit to the aid station."

Singer left with fifteen magazines and more than enough ammo. Back on the perimeter, he quietly reloaded them while Trip sat silently beside the bunker on a pile of sandbags. When he thought he had enough, he counted them. Recalling scrounging for ammo from the bodies, he loaded the rest, stacking them next to him.

Finally he opened a can of spaghetti and picked at it cold, too weary to heat it. He set the tasteless mash aside half finished.

With darkness settling over the firebase, Trip, in his first words of the evening, offered to take the initial watch. Singer tossed and turned before giving up and sitting on top of the bunker, watching the distant flares and tracers that were so far off in the mountains they might have been a dream. In the darkness he saw the faces of Rhymes, Doc, Stick, Red, and Sergeant Edwards and tried to recall their last words. How could he still be here? What debts did he owe?

"You hear what they're saying?"

Until Trip spoke, Singer had forgotten he was there.

"What?" Singer asked.

"The lieutenant froze. That's why Top was running things."

"Lieutenant Creely?"

"Yeah, the general's fair-haired boy. That West Point fucker."

Singer heard Trip spit and his boot grinding the dirt.

"The CO's dead and we're getting cut up, and the fucking lieutenant does nothing. Worse than nothing. In the Cav we'd have shot him."

"We were lucky Top was there."

"I knew that fucker was all show."

"They'll ship him out. Top will see to that. He's probably gone already."

"Hell, I heard he's still at the CP ordering people around now that we're back on the firebase. Fucker, acting like nothing happened."

"If he stays, we're in big trouble."

"Some chickenshit lieutenant isn't keeping me from going home."

Trip spat again.

Singer pulled a single round from a magazine and rolled it back and forth in the palm of his hand. Christ. They were in a bad way if the lieutenant took over the company, even if he couldn't be blamed for everything that happened today. Now he worried about Trip, too. The threat of the solution used in the Cav was not an empty one. Trip was so determined to make it, he would kill anyone who might threaten his survival, regardless of the uniform they wore. Incompetent and dangerous officers were at the top of Trip's list. Singer didn't want to get caught in the fallout.

That the lieutenant froze in battle was frightening on many levels. If he stayed they would have to follow him and rely on him when they hit the shit again. More frightening was the knowledge that even the best-schooled and most competent on the training grounds could disgrace themselves in the face of enemy fire. How did you live with such shame? It would be better to be killed. Singer hadn't frozen, but he doubted he had fought as well as he should have. Rhymes, Stick, Sergeant Edwards, and Red were dead. He might have saved them had he been better.

He hated Lieutenant Creely for showing how easily disgrace could come and for the fear that pressed against his chest. Pulling back the cocking arm,

Singer checked his M16 again to be sure a round was chambered. He touched each grenade on his web gear, assuring himself they were there. It was bad enough the NVA were trying to kill them, but they were endangered by their own leaders. Maybe he would help Trip with his list.

Eventually he slept, but woke early while it was still dark. At first when he heard Trip stir, he thought it was Rhymes. It was only with the rising sun that the reality of the day after settled over him.

Trip offered his morning greeting. "Twenty-four and a wake-up and I'm out of this fucking place."

Hueys came just after dawn bearing men reportedly from a replacement unit in Da Nang, their eyes as bright as their weapons and their boots. Singer almost had to turn away. Had he ever looked like that?

"It's not very many replacements," Singer said.

"Get used to it," Trip said. "There's not a unit in Nam that isn't understrength."

Singer watched with interest to see if there would be a new captain in the group. But there wasn't an officer among them.

A black buck sergeant looked around uncertainly before he was directed toward Sergeant Milner.

"A Shake and Bake," Trip said. "Got his rank from a school. Things just keep getting better."

After the last chopper departed, a small group of shiny uniforms was left gathered around Sergeant Milner. Ghost tried to slip back in his bunker, but Sergeant Milner caught him first, giving him a tall white guy who had a gliding dancer's step, even laden down with gear. Later on, Singer heard Ghost call him "California."

Then Sergeant Milner brought a smaller guy over to Singer's and Trip's position. "He's with you," he told Trip.

"We don't need any new guy, Sarge."

Sergeant Milner was already five feet away and didn't look back.

"What's it like?" the New Guy asked.

He was a slight, wiry guy, the kind of build that would make a good tunnel rat. He bowed under the weight of his ruck, which rattled when he moved. His helmet shadowed his small face that seemed all teeth, yellow and uneven. He held an M16 in one hand at his side, looking at Trip eagerly. Singer thought of Stick's eagerness to carry the radio.

"You know, the fighting," the New Guy said when Trip only stared at him. "You guys wasted some gooks yesterday, huh? Man, I'm going to—"

"Shut the fuck up!" Trip was in the New Guy's face, his fist twisting the Cherry's fatigues.

The New Guy's mouth hung half open, wordless. His face paled and his eyes bulged. Singer watched without sympathy.

"Hey, I didn't mean nothing," the New Guy squeaked, his voice an octave higher than before.

Trip's fist was against the Cherry's throat. The New Guy dropped his rifle on the ground and raised up on his toes. His helmet fell and his chin shook. Singer thought of Rhymes lying in the crater and tightened his hands on his M16.

"If you want to make it through the day, keep your fucking mouth shut," Trip said, slowly emphasizing each word as if letting the pressure out in small measured bursts.

"It's not worth it," Singer said. "Don't fuck up your ETS."

Trip released the Cherry with a shove that sent him staggering backward, his ruck rattling, though the New Guy kept his footing.

"And repack your fucking ruck so you don't sound like a herd of cows," Trip added over his shoulder, looking certain the Cherry wouldn't have the balls to use his rifle. "Fucking gutless officers and guys like this. I won't die with this fucking outfit." Trip walked back to his M60 on the bunker top.

The Cherry stood there shaking and rubbing his throat before stooping to pick up his rifle, all the time glancing nervously at Trip. He pulled at his uniform and web gear, then took a few quick steps toward Singer.

"What's wrong with that guy? He's crazy. Hell, I only asked about the fighting."

Singer looked past the New Guy not wanting to commit his face to memory. "You don't have a clue what happened yesterday. He's seen more than you'll ever see. Be quiet and pay attention and you'll be okay." Then he quickly walked away, leaving the New Guy standing there alone to figure the rest out by himself.

At the helipad he was hoping to scrounge some LRRP rations, extra Cs, or any unattended equipment he might trade for beer. A Huey waited on the pad, its engine quiet. But any supplies that might have come in with it were already stored and secured. A crew chief was bent over one of the guns checking the ammo belt. A gunner stood off to the side talking with a grunt who carried no equipment. The grunt's left hand was heavily wrapped in white dressing bright as a beacon in the early morning sun. When the grunt turned his head, Singer recognized the profile.

"Hey, Sarge. Sergeant Royce," Singer called out.

But Royce turned his face away.

The pilot and copilot walked up to the helicopter, said something to the crew chief that Singer couldn't hear, then climbed into the cockpit, donning their flight helmets. The crew chief bent on one knee to look under the Huey.

"What happened?" Singer asked when he got up next to Sergeant Royce.

The gunner moved toward the Huey, motioning Sergeant Royce to follow. Sergeant Royce looked at the waiting Huey and the beckoning gunner, then back at Singer. Sergeant Royce's eyes had that same lost look Singer saw in them at the crater.

"I'll never survive another ambush," Sergeant Royce said, then ran toward the helicopter, his bandaged hand waving like a white flag.

The helicopter's rotors turned, slowly gathering speed. Singer's mind filled with the roar of the engine and he turned away from the image and the dust that swirled around him.

Near his position he passed a lieutenant with clean, crisp fatigues and shiny jungle boots who was walking briskly. At the bunker, Singer found Trip and the New Guy sitting in a tense, quiet truce.

"Who was that?" Singer asked.

"The Cherry lieutenant taking over fourth platoon. Wanted to tell us personally how excited he was. Jesus. Another fucking winner."

"Where the hell did he come from?" Singer asked.

"Just came in. You should be happy."

"What do you mean?"

"We're heading out in thirty. Back to the ambush site."

14

May 6, 1968
0719 Hours
Vietnam

It wasn't good. Going back the same way was inviting trouble. Singer ran his sweaty palm across his thigh then returned his hand to his rifle's grip, thumbing the safety.

NVA were in every shadow. He was sure of it. They were waiting, knowing they'd be coming back. If he had his way they'd recon the whole way by fire, walking artillery along both sides of the road ahead of them, the lead element shooting up each stretch of jungle they moved toward and through. That would clean them out.

With Lieutenant Creely leading them, what chance was there of things going well? Someone had decided to give the lieutenant another chance. No one had asked him. Trip said he wouldn't go out if Lieutenant Creely was in charge, but eventually reneged, saying he could survive twenty-four more days even with a chickenshit CO.

Despite their shaky leader and the foolhardiness of using the same route, Singer was excited. He needed to see the place again, before too much time passed and things changed. Doing anything was better than sitting on the firebase, where there was too much idle time to think and hear the voices.

Even now, there had to be something he could do to still save Rhymes and the others. He was convinced he would discover it there.

The terrain looked different today, all of it altered in some way Singer couldn't explain. The road was a red-brown slash through an expanse of formless, mottled greens that stretched to each horizon, the mountains a line of jagged teeth below a blue abyss. The early morning sun pushed out long, ghost-like shadows ahead of them.

In the northwest, low, gray clouds hung among the peaks, a residue of yesterday's storm. A reminder of unsettled things. He hoisted the ammo pouches on his belt, checking their weight, and counted the loaded magazines he'd hung in a bandolier. Two belts of M60 ammo for Trip's machine gun crisscrossed his chest, adding to his load. When they found trouble, he would help Trip on the gun.

Singer ran his fingers across each eye, pushing away the sweat, but they still burned. The scene remained unchanged. The fatigue he bore today was weightier than his pack.

At least today they were sweeping the road, looking for mines and booby traps like the ones that killed Doc Odum and Captain Powers. Far ahead, he could see the man alone in front of the company with headphones, swinging the detecting unit back and forth inches above the road surface. Occasionally the whole company stopped while the man swung the detector slowly over the same ground, titling his head. Sometimes the man knelt and probed delicately with a bayonet.

Someone should ask the guy where the hell he was yesterday. Singer waited for the explosion from the road or the jungle, gritting his teeth, hoping for release. Stopped again after moving just a short distance, Singer stood coiled, ready to charge the treeline, knowing it was coming. Already feeling the rush. He rocked back and forth, shifting his weight from his front leg to the rear in a steady motion.

A ways behind him the New Lieutenant stood casually consulting a map, looking conspicuous in his shiny fatigues and new helmet. His RTO, who looked nothing like Stick, but still reminded Singer of him, stood next to him similarly attired, inviting disaster. They would be the first to die.

Singer took two steps forward, increasing the distance between them.

Ahead of him, Trip held his M60 on his hip, turning his head slightly back and forth as if testing the air. The New Guy stood in front of Trip, his head bowed, scratching at the ground with his right foot. A small man anyway, he looked smaller in the wake of Trip's threat.

Instinctively, Singer began to search for Rhymes before catching himself. He tried to spit the bitterness from his mouth without success. *Hold on. I'm coming,* he thought to say, the words floating in his mind. Instead he cursed and rocked forward on the balls of his feet.

Top marched up and down the company, a shorter distance than in previous days, looking at each man as if checking who survived and sizing up the replacements. Then he repeated it. If Top was worried about Lieutenant Creely today it didn't show, except in the distance he kept from him. Singer watched Top pause occasionally, saying something. Without Top yesterday, more of them would have died. Maybe the whole company would have been lost. Top didn't stop beside Singer, but he slowed and they exchanged a glance. The corners of Top's mouth lifted slightly, and he nodded.

Their snail-like progress had Singer ready to run screaming down the road firing his weapon. He needed to race ahead. Rhymes, Stick, and Sergeant Edwards were lying there waiting for him.

Things that started yesterday were still unfinished. More would die today. He could feel it in his bones, in the hardness of the weapon in his hands. He could see it in the approaching clouds, which had grown darker and foreboding. Today there would be retribution.

His pack grew heavier through every klick. Each stretch of jungle looked more menacing. He sucked in air, unable to get his breath. Even knowing where they were, he felt disoriented. Maybe it wasn't the landscape but himself he was no longer familiar with.

He tried to steady himself, watching Trip's back as he had Rhymes's, promising a better outcome. He moved when Trip moved and stopped when he stopped, watching the jungle and squeezing his M16 so tight his hands hurt.

A lifetime of reflection and suffering passed before Singer finally saw the place where yesterday morning he came out from the jungle with fourth platoon, leading the company on what had looked to be an easy mission.

The stretch of road that held the ambush they walked through and then ran back to lay before him looking as innocent as it had at first yesterday. But today he wasn't fooled. The screams rose from the jungle and rattled in his mind. He heard the roar of gunfire and felt the concussions of explosions, but ahead of him Trip never went down or even flinched. Singer's heart accelerated. A wave of death rolled over him and only his anger kept him afloat. His survival burned like a raw wound.

His stomach knotted and he squeezed his weapon even tighter. He saw the stretch of jungle where the crater was. His feet grew light. When Rhymes yelled for him again, the world shifted and he lost his equilibrium.

He broke ranks and raced toward the crater. The screams for help changed tone. The voice sounded like his own. He could still save them. Rhymes, Stick, Red, Sergeant Edwards. All the answers were at the crater. His rifle swinging with each stride and his ruck bouncing on his back, he drove his legs, chewing up the ground.

"Goddamn it, stop that man!" Lieutenant Creely screamed. "Get that man back in formation!"

The CO's voice was a rifle volley in the morning heat.

Still Singer didn't waver. The crater loomed. The men beside it screamed louder. Legs pumping, he drove forward on his mission.

Then his rucksack was caught from behind and he spun halfway around and fell, his legs collapsing under him. Lifting his head, he pushed back his helmet and tried to see the crater, but the jungle was still so far away, farther than when he started. He lifted himself on to his elbows and drew his right leg forward, looking ready to take off.

"Fuck, don't make me run again," Trip gasped. "If you get crazy you'll get us both killed." His chest heaving and his mouth agape, he lay there keeping a hand on Singer's ruck. "Fuck, next time maybe I'll just shoot you. Be a lot easier."

Singer looked up at Trip's face, his flush cheeks and the beads of sweat that ran down his sharp nose and dripped in rapid succession. There was no hint of a smile, and he knew Trip was only half kidding. Singer pushed himself up, struggling against the weight of his ruck that worked to keep him on the ground. From the road bewildered faces stared at him, some men shuffling their feet. Singer looked back toward the crater. The voices had gone silent. Had Trip or anyone else heard them?

"Goddamn it. I won't have this happen in my company," Lieutenant Creely yelled, but it was unclear who the CO was speaking to. Sergeant Milner moved among fourth platoon, saying something to each man.

"Singer. What the hell are you doing?" Top stepped up and studied Singer closely, ignoring Trip.

Singer ran his hand across his face rearranging the sweat. "It's just the guys, Top." He glanced at where he knew the crater was.

"I know. You'll get your chance. Now get back in formation. We've got work to do." Top placed his hand briefly on Singer's shoulder. "You're okay, right?"

"Yeah, I'm okay, Top."

He bit his lip against asking what Top meant by "you'll get your chance." What did Top know? Did Top hear the cries for help, too?

The three of them walked back to the company where men looked away, the Cherries looking confused. Singer didn't look away but held the gaze of any man that looked at him. Fuck them. So many damn Cherries. How had he become one of the few old guys in just one day?

He and Trip rejoined fourth platoon. Top continued back toward the CO, where Top leaned in and said something to Lieutenant Creely, who turned away red-faced and silent.

"You okay now?" Trip asked, stepping closer, still looking flush. Singer could see the questions in Trip's face. Maybe even fear. Then the muscles in Trip's face tightened and his eyes narrowed and whatever he'd seen was gone.

"Let's fucking do this," Singer said.

"Stay cool. You got a lot of days to do."

The company broke up and deployed from where they stopped to watch Singer's lone charge. Lieutenant Creely and the other three platoons headed south, leaving fourth platoon standing on the road alone, Singer with thoughts of the similarities to the day before. Maybe the CO was hoping to replay things, too.

Singer watched them trail off, disappearing into the jungle. It was good to be free of the CO. Still, Singer would have been happier had he left another platoon and Top with them. He imagined Trip was glad to see the CO head off, as well.

Barely two squads, they stood in the sunlight and the heat too long while the New Lieutenant and Sergeant Milner conferred, neither looking sure what to do. Alone on the road, surrounded by jungle and mountains, it was hard not to feel insignificant. Singer thought of drifting on a featureless sea.

"We're better off alone," Singer said.

Trip didn't answer and just kept watching the road ahead as if he imagined it leading home.

Sergeant Milner continued his conference with the new platoon leader, who kept looking at his map, then pointing north, as though confirming some location.

"God save us," Singer whispered.

He thought of Sergeant Edwards as Sergeant Milner walked toward him, and how nothing would ever be the same.

"Trip, take Singer and the New Guy and sweep west through yesterday's positions there." Sergeant Milner gestured loosely toward the center of the ambush site. His squeaky voice irritated Singer as much as the fact that he wasn't Sergeant Edwards. Sergeant Milner offered no explanation as to why he was sending only three of them, or what the few other men who made up the platoon would do. Singer didn't care. He tightened his face to hold back his smile. It was what he wanted. A chance to go back to the crater. Without Sergeant Milner or the New Lieutenant looking over his shoulder, he could do what he wanted. Maybe there was hope.

"I got the point," Singer said. "What do we do with him?"

"Don't run off," Trip said to Singer, then looked over at the New Guy, who was turning slow circles in the center of the road, blinking too fast. "Well, he ain't no good on point and I sure don't want him behind us."

"Shouldn't we all stay together?" the New Guy asked, then resumed turning.

"Great. A fucking Cherry for a slackman," Singer said. "Just don't let him shoot me in the back."

Singer led off, as he'd done so many times through the months in Nam, forgetting about the Cherry at his back. Today there were more important things. He would be methodical despite his anxiousness. With steady steps he crossed toward the jungle, holding back the urge to charge and fire. Survival, at least in this moment, wasn't a question. Yet the challenge seemed more daunting.

The ground with its clumps of grass, clods of dirt, and torn roots offered up no quick answers. Why had so many died? Why was he alive? What price had the enemy paid? The answers were here somewhere. He had to find them.

It was like passing into another world when he slipped from the stark brightness of the tropical sun to the darkness of the towering layers of jungle vegetation. The scene blurred, trees and leaves losing their shapes and fading into shadows. He was charging into the ambush, then moving under fire to the crater with Sergeant Royce and Red. He pushed a thumb and forefinger against his eyes, then found himself alone just inside the shadows. Behind him the New Guy and Trip were lit in the sunlight, looking anxious.

The crater was west of him, waiting. But the voices of the dead were silent. If he could feel his rifle firing and listen to the rounds explode, he could keep his balance. It was more than vengeance that he carried.

Within a few steps he found the first spider hole that he knew would be there. The only surprise was that there were so many. Carefully, his rifle ready, he peered into each hole, thinking of the NVA who rose up after the battle to shoot Bear. The guy had balls or was crazy. Maybe they all would end up that way.

In today's stillness, it all seemed so meaningless. But once started, how can you ever stop it? Singer leaned over, pointing his rifle into another hole, then backed away, disappointed. Not a single NVA to die in payment. He kept working west toward the crater, checking every hole. After fifteen he lost count, knowing it didn't really matter.

The crater seemed so far today from where they started. Yesterday it was just a few short sprints, distance blurred by gunfire and fear. Had they really been so spread out, stretched so thin that any enemy push would have swallowed them? How had he crossed so much ground under fire unscathed, while Rhymes, Stick, and Sergeant Edwards, with the protection of the crater, died? Nothing made sense.

Crouching slightly, he slipped under an overhanging branch, careful not to brush against it. He clung to his rifle, knowing it was all that mattered.

Singer froze in mid-step, aiming his rifle. Barely breathing, he stood motionless, waiting for some movement. A line, broken and obscured by leaves. No real form. Just something that didn't fit. How many bucks had he discovered that way? The edge of a back. The curve of an ear. The smallest thing out of place. Waiting long enough, the buck would move, revealing itself and offering the shot. Or sometimes studying the vegetation, the broken outline, he could discern the animal and kill it where it stood.

Seconds passed. His pulse pounded in his ears. A foot shuffled in the litter and a branch scratched against something hard. He cursed the New Guy behind him.

Nothing moved before him. When he shifted to his left he could make out a sandaled foot and more of the leg he'd first seen. His finger tightened on the trigger. Still he waited, playing a game of stealth. He wanted the man to know it was Rhymes's friend who killed him.

When he eased forward he found two of them, but there was no need to fire. He nearly emptied a magazine into them anyway. But the ray of light gave him pause, the suggestion of something nearly divine, though God seemed absent in this place.

One man lay on his back. Puffy hands, fingers slightly curled at his side. Legs extended in a peaceful pose except for his blood-encrusted shirt. Despite the distortions brought by death the day before, Singer knew the face.

They'd stared at each other days before across a stream.

Singer bit down hard, tried to swallow, and vowed the end of mercy.

A thin beam of sunlight that had somehow filtered through the jungle canopy illuminated the man's face, reminding Singer of saintly depictions in a grade-school missal. Singer raised his eyes to the small break in leaf cover high above and followed the beam of light back to the man's face. The man's boyish face stared into the light with cloudy, sunken eyes, giving no indication of whether he had sought the sunlight or taken any comfort in it. His mouth was open slightly, his lips drawn back in death. A gold tooth glistened in the sunlight.

The second soldier, just a few feet from the first, lay on his stomach with his head in the same direction as the first man's. He was slightly smaller, perhaps younger. His head was turned to the side. Flies buzzed about an ugly wound just above his right eye that had obliterated part of his forehead and the top of the eye socket, exposing a drying mass of goo that had once defined the man. Singer watched the flies buzzing, settling, and crawling on the pulpy mass of mangled tissue before rising and settling again. The man's arms were drawn up on either side of his head, elbows bent, the right reaching farther out beyond the left. Both hands were closed into tight fists, as though gripping the earth. His right leg was pulled up tightly, bent at the knee, his foot poised to push forward. His left leg was extended but twisted oddly below the mid-calf, where his pant leg was caked with dried blood and his left foot lay turned in an unnatural position. The vegetation was matted and torn behind him, marking the path he had crawled before a headshot had ended his journey.

When Singer turned he caught the New Guy edging up behind him, his face ashen and sweaty, eyes locked on the scene. The New Guy ran off a few steps. Singer bent back over the bodies, ignoring the sound of vomit splashing on the foliage and the New Guy's soft gagging.

"Jesus Christ. Fucking Cherries," Trip said as he moved up toward Singer. "Watch our backs!"

Straightening up slowly, the New Guy wiped his mouth on his arm and moved off, looking at their trail back to the road. The New Guy appeared more comfortable watching the jungle than the bodies, but Singer figured that would change soon enough, if he survived.

"Shit, it's only a couple of dead gooks," Trip said, stopping next to Singer and eyeing the bodies, then looking quickly about to the front.

Trip shifted forward and kicked softly at the first body as though fearing the man might still be alive. Then he poked his foot at the second man's damaged face, causing the flies to rise and buzz about wildly.

"This war ain't worth losing your head over." A deep rumble came from Trip's chest and his mouth curved up, not quite a smile.

Singer wasn't sure who Trip was talking to and was afraid to ask. Maybe Trip was just trying to remind himself, as Singer had been thinking there was nothing here worth dying for. Nothing except each other. Was that why these men had died? Was anything different for them?

Singer knelt down next to the first body while Trip crouched beside the second. There were no weapons, web gear, or helmets, all apparently taken by the NVA. Aware of the ray of light and the shining tooth, Singer shifted position as he reached across the man so as not to block the light, though he wasn't sure why that was important. Cautiously, he checked around and under the man, fearful of booby traps, before prying at the man's shirt pockets, sealed with dried blood, checking for documents, letters, or photos, anything that might be of some military value or that would give the man an identity. He pushed his hand awkwardly into each of the man's pants pockets, repeatedly glancing at the man's illuminated face.

The man took their secret to the grave. No one would know that Singer could have killed him days before. Would it have averted any of this?

"Nothing," Trip said, resting next to the second body, waving at the swarming flies. "No souvenirs today."

Singer looked over at Trip, glanced at their back trail, and saw the New Guy turn away quickly. The search of the two bodies finished, they stood up almost in unison, Trip looking off toward new ground.

Singer couldn't move on so easily. Nameless corpses left behind. The afterbirth of battle. Not a clue as to who they were or what their lives had meant. Nor what their deaths had meant. Both sides abandoning the ground they died for. Who had loved them? Would their loved ones ever know what happened to them, or would they suffer through the years not knowing?

"Let's keep moving," Trip said.

But Singer stood unresponsive, raising his gaze up into the canopy, once more following the narrow beam of light that shone on the man's face, causing his gold tooth to shine against the dull pallor of death. What did it mean or say about death? A message lay here, if he could only read it.

Transfixed by the light, he saw himself lying there, the sun on his face. He gave no thought to the man or what the gold tooth told of his past. He thought only about this time and this event and their meeting here a second time. The secret that died with the man. They both had lost something and it was important to remember this event, if not this man.

"It's done," Trip said. "Let's go."

But the man continued to smile at Singer. Mocking him. Maybe the man thought he could smile his way out of this meeting, as well. Without warning, Singer raised his rifle and smashed the butt into the man's mouth, breaking his smile. One measured blow. The crack of the rifle against the man's teeth was as loud as a gunshot.

"Shit," the New Guy said. He bent over, retching up another stream of vomit.

Trip watched wordlessly.

Singer pulled the gold tooth from the dead man's mouth, then held it up in the ray of light. Eventually he closed his fist around it, squeezing it before pushing it down in his pocket. He looked at the man's broken smile, the space where the gold tooth had been. The man's face was dark, the beam of light gone. A current of sadness passed through him and he turned away.

"Now it's done," Singer said, starting west toward the crater.

"Cherry," Trip called out to the New Guy. "Let's go."

The New Guy came forward, giving the bodies as wide a berth as the vegetation allowed, but staring at the damaged mouth. He closed on Trip until he stood too close.

"Why'd he do that?"

Did the Cherry think Singer couldn't hear him? Singer stopped and looked back at the New Guy, seeing his face for the first time. He looked too young to be there. His face was pale with soft features. His cheeks still held the chubbiness of youth. The bravado he'd tried to project in the first moments of his arrival was nowhere to be seen. Yet his eyes were bright, unlike Trip's or so many of the others. But maybe it was just the near presence of tears. He looked like he might bolt, like he didn't want to be there, but who of them did?

How could Singer explain what he'd done? He wasn't even sure he understood it. Images of his father flashed through his mind and the stories told among his father's friends of collecting teeth from Japanese bodies in their war years in the South Pacific.

This is war, he could say. Or he could tell him, *we are all our father's sons.* But what was the point? The New Guy would never live long enough to understand. In the New Guy's features he saw the mingling of life and death. He turned away, not wanting to be reminded of his past self or to remember the New Guy's face.

15

The crater was close. He could feel it. Rhymes was calling his name again. Sergeant Edwards began pleading. Desperate, whispered words. Singer quickened his steps.

"Shouldn't we go back?" the New Guy asked. "What if everyone leaves?"

Singer wasn't going back. He was just getting started.

The voices pulled at him and he bulled his way through the brush, forgetting caution. When he stepped, his left foot found only air where the ground should have been and he staggered. Without the tree to grab onto, he might have fallen in. He pushed the brush aside with his rifle and found one hole, then another. Christ, they were everywhere. But where the hell was the excavated dirt? How had he missed these yesterday? He must have been too focused on seeing bodies or the fleeing backs of Vietnamese.

In the end he counted five additional spider holes, but knew there were more. You could lay beside them and never see them. How close had he been yesterday? His neck tingled with a million pinpricks and his fingers grew almost numb.

Just beyond the enemy fighting holes through the vegetation he could make out the broken outline of the crater. Rhymes screamed. Singer heard the crawling.

Bullets ripped through the vegetation, shredding leaves, tearing at limbs and pounding the ground. The jungle swallowed the bullets without comment and Singer smiled as he slammed in another magazine and pulled the trigger with all his might.

Trip slid up beside Singer but didn't fire. "What do you got?"

"I'm going to kill them all."

"You see something?"

"They're here."

Trip stood still, appearing to listen to the quiet that descended when Singer stopped after the second magazine.

"Shit, there ain't no one here." Trip peered into one hole, then a second. "They're empty."

"They're here," Singer said, breathing heavily. "The crater's right there. This is where they are."

"What's going on?" the New Guy asked from behind them.

"Nothing," Trip said. "I'll take the point," he said to Singer. "You watch him."

"No! I got the point!"

"Okay. Okay. Take it easy, though, I don't want that Cherry Lieutenant or Sergeant Milner over here."

Singer edged around the holes, keeping the crater as his reference point. Each hole was progressively darker and deeper, yielding nothing but taunts. At the last hole he stood staring into it. If each hole was an occupied grave waiting only for the dirt to be shoveled in, which he would have done, taking joy in the labor, would he had been satisfied? How many bodies would it take to fill the emptiness? He kicked at the edge and listened to the dirt fall softly to the bottom and to the pounding in his head.

All morning he wanted to run to it, but now when he was so near to it, he wanted to turn back, or a least wait a little longer. He moved to the crater cautiously, afraid each time he took a step the earth might explode or that his head would. When he reached the crater's edge he stood still, surprised at how bare and common it looked. Like a million other craters that pockmarked the countryside. Why was he so afraid of it? No tears came. Yet he sagged under a sense of grief and disappointment. Had he truly expected to see Rhymes, Stick, Sergeant Edwards, and Red? What had he believed he would find?

Shell casings littered the bottom, some of them pressed into the dirt under imprints of boots. Was it just yesterday he had stood there? The vegetation was compressed and stained where Stick had sprawled on his back, gripping the radio handset even in death, and where Sergeant Royce and Red had tended to Sergeant Edwards as he had begged for it to end.

He bent down and picked up an AK shell casing next to the crater and rolled it in his hand, then felt the small depression where the firing pin had struck the primer, starting the explosion that sent the bullet toward its target. He looked into the end of the casing and saw nothing but darkness.

Singer slid down into the crater, entering slower, more carefully than he had yesterday, as if he were sliding back in time. He listened for Rhymes and the voices of the others, but the crater was quiet now. Even the crawling of the enemy was absent. A slight, momentary breeze rustled the leaves at his back and he turned quickly, expecting someone to be there. He watched a leaf twist, then hang still. The smell of cordite mixed with the coppery smell of blood rose off the vegetation or up from the earth, and for a moment he could smell the battle as strongly as he had yesterday, as though gunsmoke hung over the battlefield like a permanent veil.

From the crater he looked out to where he knew the enemy fighting holes were and thought of the men who had occupied them. The enemy rose from the holes, reaching up with hands dirty from their lives in the jungle and a night of digging, pulling themselves up and forward, coming toward the crater. Fear began to fill Singer's mind like thick smoke seeping into a closed room, black and acrid, threatening to blot out all life. He felt the rush of his frantic firing and his desperation to kill the NVA around the crater. He ached for another chance and hated himself at the same time for what he wanted to do. He could hardly remember who he was or how he'd come to be here doing these things.

He shook his head to erase the images, but the residue of terror clung to him like chalk on a blackboard from yesterday's lesson.

In a few weeks the compressed vegetation and the stains on the ground and the litter of shell casings at his feet would be mostly gone. The rains would wash away the stains, the vegetation would rebound, and the dirt from the sides of the crater would wash into the bottom, burying the casings, and there would be no memory on the land. Just another shell hole, indistinguishable from all the others. Memorable only to the few who were here and survived. Sergeant Royce had already fled, but Singer doubted he or Sergeant Royce could ever escape the crater.

Above him, outside the crater, Trip and the New Guy stood with their backs to him, silent sentries with different memories of yesterday.

He had been sure there would be answers here. But there were only the questions of how he had survived and what it might mean.

"You finished?" Trip asked.

On his second step up the crater wall, Singer slipped, his knee pressing into the soil, his hand catching the edge, his face near the dirt. He hung there as he had yesterday, between two worlds, neither dead nor living. It would be so easy to let go and slide back into the bottom.

"Hurry up," Trip said.

Before crawling out, Singer twisted to look once more at where Rhymes smiled throughout the battle. Nothing indicated that Rhymes had ever been there except for Singer's memory.

"Thanks," Singer said when he neared Trip, who was watching the New Guy like a nervous parent.

"Fuck, let's head back," Trip said. "I've had enough of this place."

"I want to look around some more."

"Shit, there's nothing here but ghosts."

Singer walked away, certain there was more. Only two bodies. There had to be more.

"Goddamn it, Singer," Trip said, hurrying to follow, motioning for the New Guy to keep up.

Singer pushed ahead, not caring whether Trip came along or not. Not caring what happened anymore. Even if he couldn't find Rhymes, he would find the NVA. He had killed more and he wasn't leaving until he found them. It was one of the few things anymore that would bring him any comfort.

"Five minutes, then we're leaving with or without you," Trip said.

Twice Singer paced around the crater checking holes, uncertain of which he'd checked before. He pushed through a matted ring six feet across, where he knelt and fingered dried blood. He made a circle but found no trail.

"Fuck," he said and tried to spit, generating only grit.

Again he crossed the area fifteen feet out where he thought the man should be. "Okay," he was about to tell Trip, but then he saw the fresh-turned ground. East of the crater maybe thirty feet away was a recent dirt mound. At first he thought it might just be excavations from the fighting holes. But after he pushed through the brush he saw the shallow, disorganized scrapings and the mound's low, elongate form.

"Yes," he said, kneeling beside it and laying his rifle to the side.

There was no choice. He had to know. He considered calling Trip over but quickly dismissed the thought, already hearing his reproaches. A quick glance around assured him he was alone. With no wires or any metal to suggest a booby trap he made a move, tentative at first. The dirt was dry and loose against his fingers. He pulled a handful from the pile, holding his breath as the dirt slid off the mound. When nothing happened, he moved a second handful, and then a third, working with more confidence.

He felt the soft flesh before he saw it, recoiling slightly at the different texture. His hands worked more quickly, exposing the man's face. The countenance was ashen and distorted, and dirt clung to the dead flesh. The head was damaged by repeated bullet strikes. The right ear hung on a piece of skull. The bullet hole was there, high in the check just below the right eye, though the face looked much different than it had the day before. The surprised expression Singer saw at his bullet's impact was lost in death.

He wanted this man dead, as well as his comrade, but he didn't feel the satisfaction he was expecting. The man had killed his friends. How could he explain it? After the wave of sorrow passed, leaving no feeling in its wake, he resumed his work of uncovering the man.

The chest was slight, the stomach distended like a famine victim. It was more the body of a boy than a man. He had seemed so much more imposing at the crater edge with an AK-47 in his hands. His left shoulder and left arm were riddled with bullet holes, dirt caked in the dry blood.

Again Singer paused and scanned the ground behind the body. "The fucker," he said when he couldn't see a second grave.

Locked at his side by stiffened arms, he found the man's hands, small and empty. Any gear the man had carried or worn had been stripped away. There was nothing to salvage or collect. He pried apart the man's pockets and slipped his fingers in, not expecting much. In the man's breast pocket he found a photo. A picture of a man and a woman that had no military value. He quickly slipped it in his own pocket so Trip wouldn't see it.

When he slammed his fist against the man's chest there was a dull thud absorbed by the dead flesh. He hit the man again rather than give in to the tears pooling behind his eyes.

"Jesus Christ, what—"

Singer grabbed for his rifle and spun around too late. "Goddamn it," Singer said. "I nearly killed you."

Trip snorted. "You'd been dead long before that."

The muzzle of Trip's M60 was slightly to the side, but Singer saw the truth in it. His heart was still pounding so he could hardly speak. He knew he'd been careless.

"What the fuck are you doing? Lucky I ain't the lieutenant."

Singer tried to hide his grimy hands. "I found him like this."

"What is it with you and dead guys?" Trip asked. "You'll have ghosts and that Cherry Lieutenant on our ass."

"When'd you get superstitious?"

"Even a Cherry knows it's bad luck to dig up graves. Fuck, the investigation alone would drag on for months and I'd never get out of here. I won't let you fuck up my leaving."

The New Guy standing behind Trip's shoulder blinked rapidly, but he didn't look away.

Singer set his rifle down and started scooping up dirt with his cupped hands to cover the man.

"Leave him. We're heading back," Trip said.

"It'll be worse luck if we don't rebury him."

"Christ. Okay. Help him," Trip said, looking at the New Guy.

The New Guy took a couple of steps back, shaking his head slowly. His prominent Adam's apple rose and fell on his neck.

"Everyone's a fucking problem," Trip said.

"I got it." Singer quickly shoveled enough dirt with his hands to cover the man's face and most of his torso, though he could still see the man's distended stomach and fingers of his right hand. Then Singer wiped his hands on his pants, leaving muddy smears on the sweat-soaked fatigues, and picked up his rifle.

"Maybe we can leave now, if everyone's fucking ready," Trip said.

"Just a little more," Singer said.

"Your time's up."

"You know there're things here."

"What's a few more dead gooks? It won't change anything. We're still stuck in this fucking place."

"I need to look."

"You're done."

The New Guy shuffled his feet. "We should go back. Tell the lieutenant."

"Tell the lieutenant what?" Singer asked, taking two steps toward the New Guy.

"I just mean we should report, aren't we supposed to—"

"You don't know shit. You didn't see nothing. You don't say nothing." Trip said.

Singer and Trip exchanged a look.

The New Guy paled. His Adam's apple bobbed.

"You understand?" Trip asked.

A weak nod was all the New Guy answered.

16

K eep moving," Top said.

The New Guy had nearly stopped, his hand reaching for his knees, his mouth open, sucking air. He straightened up with obvious effort and took tired steps forward. Singer could hear his labored breathing and wondered if men could die from exhaustion.

"Let's go. Keep moving."

Top stood just off the trail, feet staggered on the slope, his rifle held loosely in one hand, waving men forward with the other. His back was straight and his breaths even despite the climb.

Singer slowed to keep from getting too close to Trip, who followed the New Guy. With the M60 braced on his shoulder Trip was still taking energetic steps, as if he drew strength from the big gun or from his increasing closeness to going home.

The black gun shined from the hours Trip spent running an oily rag across its action and exterior. The crossed belts of rounds hung like deadly golden sashes, cleaner than those Singer lugged, which brought on Trip's admonishments. How Trip kept his so spotless Singer couldn't figure out. Singer worried first about his M16, even though he knew his job these days was to stick with Trip and when they hit the shit to be there on his left, clipping together belts of ammo to allow Trip's uninterrupted firing.

"The machine gun's the most important thing," Trip said a few days after picking up Shooter's M60.

Trip stopped wiping the action and looked at Singer. "We keep the gun firing no matter what. Even if you're hit, I stay on the gun, and if I'm hit, you man the gun. You leave me be and keep the gun going. You understand?"

"Right, the gun is more important than you or me."

"Keep the gun going at all costs. Without the gun we're fucked."

Trip looked at Singer for a long moment as if waiting for an additional affirmation before returning to rubbing the oil rag across the M60.

Three nights ago, Singer dreamed of Trip lying beside him, dying, as he fired the gun trying to stop the wave of NVA charging their position. He never told Trip of the dream, but he thought of it and what it meant.

Today he followed Trip past Top, wanting to ask where they were going in such a hurry, but Top was already looking past him and waving men on, so he pushed by without a word. Wherever they were going, Top would be there.

That was critical to Singer. Lieutenant Creely was acting again like he was in command, but how could they trust a man who failed once? Another big test had yet to come but Singer doubted the CO would pass. Trip said, "Nothing's changed. Count on more trouble." So Singer counted his clips, stayed close to Trip, and kept an eye on Top's whereabouts.

Top's posture gave no hint of tension, but Singer could feel it crackling through the company like the static of an electrical storm. He wondered when the first blinding flash would explode amongst them and who would survive. He leaned into the hill and struggled for good footing, climbing in the dim jungle light. The ache in his calves had spread to his thighs and his shoulders burned with the weight of his ruck.

For a couple hours they had been pushing without rest, racing toward some objective, hacking through tangles of jungle, clawing their way to higher ground, trading caution for speed. He knew this kind of movement could only mean trouble.

When they finally stopped at the edge of a clearing on a small plateau, Singer dropped heavily to the ground and sat there open-mouthed, struggling for air. He watched impassively as the New Guy bent over, retching with dry heaves. A few feet away, Trip paced.

"Fucking bullshit. Nine days and a wake-up. I should be in the rear packing for home."

"Fuck you," Singer said.

Trip looked down and smiled.

The whacking of machetes rang out around the clearing and Singer and Trip looked at each other, knowing what it meant. The frantic rhythm sang across the valley and echoed off adjacent hills, announcing their presence. The ringing of blades against bamboo covered Trip's curses as he strolled off.

Singer heard the choppers coming even before the machetes were silent. The *whump whump* of incoming Hueys grew louder, drowning out the machete work, and then even Singer's thoughts.

The first bird hovered above the LZ and Singer stood to watch the crew chief push boxes of ammo out the door, not waiting to hand them off to the work detail that rushed up below swirling blades, then jumped back to avoid the tumbling crates. Even before the last box smacked against the ground, the bird lifted sharply and sped back to the east, door gunners bent forward over their guns, searching for targets. Men ran from the clearing toward the perimeter with crates of grenades and ammo cans. Another bird moved in right behind the first. Men on the ground scrambled to clear the LZ as cartons of Cs rained to the ground.

Trip edged up beside Singer and watched the second Huey unload and depart before speaking.

"Fucking bad signs. I should be going out on one of those birds."

"You'd let me have all the fun alone?" Singer asked.

"Damn straight. You and the New Guy."

"God save me."

The guy Ghost called California glided up, shirtless, bracing a wooden crate on one shoulder and an ammo box in the other hand. He dumped them close without comment. Men Singer didn't know followed and the pile grew.

"Wait your turn," Trip said, then took the box of Cs the New Guy had reached for.

The Shake and Bake stood beside the piles like a hapless sentry, while Singer grabbed what he wanted and went over and sat down near Trip. After checking the pins, Singer hung two grenades on his ruck because his web belt was full. Then he filled a new magazine, testing the spring before setting it in a pile. Everywhere Singer looked around the perimeter, men where stuffing ammo into web gear and rucks and there was a symphony of clicks of rounds being snapped into magazines. The last chopper was gone, along with Trip's hope of leaving.

"You need any more?" Trip asked.

Singer looked up, his fingers still pushing rounds home. "Where you think we're going?"

"I heard a guy say the A Shau. Claimed the 101st is in some shit."

"Ah Shau," Singer said, "never heard of it."

"A Shau. A valley near Laos. NVA stronghold. Better hope it's wrong. Even the Cav stayed out of there. If the 101st needs help, things must be bad."

"Shiiiit." Singer flipped a round in his fingers.

"Shit is right. I'm too fucking short for places like that."

"I'm too young."

"You want more ammo?" Trip asked.

"I got more than 600 rounds already, but I'll take a couple more grenades."

"Grab another belt of M60 rounds. I got a bad feeling about this. Check on the New Guy, too. See that he's carrying enough."

"Already did. He only wants to carry 200 rounds, already complaining his gear's too heavy."

"Fucking new guys. Make him carry 200 more, even if you have to shove them up his ass, but take his grenades. I don't trust him."

"Birds coming in, ten minutes ETA," Sergeant Milner's shrill voice came like fingernails on a chalk board. "Hurry up, we're first out."

Trip made a pistol shape with his empty hand and mock fired it at the departing Sergeant Milner. After shoving one last belt of ammo in his ruck, he tied it up. With the action of the gun cleaned and oiled, he fed a short length of ammo into the gun. He heaved on his ruck and slung two ammo belts over his head, shouldered the big gun, and ambled to the clearing edge.

"Load and carry these," Singer said, shoving two hundred more M16 rounds at the New Guy, letting them drop in his lap without waiting for him to reach up to take them. "Hurry up or you'll be sitting here alone."

Singer shrugged on his ruck, then threw two belts of machine gun ammo over his shoulders and hurried after Trip, leaving the New Guy to catch up on his own. *Nam. It don't mean nothing*, he reminded himself.

At the tree edge, he slid up beside Trip and looked expectantly across the clearing and up at the patch of placid sky. His stomach rolled. He clenched his sphincter, trying not to think about his bowels. Once they were on the ground, or when the shooting started, he'd be okay. The waiting and not knowing was often worse than the actual mission. He hoped that would be the case again, but somehow he doubted it.

He fingered the trigger guard of his M16 and ran his left hand along the strings of belted rounds across his chest, assuring himself they were there even though his shoulders felt their weight. Across the clearing, the grass stood motionless and an expectant quiet settled in, as if time stopped for just a moment on the collective wills that hoped to prevent what was coming. Someone popped a smoke grenade and a purple plume rose nearly straight up until it topped the clearing and drifted lazily east, dissipating.

Singer stood next to Trip, wordlessly waiting, wishing he could rid himself of the nausea without embarrassment. He glanced at Trip, not sure what he hoped to see, but his face betrayed nothing. The New Guy lumbered up next to them, but neither of them acknowledged his arrival. The distinctive *whump, whump, whump* rose from the distance, growing steadily louder, coming for them. Singer flexed his fingers, wiping one hand and then the other on his thighs. Trip brought two fingers to his lips and then planted them on his gun.

Top marched into the clearing and stood, arms raised as though beseeching the gods in a fashion his native ancestors had likely done on western plains. The Huey's rotors pounded the sky, the thumping like tribal drums leading paint-marked warriors to a fighting frenzy. Singer's stomach swirled and he clenched his teeth. The line of birds dominated the sky before dropping toward the clearing, six ships squeezing in, whirling blades close to clipping trees.

With a tight-lipped nod, Singer and Trip broke for the first bird as its nose flared up sharply before its skids leveled out just above the flattened grass. They mounted the bird with a smoothness that belied the loads they carried. Singer leaned out and heaved the New Guy up onto the bird as he struggled to climb the skid and risked being left behind. The New Guy rolled onto the floor in a tangle of gear, and a bandolier of ammo fell from his ruck and out the door as the Huey lifted and broke west in a sharp turn. Singer held onto the New Guy's shoulder strap as the bird tilted and the bandolier dropped into the clearing.

The line of birds climbed and raced toward Laos, moving farther from ground Singer knew. Singer gazed out the door at the pockmarked jungle streaking past to avoid the faces of the six men around him. He squinted against the wind and tried to gather a strength that today seemed hard to come by, hoping to be brave, or at least not to fail. Far below him, just above the canopy, he could see the Cobra escort looking small and insignificant.

The rotors whirled above his head, and he could feel the thumping of machinery, hear the blaring music and noise of the midway. Susan was beside him, her hips pressed into his in the small seat, and he could smell her perfume, a light floral fragrance made stronger by her body heat in the hot August night. They raised their hands and screamed as they started the descent, the rollercoaster quickly gathering speed, leaving their stomachs far behind them. At the bottom of the loop they lowered their hands and laughed and as they started another steep, laborious climb, slowing to a crawl, he reached over and took her hand and she leaned into him, laying her head on his shoulder. He turned and kissed her, softly at first, then harder, pressing his tongue into her mouth. He could feel himself getting hard. Then they were tumbling forward again, gaining speed, and she clung to him, screaming.

Still in a sharp dive, the pitch of the rotors changed as they turned south. The scenes of the midway and taste of her lips fled and Singer turned, startled, as the door gunner on his right opened up with his M60 at targets Singer couldn't make out. The ground spun by below his feet. Above him, out the left side door, he could see only blue sky. The air was suddenly heavy and it was harder to breathe. His skin tingled with the electricity of some building event.

He prayed for a cold LZ. Across from him, Ghost crossed himself repeatedly and his lips moved in what Singer knew was a Spanish prayer, though he couldn't hear it over the noise of the gun and the rotors. The New Guy, his arms splayed, gripping the chopper floor and his loose equipment, looked up at Singer as if searching for reassurance. Singer had nothing to offer, not even for himself. The Californian looked unfazed, with a closed-mouth smile and his left arm out, swaying as if balancing through a big curl. The man was odd.

The door gunner leaned out into his gun, shooting at something below and behind them. The rotors slapped the air. The ship shuddered, dropped six feet, then caught itself. Both door gunners were firing now, sweeping their guns back and forth in fast arcs.

Singer strained, listening for the *ping* of incoming rounds. He wished for the feel of ground and not to vomit. His body tensed against the expected impact and he unconsciously cupped his balls against the round that would come up through the floor.

The bird leveled out and treetops raced past just below them in a green blur so close he feared they might catch a skid and be hurled into the canopy in a mix of whirling blades, twisting metal, and breaking bodies. Ghost's eyes were pressed tightly shut, his face taut, only his lips moving rapidly in a continued litany for salvation. Singer dragged his parched tongue across cracked lips. Next to him, Trip shifted the big gun and pulled one leg up under himself and looked out, stone-faced. It was unlikely he was praying or believed in anything beyond himself and maybe the big gun.

The canopy fell away suddenly and they were over a clearing in a high saddle that seemed too small to accommodate all the birds. The Huey fell into the clearing, flared, leveled off, stalled, but Singer could feel it ready to climb.

It looked too high to jump, but this was it, so he tumbled out, bodies falling beside him. The prop blast of the departing bird swept over him before he hit. Then he was running, Trip at his side, both of them firing, trying to gain the cover of the trees. Running and firing. Fear faded into some deep recess of his unconscious, his stomach was forgotten, and he felt the thrill of firing and of being alive.

Singer hardly felt the slap of branches, or the inch-long thorns that ripped his arms, or his body slamming against the ground. He quickly crawled closer to Trip and snapped a link of rounds to the machine gun. Trip stopped firing with a long string of rounds left, but kept his head down on the gun and his finger ready on the trigger.

Singer re-grasped his rifle and looked into a jungle understory that was indistinguishable from every other piece of jungle he'd lain in. The firing gave out sporadically around him until every gun was silent and he could hear his breaths, shallow and rapid. Were the NVA waiting for the Cobras and Hueys to get farther away before attacking? Or were they gathering around the LZ to wait in ambush?

In the distance, the sound of the Hueys and Cobras was fading until even straining, Singer couldn't hold on to it. A lifeline slipped away. The LZ was deathly quiet. Small and encircled by a noose of trees. His breath, dry and raspy in his throat.

A sense of aloneness so pervasive and frightening swept over him that he turned to assure himself that Trip was still there. He listened to the silence, counting raspy breaths, groping to hear the sound of the returning Hueys. The minutes dragged by, each one a lifetime, as he waited, wondering if the Hueys or the enemy would get there first.

Trip lifted his head slightly from the machine gun and seemed to listen. "Too quiet," he whispered without turning.

Singer's hands sweated on his rifle. He listened for anything, hoping to hear the rhythmic *whump* of rotors that would mean they wouldn't be abandoned here. A bead of sweat rolled down his nose and hung there a moment before dropping onto his rifle. There was a muffled cough to his left, followed by a soft curse, neither answered by gunfire. If the NVA were here they were waiting, biding their time. Twice he thought he'd heard them coming, the faintest of sounds at the edge of his hearing, but both times the sound disappeared so quickly it left him wondering if he'd really heard it. A fly buzzed and settled on his cheek but he didn't dare swipe at it.

Finally the thumping of rotors was there, far away, but coming. Definitely coming. He clung to the sound until the Hueys were beating the air around him and he knew without looking that more of the company was jumping into the LZ. With the arrival of more men reinforcing the perimeter, Singer believed for the first time that morning that he might just survive. How many air assaults would he have to make in a year? How long could he beat the odds?

The choppers departed more quickly than they arrived and there was the noise of voices, movement, and the rattle of equipment as the company assembled and prepared to depart the LZ. Singer felt the ground against the length of his body, knowing he would soon give up the relative safety of his prone position to troll for the enemy.

"Welcome to the A Shau," Trip said, greeting the new arrivals as though a self-appointed welcoming committee, though only Singer could have heard him.

Singer stood reluctantly and within minutes was moving downslope, part of a long, twisting line of tired-looking men descending uncertainly into a dark and foreboding jungle.

"Welcome to the A Shau," Singer said, hoping he'd be around to say goodbye when they left.

17

They'd been lucky so far, but signs were there. The trail they cut and started down, descending into the A Shau in the midday jungle dimness, was hard-packed bare dirt, the vegetation worn back at its edges. A pathway traveled by an army.

When Trip reached it, he stopped and stood there looking reluctant to take the next step, as if on the edge of a deep abyss. Above him, Singer dug his feet in and leaned back into the slope, waiting, taking some of the weight off his shoulders, straining to see down the trail in both directions. He worried Trip was considering going it alone, breaking a trail rather than following the company down a well-traveled path in a reputed NVA stronghold. Who would he follow?

"Why a trail like that out here?" the New Guy asked from just above Singer.

"Gooks," Singer said. "Lots of them."

"Couldn't it be animals?"

"Not a chance. Be quiet and stay alert."

Singer wiped the sweat from his face, adjusted one of the ammo belts that hung over his shoulders and then checked the safety on his rifle, clicking it off and on. Trip looked back at Singer before stepping onto the trail, concern etched in his face. Singer pulled himself up and side-stepped carefully down the slope, leaning slightly to keep the weight of his pack from toppling him forward.

While it was easier going, Singer was certain following the trail could only lead to disaster. Being this far back in the column offered some safety to an initial assault, but with it came blindness to what was happening at the front. At any moment he expected to hear gunfire and screams from the point. They were being sacrificed in some effort he didn't really understand anymore.

The layered jungle canopy muffled sounds and created a crushing stillness. It made him want to yell just to hear his own voice.

Ahead, the silhouettes of the forward platoon disappeared into the distance, the shadowy forms merging into the dark wall of jungle. Forms hunched under the weight of the things they carried, plodding on like over-burdened pack animals on a long trail.

Singer followed, knowing no other option, each step taking more effort. The air seemed to hold little oxygen, and he worked harder for each breath. A dull ache was growing in his bones, the kind he imagined old people felt when barometric pressure changed before a storm. He flicked the safety on his rifle and looked at the uphill slopes around him where hundreds of NVA might be watching, undetected. Were they the hunter or the hunted?

The dread grew heavier than his pack and he bowed under it. He waited for the jungle to explode, resigned to it, but without little stomach for it today. Vengeful feelings lost to his fear.

The enemy was there watching, waiting. He could feel them. Yet he couldn't catch any figure or movement around him on the slopes. He wanted to tell Top, but Singer hadn't seen him since he moved past, heading toward the point, more than an hour ago. *Top must already know the enemy is here,* Singer figured.

His dread didn't lessen when they finally left the trail that descended steeply toward a deep, foreboding chasm, where apparently even Lieutenant Creely was unwilling to lead the company. More likely it was Top who had stopped their descent.

Instead of following the trail further down, they turned right and began to climb. Trip shifted the big gun to his shoulder, set his right foot upslope, paused as if gathering strength, then pulled himself up with his free hand. He repeated the process, reminding Singer of a climber on an alpine slope, making progress so agonizingly slowly that when he'd watch the documentary in his high school history class he'd wondered if the man had frozen stiff in mid-step.

Before starting the climb, Singer stared down the trail, a narrowing dim line merging into a black void, thankful he didn't have to go there. He followed Trip, moving his rifle across his body to keep the muzzle out of the dirt, finding himself struggling against the steepness of the slope and having to use the same slow process as Trip to pull himself up.

The steepness offered a small hope that if the NVA were going to reach them, they would have to make the same brutal climb. The top might save them. If the NVA weren't waiting for them at the top already. For a moment, Singer had the vision of grenades being rolled down the slope, exploding around him. He trembled at the thought. He clung to a thick vine and wiped the sweat from his eyes, and hung there, his mouth open, his chest heaving with shallow, rapid breaths until the image passed. Below him, the New Guy clawed his way up using both hands, his rifle slung across his shoulder, followed by indistinct figures, the last of the company. Singer forced himself to move.

Hand over hand they climbed, inching their way higher. Singer's legs burned, screaming in protest at each step. He fought against an agonizing fatigue and the weight of his pack that pushed him down, threatening to stop his progress. He thought of a minor wound, a medevac, a hospital bed, and of being able to rest.

A lizard called from above them, "Fuck you, fuck you," and another answered from an opposite mountain, "Fuck you, fuck you." More joined the chorus, calling as he climbed. If he hadn't known it was lizards, he might have believed it was the NVA taunting them. It had nearly the same effect.

The dimness of the jungle grew gradually, nearly imperceptibly, until Trip was a dark, formless shape above him that he had to strain to see, forcing him to push even harder to stay close and not lose contact. A rock shelf blocked his way and he struggled to get over it, believing he couldn't go any farther.

Then a hand was there, reaching out of the darkness, open, palm up, thick fingers extended. He grabbed it and the hand tightened around his and he could feel the strength as it pulled him up over the ledge. He saw Trip's face, a tired smirk, and he was on his stomach, on level ground for the first time in hours. He lifted his head and vomited.

"Some mountain," Trip said. "Let the fuckers come up this."

Singer pushed himself up to his knees and sat there his mouth open, gasping. "Is this the top?"

"Not sure, but we're stopping here. Where's the New Guy?"

"Behind me."

Trip peered over the ledge into the darkness. "Shit."

"He was behind me."

"Hey," Trip said. "Hey, up here."

There was nothing, just the oppressive gloom. Singer sloughed off his ruck and moved to the edge, holding his M16 ready. Trip pulled a grenade and held it, its pin still in place.

"Goddamn it. If that new fucker's lost . . ." Trip said. "Hey?"

There was a soft thud, then the sound of rocks falling. Something that sounded like a whimper.

"Up here."

"Is that you?" a weak voice asked out of the darkness downslope.

"You better hope it is. Get your ass up here."

Trip waited, not putting down the grenade until he saw the New Guy's face, then pulled him over the ledge with too much force.

"You better keep up. Fuck around and get yourself lost ain't no one going to look for you."

"Give me a hand," a soldier said at the ledge, and Singer grabbed his hand.

"It was dark," the New Guy said, his eyes wide and moist.

"Fuck, it's always dark," Trip said.

"What's the hold-up?" asked a disembodied voice from the darkness that was unmistakably Sergeant Milner. "Get a perimeter set up, two-man positions." He pointed at the New Guy. "You, shift right. Pair up with the man over there." The New Guy shuffled off without a word.

"Where's second squad? We need to send out an ambush." Sergeant Milner said.

"Don't know, Sarge, just got here," Trip said.

"I want the M60 over there."

Trip picked up the gun and his ruck and moved off quickly, gesturing with a slight motion of his head for Singer to follow. They walked past dark forms sprawled amidst the trees and rocks, holding their weapons, a few already eating Cs. The hilltop held the murmur of movement, whispered words, and the muffled sounds of shifting equipment.

Here," Trip said, dropping his ruck and the gun. "Watch out for Sergeant Milner or he'll be trying to send us on some crazy nighttime mission. If he wants an ambush, he should go. This short fucker ain't doing anymore night-time patrols." Trip pulled the machete from the side of his pack and hacked at brush and a small tree.

Singer sat down hard, still breathing heavily, putting his back against a tree. "I didn't spend all day climbing just to go back down. Let them come to us." He pulled a grenade from his web gear and set it in front of him, then lined up another until he had six grenades laid out. Then he dug the claymore out of his pack.

Trip set his M60 in position and lined it up to fire downhill, checking that he could move it without getting hung up. He set it aside and swung his long blade once more, then checked the gun's movement again before sheathing the machete. He strung an additional length of rounds and laid belts of ammo near the gun. He handed his grenades to Singer, who added them to the pile.

"I'm too tired to dig in," Singer said. "That hump kicked my ass."

"We're okay. With all the rocks and roots you couldn't dig, anyway," Trip said. "I'll put out the claymore."

"No, I'll do it, you're short."

"I'll check the next position to see how we're tied in and tell them we're going out in front to set a claymore."

When Trip got back and on the gun, Singer moved cautiously, dropping down below their position with his M16 and the claymore, feeling his way, mindful of his bearings. On his knees, he set the claymore on a likely approach, angling it for maximum effect, imagining the carnage and the payback for Rhymes, Doc, Red, and Stick. After inserting the fuse, he camouflaged it carefully and then ran the wire, hiding it as he went back to his position. He set the trigger near the grenades and sat down next to his ruck.

"How's it look?" Trip asked.

"It's an easier route than we came up," Singer said. "The slope won't slow them down much, but I put the claymore in a good spot."

"Keep the trigger handy."

Singer dug a can of Cs from his ruck and held it up close to his face before running a P38 around the lid and spooning out a mouthful. It was as tasteless as paste and about the same consistency. He swallowed with the help of a slug of water from one of his canteens, then took another spoonful of food.

"Have a burger for me when you get home," Singer said.

"Right after the steak and beers, count on it," Trip said. "Eight and a wake-up. I should be in the rear stacking forms or sorting supplies and waiting for my bird. This is the last fucking mountain I'm ever going to climb."

"What will you do?"

"My old man will want me to work, but after this I don't know. Maybe get me a fast bike and see some country. Fuck, I don't know. I know I won't spend years bent over the same damn machine like my old man."

"A bike and open country sounds good. No trees, no mountains, just flat country and sunshine. I don't ever want to see woods again. I hate this fucking darkness. How do those fuckers live in this dreary place? I want to be able to lie on my back, look up and see the sun. If I can see the sun, everything will be okay."

When Trip went quiet, Singer imagined he was thinking about the steak and beer he would have in just a few days or girls back home he only alluded to in crude sexual references. A number of girls wrote him, perfumed letters which came in distinctly different envelopes, often including photos. Trip would read them and get that half smile, half smirk of his and stare at the photo before adding it to the small bundle he carried and guarded judiciously. Yeah, maybe he was thinking about the girls.

Nine days and Trip would be gone. Singer thought of the 247 days he had left and couldn't even imagine it. How many more patrols would he make? How many more mountains would he have to hump? How many more cans of shitty food would he have to eat? Singer put the empty can from his Cs in his ruck and wrapped his poncho liner over his shoulders against the evening mountain chill, pulling his M16 onto his lap.

"I'll take first watch," Trip said. "Get some sleep, I'll wake you in two."

Singer curled up on his side in his liner holding onto his rifle, his head on his ruck. "Singer, Singer," Rhymes called him, his voice faint and distant. Soft pleadings. "Hold on, I'm coming," Singer told him.

"Singer, it's your shift," Trip whispered.

"What?"

"Wake up. Your shift."

"Okay, okay." Singer sat up and rubbed his eyes. "What time is?"

"2210."

"Everything quiet?"

"Yeah."

Trip handed Singer the watch and claymore trigger and lay down behind the gun. Sat up and pulled a rock from under him and lay down again. "Wake me for my shift at 2400."

Singer pulled his rifle into his lap and a bandolier nearer, then sat blinking, trying to clear his head. He could already hear Trip's sleep-breathing, slow, shallow exhalations, though he could barely make out his sleeping form, a dark, vague shape amongst other vague shapes. It seemed even darker now, if that was possible. The slope was indiscernible. Shapes merged, blurred, disappeared, and reemerged only through his imagination. The darkness was monotonous and he shifted his eyes back and forth to relieve the fatigue. He shook off the poncho liner, hoping the chill would help keep him awake. He held the watch up to his face: 2225.

He opened his eyes with a start and quickly raised his head, blinking at the darkness that refused to retreat. The watch read 0147 hours. Shit. He started to shiver and needed to pee but was afraid to move. How long had he been asleep? Trip was still curled where he'd first lain down, his breathing slow and nasal. It wasn't that, but there'd been something. Shit, how had he fallen asleep? He strained to hear anything out of the normal, knowing he was lucky to still be alive. There it was, or was it his imagination?

Singer leaned over and touched Trip sleeping form beside him, "You hear that?"

Trip raised his head. At the noise he screamed, "Blow the claymore! Blow the claymore!"

The claymore boomed, shattering the night, a flash of brilliance, debris raining against the trees.

Trip opened up with the M60 in frantic burst, the muzzle blast lighting their position. A claymore blew on their right. Singer threw a grenade. A brief quiet reigned before someone down the line fired a short burst from an M16. Singer listened, ready.

Singer spun toward the rear, feeling the trigger pressure along with terror. They wouldn't get in on him again.

"Jesus," Sergeant Milner shrieked. "Don't shoot. Don't shoot."

Singer let out a breath and lowered his rifle.

Sergeant Milner hung there a moment, a dark shape on the edge of Singer's vision, like he was debating returning to the safety of the platoon CP and forgetting about everything until the morning. He straightened up a bit and edged closer, still looking frightened. "What happened here?"

Singer looked at Trip.

"We had a probe," Trip said.

"Show a little fire discipline. It was probably nothing."

"Right, Sarge, just like May fifth was nothing. If we'd had a little less fire discipline then, some of the guys might still be alive."

Sergeant Milner sagged, his mouth hanging half open, before he turned away without a word.

"Fuck that guy," Trip said. "You see him May fifth? You see him shoot his rifle even once? He did nothing. Now he's going to tell us we shouldn't fire. Fuck him. I'm going home. No way I'm getting zapped my last days in country. No fucking way."

"Christ, what was that?" Singer asked.

"Don't know. Gooks feeling us out. Whatever, they sure took off."

"Moved across the line pretty fast."

"Probably a group spread out, unsure where we were."

"But they never fired."

"Why give themselves away until they're ready? They were just feeling us out, seeing what kind of response they'd get."

"Shit, that was close."

"Too fucking close. You were supposed to wake me at 2400."

"I was—"

Don't fall asleep again. Get me—"

"I was—"

"Don't fucking sleep. Get me up if you can't stay awake. We could've had our throats slit. Happened in the Cav. Gooks slit the throats of three guys on the perimeter. We found them dead in their foxhole in the morning. No one heard a thing."

"Fuck. I'm sorry, I don't know what happened."

"Don't let it happen again. Sleep all you want after I'm gone, but not before."

"I'm awake if you want to sleep."

"No more sleep tonight. They'll be back. They know where we are now." Trip clipped two more ammo belts to the one trailing from the gun, then felt the barrel. "Be sure to shoot low, downhill, or you'll shoot over them."

Singer released the magazine from his M16 and pressed down on the round, assuring himself it was full, then checked the chamber before slowly pushing the magazine back home, letting go when he heard the quiet snap of the catch. He pulled the grenades closer, rearranging them one by one while Trip lay silently at his gun.

"Who will you see first?" Singer asked.

"What do you mean?"

"When you get home, which girl?"

"Fuck, I don't know, maybe I'll just shuffle the deck and take them one at a time as they come up."

Singer could see Trip's teeth and tell he was smiling again. "Sounds like a serious problem."

"Yeah, but I plan to give it my full attention."

"Save some for me."

"Sure, come out when you're done and I'll hook you up. Easy."

"Count on it, then."

They settled back into silence, Singer thinking about home and the prospect of heading out to see Trip after the war. Maybe he'd even look up Rhymes's family, Doc's, too. What would he tell them? He listened to the night and stared into the darkness, taking comfort that Trip was beside him doing the same. Shadows formed in the darkness, taking on strange shapes that flowed, seeming alive. He strained against the blackness, trying to find the outline of things, something to hold onto that would orient the world, but the blackness was fluid. Reality and imagination merged. They were coming for him. He knew it. Moving up the slope with determined faces, carrying AKs and RPGs, intent on killing him. He opened the bolt of his M16, felt the round, then pushed it forward before fingering the grenades, as if counting them to be sure they were all still there.

"Do you hear that?" Singer asked.

Trip cocked his head slightly, but didn't answer.

"The crawling?"

"No," Trip said, "Nothing." But he shifted up tighter behind the gun.

It wasn't the wind or his imagination. It was real, even if Trip couldn't hear it. Bodies dragging themselves forward over hard earth. They were coming for him again. He pointed his rifle toward the sound, his hands sweaty despite the mountain chill.

He turned quickly to find only empty blackness. Too slow. He had to be faster. Could he do it again? Could he make the same kind of lucky shot? He doubted he could and that unnerved him. Next time they'd kill him. He checked his rifle's chamber again then tested the magazine to be certain it was seated properly. When dawn finally came, he was exhausted.

18

May 23, 1968
A Shau Valley, Vietnam

With the dawn the slope slowly materialized into jumbled boulders, tangles of vines and stems amid massive trees, all in shades of gray. Nighttime blackness gave birth to a pervasive gloominess. Shapes took form, but details remained lost in the depths of perpetual shadow. When it never really got light, Singer cursed the jungle and felt the thread of hope evaporate. He tried to imagine the sun, an invisible god that inside the jungle tomb was nearly beyond knowledge or memory. To die here, entombed in the darkness, would be to die without salvation, without hope. If he could only look up at the face of God, feel it's warmth on his face, he could give himself up to death. But not here. Not in this godless darkness.

Trip met the dawn with silence. Singer waited for his proclamation of his few remaining days, but Trip never gave it. Instead, he ran his oily rag back and forth across the gun.

Since May fifth, Singer felt like he and Trip were the lone survivors of a shipwreck drifting about, looking for solid ground. Trip was nearly there. Seeing anyone survive and leave intact made it seem possible. If Trip could make it, maybe Singer could, too.

With his grenades hung back on his web gear, Singer retrieved his belts of machine-gun ammo and draped them on his pack.

"I'm going down to check the claymore," Singer said. "Maybe there'll be something."

Trip nodded without looking up.

At the claymore site there were no indications of what had approached last night: no bodies, abandoned equipment, or blood. Just a shattered piece of jungle: sheared stems, frayed and ragged ends, the litter of torn leaves and leafless branches.

"What does it matter?" Trip said when Singer told him.

It was the Shake and Bake who gave them the bad news, his dark face soft and slack. Too green to know the truth of it. "Platoon patrols. Ten minutes. Be ready."

Trip turned his back and picked up his machine gun as though just holding it would save him.

There was nothing to say. They were going out alone. Singer let the man depart without a question. Nothing he could ask would change things, and the Shake and Bake would know little else about the mission. They were all mostly the same, anyway: walk until you find something bad or it finds you. Someone was always telling them to be ready, but how could you ever prepare for what was coming? He pulled out a letter from his helmet, reading the same words, unable to concentrate.

Giving up, Singer hoisted on his ruck and waited beside Trip, ready to move out. Neither of them spoke. Singer worried that anything he said might give life to his fears. This place held the promise of death. It offered none of the potential for payback of a line of targets on open ground. Here they were the hunted, despite any illusions they might cling to otherwise. The ache, deep in his bones, was unrelenting. He doubted Trip would leave before things exploded. None of them would make it out.

Men trailed past, pausing to space themselves, using the easier slope near Singer's position to start their descent for the day's patrol. One after another, the jungle swallowed nameless figures, leaving little trace they had ever been there. Singer's turn was coming.

He stared, unable to look away even though he knew he should. Men moved by like a procession of convicted men being led toward the chamber where their lives would end. Watching revealed some flaw in him. Still, he had to see. He counted each rifle as it moved past, held by a faceless body hung with ammo and grenades, and he felt his own strength seeping away. How many of them would come back?

Singer turned toward Trip, who was examining his hand. "Platoon-sized patrols is nuts. Doesn't the CO know where we are?"

"He's casting a wide net to try to find his lost honor."

"Slim chance of that. Any idiot could tell him what we'll find."

Fourth platoon was the last to leave, taking a different line. The Cherry Lieutenant, his pale face shining ghost-like in the gloom, moved out behind the point squad, balancing his map in one hand and his M16 in the other, his RTO on his heels. Sergeant Milner followed, looking like an old desk jockey who'd never grown comfortable with the field. The Shake and Bake waited to bring up the rear. Singer felt too weak to stand, knowing he would have to follow them and his life was in their hands. They would be lucky if they didn't become hopelessly lost. Years later, he imagined, people would still be wondering what happened to the platoon that never came out of the A Shau. Or maybe no one would care. What he wouldn't give for Sergeant Edwards's leadership and confidence under fire. But that was all over.

"This is fucked," Trip said. "Why can't the 101st take care of their own AO?"

None of it made sense to Singer, either. Pulled from their home AO and dropped off alone in strange terrain outside the range of their own support elements. And now, breaking up into platoon-sized patrols. It was feeling more and more like they were bait in some scheme they would never be let in on, and, like bait, they would be sacrificed for some larger prize.

The New Guy eased over from wherever he'd spent the night, looking fresher than Singer felt, and he hated him for it. Maybe the guy could sleep without nightmares.

"I'm supposed to stay with you guys in the day," the New Guy said.

"Who said that?" Singer asked.

"That Negro sergeant."

"Christ, where are you from?" Singer asked.

"I thought we were rid of you," Trip said.

"He said I was—"

"Just shut up and follow Singer."

"Fucking great," Singer said.

There were only a few men waiting when Trip fell in line. "Watch my back."

"Got it," Singer said, bothered that Trip would ask, then laughed at the prospect of asking the New Guy to cover his. At least they were in the rear of the platoon, away from the point as well as Sergeant Milner and the New Lieutenant. Still, he knew when the point hit something he and Trip would be expected to move forward under fire to bring up the gun.

Singer followed Trip, staying close enough to get to Trip and the gun, closer than he would have otherwise. He turned to be sure the New Guy followed. The New Guy was looking down, fussing with his web gear, and hadn't started. Even with more than two weeks in the field the guy still hadn't caught on. He might never. Singer was about to yell when the New Guy lifted his face, showed something near panic, then ran forward clutching awkwardly at his web gear.

"Not so close," Singer said.

The New Guy nodded and held up a second but next time Singer looked back the New Guy was right on top of him, looking like he wanted to walk right next to him if he could. After the third time Singer gave up at getting the New Guy to stay back, but never stopped worrying that the New Guy might get him killed.

They moved slowly, the point leading them through a maze of trees far older than any of them. The heat built quickly, radiating down through the canopy and up from the earth, cooking like a covered pot. Sweat clung to Singer's body and soaked his fatigues with nowhere to go in the already saturated air. Fatigue came as quickly as the heat and Singer sagged under his ruck, at times carrying his rifle one-handed at his side. The familiar pain in his shoulders grew, screaming for relief that was months away. He reached up and pulled at a strap, momentarily relieving some of the pressure, and bounced the pack slightly, trying to resettle it in a new position, but it bit back into his shoulders in the same place.

In the absence of the sun, orientation was nearly impossible without a compass, but Singer thought they were heading mostly west. He wondered if they might have crossed into Laos already or if anyone would know if they had. The jungle took on a monotony of dull greens, deep shadows, and vertical lines that challenged his vigilance already diminished by heat and fatigue. At times he found himself gazing unfocused as though he just woken up, and he wondered how long he'd been walking without thinking or looking. *Stay alert*, he reminded himself.

Through the hours he watched Trip's hesitant steps, each saying *seven days and a wake-up*, and he felt the weight of responsibility made nearly unbearable by his failure to save the others. If he could save Trip, there might be a small measure of redemption. Trip kept shifting the gun from his arms to his shoulders and back again as though he couldn't get comfortable with the weight or was anxious to be rid of it. Seven days and a wake-up. He looked back at Singer only once, nodding in the kind of tight-lipped gesture made between men standing on the gallows, resigned to their fate with nothing left to say.

A few times Singer looked behind him to see the New Guy still there, though slipping farther back, but he didn't hold up or wave him forward. He couldn't see the other men of the platoon. Maybe they weren't even there and Trip, he, and the New Guy were just a three-man patrol.

They slogged on, at times climbing, but mostly going down as if they were looking for the bottom. Progress was slow, and after four hours they had barely gone two klicks.

Trip stopped abruptly in mid-step, his head turned looking down at his gun barrel, which was pointed at the ground next to his feet. Singer took a step back. Somewhere in the distance came the short, shrill call of a lizard or a bird. Trip brought his head up in slow motion, following the tangle of vines next to him, then lowered it on the same path. He took a half step back and Singer turned his face. The vines that had snared the barrel of his M60 refused to release it and Trip pulled at them repeatedly, grumbling, "Fucking jungle." The barrel finally came free after he twisted the gun and pulled again, but still he stood there.

The movement behind Singer caused him to turn, rifle waist-high. The New Guy was there, just a few feet away, his helmet cockeyed, nearly covering one eye. "We taking a break?"

"No. Stay back and watch where you step," Singer said.

The New Guy looked down at his feet, "When will we stop?"

"Not 'til tonight."

"Couldn't we use a trail?"

"You want to walk into an ambush?"

The New Guy wiped his nose with the back of his hand, then glanced at his feet again. "A trail would be easier."

"Easier to die."

Singer turned back to follow Trip, who had started moving again. One by one they slid down a steep slope into a dry creek bed that held rocks, some boulder-sized, worn smooth by ages of rainy-season flows. Singer worked his way carefully down, planting each foot sideways and grabbing what he could to stop him if his feet slipped. As he sized up his next step, he saw Trip's feet fly out from under him and Trip slide the length on his back, slamming into a small boulder at the edge of the creekbed with a soft thud. Apparently uninjured by the fall, Trip was up and moving when Singer safely reached the bottom. The New Guy sat down at the top of the slope and inched his way down.

The footing in the creek bed was good, though uneven. In the wet season the creekbed would have been a nightmare, even now they had to be careful not to wedge a foot in one of the crevices and twist or break an ankle. Singer looked up at the closed canopy. A medical extraction would be difficult.

The rock-strewn corridor was tunnel-like, an open passage enclosed in gloom. For the first time, though, since starting out that morning, Singer could see men ahead of Trip as the patrol followed the creek bed's gradual grade down. Stepping from rock to rock, he tested each stone before shifting his weight, careful not to slip or send loose rocks clattering down.

It was a lot like walking along railroad ties, and Singer thought of when he was twelve and had crossed the long trestle that ran high over Rabbit Creek. Before starting out on the trestle, he'd never realized how long or high it was as it crossed the valley, running nearly parallel to the creek before finally gaining solid ground again on the opposite hill. Partway across, looking down through spaces between ties at the valley floor two hundred feet below, he had been nearly paralyzed by fear. Solid ground was so far away in each direction that going back or forward seemed impossible. He couldn't recall now why it had been so compelling to cross, only that he had done it, forcing himself to step from one tie to the next looking only at the ties, not the empty spaces and open air that made him dizzy. He heard it coming just as he reached the other side, and he turned and watched the freight train barrel onto the trestle. He watched the cars race pass in a blur, accompanied by the hypnotic clatter of the wheels on the rails. Afterward he sat there for a long time staring back over the trestle, wondering what might have happened if he'd been a little slower. There was no escape that he could see. Every choice was just a matter of the way he would die. When he finally gathered his strength, he walked back home the long way around, avoiding the tracks and the trestle and once home went straight to his room. He never told anyone how he might have died that day. In the creek bed now, balancing from one rock to the next, he could feel the freight train barreling down on him.

A flat rock offered secure footing, and he looked up from his feet first at Trip, who hugged the big gun with his right arm and had his left arm outstretched trying to keep his balance, and then the men beyond him, and finally up into the canopy, wanting to imagine the sun.

He snapped his rifle to his shoulder, flipping the safety to full auto in one smooth movement, but held his fire, waiting for a face to appear. His heart drummed in his chest. The structure was about thirty feet up in the limbs of a giant tree at the creek's edge and offered a commanding view of the creekbed and surrounding terrain that would have allowed the NVA to observe the patrol's approach for some time already. Despite its large size, it was protected from detection by camouflage that blended nearly perfectly with the vegetation and the tendency of men not to look up. The point element and those who followed, including the Cherry Lieutenant, must have missed it, or they would have stopped and passed the word down the line. They had walked under it unaware, toward whatever it guarded.

It was only the lines of the long observation and shooting slot, a dark horizontal slash across the jungle canopy, that gave it away for what it was. This structure was bigger than any treehouse Singer had ever seen and would have comfortably accommodated a couple men, but still he wouldn't have seen if he hadn't paused and looked up. Had they camouflaged the slot, he might have missed it altogether. The whole box-like shape took form as he brought his rifle to bear on the opening. Still no enemy looked out. Ahead of him, Trip kept moving, tightroping across the sea of rocks, the M60 clutched at his right side, his left arm extended, gripping air.

It was hard to keep his aim as his whole body shook, knowing what an observation post of this size would mean. This was no small, temporary camp. He was part of a platoon of less than twenty men walking into a large, permanent base the enemy would surely fight to defend.

It was just a few seconds, but he couldn't wait any longer for the enemy to show himself. While he waited, the men ahead of him were moving unknowingly toward disaster. He scrambled across the rocks toward Trip, moving quickly, no longer conscious of the weight he carried or the fatigue that just moments before had been so numbing. Even the persistent ache in his bones had disappeared. The storm had arrived.

"I got to warn the lieutenant," Singer said, pausing just long enough to point out the structure to Trip.

"Oh, fuck," Trip said.

Singer hurried past men, searching ahead for the radio antenna of the RTO that would indicate the lieutenant's position. No one said anything, not even Sergeant Milner, as he ran forward. The Cherry Lieutenant was stopped, studying something further on, and Singer touched his arm to get his attention.

"Sir, there's a large observation post in the trees behind us," Singer said, working hard to keep his voice calm.

"There're hooches up ahead, take the right."

The Cherry Lieutenant immediately returned his attention to the left, which must have been where the point element was moving.

It was not the time nor Singer's place to ask if the lieutenant saw the structure and why no word was passed back, or why they hadn't stopped to consider things. Did he really think it wise to amble into a major enemy base camp with just twenty men? Perhaps all the Cherry Lieutenant could see were the congratulations and awards he might receive for such a discovery. Or maybe he had something to prove that compelled him to try to go it alone with an understrength platoon. But still, he'd have to survive to tell the story, and from what Singer could see, that was becoming more and more doubtful for any of them.

Sergeant Edwards never would have taken the platoon into an enemy base camp. He would have called in heavy artillery and jets and only gone forward after the place was leveled. If he were only still here.

The Cherry Lieutenant didn't get it. These weren't some flatland hooches marking the edge of a village that was more likely to be occupied by rice farmers than anyone that posed a threat to them. These were NVA lodgings in the A Shau Valley.

But going back was not an option anymore. The Cherry Lieutenant had already moved off to the left, apparently following the point toward the hooches they'd spotted, leaving Singer with the orders to "Take the right." Singer could feel the undertow pulling at him.

This wasn't something to do alone, and he didn't want to get separated from Trip as he had from Rhymes. To his relief he saw Trip had followed him forward, covering his back as he sought to warn the lieutenant. Surprisingly, the New Guy stood just a few feet from Trip, struggling to put his canteen back in his web gear while looking up repeatedly as if checking to see that Trip and Singer were still there. Or maybe he was starting to get it, that a fire-team had to stick together. Either way, it didn't matter. He was there and they didn't have to look for him or worry about his whereabouts.

"There're hooches, we're supposed to take the right," Singer said after waving Trip over.

"Fuck, I knew it," Trip said.

The right bank of the creek was low and gradual. Singer climbed it easily and continued up the slight grade, stepping slowly and as silently as possible, his rifle ready at his hip. The jungle was still, as though every creature was holding its breath. Even the buzzing of insects stopped.

Singer looked back up the creek, but he couldn't see the elevated observation post anymore. Still no shot or raised alarm. It had to be a trap, and they were already deep into it.

Only the three of them had come this way. The point element and the Cherry Lieutenant were somewhere behind them, moving away toward other structures. How the rest of the platoon was deployed Singer wasn't sure. All he knew was he was with a short-timer and a new guy walking around in an enemy base camp in the A Shau Valley a very long way from any other 82nd company or support elements.

He edged forward, his heart in his throat, his palms sweating on his rifle. He blinked against the sting of the sweat that ran down his face, trying to clear his vision.

A few meters beyond the creekbed, Singer pushed carefully through a thin wall of brush and came upon a major trail. He stopped and checked to see that his M16 was on auto. The trail was bare dirt, hard-packed and worn down by years of use so that it was depressed slightly into the earth. Visibility was less than it had been in the creekbed, but he could see down the trail a short way in each direction. It looked empty. To the right it dropped down toward the creek in the direction they'd come, and to the left it ran away from the creekbed, continuing to climb before disappearing over a slight rise.

He leaned back toward Trip and whispered, "Trail. Make sure the New Guy watches behind us."

Trip nodded acknowledgement.

Singer tensed his grip on his M16, took a deep breath of rancid air, and stepped onto the trail. He edged his way up, going even more slowly now, stopping once to look back to be certain he wasn't alone, relieved to see Trip right behind him and the New Guy behind him, all of them staying close. He had enough to worry about what was in front of them, but he hoped the New Guy was watching their back trail so some NVA didn't come up the trail behind them and shoot them in the back before they knew he was there.

At the top of the rise was a trail intersection, both paths looking similarly worn. Singer went left again, on instinct, unsure where either trail led, but knowing already they were somewhere they shouldn't be. Each step took them farther from their small, scattered platoon, deeper into the camp. They'd be lucky to be killed outright rather than taken prisoner and suffer all that would mean. This was far from any retribution he'd dreamed of. He nearly panicked, thinking of the gold tooth and photo he carried that would invite harsh reprisals, but there was nothing he could do.

Singer sucked open-mouthed at the thick air, nearly gagging. Disaster was looming larger and larger and any chance of escape faded with each step. Still, he went forward because the only other choice was one he feared more than death.

The line of thatched roofs mostly hidden by the jungle vegetation was the first evidence he saw of a base, but then he could make out the broken forms of more hooches up ahead. He fought the urge to run, struggled to swallow, then inched forward, knowing any moment things would explode. These might be his last minutes, his last memories, and he was trying to prolong them.

Another trail intersection, and he stood there peering carefully in each direction, expecting to see enemy soldiers sauntering down one of the trails. The ghostly outlines of hooches stood around them in every direction. It wasn't possible the place was empty. Even if the main force was out on a mission, there would be a significant contingent left behind. Maybe everyone was at some central location. Things weren't right.

Sweat ran down his face, and he stopped and wiped his trigger hand on his pants, considering his options. Should they continue along one of the trails, getting a better picture of the size and nature of the camp, or should they start searching hooches? What he really thought they should do was get the fuck out of there right now, then hit it from the air and come back in force so they could roll through it. He wanted to be anywhere else than where he was right now. The freight train was bearing down on him and his legs wouldn't move.

Die bravely, he thought. Let people know he died bravely. He swallowed down his fear.

He was confused. Had he gone left or right at the last fork? He tried to envision the way out, constructing a mental map of the trails and what they'd seen of the camp so far. The network of trails was complicated, with so many twists and turns that he wasn't sure exactly where they were or if he could find his way back out, even if he had all the time in the world. Which way should he go? Every direction looked equally dangerous, and he was frozen with indecision. If he didn't move, he might live a bit longer.

The decision was made for him when Trip edged past him and started down the trail to the right, as though no longer content to follow and determined to lead them safely out or take himself home. Singer followed Trip after checking each direction again and pointing at the back trail to remind the New Guy to watch it and touching his finger to his lips for silence. He prayed the New Guy would be quiet for once. The New Guy had stared back wide-eyed, as if uncomprehending, but finally turned to look behind him in little more than a quick glance.

They crept along the trail, between walls of brush that screened them from the hooches, Trip in the lead ready with the big gun, Singer staying close behind hoping for some escape, certain there was none. The sound stopped him cold and he stood mid-step, not daring to put his weight down, listening hard. It had been a sound like that of a ripe acorn dropping from an oak tree into leaf litter in the fall. A footstep, or something dropped or thrown? Leaves hung listless. A spider clung unmoving near the center of its web, stretched across the brush, waiting. Had he really heard something?

"What was that?" Trip whispered, leaning in close.

Singer shook his head slightly, still wondering, wanting desperately for it to be nothing. He barely breathed the word. "Nothing."

Trip turned back and took a step. Slow, deliberate.

Chattering in Vietnamese exploded like gunfire from the other side of the hedge. There was no denying it or assigning it to fear-fed imagination. The NVA were here, as Singer knew they would be from when he first saw the observation platform. The freight train hit in a crushing impact.

Before the NVA finished speaking, Trip and Singer opened up with their machine gun and M16, ending whatever it was the NVA was about to say.

Behind the hedge they saw the blur of movement, men falling hit or grabbing for weapons.

Singer tore into them with gunfire.

Trip's machine gun stopped after the first burst.

The New Guy never fired.

Only he was shooting. "Fire! Keep firing!" Singer loaded a second magazine and slammed the trigger tight. "Fire, goddamn it! Fire!" If they didn't overwhelm these guys and those who came to their aid, they were done.

The New Guy fired a couple shots, then quit.

Still Trip didn't fire.

Singer looked to see if he was dead. "Fire!"

Trip pulled at the operating handle again and again without results.

"Keep firing!" Singer screamed, maybe at himself as much as at Trip and the New Guy.

The New Guy's M16 gave up a short burp.

"Keep firing! Keep firing!" Singer burned through his fourth magazine. "They're coming, we need the gun."

"Fucker's jammed." Trip slammed his fist against the gun.

"Keep firing!"

The New Guy fired a shot, two more, then stopped.

"Fire, goddamn it." He couldn't stop a charge of NVA alone. These first moments were critical if they were to survive and escape.

A few more reluctant shots came from the New Guy.

"Keep firing!"

"Goddamn this fucking gun," Trip said.

Singer heard Trip slam the M60 against the ground.

"Keep firing!" What the fuck was wrong with the New Guy? If he didn't need him, he'd kill him.

"Keep firing!" If the NVA mustered any return fire or a charge, they'd easily overwhelm them. With a full magazine seated, Singer pulled the trigger with all his might.

"Keep firing!"

A few more shots came from the New Guy before he stopped again, as though he was rationing his ammo.

"Fire, goddamn it! Fire!" These men had to die, deserved to die for all that had happened.

Trip tugged at the operating handle and slammed the machine gun with his fist. "Goddamn this worthless fucking gun."

"Watch the trails." Singer sprayed bullets on the hooches. The killing wasn't over. Only his firing was keeping them alive. This time he would kill them all before they got behind him. He dropped another empty magazine on the growing pile and pressed a full one home.

"Fire, goddamn it!" he screamed at the New Guy, terrified they would be overrun in the brief silence as he changed to a full magazine. "Keep firing!"

The New Guy fired a few more hesitant shots.

"It's fucking hopeless," Trip said.

"Keep firing!" Willing the enemy dead, Singer squeezed the trigger tighter. He wouldn't allow them to recover and mount an attack. He would keep Trip and the New Guy alive where he failed the others. This was his chance for some redemption and he would not lose it.

"Cease fire, cease fire."

"Keep firing!" Singer screamed. He would not be stopped or fooled so easily. The New Guy started to fire again.

"Cease fire." The strained voice was closing on them.

The New Guy held his fire.

Singer did not. "Keep firing!" It didn't matter who was trying to stop him. He would keep going as long as he was alive and had ammo. He refused to die in this dark, fucking godless place. He held the trigger back and screamed and felt alive. Never had he been so alive.

"Cease fire! Cease fire! Cease fire!"

How long had the voice been screaming right behind him? Only now was he aware of how close it was. Still clenching the trigger, he looked back to see the Cherry Lieutenant, red cheeks, his mouth open, trying to breathe or about to yell again. The RTO and another man were at his back, all of them with their rifles held loosely, one-handed.

His rifle was quiet, even though he still held the trigger back. Slowly he loosened his grip. He dropped the empty magazine and closed the bolt on a fresh round. The hooches were silent, the trails empty. No sounds of running feet. Just the rattle of Trip still trying to clear the jammed M60.

"What the hell's going on?" the Cherry Lieutenant asked.

"We got NVA in front of us." Singer remained prone with his attention back on the hooches where the NVA had been talking just minutes before. *Jesus Christ*, he wanted to say, *we are in the middle of a fucking NVA base camp, what do you think is going on?*

The New Guy started to get up, then paused, half sitting. Trip pounded and pulled at the M60.

"How many did you see?"

"Not sure, a couple."

Singer swung his head, scanning for any movement.

"We've got to get out of here," the Cherry Lieutenant said, turning back toward the direction he'd come from.

The Cherry Lieutenant wasn't entirely stupid.

Singer, Trip, and the New Guy jumped to their feet, but the Cherry Lieutenant was already moving back down the trail with his RTO and the third man.

"Hurry. Let's go. Let's go," the Cherry Lieutenant said, waving them on.

Singer noted the difference in the Cherry Lieutenant. The mask of arrogance and confidence was gone. Something the Cherry Lieutenant saw must have scared him, or the firing brought home the danger of their situation, and he was rethinking the wisdom of being in an enemy base camp with just a handful of men. Maybe he no longer saw himself being decorated for the discovery, but had a vision of himself spending his remaining years in a bamboo cage or as some unrecovered corpse left to fertilize the A Shau Valley.

Singer held up for Trip, but the New Guy ran down the trail toward the Cherry Lieutenant.

"I'm fucked." Trip gave the operating handle a hard pull. His face was flushed and sweaty, his eyes red and irritated. "I'm going to die my last days in-country because the army can't give me a fucking gun that works. Not even a forty-five. Every machine gunner is supposed to get a forty-five."

"Stay next to me. I got you," Singer said.

"I can't even fucking defend myself."

"I got you. Stay close."

"I'm your fucking shadow." Trip pushed Singer on down the trail. "Go, go. Let's get out of here."

Singer started running, Trip at his back. At the first turn he caught up with the Cherry Lieutenant and the three other men. Four faces pale with fear turned away in unison. Then the six of them were sprinting. The Cherry Lieutenant had the lead, pounding feet, equipment flapping, rucks bouncing heavily on their backs.

"Fuck the noise, just run," someone near the front said.

Singer was thinking speed and distance and worried about Trip with a useless gun. At each turn he blindly followed the New Guy, trusting the Cherry Lieutenant up ahead knew the way out, thankful he didn't have to lead. No one blocked the trail. The hooches passed in a blur.

Singer didn't have to check to know Trip was right behind him. His heavy steps and gasping breaths were so close he thought Trip might run over him.

"Don't leave me," Trip panted.

"We're together all the way."

Any second, Singer expected gunfire would rip through their backs and they would be done running. Even carrying his M16, Singer was scared. He couldn't imagine how Trip felt, lugging a worthless weapon that only made him a target. There was no reason to think the fight was over. When it came again, Trip would have to huddle helplessly, sharing the cover of Singer's M16 and perhaps hoping to get a weapon off the first KIA.

They ran, making two more turns at trail intersections, but they still weren't out of the base camp. It hadn't seemed this far coming in. Could they be running deeper into the camp rather than heading for the way out? That thought produced a near panic that almost brought Singer to his knees.

"Go! Go!" Trip said.

Singer felt Trip's hand push at his back and ran harder, wondering if they could outrun this nightmare. The NVA were certainly already in pursuit or waiting in ambush as they ran toward them.

The RTO stumbled and the New Guy ran into him, sending them both sprawling. Trip banged into Singer, but they caught themselves, holding each other up. They helped the RTO and New Guy to their feet and together they sprinted down the trail, closing again on the Cherry Lieutenant and the man running with him.

Just when Singer was certain they had come the wrong way, he saw them kneeling near the trail, rifles up, faces low, sighting down the barrels of their weapons. He prayed they wouldn't fire, unnerved by the pounding feet and bodies rushing toward them.

"Hold your fire," Singer said, as much a prayer as direction to the still-unpredictable New Guy.

The remainder of the platoon held a small defensive perimeter both sides of the trail. A couple men lifted their faces from their rifles and turned to look behind them. How long they had been waiting there, ready to flee, and why it was the Cherry Lieutenant who came to get Singer, Trip, and the New Guy once the shooting started Singer had no idea. So much of the day made little sense. At least they were together again and presented a slightly larger force with a little more firepower. They would need it, he was sure.

The Cherry Lieutenant ran through the group, barely slowing down. "Let's go. Let's go."

"What happened back there?" Sergeant Milner asked.

Not even the New Guy slowed to answer. Singer ran past with Trip on his tail, both of them ignoring Sergeant Milner. The platoon was up and Singer heard the rush of men racing behind him. That their lives hung in the balance couldn't have escaped even the inexperienced. With men behind him and Trip now, Singer was relieved their backs were covered. His heart pounded in his chest and his legs felt like they could run forever. Singer was gasping, his chest heaving, but he could run faster if those ahead would only move.

They stuck to a trail, one they hadn't been on before. It led away from the camp and allowed them to run. No one asked where they were going or spoke of the danger of running into an ambush or a returning NVA patrol. Leaving where they'd been and to still be alive was enough for Singer and apparently the rest of them, as well.

Finally exhausted, they stopped and trailing men caught up. They gathered in a tight group with restless feet and darting eyes.

The Cherry Lieutenant hurried toward the back. "Is everyone here?"

"I guess," Sergeant Milner said, looking at the last two men behind him.

"Make damn sure everyone stays together. Don't lose anyone." The Cherry Lieutenant's words came in a breathless rush.

Singer stood with Trip at his elbow. "Fuck, we should have lit them up."

"You were fucking crazy back there." Trip's laugh was hollow.

"I mean the hooches. We should have burned them, given the jets a target." He wiped at the sweat dripping off his nose. "They'll never find that place from the air. The Cherry Lieutenant won't know where the fuck we were."

"Fuck, let the gooks have it. We should all go home," Trip said.

"Let's go, move, move," the Cherry Lieutenant said, jogging toward the front.

The brush whirled past. Trunks and foliage merged without detail. A branched slapped at Singer's arm. Trip huffed behind him. He kicked his legs, propelling himself up the trail, watching the New Guy's back. It surprised him that the New Guy could run like he was. Finally, something he was good at. The jungle had a different, more acrid smell. A scent he'd smelled before.

Where were the gunships and jets that should be hitting the camp, covering their retreat?

They were on their own, as he knew all along but had pushed from his mind. Unlike May fifth, no help was coming.

They ran for a long time before finally slowing to a fast walk. Shortly after slowing down they left the trail and climbed up a hillside, hiding in the brush, watching the trail below them, waiting for the enemy who would be following them. Singer could hear the heavy breathing of the men around him as he tried to slow and quiet his own breathing. His rucksack lay heavily on his back, sliding downslope against his neck, pushing him into the earth and making it hard to rise up over his rifle. Trip had given up on trying to repair the machine gun and lay next to him clutching a grenade in each hand. The worthless M60 sat there looking deadly. Singer laid his head down briefly, resting his neck and inhaling the smell of the earth and damp, decaying leaves, a sweet smell free of the pungent odor he smelled while running.

He looked back down the trail where NVA would materialize. When they came, he would kill more. Waiting with his rifle ready was far preferable to running.

"Wait 'til they're right in front of us. We want to kill as many as we can," Singer whispered.

The New Guy turned and looked at Singer, his face full of bewilderment.

They lay there waiting. Watching. Trip removed the pins from one grenade, held it ready. It was a hastily arranged ambush. Not a perfect setup, but it still held possibilities. Singer felt in control again, but maybe it was just another jungle illusion.

How many had he killed in the camp? He regretted there'd been no time to inspect the hooches and check for bodies before they fled. It would have been dangerous. They didn't have the manpower for it, or the firepower, with the machine gun down and the New Guy's hesitancy. The uncertainty of the kill stripped him of any satisfaction.

Singer brought his head down and wiped his face on his arm, then resumed staring down his rifle at the trail. Trip swiped at an insect near his face while still clutching a grenade, a small awkward movement in slow motion. On the other side of him, the New Guy shifted his legs, the scraping of boots and knees magnified in the silence. Singer looked at him, turning his head slowly, and the New Guy stopped moving. The sweat ran into Singer's eyes and he blinked at the irritation, trying to keep the trail in focus. He knew they were coming. They would be rushing forward, caution forgotten in the pursuit. He hoped they would be bunched up carelessly, all of them anxious to get in on the kill, but they would die as their friends in the camp had died. He just had to be patient, quiet, and still, and then give them no chance to return fire or maneuver. He knew how to be patient, having hid watching trails before. In the end, he had always won. They would come, he knew, as sure as he knew their only chance was to kill them all. He sighted down his weapon, the safety off, his finger in light contact with the trigger, waiting.

19

May 23, 1968
A Shau Valley, Vietnam

When the fourth platoon finally found the rest of Charlie Company, Singer's lungs burned and bolts of pain shot through his thighs with every step. Still, he was ready to run more.

The news of the base camp discovery and fourth platoon's running retreat reached the company before them. Singer could see it in the worried faces and hear it in the animated discussion between Lieutenant Creely and the Cherry Lieutenant. Even Top's brows settled low over dark eyes as he listened and his lips pressed tight as if to hold back a thought.

Singer still believed the NVA were chasing them, as apparently did Lieutenant Creely, since the company moved quickly to high ground and was given orders to dig in and set out all the claymores. Assigned to two-man positions again, Singer and Trip set up together while the Shake and Bake took the New Guy to set up with him. Trip seemed relieved to put down the jammed M60 and pound the ground with an entrenching tool. Singer and Trip took turns digging. Every time Singer thought they might be done, Trip said, "Make it deeper." Frequently they stopped to listen for the sound of approaching NVA or concussions of distant explosions from jets and artillery that should be pounding the base camp. Instead, all they heard were the sounds of hurried digging.

"They should have shelled it already," Singer said.

"Think anyone knows where the fuck we were? Even if they did, we're at the bottom of the list. The 101st won't be anxious to help a company from another division. They'll take care of their own first," Trip said.

"Fuck this shit."

"Even Top can't help us here." Trip lifted his entrenching tool high over his head before arching his back and bringing it down, hitting with a tremendous

186

whump. His arm and chest shook. Holding the M16, Singer watched Trip lever the tool loose and lift out dirt, piling it onto a growing berm.

Were Top's connections out here really as worthless as the jammed M60? Singer expected the 101st artillery would obliterate the camp so their mission would merely be a mop-up. The silence was painful and nearly as frightening as the gunfire.

"Maybe it's still coming."

"We're fucked," Trip said. "Think about it. We're an orphaned company led by a no-name lieutenant operating in another division's AO. We're at the fucking back of the line for support."

Singer shivered and turned to hide his shaking hands. Tomorrow they would go up against the base camp without fighter jets, gunships, or artillery. If the NVA understood the silence, they would be emboldened by it. Laughing and waiting. Christ, they were being screwed by some petty unit rivalry. What the hell would they be dying for? He watched Trip as he swung the entrenching tool again, the muscles in his back rippling. Each other was all they had.

"My turn," Singer said.

Trip took a couple more tired swings and climbed out of the hole, wiping his forehead, leaving a dirty smear.

"I should have shot myself before this fucked-up mission. I knew as soon as I heard Lieutenant Creely was staying after what happened May fifth that he'd volunteer us for something crazy. Someone should have told him that once you're marked a coward, nothing you can ever do will change that. Now we're going to die because the man can't live with lost honor."

"Let me dig."

After exchanging his M16 for the entrenching tool, Singer climbed into the hole and swung the tool in a short, one-handed motion while Trip stood guard, examining the palm of each hand. Singer stopped digging and looked up when the new Shake and Bake approached their position, taking small, uncertain steps.

"Trip, get up to the CP with your M60," the Shake and Bake said.

"There is a God," Trip said, breaking into a broad, schoolboy smile. He handed the M16 back to Singer and picked up his M60, ruck, and web gear. "See you back in the world."

"Just the M60 and all the M60 ammo. Leave your gear here."

"What? I'm not going out?"

"Just the M60 and ammo was all they told me." The Shake and Bake left with quick strides.

Trip dropped his ruck and web gear. "Fucking motherfuckers!" Trip kicked his web gear. "One tour already and they're going to make me stay in this fucking place 'til my last fucking day."

Singer climbed out of the hole and pulled the belts of ammo from his gear and gave them to Trip, who headed toward the CP head down and kicking at the ground.

After Trip left, Singer sat on the edge of the hole with his M16 watching the jungle. He wasn't digging unless someone had his back. A lone Huey approached. Singer couldn't see it, but he heard it coming and waited for the fire that would drive it away. Eventually it hovered over the CP, marking their position for the NVA, if their digging hadn't already. He checked the magazine in his M16 again, ensuring it was full, flicked the safety switch back and forth a couple of times, then pulled his web gear and bandoliers of ammo closer.

Trudging back, Trip returned carrying an M16 and a couple bandoliers of ammo, but didn't look cheered to have a working weapon. The chopper, he told Singer, brought in a couple more Cherries and took out a man who gave Trip his M16 and carried out the useless M60. "Can you believe they let some fucker leave?" Trip wasn't sure if the man had reached his DEROS or come up on a timely R and R roster. Either way, Trip said, "The guy's the luckiest fucker alive."

After they finished digging in deeper than ever before, they settled on a guard schedule, but then sat up together in the darkness, neither of them able to sleep. Singer figured it was the same with most of the men of the company—certainly with all the men of fourth platoon who understood how narrow their escape had been and the likelihood of an attack. Neither Singer nor Trip ever lay down. When one of them had to move, they shifted position in slow motion, careful not to make any noise.

At dawn, Singer crawled off a short distance then shifted up on his knees and knelt there pissing, sighing with relief, having waited hours for the darkness to pass. Still holding his M16 in one hand, he tucked himself in with some difficulty. No way was he letting go of his rifle after yesterday, even to pee, especially since he heard that the May fifth ambush was triggered when a man from first platoon went out to relieve himself and stumbled into an NVA position. Back at their foxhole he slid in beside Trip, glad Trip had insisted on such a deep hole. If they could stay here, they might be all right.

"Thank God it's over," Singer said, looking up at the faint light that leaked through the canopy.

"It's just beginning," Trip said.

"I mean the night. I thought they'd hit us."

"They're waiting. They know we'll come."

Singer cocked his head. The dawn was as quiet as the dusk. No whistling of incoming artillery rounds. No rotors of Cobras racing toward them. No roar of approaching jets. Just the buzz of fucking mosquitoes.

Trip was right. Soon the order would come and they'd head back toward the enemy base camp. This time the enemy would be expecting them. It might be his only chance to eat, so Singer opened a can of Cs after digging around in his ruck and rejecting the first two he pulled out. This can said beefsteak, potatoes, and gravy, but the resemblance was slight. He forced himself to chew and swallow.

"Aren't you going to eat?" Singer asked.

Normally by this time every morning Trip had already bragged about being short and announced his days, but this morning he sat in silence, rubbing his hand over his M16.

"Thanks," Trip finally said.

Singer looked up from his Cs, stopping with the spoon halfway to his mouth. "For what?"

"I figured we were dead."

"Yeah, me too. We never should have gone in there."

"I'm so close to going home I can smell it, but . . ."

"Just a couple more days and you'll be back on the block chasing skirts."

"I'm not going to make it." Trip picked up a handful of dirt and let it slip through his fingers.

What were the odds of surviving one more incursion? Singer dumped out the rest of his food and covered it halfheartedly before shoving the empty can and spoon back into his ruck.

"We'll be okay," Singer said, though he didn't believe it.

"Yeah," Trip said, starting to fuss with his ruck and web gear.

The Shake and Bake squad leader moved past quickly, leaving word that they'd be moving out in fifteen minutes on a three-platoon patrol, with web gear only. Three platoons would attack the base camp. Maybe sixty men. They'd leave their rucks on the hilltop that had been the NDP and second platoon would stay behind to hold the hill and act as a small reaction force. The Shake and Bake had no answer for what would happen to their gear if second platoon had to come to their aid. His dark features were little changed by his two weeks with the company and he looked like a school kid despite his E5 stripes.

"Think he'll be all right?" Singer asked.

"He's a fucking Shake and Bake who ain't seen shit. Stay together. We might have to do our own thing."

Moisture hung in the air over the mountaintops and in the valleys as they packed up their rucks. Dim light streamed in through the hole cut in the canopy over the CP.

"Take these," Trip said.

Singer looked up at the small bundle of envelopes in Trip's hand. "Why?"

"Just some photos and shit. If something happens I don't want some REMF to have my stuff. There're some chicks would show you a good time."

"You keep them. You'll be home in a week."

"I won't make it."

"I got your back."

But then Singer thought of Rhymes. Maybe Trip did, too, because they both went silent. Trip still held out the stack of worn envelopes.

"Just for today. Give them back to me before I leave."

* * * * *

In silence, Singer and Trip carried their rucks to the center of the NDP and added them to the pile. To Singer there seemed something final about the act. The piling of the dead's gear after an attack.

Singer and Trip stood together at the perimeter in their web gear and bandoliers with the rest of fourth platoon, waiting for word to move out.

Nearby, the New Guy fiddled with his web gear. The morning was even quieter than the dawn. There would be no pre-assault artillery barrage.

The news that they would have the point came as little surprise to Singer, since they were the ones who supposedly knew the location of the enemy camp, but it seemed to deepen Trip's despair.

"Okay, let's move out," Sergeant Milner said, but held back. His face slackened after giving the order.

The men of second platoon were already digging new holes in which to wait out the day, in a smaller perimeter around last night's CP. Singer watched a man digging, shirtless, his back holding a dull glow of sweat, the pile of rucks behind him. How long could they hold the hilltop against an all-out NVA assault? Even with defensive positions, the few men of second platoon wouldn't last long. Still, Singer would have preferred his chances on the hilltop to attacking the base camp.

The guy Ghost called California was ordered by the Shake and Bake to take the point and started down the slope looking grim-faced and ashen despite a tan. In slack position, Ghost glanced around nervously as though already searching for an avenue of escape, before resignedly trailing California.

Singer stepped off to follow Ghost down the mountain to find the NVA. Without his ruck he felt light, unanchored, as if he could almost fly. His arms and legs were flailing as he tumbled into the void. He focused on Ghost's back and his rifle that felt hard and hot against his palms. Behind him he could hear Trip, sliding at times, and trusted the New Guy and the rest of the company were following Trip, but he didn't turn to look, concentrating instead on Ghost and on his footing.

At the bottom of the slope they moved east, as they had yesterday, only today they already knew what awaited them. Occasionally he got a glimpse of California in the distance, a phantom-like image drifting in and out amongst the trees.

Ahead of him, Ghost moved in halting steps, swinging his head from side to side too quickly to really see anything. When the understory became thicker, Singer moved up tighter to keep Ghost in sight. A light haze still hung in the canopy and, the jungle brightened little beyond the dim light of early dawn. The morning seemed dream-like. The beginning of a nightmare.

This close to the point, his chances of surviving the initial onslaught were slim. The support of three platoons behind him would likely make little difference in the end, though there still was some comfort in their presence. Even if he survived, so many months of the same lay ahead of him. He pitied Trip to have made it so far just to end up like this.

He tried to calculate how far the base camp might be to measure how much time remained in his life. But he was confused by aspects of terrain and yesterday's panicked retreat, which he figured made it seem farther away than it was. None of them knew exactly where the base camp was except in a vague sort of way and they had no idea where its outer perimeter sat. It was too much to hope for that they wouldn't find it. The fight was inevitable. Only the number of minutes remaining was an issue for debate.

More than likely, the NVA had set an ambush between their base camp and Charlie Company's night position and would hit them before they ever reached the camp. Somewhere very near the NVA were sitting, weapons ready, waiting for them to get closer, likely already watching them. They were living on borrowed time. The world would change at any moment. He watched Ghost and the jungle beyond him and took careful, measured steps forward.

They'd gone maybe two klicks. After crossing a narrow valley, they'd climbed a small hill and were moving down the opposite slope toward another valley. Large trees rose from the jungle floor like pillars that supported the dark shroud overhead. Tangles of vines hung from branches high above and clumps of bamboo and underbrush created short sight-lines, yet movement was mostly unrestricted.

They snaked their way down the incline, moving left then right around trees and undergrowth. Far ahead, Singer caught a brief glimpse of California cutting sharply left across the face of dense vegetation. Singer checked his left flank then looked ahead at Ghost, hoping Ghost was keeping California in sight, though he was staying so far back Singer wasn't sure how he could.

With his rifle in both hands and the muzzle pointed at the ground, Ghost shuffled forward, with quick, jerky turns of his head. Suddenly Ghost froze. His arms started up to bring his rifle to his shoulder, but before they barely moved everything exploded. A torrent of AK and machine gun fire swept over them.

On the ground, far too exposed, Singer flattened out, returning fire while AK rounds tore up the earth beside him.

Behind him, Trip's screams pierced the gunfire. "I'm hit! I'm hit!"

Far ahead on the left, Singer could hear the distinctly different fire of an M16 and knew California somehow survived the initial flurry. The foreground where Ghost had stood before the gunfire was empty. Ghost had disappeared. Upslope from Trip, where the rest of the company should be, was quiet. Only he and California were returning fire. And they were far apart and isolated.

"Stop firing!" Trip screamed.

A pause came when every gun was quiet. For a moment even Trip stopped screaming. The silence was sudden and nearly as shocking as the explosion of fire. Singer gulped in air, raw against his dry throat.

Once Singer opened up again, shooting into the thick brush that hid the NVA positions, a few more M16s fired from behind him far up the slope. Immediately an NVA machine gun fired rounds raking past Singer, small puffs in the litter on the jungle floor, climbing rapidly upslope.

"Stop firing! Stop firing!" Trip screamed.

After Singer stopped, the enemy machine gun stopped as well, and again Trip rested his voice. When he fired again, the NVA answered with their machine gun.

"Stop firing! Goddamn it, that machine gun's right on me. Jesus, if you don't stop they're going to kill me."

Again Singer held his fire and all the shooting stopped, as if he were the sole conductor of a deadly orchestra. He felt the pressure of his chest against the earth and the rapid pounding of his heart. A mosquito buzzed his face. Sweat ran into his eyes and down the bridge of his nose, but he held still, not wanting to give the NVA a better target. The next move seemed his to make.

"If we don't fire, we won't get out of here," Singer said.

"Fuck, they're going to kill me," Trip said.

"Can you move?"

"They'll kill me if I do."

"Where are you hit?" Singer asked.

"My leg."

"I'm coming back."

"No! No! Don't come back. You'll draw fire on me."

"Okay, okay, I'm staying here."

The NVA held their fire, perhaps waiting for someone to expose themselves, knowing a wounded man was good bait. Above Trip, the Americans were quiet, as if hanging on Singer's conversation. California was silent, either dead or hoping to become a forgotten man.

"Can you reach your leg to stop the bleeding?" Singer asked.

"No. I can't move. If they fire again, I'm dead."

"I'm coming to get you."

"No! No! Stay where you are. You'll get me killed."

"Okay, okay." Singer lay there, trapped as much by Trip as the NVA.

The NVA patience gave out. Enemy fire raked the hillside.

"Oh, shit," Trip screamed.

Singer fired back, aware that some of the men above him were firing, too.

"Stop firing. Please. Stop firing. Oh, Jesus, stop."

Only when the NVA stopped did Singer quit firing. Despite Trip's pleading, he couldn't let enemy fire go unanswered. The area grew quiet once more in a repetitive pattern from which Singer took no hope.

"Hey, Point," Singer yelled. "You still with us?"

"I can't move," California said, a quaver in his voice.

"You hit?"

"No, but they're right on top of me."

"Hang in there," Singer said, not sure how any of them would get out of this.

They lay there, each side firing sporadically, neither side advancing or gaining any advantage. Singer and the others fired only when the NVA fired. Each time, Trip screamed for them to stop. Singer tried to close his mind to it, torn between the need to fight and Trip's pleadings. He would have to do something about Trip before he could fire at will. He wanted to go back to him, but Trip was adamant he shouldn't, terrified it would bring enemy fire that would kill him. Singer was stuck, rendered ineffective, uncertain what to do.

After each volley, Singer's position felt more lonely and exposed. No one was on either side of him. Ahead of him, far too close, was a tangle of brush that hid the NVA. Ten feet to his left was a large tree that looked inviting, but trying to get there might mean dying, so he burrowed into the ground where he was.

California was so far off to the left front that any kind of support or connection was completely lost. Ghost had let California get too far ahead and then disappeared in the first volley of fire, breaking any link between them. California was pinned down closer to the enemy and even more alone than Singer.

Up the slope behind Singer and Trip, where the New Guy was, a few men of fourth platoon had formed a small perimeter, taking cover behind trees, roots, and rocks, but they weren't coming any closer.

During one of the exchanges of fire, Trip suddenly stopped screaming. *Dead,* Singer thought. He sagged as if he'd been hit. But when he twisted his neck to look, he saw the Shake and Bake crawling upslope to the impromptu perimeter with Trip on his back. Singer leaned into his rifle with new recklessness. Able to fire without restraints was a help, though he still had no idea how he'd get out.

Enemy fire was intense, and he remained exposed. Some of the enemy fire was so close he could feel the air stir and dirt kicked up on him. And then there was California. For him to move to California would be suicide, and even if he could make it, the two of them would be stuck, isolated far from the main body. The NVA fire wasn't showing any signs of weakening. They needed more people up front if they were to have any hope of suppressing the enemy fire. It didn't look like any squads were coming forward to reinforce his position and put more effective fire on the enemy. Who above him would see that need and order it?

"Pull back!" someone, whom Singer didn't recognize, yelled from far up the slope.

Singer looked off toward where he knew California was trapped. "I can't," Singer yelled. "I got a man out in front of me."

He waited, but the upslope voice never answered. No one moved or offered any help. Fuck, worse than leaderless again. Trip was right. They both should have refused to go out with a CO who'd already failed. With gritted teeth he held the trigger back even after his M16 was empty. When the quiet resettled, he made a plan.

"Hey, California," Singer yelled, forgetting not to use any name. "You still there?"

The "Yeah" in response sounded uncertain.

"Think you can crawl straight back from where you are?" Singer thought it was the best way out for California. For him to try to come back to Singer would be impossible. He'd never make it.

"Maybe."

"Don't come back this way. Go straight back from them and then circle around to us. Okay?"

"Okay."

"I'll put out covering fire from here and try to keep them off you. Go after I fire."

Singer opened up without waiting for any acknowledgement from California, and the men in the small perimeter above him started firing as well. The NVA poured fire on the hillside and Singer kept his head low while he burned through one magazine after another, trying to buy California the time he needed.

If the NVA had forgotten about California with his lying quietly and not firing, he had again exposed his position by yelling back and forth with Singer. Still, when the shooting started, it seemed all of it was directed at Singer and the men above him. Maybe California had a chance.

He imagined California turning and crawling quietly away, gaining distant between himself and the NVA guns inch by inch. Then he heard running and breaking brush and finally yelling behind and above him

"It's me! It's me! Don't shoot! Don't shoot!"

Then the running stopped.

"I made it," California yelled breathlessly. "I made it."

Singer nearly smiled with relief. At least California had made it and he wouldn't have to go forward to get him. Crawling back to help Trip was one thing, but crawling up within a couple feet of the enemy where California had been was an entirely different matter.

Now only he was left.

Trip's retrieval and California's escape left him alone out in front of the company, closer to the NVA positions than his own. He was the closest and most exposed target for the NVA. He stopped firing and laid his head down on the ground, smelling the dirt and the decay of the jungle floor. No one would be coming to help him, and he couldn't stay here forever. It was a miracle that, despite all the fire and his exposed position, he had not been hit. If he had more time he would ponder that longer, but right now he had to think about getting out of here. He didn't like it, but it was move or die. Perhaps it would be both.

He twisted his head around awkwardly and looked back over his shoulder at the American positions up the slope. He could see the partially hidden faces, small and distant, staring down at him from their positions of relative safety. No one was offering advice or encouragement. They hugged their cover and stared, their thoughts masked by the distance though Singer could feel their fear that mirrored his own.

It didn't look good. Only scant cover existed between him and the American positions. The upslope route would compound his exposure to NVA fire, but there was no other way. He fought the urge to stand and run, pushing away the desire to rush to the cover of the perimeter and the comfort of having men beside him. How far would he get running before machine gun and AK fire caught him and brought him down? A few steps, or maybe even halfway if he was really lucky. Running was just too exposed, too dangerous. His best chance would be to crawl. With the help of covering fire, he might make it. He looked up the hill again, trying to measure the distance and the effort it would take. It was a long crawl that would be tough, if not impossible, to do all at once. He would have to do it in stages, a little at a time. He searched for resting places that offered even the smallest bit of cover, but there were none. He rested his head briefly, closing his eyes, telling himself when he opened them he would go.

"Give me some covering fire. I'm coming back."

The men above him opened up and immediately the NVA answered with fire more intense than any so far. For a moment Singer didn't move, but just listened to the roar of gunfire. He could do this. He turned on his belly, keeping his face in the dirt, and pushed off, inching forward, pressing his body against the ground, trying to blend in with the jungle floor. He pushed his M16 ahead of him in his right hand and then reached out and pulled with his left, pushing alternately with each leg. It was slow going as he concentrated on keeping his head and ass down and tried to make himself the smallest target possible. Bullets ripped through the air in both directions and he inched along through the middle of it, pushing and pulling, willing himself to stay down when he wanted nothing more but to get up and run away from it all and not stop running until it was all so far behind as to seem like some distant nightmare. He could feel the bullets impacting the ground near him, or he imaged their impacts, and even while he crawled he tensed his entire body against the force of the rounds that would strike him at any moment and pound him into the ground. His legs and arms ached and his breath came in torturous gasps that hurt his lungs. Dirt clung to his mouth and nostrils and he spit repeatedly, trying to clear the dirt, but only succeeded in taking it deeper into his throat. The firing waned and he risked raising his head slightly and was discouraged at how far off the men above him still were. Yet he had managed to get this far without being hit. Maybe he had a chance. He lay there feeling large and obvious on the open hillside, needing to move quickly again, trying to catch his breath, knowing every eye was on him, all of them likely wondering how he was still alive and if he would make it. He couldn't wait any longer.

"Give me some more fire."

With the first shots, both sides joined in until the volume of fire was again deafening and rounds raked up the hillside. He started moving, pushing off hard with his coiled leg, pulling the other up, switching his weight from side to side and reaching with his arms, clawing at the dirt, the air abuzz around him. The slope was slightly steeper here and he strained against the incline. When he looked up he could see the faces above him, closer now, but still a good crawl away, leaning into their rifles, firing just over him with focused determination. He pushed and pulled himself forward, gaining a few more feet then stopped, exhausted, a long ten yards below the makeshift perimeter. When he looked back down the slope, he saw how far he'd come and was encouraged to realize that he had survived this far and was almost there. He was going to make it. One more push.

A large tree with wide, sprawling roots stood near the center of the perimeter and was his focus as he crawled uphill. He stared at it now as he prepared for his last move to safety. On the left side of the tree, the Shake and Bake looked out where he knelt, his rifle slightly off his shoulder, the muzzle pointed downslope but over Singer's head. Other men huddled behind cover nearby, but Singer looked at the tree and the salvation it promised. The Shake and Bake brought his rifle to his shoulder. Before the Shake and Bake took aim, their gaze met. What was it Singer saw? Urgent pleading? Sadness of a last goodbye? Fuck it, he was almost home.

"When the shooting starts, I'm coming in around the right side of the big tree."

He said it loud enough so that everyone on the line would hear him, but he looked directly at the Shake and Bake, wanting to be certain he understood his plan. He was too close to making it to die at the hands of his own men. Before he could say it again to be sure everyone knew what he was going to do, someone started shooting and everyone joined in and there was little chance to be heard above the gunfire.

The M16 fire was frighteningly close and he ducked his head, raising just his eyes to keep sight of his goal. The Shake and Bake's face was pressed against his rifle, so Singer could no longer see his eyes and had to guess that he understood and would adjust his fire as Singer got up to the tree. Singer could see the muzzle flashes and slight recoil and the blur of casing spitting out the side of the Shake and Bake's M16. He could hear the cracks of the AKs and the pounding enemy machine gun reaching up at him. He crawled with the urgency of a man trying to cheat death. Three yards. Five. The safety of the tree was just above him. Survival he'd thought impossible during the past hour was nearly in reach.

In desperation, he rose to his hands and knees. He flew at the tree as fast as he could, hoping he didn't catch an NVA bullet up his ass. To his left, he could see the muzzle of the Shake and Bake's M16 sticking out beyond the tree, bouncing with its steady fire, but the Shake and Bake was obscured by the tree and the angle. The right side of the tree was empty and waiting. Singer raced toward it, hands and knees paddling furiously. A yard away he allowed himself to believe he'd made it.

But in that last second an M16 loomed in front of his face. He saw the muzzle, large and round. In the dark hole of the bore he saw his death. The rifle thrust out blindly from behind the tree. Inches from his face, there was no escaping the bullets about to explode out the muzzle. So close, and now he was dead. The muzzle would be his last earthly vision. He wished he could have seen the sun one last time.

The rifle exploded, and he heard the burst of rounds and the world went silent except for the pounding in his ears.

He could see the wide-eyed face of the New Guy, his weapon pointed in the air, the Shake and Bake's hand under the barrel holding it up so that the New Guy was unable to lower it. He realized he was behind the tree and still alive. The Shake and Bake and the New Guy stared at him as if he were an apparition.

When he closed his eyes, he saw the barrel of the M16 rising violently and firing just as it rose above his eyes. Gingerly, he lifted his helmet off his head and examined the hole in the top front and the second hole a few inches behind that. He touched his head and examined his hand, afraid of the blood he would see, but there was only dirt from his crawl. He turned his helmet over and pushed his letters aside to see the inside of his helmet liner was smooth and unbroken.

The Shake and Bake released the New Guy's rifle and the New Guy turned away against the tree. He did not look at Singer or fire his rifle despite the impact of enemy rounds against the tree.

Singer looked at the Shake and Bake, the understanding in his eyes, but couldn't form words in his mind, much less bring them to his lips, before the Shake and Bake turned back toward the enemy and fired. Singer's head hurt and the loud ringing in his ears muffled the sounds of the battle and of any words he might have said. He wanted to tell someone he was alive and see if they believed him, but he wasn't sure who to tell or who around him might even care.

"Jesus," Singer finally said, not sure himself if it was a curse or a prayer.

He lay back on the ground looking up at the dark canopy, studying the leaves, content to let the others fire.

* * * * *

An artillery round whistled overhead and Singer ducked lower, bracing against the explosion that took some time in coming and was softened by the distance and the jungle. His head hurt, and he wished he had some Darvon or even aspirin. He didn't remember the company pulling back, but they must have because he was on a different hill, the cover thicker here. He pushed himself up on his hands and knees.

"Where you going?"

It took a few seconds for Singer to bring California's face into focus. "To check on Trip."

"They already took him out. Ghost, too."

"What?"

"Medevac been here and gone. Brought a basket down through the canopy. You lay there and listened to it."

Another artillery round came whistling in and Singer dropped prone, waiting for the explosion that seemed to come from a different valley.

"Fuck."

He looked up at the canopy, imagining where Trip had gone, staring for a long time. Trip had known somehow. Now he wished he'd taken the photos and letters.

"How were they?"

"Ghost's dead. That fucker left me hung out down there. When I got out and atop the hill I found him sitting with his back to a tree, his rifle on his lap. He grinned when he saw me as if it had been a fucking joke. The joke was—"

"Trip? What about him?"

"Okay, I guess. Medic was with him. Had a bandage on his thigh."

Singer laid his face down into the leaf litter. Christ, his head was pounding. He removed his helmet and touched his fingers to his head, then examined them again.

"The Shake and Bake says we're going back."

"Where?" Singer asked, knowing the answer.

"Down there, soon as this is over."

"They'll put a different platoon on point. We had our time."

"I don't think I can do that again."

"Fuck, you and me both."

They lay there, Singer waiting for the barrage that would come once the artillery was adjusted on target, hoping when it came it would go on forever.

"You hear that?" Singer asked.

California looked at him as if puzzled, or straining to listen. "Nothing."

"That's what I mean. How many rounds you count?"

"Maybe five."

"Five exactly," Singer said. "Now nothing. No jets, no gunships, and five lousy fucking rounds. What a fucked-up operation."

"There's got to be more," California said, looking around as if he'd lost something.

"Don't count on it. They sent us out here and now forgot us."

Singer checked his bandolier and ammo pouches, counting and shifting his loaded magazines to his right side. He was okay, but he'd have to be careful. He knew how fast he could burn up his ammo.

"Where's the rest of the squad?" Singer asked.

"Shake and Bake is on our right with the guy who came in with me. That's all of us."

Singer thought for a minute trying to count, recalling the names. Could the squad be just four guys, three of them new? "Who else got hit?"

"Don't know. I didn't see anyone else." California rolled over and sat up. "Maybe they'll pull out."

"Who?"

"The gooks."

"You see that base camp yesterday? This is home. They aren't going anywhere. Even if they wanted to leave, they're trapped as much as we are. We'll have to dig these fuckers out one bunker at a time. Doesn't look like we're going to get any help doing it, either."

"I can't do it again."

"What choice do we have? At least we'll be in the back this time."

Singer didn't want to think about it anymore. The talking made his headache worse so he sat there, letting the silence tick by.

When the Shake and Bake came over with the New Guy at his side, Singer and California stood up.

"Fourth has the point again—" the Shake and Bake said.

"You're fucking kidding," Singer said.

"We'll be last squad in the platoon," the Shake and Bake said.

Singer and California looked at each other, Singer feeling as though he'd just survived another long crawl under enemy fire. He imagined California felt the same.

Second squad had barely started out when Sergeant Milner came running up.

"Hold up, hold up."

The men of second squad stopped and looked back with what might have been relief. Sergeant Milner rushed up to Singer and California, but directed his words at the Shake and Bake.

"The CO wants the same men on point. He wants to go back to where you got hit."

The shrill voice grated on Singer's brain. "That's bullshit," Singer said. California went pale.

The Shake and Bake shuffled his feet but said nothing.

"You're on point," Sergeant Milner said, looking at California. "Singer's on slack. The CO wants you to go in the same way."

"Okay, Sarge," the Shake and Bake said in a weak voice.

"That's fucking nuts," Singer said. "Let's go in a different way, come in from a flank. They'll be waiting for us if we go back in the same way. We're as good as dead already."

"The CO wants to count bodies. Get going," Sergeant Milner said.

"What bodies? From a couple artillery rounds? The CO is—"

"That's enough, soldier! Now move out," Sergeant Milner said.

California started off down the slope, but then stopped and looked back at Singer as though wondering if he was coming or not. Sergeant Milner stood there scowling, as if trying to look tough, but looking mostly comical with his pudgy cheeks and double chin and remarkably clean fatigues. Singer wondered how such ineffectual men became sergeants. Trip should have killed the fucker and the CO, too. Put an end to that annoying voice and the stupidity. The seconds drew out. Sergeant Milner, surprisingly, held his ground. Singer fingered his trigger. The man was slow and would be easy to kill. Sergeant Milner would never see it coming, then he'd go for the CO. What would happen then? Where the hell was Top?

"We got it," the Shake and Bake said, moving between Singer and Sergeant Milner. He turned to Singer. "I'll take slack. You can follow me."

"No, I got it," Singer said. "The CO wants to see bodies, we'll show him fucking bodies, even if they're our own."

Singer stomped off toward California, who waited until Singer was nearly next to him before turning and starting forward in uneven, shuffling steps. Together they edged back toward the ground where they'd been hit just a short time ago. California stopped repeatedly, as if resting, and kept turning and looking back at Singer and then beyond him at the men who followed before taking a few more steps..

Singer watched California measuring out his remaining life in the small steps and felt his own slipping away. He looked ahead to the next tree and picked his spot to stop, moving from one piece of cover to the next, determined not to be pinned down on open ground again. This time he would have a tree for cover or to die beside.

At one point he looked behind him to see the Shake and Bake not far away and the New Guy following him. Sergeant Milner was nowhere to be seen. The Cherry Lieutenant was missing, as well. He cursed them all, especially the CO who had lost all reason in his attempt to restore his honor. His and California's deaths would do nothing toward that end.

What would it mean, and who would even know where they died? This was just one more obscure battle in another obscure place that only the survivors would remember. He was certain now he would not be one of those.

He edged away from a small tree and inched up to the next. Ahead, he watched California take a few tentative steps, moving even slower than before. They were getting close. Even without seeing them, he knew the enemy was there. Any moment, the end would come. He tried to make himself smaller beside the tree. In a moment he would have to move again.

California crept three steps and stopped. Singer followed, sliding up to the next piece of cover, little more than a sapling, but something, anyway. His breaths were quick and shallow. His arms were leaden, as if his rifle had taken on more weight. He flexed his aching fingers as he studied the terrain. Even moving carefully, there was no chance to prevent his death.

When he saw it, he knew exactly where they were. The big tree with the sprawling roots where the New Guy had nearly killed him and the slope that he had crawled up under fire were just ahead. A pain spread from the hollow of his gut and settled in his chest with such a force that he nearly stumbled to his knees. He sucked in a breath of putrid air, though his lungs resisted. And still his legs felt weak.

He saw California freeze and was certain he recognized the place as well and saw their deaths just down the slope. California looked over his shoulder, his face holding some question. His eyes begged some answer before slipping to a vacant gaze. Singer felt the heavy silence.

They stood there so long Singer wasn't sure California would go any farther, until he saw him take a small step and he felt himself forced to move again. At the big tree Singer stopped and ran his left hand across its coarse bark. To stay there would bring a shame more painful than any death. He stepped away from the tree slowly, pausing beside it, looking down at the open slope and California, who stood naked and exposed, barely moving his feet. They were in their last moments.

When he escaped crawling up this slope he never thought he'd have to brave it again. It was madness to come back this same way. Now he would die going down it rather than up. Trip was luckier than he knew. Matching California's halting steps, Singer inched on, waiting for the world to explode and life to end.

Maybe they could save themselves if they just threw themselves to the ground and fired blindly. At least it would end this painful waiting. But if he couldn't coordinate such a move with everyone, those who weren't in on it or were too slow would likely die. Even if he survived, he'd only be forced to rise and go forward or to crawl out again under fire. What was the use?

At the bottom of the slope he stood on the ground where he lay before certain of his death. On his left was the tree that had been so close, yet beyond his reach while under fire. He shifted toward it in disbelief that he'd made it this far. A few meters on was the thick brush from where the enemy had fired. The area was undisturbed. There were no bodies and no sign of artillery impacts. Everything looked as when he'd first found it, but now it held the memory of gunfire and Trip's screams. A long-tailed lizard scurried across leaves and disappeared, its movement noisy in the silence. Was it possible that the NVA pulled out?

When California glanced around, Singer could see his reluctance to go further. Singer had the same thought: this was far enough. It was near where California had turned sharply left on their first incursion and perhaps he was debating that as he sidestepped toward a thin tree that offered little more than the illusion of protection.

"What the hell is going on? What's taking so long?"

The screaming tore through the quiet. Singer spun around as if shot, shocked by the volume and suddenness of the voice behind him up the slope he just descended so carefully.

"Goddamn it, I expect to move!"

In disbelief, Singer watched Lieutenant Creely come pounding down the slope with his RTO and a handful of men in tow. The men seemed reluctant followers, making little effort to keep up. Even the CO's RTO trailed some distance back. Still far up the slope but closing ground, the CO continued screaming.

"If you men can't handle the point, I'll put someone else there who can!"

"Fuck," Singer said, reaching out with his left hand to touch the tree beside him. He slid closer to it. If California was smart, he was doing the same. The NVA were close. Probably watching, as confused as he was.

"Goddamn it, I won't allow this!"

The CO charged toward the point. No one spoke or moved to stop him. The CO's RTO stopped on the hillside to the left and above the Shake and Bake. The men behind him held up, too. The CO advanced alone, never breaking stride. Singer glanced at the jungle beyond the point. California gave a helpless look and took a step back.

"I want to see the bodies, goddamn it! What's the fucking hold-up?"

The CO stormed passed Singer and marched directly up to California. The cords of his neck were protruding and taunt and his cheeks inflamed. His eyes were wild and unblinking. His right hand was balled in a fist and he gripped his M16 tightly in his left hand, swinging it haphazardly as he moved.

Singer melted against the tree and switched off the safety on his rifle. The world was imploding. They were being led by a man who had fallen over the edge and was no longer operating in the real world. *God save us*, he started to think, and then abandoned the thought, having forsaken any belief in God weeks ago.

Up the side slope on his right rear he saw where the RTO and the few men who had followed the CO had taken cover, small, pale faces peering down like spectators in bleacher seats at a sporting event. They clung to the cover on the hillside. They showed no interest in coming any closer or being anywhere near the CO or the point. The CO pressed his face in close to California's.

"What the fuck is the hold-up here?"

California looked around and shuffled back a step. But Lieutenant Creely shifted forward, glaring. His temple throbbed and his checks grew even redder.

Singer, just a few feet away, said nothing. If the enemy wasn't already there, they were closing in on Lieutenant Creely's yelling. He could think of nothing to stop the cascade of events.

"We'll never find bodies the way you're moving! Why aren't you moving faster?"

"Sir," California stammered in a hushed voice. "We've got enemy in front of us."

"I know, damn it! I want to find the bodies! I'll show you how to walk point. Follow me."

Lieutenant Creely turned away from California and brought his rifle up and gripped it in both hands and stepped out, all in one quick motion. His RTO, whose duty it was to be at the lieutenant's side, made no move to give up the safety of his hillside position.

When California gave him a bewildered look, Singer shook his head, so slightly that no one but California would have seen it. He wondered if fear was visible in his face, as it was in California's.

"Follow me," Lieutenant Creely had ordered, but Singer wasn't about to follow some crazy lieutenant who was bent on getting them all killed. All the stories about Lieutenant Creely on May fifth were suddenly believable.

Singer watched frozen in horror as Lieutenant Creely rushed forward with complete disregard to his surroundings, obsessed with some fantasy of discovering enemy bodies and winning back his honor. The impossibility of such redemption was perhaps the source of his craziness. If Lieutenant Creely didn't stop right now, the first body they'd report would be his.

No one else moved. No one called out or made any attempt to stop Lieutenant Creely. Everyone in the company stayed silent and frozen, perhaps, like Singer, in shock at what they were seeing.

Lieutenant Creely charged blindly forward, bulling through vegetation. Five feet. Ten.

The question of whether he would have to follow or not never came to Singer's mind, though it might have if Lieutenant Creely had made more ground. But the CO's mad rush was quickly ended.

A burst of AK-47 fire exploded from just in front of the lieutenant.

Lieutenant Creely fell forward, emitting a low, animal-like moan. His body hung there held up by the vegetation, or more likely, the structure beneath it. The last explosions of the AK were muffled, as though the rifle was held against Lieutenant Creely's body. Singer thought he saw Lieutenant Creely's body bounce, but then it was still, hanging there halfway between standing and kneeling. After the first moan, Lieutenant Creely made no other sound.

Singer fired, avoiding the direction where the lieutenant's body hung, though the enemy was firing from there. More Americans and NVA joined in until the gunfire became deafening, even more intense than earlier. Singer could feel as much as hear rounds impacting against the tree and was relieved not to have been caught in the open this time. It was in a pause in the firing that he realized that except for the CO, he was alone out front again. California was gone. He probably hightailed it in the moment Lieutenant Creely was shot, as Singer never heard him fire or saw him after that. Maybe he'd learned a thing or two from Ghost.

Singer peered around the base of the tree. Lieutenant Creely hung there unmoving about fifteen paces away. Under this intensity of fire it might as well have been a mile. Back behind the tree, Singer looked around, sizing up the situation. The Shake and Bake was up the slope closer than before with the rest of fourth platoon strung out behind him, rifles and parts of faces barely visible. To his right, higher up on the side slope, were Lieutenant Creely's RTO and the other men the lieutenant had dragged forward. They looked jumpy and ready to bolt. Some were turned, looking back up the slope as if measuring their escape. None of them were really engaged in the firefight.

No way was he being left down here alone again. What were the chances he could crawl out of here under fire a second time? He pushed up against the tree, trying to hide his entire body, then leaned out, peering with one eye across his weapon, puzzling over the position of the lieutenant's body and the sanctuary it gave the enemy. He held his fire, conserving his ammo.

"Hey, you behind the tree."

Singer looked up at the side slope.

"Go get the lieutenant," the RTO ordered, clearly speaking to Singer. No one else was anywhere near the lieutenant.

The RTO was acting as if he was in charge, but he was just the lieutenant's radio man. He wasn't an officer or even an NCO. He had the same rank as Singer, though Singer figured he had less time in grade, which meant Singer outranked him and thus between the two he would technically be the one in charge. But it wasn't just the two of them. If someone was to give orders, it should have been the Shake and Bake behind Singer, Sergeant Milner, the fourth platoon's Cherry Lieutenant, or Top, somewhere farther up the hill. But no one with rank came forward or spoke up.

"Go get the lieutenant!"

"He's dead," Singer said.

"He's alive. Go get him."

"Christ, he took a full clip in the chest. Let's get some men down here and push through these guys."

Singer knew that was what they should do. They should flank and maneuver on the NVA and put some pressure on them, and drive them back or kill them, not have one guy go forward and die trying to recover a body, especially a body of someone who died so stupidly. One stupid death didn't require another. It was all crazy. Here he was, a private first class, directing strategy. The RTO should be on the radio getting a platoon leader down here with some men instead of yelling at Singer to get the dead CO. Where were the leaders, the officers, the NCOs? The situation was being left to Singer and Lieutenant Creely's RTO to resolve. Everyone else seemed like shocked observers of a horrible accident, unable to move or speak.

"I'm telling you, go get him! You're in trouble if you don't get him now!"

"We'll get him when we push through them," Singer said. "Do your job. Get on the radio and get some help down here."

"Fuck you! You're screwed when we get out of here. I promise you that."

The Shake and Bake was quiet through it all. Singer saw him slip behind a tree. Who would want to draw attention to themselves from the RTO or the NVA?

Fuck the RTO. Pinned down again, alone on the point, Singer had much bigger problems than a pissed-off radio operator. He might be screwed, but he was still alive. There was a difference between bravery and stupidity and right now the distinction seemed very clear. He hugged the tree, watching his back now as well his front.

Up on the hillside the RTO glared at him, but hadn't pointed his rifle. If he did, Singer was ready and knew what he had to do. The men near the RTO seemed to shrink back, perhaps fearful the RTO might single them out next.

Lieutenant Creely's body hung there in the same position it had fallen. Everyone lay as still and silent as the dead lieutenant with the seconds ticking by and the tension building. Even the NVA seemed willing to wait, secure in their bunkers with the bait of a dead American to lure the others toward the same end.

The standoff broke when a blur of movement hurled downhill past Singer and enemy machine gun and AK fire sucked away the air. The onslaught surprised Singer and he ducked down before quickly recovering and returning fire. He fired in a measured fashion, conscious of Lieutenant Creely's body and the running man, his shots swallowed by the roar of enemy fire.

When the figure crashed at the base of the brush structure that held the lieutenant's body, Singer recognized the profile of the company medic whom he'd seen walking with the CP group, but didn't know. Doc lay there next to the lieutenant's feet, his chest heaving.

What would Doc do now? Up against the base of what had to be a bunker, the medic was momentarily sheltered from enemy gunfire, but the NVA had to know he was there and would eventually try to return to the Americans' positions. They seemed to be waiting. How could he possibly make it back with the lieutenant's body? Doc looked trapped. Singer watched, nearly forgetting to fire.

Finally Doc reached up and grabbed hold of the lieutenant's web gear in what looked to be an effort to pull the lieutenant to the ground. Before he could secure his grip, a hand flashed from the vegetation just above him. A grenade dropped toward Doc. Singer watched it fall and waited for the explosion, certain Doc was a dead man. But Doc rolled hard away from the bunker, twisting over twice and curling into a ball. The grenade exploded, sending up a small plume of smoke and dirt, Lieutenant Creely's body absorbing part of the blast. Before the concussion had settled or the smoke cleared, Doc was scrambling back next to the lieutenant.

Without help, Doc wouldn't make it. To this point Singer's fire was ineffective. He had to do more. If he was careful, he could fire on the bunker without hitting Lieutenant Creely. Even though he believed the lieutenant had died in the first enemy volley, he didn't want to hit his body. Singer shifted his fire cautiously toward the bunker, trying to measure his shots and control his breaths, which was proving difficult to manage. Maybe if he was accurate with his fire he could keep the NVA off Doc.

Again Doc reached up from the base of the bunker to grab the lieutenant. Again the hand came out with a grenade. Singer fired at the hand, but it released the grenade before disappearing. The grenade fell toward Doc's chest, turning over once. Doc, instead of rolling, jumped up, turning to run. His head went back when the round struck him in the face. His legs folded and his body collapsed just two feet from the lieutenant's.

Singer stopped firing too late to take back the round. He lifted his face slowly from his rifle. The firing around him continued unabated, but he couldn't hear it. The world had gone silent. Doc didn't move, and though his face was hidden, Singer could still see his last look of surprise. It was the same look he had seen on the face of the NVA in the crater when the round had struck him. Neither had expected to die.

He turned his rifle on its side and studied its lines, the dull blackness of the metal and hard smooth plastic of the stock. It couldn't have been a round from his M16. It was the NVA. They had killed Rhymes, Stick, Red, Doc Odum, Sergeant Edwards, and before that Sergeant Prascanni, and now Lieutenant Creely and the medic. They were the killers.

He pulled the magazine from his rifle and dropped it beside him, though it still held rounds. He pulled a new magazine out of his ammo pouch and pushed it home until it clicked, and then he heard the heavy beat of the NVA machine gun, the AKs, and the Americans' M16s. It was the NVA. They were the killers. They were the killers. He fired at the bunker, not caring anymore about being careful, only caring about the steady recoil of his rifle that would end it all.

The firing waned, both sides pausing as if the fighters were exhausted and needed to catch their breath. Singer pulled inside the tree and surveyed his situation. On the side slope, the RTO lay holding the radio handset away from his face like it were a dangerous object, and the others who had come forward with Lieutenant Creely cast repeated glances at him as if waiting for some release. Further up the slope the blurred images of others hunkered down. He saw the prospect of another long, lonely crawl to safety and didn't like his odds.

The air was thick and charged with tension that seemed ready to ignite. The skin on Singer's arms prickled, and he found it difficult to swallow. It felt as if all of them were hanging by a thin thread somewhere between life and death, each of them waiting for the thread to break and send them falling into some dark abyss. A collective fear hung in the air, fed by the intensity of the NVA fire, Lieutenant Creely's bizarre behavior and death, and the failure of any leader to take charge. It was like a gas-filled room just waiting for the spark. Singer knew it was coming.

The radio squawked.

Singer turned and looked up at the hillside. The RTO was lifting the handset toward his ear, though there was no need. The sound carried through the charged air like voices across a still lake.

"Pull out!" the voice from the handset said.

The room ignited. The thread broke.

The RTO and the men with him on the side slope rose as one, turned, and ran. The NVA fired. AK and machine gun fire scoured the hillside.

"No!" Singer screamed. But none of them stopped, and he watched the puffs of dirt from the machine-gun impacts chase up the hill until they caught the RTO and holes exploded in his legs and up his back, smashing the radio. The RTO crumpled. Still the other men ran, and the enemy fire chased them.

Singer had seen enough. He had envisioned an orderly withdrawal, with some men firing as others moved, as he'd practiced with Rhymes and Bear on exercise in Florida. And which Rhymes had expounded on later back at Fort Bragg in a scholarly kind of dissertation. Fire and maneuver. It worked the same in advance or withdrawal. He would have stayed and put out covering fire and waited for his turn, but all that changed when the simmering fear became an undisciplined retreat. He wasn't about to be left down here alone again. While the enemy was concentrating on the men fleeing up the side slope, he made his own escape.

After he crawled away from the most intense fire he scrambled back and around on a route similar to that which California might have taken when they were first trapped. He called out as he climbed toward the American positions and didn't stop until he was well inside their perimeter. Then he just lay there oblivious to the sporadic firing below him, thinking of nothing.

"What happened down there?" Top asked.

Singer sat up and looked at Top's deep-set eyes, prominent nose, and strong cheekbones. A warrior's face. Where had Top been?

"The CO came down screaming, took the point, and the NVA shot him point blank. He fell on their bunker."

Top shook his head and something passed across his face. Disgust?

"He was dead before he hit the ground. Doc tried to get him, but he's dead, too."

"Where's his RTO?"

"Dead. Machine gun got him as he ran up the hill."

"You sure?"

"He was hit maybe ten times. No way he's alive."

"Jesus," Top said. "The radio?"

"NVA probably have it already. It was fucked-up, Top. We needed some firepower down there."

"Okay, hook back up with your squad."

"It was fucked-up, Top."

"Yeah. You did what you could."

"They're in bunkers. You can't even see them. We need some heavy firepower."

"I know." Top moved off in a low crouch.

The bodies lay below them. The NVA would be waiting. Singer counted the few full magazines he had remaining, knowing what would come. But they didn't go back down. Instead they turned and left. Leaving the base camp and its bunkers. Leaving the bodies of Lieutenant Creely, the RTO, and the medic. Singer felt he was leaving something more behind.

They made plodding steps, feet dragging, heads down. Singer felt the exhaustion and despair coming off the men around him mingling with his own. It was different than the tension that charged the air after Lieutenant Creely and Doc were killed, when fear was palpable. This was the residue of disaster. Of defeat. They were trailing away like a line of refugees fleeing death.

The images of the men they were abandoning to the enemy were stuck in Singer's mind even as they moved farther from them: Lieutenant Creely carelessly taking the point, the sound of the AK so close, and the guttural moan as he collapsed; Doc unexpectedly standing and the look on his face when the round stuck him; the RTO fleeing uphill, machine gun rounds chasing him and tearing holes in his back; the RTO, along with his threats, crumbling into the earth. All of it had saved him.

Even moving back through the jungle, putting one foot in front of the other, he didn't feel he was leaving. He saw himself as one of the men left behind. One of the bodies. He was a dead man three times over. Surviving made no sense and he couldn't process it. If Lieutenant Creely hadn't so bizarrely taken the point, it would have certainly been his and California's bodies the company was leaving with the NVA. Why the NVA had not killed them all as Lieutenant Creely stood before California chewing him out for moving too slowly, he couldn't understand. That he was alive made no sense at all.

Now they were walking away. His shoulders slumped under some new weight. Abandoning men, even dead men, wasn't right. Yet what effort had he made besides calling for more men and firepower that never came? He could have done more. Someone had ordered them to pull out, but he had refused the same order earlier when California was pinned down in front of him. He believed in the promise that they would never leave anyone behind. Now that promise was broken. He was leaving more than just the bodies of men he watched die. There were things within himself he was abandoning.

The terrain rose and he felt the sharp angle of his feet and his body leaning into the hill and the weight of it pushing down on him, trying to force him back. He edged along with little awareness of the men around him except for the helmeted form in front of him that he followed mechanically. Their retreat could be little more than a temporary withdrawal to reorganize before going back in. Nothing was over yet. Soon they would halt, regroup and turn and make another attempt to somehow breech the bunker line of the camp, or at least recover the bodies. There would be no end. Just a deadly back and forth with each direction frightening and holding its own dangers.

He wasn't sure anymore whether they were retreating or attacking. He thought they had stopped once or twice. He could recall gunfire, but his mind had wandered or he had dozed off and now everything was distorted, like he was hearing and seeing it across the heat warp of a desert. It was like he was watching a movie in which he had a part. The movie was blurred and hard to follow. There was more gunfire, but it was far off, and he could lie there and listen to it knowing it didn't concern him. Then he was walking again and it was nearly dark and his left arm was weighted down by the body he was helping to carry.

Fuck-you lizards called from across the valley as Singer and the rest of the three-platoon patrol struggled up the hill in the fading light. "Fuck you-uuu. Fuck youuuu. Fuck youuuu." The voices were shrill and taunting. Singer was sure it was the NVA mimicking the lizard's call, mocking them, saying this was their valley and they weren't leaving, and the Americans would never be able to make them leave.

At the top of the hill, Singer tried to count, to organize his memories, but everything was confused. How many times they had gone back in today, he wasn't sure. Nor was he sure how many more casualties they'd taken. How he had survived and who might have died he didn't know. He recalled moving across the same ground wearing down their own trails and knew they had never gotten as close to Lieutenant Creely, the medic, or RTO as he had been when they'd died. He recalled the firing, but wasn't sure if he was confusing events from one assault with another. If they killed any of the NVA they must have been quickly replaced, as their firing never diminished.

He remembered the quiet as they waited and his bitterness when there were no whistling rounds overhead or explosions of artillery. No jets. No gunships. Nothing. Just the sickening stillness and the knowledge they would attack again.

It seemed like days ago that Trip had been hit and screaming for him not to fire or come near him, but he was sure they had shared a foxhole last night. Singer looked over as if to confirm this, almost expecting to see Trip, uncertain if he had only dreamed he'd been hit and screaming. But it was California who sat there ashen and hollow-cheeked, looking years older, intently pushing rounds into a magazine, his rifle near his hands. Trip was gone. They were all gone now. Trip. He was probably already lying on clean-pressed sheets in an air-conditioned post-op ward, or perhaps on a medical flight to a hospital in Japan. He was most likely already giving the nurses a hard time, collecting names and numbers and making promises to visit. He made it out the hard way, but he made it.

Singer gazed down into the darkness and had to put his hand out on the ground to steady himself, feeling as if he might tumble into the void. California was still there, head down, the magazine he fed nearly lost in the blackness. The repetitive click of new rounds being pushed home. For a moment Singer wasn't sure where he was, which hill, which valley. Then he remembered the A Shau, the climb, the weight of the body he helped drag up the hill and digging a fighting hole. He remembered it all.

They were back on the same hill they had left at first light so long ago, reunited with second platoon and their rucks. The second platoon held the hilltop unchallenged throughout the day, able to hear the fighting not far away that marked each assault. A few of them would have heard the radio traffic, but most would have had to wonder at what was happening and who was dying and whether they would be called to help or if they would come under attack where they were.

Reunited, the men of the Charlie Company tightened the perimeter, digging new holes. There were fewer of them tonight. Singer listened as the medevac and resupply choppers came and went. They came in high and wide, guns working hard as they broke toward the hill, pausing only a moment and then racing away with their loads of men who would not have to face another day of assaults against the enemy base camp. Some of whom would never have to face anything again.

He'd recovered his ruck and opened a can of Cs, feeling an emptiness which might have been hunger, but his stomach protested at the first food of the day and he fought to keep from retching. He forced down a few more spoonfuls before abandoning the activity, thinking it not worth the effort. After burying the half-full can, he reloaded his empty magazines with the ammo that came in on the resupply. Then he went through each magazine, testing it for tension that would push the next round up, feeding the bolt that would slam the round into the chamber ready to fire. Finally he set out his grenades at the edge of the hole. He felt calmer and more focused when he finished these things, more able to face the night and the prospects of tomorrow.

He ran his hand over the rough stubble on his face. Even in the darkness, he saw the caked blood on his hands. He scratched at it, uncertain when he came by it or whose it might be. With water from a nearly empty canteen he washed his hands, then wiped them on his pants, leaving dark stains. Beside him, California sat bent over his rifle as if trying to memorize its parts, a pile of newly filled magazines beside him.

"I'll take first watch," Singer said. "Get some sleep."

California didn't answer, continuing to stare at his rifle.

Across the valley, lights moved on an invisible mountain as if suspended in space. Singer watched the lights traveling up and down, coming together and separating, with more fascination than fear. It was amazing that the NVA would move about so brazenly with lights. But then, it was their valley. Singer waited for the tracers to descend from the sky or the flash of explosions from an artillery barrage that would extinguish the lights, but the skies stayed quiet and the lights went unchallenged. They were forgotten men.

Singer gathered his poncho liner up over his shoulders against a sudden chill and pulled his M16 tight to his body.

A lizard called, "Fuck youuu."

20

June 7, 1968
A Shau Valley, Vietnam

At the sound of the rotors, Singer raised his head, hoping to see the bird, but he saw only a dark tangle of branches and leaves above him that obscured the sky. A fog clouded his brain, as if he'd suddenly been awoken from a deep sleep. He ducked at the heavy crack of rapid gunfire despite the distance and heard the rotors whine in protest, then fade into an uneasy silence. He remembered he was in the A Shau.

With his M16 in his right hand, he slowly turned his head. A few paces away, another GI sat hunched over, his head down, so Singer couldn't see his face, but he could see the thin curl of cigarette smoke just above his head. Were they just taking a break or encamped? He rubbed his hand across his face and then pushed his thumb and forefinger against his eyes. He couldn't remember what he had been doing before the sound of the helicopter or how long he might have been asleep.

He remembered the lights. When had he watched them? Lights moving like fallen stars struggling to regain their positions in the sky, climbing slowly up and falling back, then rising again. A silent, eerie ballet. He was sure he hadn't dreamed it, but the memory ended with the lights still dancing.

There were other disjointed memories. Movement across nearly level ground and then on slopes so steep he had fought to keep from falling. Tangles of vines, impenetrable thickets of bamboo they moved around and tree trunks so large two men couldn't encircle them with their arms. And trails they encountered and sometimes traveled on not knowing where they led. At times he crawled, he remembered, uncertain of what direction he was going, or whether he was moving away from the enemy or toward them. In the end it hadn't mattered as the enemy was everywhere, always there cutting them off. He shuddered at the recollection.

He looked over to see if the hunched figure was there, unsure if he had imagined him. The man was farther away or the light had changed. He thought to call out to him, but then thought better of it.

Time. Think. He wasn't sure what day it was or whether the dim light was dusk or dawn. At some point he had started tracking time only by the presence or absence of gunfire. He was floating, adrift in some nightmare. He tried to grab onto something. If he could remember how he came to this moment, maybe he could find his way out. But there were only the pieces of memories that he couldn't connect and the bone-numbing fatigue, an exhaustion that came from the depths and filled his being so that it was a great effort to move or even think. He wasn't sure he could get up again when they had to move. All he wanted was to sleep and then wake up somewhere where the sun was shining and where there was no gunfire and no smell of death. He could smell it now emanating from the jungle, coming off his clothes, and carried on the air from the dead and dying who must lay somewhere nearby.

How long had he been here? He'd heard someone say it was ten days, but that didn't make sense. How could it be ten days already? He could remember riding helicopters into the A Shau and Trip still being there and finding the base camp, and then Trip was gone and the CO was dead. The CO's RTO and Doc, too. He remembered that. But he couldn't remember how many days it had been since then, though they still hadn't retrieved their bodies. At least, he didn't remember retrieving them. They tried, but each time the NVA drove them back. He couldn't remember how many times they went back down or if they'd ever even gotten close. He didn't think they had.

Ten days? Maybe. There had been other deaths and more bodies. He'd carried some. Drained by the weight of them, trying not to look or think, secretly happy it wasn't him. He'd seen others lying there wrapped in ponchos, boots hanging out, a face only half covered, waiting for an evac helicopter that couldn't get in. He'd been there when some of them had died, but they'd had no names, or none he could recall, and the places had all looked the same, so he was confused about where things happened and about how near they'd been to reaching the ground where Lieutenant Creely and the others lay. So many more bodies. It could have been ten days already.

He struggled to bring some order to the memories, but there were so many loose pieces that just didn't fit and it was difficult to order them. They were moving now. When had they moved out? He stumbled downslope, grabbing a tree to slow his decent, trying to remember if he'd been told where they were going and why. Focus. It bothered him that he didn't know things that had just happened. There were so many things he couldn't remember, like who he was before he came to this place and did these things. He wasn't sure who he was anymore. He thought he might be losing his mind.

There were recollections of gunfire and explosions, and the sound of choppers that he couldn't see, and the crawling to get closer or to escape, and the impact of rounds so close he couldn't believe he wasn't hit. How was he still alive? Short, intense flurries of gunfire came and went. Other gunfire came in unrelenting storms that lasted forever. There were memories of times when he fired frantically trying to survive, the sound of his firing lost in the roar, so that afterwards he wasn't even sure he had fired except for the pile of shell casings and empty magazines. One battle or many? The same day or different days? It was a puzzle he couldn't assemble.

There was the smell of earth and the minute detail of the ground where he lay. The leaf with the slightly curled tip and the network of veins that once brought life to the leaf, the rust-colored marks on another that looked like blood, and the stone so smooth as if it had been tumbled in a stream, but there was no stream. When had he seen these things? A dream? Maybe he was drifting in some afterlife.

Take another step. Then another. He tried to focus on the movement and the jungle, but the memories raced through his head unchecked as if they were the present. There were recollections of explosions of grenades and the screams of wounded and the *whoosh* of LAWs and the close-quarter detonations and the absence of air that made it difficult to breathe. Still the NVA fired from their bunkers. Always there. Always waiting. Lieutenant Creely, his RTO, and Doc lay waiting, too, rotting in the heat, unconcerned at how long the battle might last or who else would die. Singer sucked in air, open-mouthed, feeling he couldn't breathe. Breathe. He had to breathe or he would die. Maybe he would die anyway. Maybe he was already dead.

The ground was level now and he followed the man in front of him, keeping the distance close. For a moment he thought it was Trip and he was going to ask him how many days they'd been here. Trip was short, he would be carefully counting each day. He would know. He had nearly called out when he heard Trip's screams, pleading, but distant, and he remembered Trip was gone. It might be the man he'd seen sitting near him hunched over a cigarette. Had that been today? California? Was he still alive? He slowed up and let the distance increase.

He remembered slipping through the cloud of red, yellow, green, and purple smoke and the burning in his throat and nostrils and the fear that he still could be seen. Sliding forward, trying not to lose the man in front of him, and instead losing the earth and all sense of up or down. Still, even in the haze, the NVA bullets found them. Disembodied screams and men running into each other. The colors swirled and pulsed and threatened to swallow them all. He didn't know how he or the others escaped. When he closed his eyes, he still found himself trapped in the multicolored smoke and felt the panic rising in his throat.

He clutched his rifle, trying to focus on where he was and his movement, but still the images rushed through his mind. Yesterday or last week? He wasn't sure, but he was sure it was here in the A Shau that he saw the man propped up against a tree half lying, half sitting, his head hanging on his chest as if he was asleep. His face was hidden, his helmet off, his brown hair wet and matted. His web gear was unbuckled and laying open. His shirt was gone, his chest deathly white, wrapped in dressings, another dressing on his thigh where his pants had been cut open to his crotch. Smears of dull red marked his body. Two men crouched beside him, one touching his face as though trying to lift his head.

"Do something," the man said. "He's dying."

"There's nothing I can do." The other man, a medic, it seemed, turned his head, and Singer could see the strain and weariness. "Thirteen hits." The medic shook his head. "How can he be alive?" His body slumped and his head sagged.

Singer stopped and stared sharing the medic's exhaustion and disbelief.

"I've used all my dressings. Nothing I can do." The medic's voice trailed off so that Singer could barely hear him.

The medic pulled a cigarette out of a pack that he returned to his fatigue jacket pocket. The flash of a flame from a lighter and then the acrid, sweet smell of grass. It mingled with the stench of death so that it was compelling and repulsive at the same time. Singer could smell it even after he was well beyond the scene. He was sure he hadn't dreamed it. He remembered wanting to sit down next to the dying man and share the joint, but instead he moved on, certain he was moving toward his own death. They were all dying. Some just faster than others.

The slope had changed, but he wasn't sure when. He was climbing now, planting his foot. The calf of his rear leg tightened, and he pulled until he dragged it ahead. Each step took a great effort, and he paused to catch his breath between each step, as if he were climbing at some great altitude where the air was thin. He carried his rifle one-handed, freeing his other hand to grab onto trees to pull himself up. He was relieved not to be burdened with the weight of a body, as he had been on so many climbs. So many things already weighed him down and made it difficult to move that the weight of a body was nearly impossible to bear. He thought about stopping, just lying down where he was and putting his head down on the ground. Sleep would be immediate and he would escape, even if only for a short time. But he kept moving mindlessly, something in him refusing to quit as though he held the hope if he just kept moving he could eventually walk away from everything. He sucked in air that burned across his throat and took another step.

How many days ago had it been when the burst of gunfire brought the sickening *whap* of the impact of a bullet with soft tissue and bone and the sudden loud exhale, not really a moan or a scream, just a rapid release of air? The memory was there, drifting, unattached to any date or other event. "In the trees," someone had yelled, and then they were all firing wildly into the canopy. A rifle fell out of the trees as if dropped from the sky and he stopped firing to watch it fall. It clattered on impact with the ground. The firing lessened and he heard a soft thud and the crack of breaking branches and finally a body tumbled out of the trees, falling sideways toward the ground, until it was caught suddenly by a rope tied to the left leg and bounced heavily before settling at the end of the rope, five meters above the ground, arms reaching toward the earth. More gunfire and the body danced. Singer remembered laughing at the sight of the man twirling on the end of the rope, but he wasn't sure now why it had been so funny. He caught himself and looked around, wondering if he might have laughed out loud. If he had, no one took notice. The few men he could see were climbing, heads down.

There had been other climbs like this on similar mountains when his legs protested and he sucked air, trying to keep moving, to make it to the hoped-for safety of the top. How many had he climbed? Maybe it was all the same mountain but just different days. Memories raced past like telephone poles along a highway. Pinned down by enemy fire. Near escapes. Torturous climbs with bodies that sagged and bled, resisting being carried. The waiting for medevacs that turned back in the face of heavy enemy fire. The moans and pained calls of the wounded in the night. The promises of resupplies that didn't come. Counting his full magazine. Rationing his food and water. Digging in at night, waiting for a mortar or ground attack. More movement until gunfire erupted and they hugged the ground again. The dim dreariness of the days and the darkness of the nights.

It would never end. He raised his head and tried to see the top where they would end their climb, but all he saw was the back of a man ahead of him and the dense foliage that had become his world. He saw the muzzle flashes so close they were nearly blinding and felt death pass over him, and he fired as he tried to crawl to cover. He pressed his fingers to his eyes to push away the image and the fear that made it difficult to move. That had been just hours ago, but now he wasn't sure. He'd been here so long he wasn't sure of anything anymore. It might have been ten days or it could have already been a month in the A Shau. The repetition of movement, gunfire, and evacuation of wounded and dead in a place without sun where there was only a small difference between night and day had swallowed time. It was lost to him as he was lost to himself.

He recalled times of thirst, when his mouth went dry and his tongue swelled up and started to crack and his insides began to shrivel and he could feel them shrinking and twisting upon themselves and he thought he might die if he didn't get a drink, and he knew he would kill for a glass of water. He had already killed for so much less. He had raced to the stagnant puddle that wasn't deep enough to cover his hand, knelt beside it, pushed the film of scum and bugs aside, lowered his mouth, and sucked with all his remaining strength, tasting the decay and feeling the grit, and he remembered the river and the bodies and Trip drinking and spitting it out, raging about water fouled by death. Still he continued to suck and swallow, getting what moisture he could from the sludge. When he finished drinking, he pushed some of it into his empty canteen, getting as much mud as water, but it was better than letting his insides dry up and crumble to dust.

When had that been? He took out his canteen and swirled it slightly, trying to measure the small amount of water remaining. Maybe there would be a resupply today. He took a mouthful and held it, prepared to spit it out. It was warm, but without grit, and he swallowed it, feeling it sweep down his throat to an empty stomach. A wave of hunger moved through him, and he tried to remember when he'd last eaten. They had been rationed to one meal of Cs per day. If he could remember the meals, he could count the days. It would be something to grab onto to order things. But all he could remember were the leaves beside the trail that he'd grabbed and eaten, chewing and choking them down despite the bitterness, trying to ease his pains of hunger. When had that been? They had made more assaults against the base camp and attempts to reach the bodies and he had been sick for days, or what seemed like days.

It must have been the muddy water or the leaves that had burned and twisted his insides until his bowels gave out. The first time it happened he was in a firefight, the platoon circled up on a small knoll, the firing heavy, but not as heavy as it had been some days. There wasn't much warning or time to consider the options. His stomach cramped and he felt the impending rush move down his bowels. He was up and crawling to the center of the small circle, believing the indignity of shitting his pants was worse than getting shot. Using a tree for cover, he rose to a squat and threw down his pants with no time to spare. His intestines emptied in one long, angry rush, testifying to the battle that raged in his insides. Then the bees were on him, large and swarming, looking like small birds, and he was dragging himself, bare ass, pants at his ankles, across the position oblivious to the gunfire. In that moment he was only aware of the sharp stings on his ass and bare legs and his need to escape. He nearly overran the perimeter. The bees were gone, but he was left with countless painful welts. He got his pants up and rejoined the firefight. No one had notice his ordeal with his bowels and the bees.

On the climb back to the NDP, his intestines let loose without warning and the foul smelling liquid shot down his legs and splashed against his pant cuffs, which were tied around his ankle to slow the advance of leeches up his legs to his crotch. The stench was nauseating and hung with him as he climbed. Waves of weakness passed through him, and then another hot rush down his legs. The smell got worse and he wished he could escape himself somehow. When they set up on the hilltop no one would share a foxhole with him so he dug in alone. His bowels continued to empty without warning throughout the night. In the morning, he woke to the overbearing stench and found his pants plastered to his legs. When he stood, his legs wobbled, and it took a minute to gather the strength to move. He walked through the hours, barely noticing the sudden rush of hot liquid, waiting for the next break, even hoping for a firefight so he might lie down. The stench was constant, like a slit trench he couldn't walk away from. Eventually he started not to notice it. It was the weakness that plagued him and had him focusing all his effort to stay standing and keep moving. After the second night he'd given in and gone looking for some help.

"Damn, you smell like shit," the medic said when Singer found him at the CP. "Stand back a little."

He was the same medic Singer had seen on the trail with the man who had been hit thirteen times. Up close now the doc looked older, his eyes without life.

"I've had it for a few days now," Singer said, making no effort to look at the name tag sewn on the doc's fatigues.

"You probably got an intestinal infection and a fever."

"Shit, tell me something I don't know."

"I can give you some aspirin for the fever," the doc said, leaning over to dig in his kit.

"You got anything for my guts?"

"Nothing. Sorry, I'm out of almost everything. Supposed to get resupplied but haven't yet."

Singer took the aspirin and was just a few steps away from the doc when he felt the familiar streams down his legs and the accompanying weakness. Back on the perimeter, he sat alone in his foxhole and tried to ignore his condition and the smell. He hadn't asked the doc about an evac and the doc hadn't offered. He could still walk and shoot a rifle, so he knew he was staying. When the platoons had swapped positions he'd seen a few bandaged men moving past on the trail and knew even some wounded were being kept for the firepower.

They were stopped again and Singer clung to a tree beside him to hold his place on the hillside. Now he smelled it. The stench was still there, but his guts were quiet and the cramping was gone. He couldn't remember now how long since he was last sick or when he'd last eaten. They must be near the top now. He hoped the peak was unoccupied and they wouldn't have to fight for it. He had enough of fighting. He let go of the tree and pulled at his pants legs, surprised to find that the pants were clean and not stuck to his legs. He couldn't recall changing. They were moving again and he pulled himself up. He paused, then took another step, thinking he could rest at the top. It shouldn't be far now.

Memories of gunfire spurred him up the mountain toward the summit, where they would stop and dig in. Better to fight from defensive positions on the high ground. Still, if the NVA came they would easily overrun the understrength, unsupported, and worn-down company. He didn't think they were coming, though, and comforted himself with that thought. They had their bait and seemed content to wait in their bunkers and kill a few more Americans each day as they came for the bodies. It was going to take more firepower than they had to get the NVA to give up their positions and recover Lieutenant Creely, his RTO, and Doc. He saw the deaths now like it had been this morning, but it was days, if not weeks, ago. With so many memories of other events since then, it had to be weeks ago, but he wasn't sure it even mattered anymore. They were all trapped here in some repeating nightmare they would never escape. Or maybe he was already dead and this was the kind of afterlife soldiers were doomed to. He really was losing his mind.

Singer dragged himself forward, gaining another meter, as disjointed memories continued to float across his mind. He had heard the story about Top, but he wasn't sure who had told him. Whoever told him said he heard it from a guy who saw it play out at the firebase while he waited to return to the field after treatment at the rear aid station. That part was clear, and he remembered smiling when he heard the story. He smiled now recalling it. If his faith in Top had suffered with what had happened the first days in the A Shau, the story restored it.

Top had saved another one of them. The storyteller said it was a second-tour guy who had been in the thick of the May fifth fighting. The man was sent back to the company's firebase with just two weeks to go, still recovering from his May fifth wounds. As Singer heard it, the man still favored his right leg and had trouble with his hearing, yet the executive officer was sending him back out to the embattled company in the A Shau. At least, that had been the XO's plan until Top rode in on a helicopter to expedite the company's resupply. Everyone near the helipad reportedly stopped to watch the heated exchange between Top and the XO, after Top told the short-timer May fifth survivor to turn in his gear and wait out his last few days there. The XO went to stop the man, but Top charged and cut him off.

"This man has more Nam time than you have in the army. On May fifth he held off repeated enemy attacks on his lone position and helped save the company. You should hope to be so brave. If he doesn't stay at the firebase and go home safely without harassment, you'll be doing lone patrols up on the DMZ," Top said. "Don't test me. Better men than you have tried and lost," was the last thing Top said before the XO sulked away.

The short-timer was spared the A Shau battle and assured of going home thanks to Top. That Top had taken on a lieutenant, an XO, to do it was pure Top. It was the Top that Singer knew and admired. Singer imagined Top nose to nose with some Cherry lieutenant who didn't understand Top's reputation or power that went well beyond his rank. That one of the guys, a second-tour vet and survivor of May fifth, had been protected and would make it home was a small victory. But coming at a time when there was so little hope it took on greater meaning. Top was still looking after them.

The best part to the story the man who told it said was when Top ran back to the chopper where two men were placing the last crate of grenades on board. The helicopter began to rev. Top started to climb up, then stepped back down.

"Those clean fatigues?"

The two men who had just finished loading the ammo looked back toward Top.

"Those clean fatigues? Top yelled over the noise of the rotors.

"Yeah, I guess so."

"Take off your pants," Top said, pointing at the slimmer man.

"What?"

"Take off your pants. I have a man who needs them."

"But, Top—"

"You can give me your pants or you can get on this chopper, but either way those pants are going to the field."

Top climbed on to the chopper with the pants in hand, nodded to the crew chief, then looked out and exchanged a thumbs-up sign with the short-timer standing alone watching the chopper depart back to the A Shau.

If Singer wasn't hanging on to a tree, he might have fallen down he was laughing to himself so hard. Singer looked at his pants and couldn't stop the convulsions that shook his body. He had to remember to thank Top again.

Maybe on the same day he'd seen the doc, or maybe a day or two later, Singer vaguely recalled bumping into Top on a hilltop. It occurred to him now that Top must have come looking for him. Not much escaped Top. Top would have known about him being sick, just as he must have heard about him shooting up the base camp on that first day and refusing to stop. Perhaps he had smiled at that. But Top surely also heard that Lieutenant Creely's RTO threatened Singer the day Lieutenant Creely and his RTO were killed. And Doc. Singer replayed those threats over and over, but was still certain he'd done the right thing insisting they bring down more men, more fire-power, and maneuver on the enemy. Even so, he expected there would be repercussions. Someone would be looking for a scapegoat for Lieutenant Creely's death and unrecovered bodies and Singer would be it. Singer figured Top would come talk with him and he had waited for him to come that day and the next, but he never did. Nor did anyone else ever mention it. The issue had died along with Lieutenant Creely's RTO and lay on the hillside. He owed the NVA something for that.

The day he bumped into Top or Top had come to check on him, he'd already been sick for a few days. He felt weak and ragged-out, though he'd grown use to the smell. He was embarrassed to have Top see him sick like that. But he remembered thinking that even Top's stoic demeanor looked like it was cracking a little under the strain of the A Shau, the daily firefights, and the lack of support. For a moment as he studied Top's face, Singer forgot about his own situation.

"How you doing?" Top asked without making any mention of the smell.

"Okay."

"You holding up?"

"Yeah, I'm doing all right, but I could use a clean pair of pants."

"I'll see what I can do," Top said.

Now he had clean pants. Though he couldn't remember who brought them to him, he wouldn't forget the story of the REMF surrendering his pants to Top at the helipad.

With great effort, Singer pulled himself up over a ledge and saw there was no more mountain. He'd made it. He wanted to lie down right there and not go any farther, afraid that if he didn't he would pass out. But someone directed him to a spot on the perimeter and he slumped to the ground, for a time unable to move even to reach for his canteen. He could hear the sounds of entrenching tools striking rocks and the hacking of machetes as men dug in and cut firing lanes. He needed to dig in.

"Help's coming."

"What?" Singer asked, not realizing someone was beside him.

"The 101st," California said. "Shake and Bake says they're sending a battalion."

"I thought you were dead."

"Shit, more alive than you. You smell like you died a week ago."

"How long has it been?"

"Since you've been sick and talking crazy?"

"No, since we've been here."

"Two weeks or so.

"Really?"

"Almost three. You been out of it almost a week. You any better?"

"Yeah, I think so. But I need a shower."

"They're sending help, so maybe we'll get out of here."

"I'll believe it when I see it."

"They got to be sending help. They can't just leave us out here forever."

"Been forever already."

California had nearly finished digging in when Singer started on his own. He worked slowly, clawing at the dirt, working around the roots and rocks trying to get deeper, but in the end he gave in to his exhaustion and settled for a shallow hole.

"Want some help with that?" California asked.

"It's okay for one more night."

"Shit, I been digging your hole all week."

"Bullshit."

"Well, you were pretty sick and I wasn't sharing a hole with you smelling the way you do."

"Day I can't dig my own hole, just shoot me."

"You're dead already, then."

"We're all dead."

"Help's coming. Tomorrow, they say."

"Right."

Singer sat with his feet in the hole he'd dug, his rifle beside him, and ate a can of pressed meat that vaguely resembled chicken. He ate tentatively, worried whether his stomach could handle it and his bowels would hold, eventually finishing it all with no immediate ill effects. In the bottom of his ruck he had a can of pound cake he was saving for when the battle was over and he was away from the A Shau. He almost dug it out just to look at it. One more night. He allowed himself to hope.

That night he slept little, sitting up even on California's watch, listening to the night, praying for the dawn and for the help that was supposed to come, even though he had sworn off prayer. He watched for the lights, but tonight there were none. "The lights. Did you see them too?" Singer asked quietly.

"For a couple nights, a week or so ago." California whispered.

"I thought I maybe dreamt it."

"You were mumbling some weird shit. Had to wake you more than once."

"Ballsy, carrying supplies up and down using fucking lights."

"Eerie."

"They knew."

"Knew what?"

"That we'd do nothing."

"We won't last much longer. They got to be sending help."

"I hope," Singer said, fingering his only remaining grenade again.

Sometimes living without hope was easier.

In the morning Singer waited, expecting the word to saddle up and move out, but there were no orders or information. He sat there with California not knowing what was going on, the minutes dragging by. The first explosion surprised him. Solitary and a klick or so away, about where the base camp would be, he guessed.

"Finally," he said.

Then came more blasts, one after another, pounding the camp. Singer listened, trying to determine how many artillery positions were firing. The sound of the explosions grew, blurring into a single sustained roar that went on for a long time, and he couldn't imagine surviving it. He was angry, even as he wanted to cheer. How many days had they waited for this, going in day after day without support, when it was there all the time? Who was running this fucking war?

When the artillery barrage finally ended, a dramatic silence followed that had Singer wondering if he had lost his hearing.

"Here we go," Singer said, surprised that he could hear his voice.

He opened the bolt on his M16 to see the round seated in the chamber, then he pulled his ruck closer and checked the lashing, but still no word came. Then he heard them. He looked at California and saw that he heard them, too. Cobras came with the first assault and Singer listened to rocket explosions and minigun fire and the successive waves of Hueys. The sound of choppers filled the air in what had to be a multiple-company assault. After letting Charlie Company go it alone for two weeks, the 101st was finally sending in the cavalry.

The small-arms fire started almost before the last Hueys left. Some NVA must have survived and not fled. Singer wasn't surprised. The Cobras came back on repeated runs with more rockets and minigun fire and Singer marveled at the firepower the 101st brought with them, even as he cursed them. The companies from the 101st wouldn't go at it unsupported as the 82nd had. They all paid for Lieutenant Creely's May fifth failures.

The battle built throughout the morning, and at times Singer could distinguish at least two battlefronts. He imagined an attacking force driving the NVA in a running battle toward a blocking force that was cutting down the fleeing NVA. The fight had been Charlie Company's for so long that, to Singer, even worn out and dispirited as he was, it seemed wrong not to be a part of the end, when there was finally a chance to even the score. It was funny how a little hope and a lot of firepower could change one's thinking.

For the first time in many days, since the screwed-up day with Lieutenant Creely when so much had gone wrong, he started to feel it again. He wished he were part of that blocking force, set up, hidden, waiting, with the NVA coming to him rather than the other way around like it had been for too long already. This time he would have the power. He would let them come until they were right in front of him, unaware, before he'd open up and cut them down. He felt the power of his rifle and saw them falling in piles and still he killed them.

"What are you smiling about?" California asked.

"Nothing," Singer said. "Payback."

"You must be feeling better."

"Yeah, I'm feeling better."

By late morning the fighting had diminished until there were just scattered, brief flurries of gunfire farther and farther apart and more and more distant. While the 101st waged their battle in the distance, Charlie Company sat tight on the hilltop and were resupplied with ammo and water, but no Cs, which Singer took as a sign they were leaving. He filled his empty magazines and hung grenades from his web gear, glad to be fully armed again and not have to worry so much about fire discipline. He drank from one of his freshly filled canteens as he worked and felt stronger. Payback even at someone else's hands was still payback.

When the distant gunfire waned, Singer ate his pound cake. The battle for the A Shau, at least Charlie Company's involvement in it, was mostly over.

The last Huey that came into Charlie Company that morning brought coils of ropes and grappling hooks and three more body bags. Charlie Company had just one more job to do. This time they met no resistance. Singer hardly recognized the place where Lieutenant Creely had died and he had narrowly escaped. There were downed trees, splayed trunks, and craters everywhere. It was funny how a place could change, yet stay the same in Singer's mind where somehow time stopped and couldn't move on. Singer looked up at the broken canopy and the narrow rays of sunlight streaking through to the jungle floor and thought of May 5th and the sunlight on the dead man's face. Here there was no face or even any bodies—at least, not a whole one. They wouldn't need the grappling hooks. If the bodies had been booby trapped, they had been detonated already by artillery hits. The company set up a wide perimeter while Singer and a few others spread out within it and searched for body parts and pieces of uniforms and equipment. One of the men found a head but refused to pick it up. The Shake and Bake finally put it in a bag. A man stood off to the side retching, but Singer smelled so bad himself he barely noticed the smell of rotting flesh. Singer found a finger which, when he dug it out from the loose earth, was part of a nearly intact hand, a thumb and three fingers. There was a ring on one of the fingers. When he tried to examine the ring the rotting flesh pulled away and he quickly put the hand in a bag. Still, he'd seen enough of the ring to see it was from West Point.

Back and forth Singer worked across the broken ground, trying to remember what he should be looking for. He couldn't tell anymore where exactly any of it happened. Where he had lain and others died. What had been won or lost here. With the fighting over, the mop-up was all that remained. It was an exhausting, gruesome task, and Singer kept waiting for someone to call an end to it. A man walked by carrying a swollen and discolored piece of flesh that would have been unrecognizable except for the jungle boot attached to one end. Maybe it would have been better to just leave the pieces to the jungle to be part of the earth where they'd died. They all belonged more to this world than the one they'd left when they were sent here. Would he ever be able to forget and not be a part of this place?

They picked up what they could find and put the pieces in three bags without making any effort to differentiate one man's parts from another. Graves Registration would have to sort them out. Lieutenant Creely's RTO had pale olive-colored, NVA-like skin, which complicated the hunt. Some of the pieces they put in the bags might have been from NVA, but no one said anything. It was a quiet, somber search that framed Charlie Company's and especially fourth platoon's time in the A Shau. Singer wanted it over. The pleasure in the payback of the assault by the 101st had already faded in the face of the search to recover the men who had died on the second day and laid rotting and unreachable for so long. He wanted to leave and try to forget what had happen here.

In the end, it was Top who said "enough" and told the men to close the bags. With the body bags in tow they headed out and left the valley behind them. By late afternoon, those who had survived the A Shau were back on Firebase Bastogne.

21

June 8-9, 1968
Firebase Bastogne, Vietnam

H e's dead," one of the soldiers gathered for mail call said. The clerk looked down at the letter, studying the name as though doubting the man was right. Finally he fumbled with the letter, trying to put it in his pocket with the stack of others already there, before pulling another from the mail bag and tentatively reading the name.

"Yeah," Singer said. He pushed forward and reached through the crowd of men gathered around the clerk. The envelope was powder blue, like the sky, like her eyes, and he didn't need to look at the return address to know it was from her. He moved to the back again and stood waiting.

The clerk read more names and men called out and pushed forward with extended arms and letters were passed back. There were a few packages, some partially crushed. The men receiving them brightened at the prospect of some kind of treat from home. Singer waited, hoping for a package and more letters. A man tore a letter open and strolled away from the gathering, reading as he walked. Men stood waiting, some empty handed, looking desperate.

The clerk read Trip's name.

The group was quiet. A few men looked around at each other as if checking who was there. Singer stood mute.

The clerk called Trip's name again.

Singer turned away, feeling the loss. Trip had been the last guy he cared about.

"Gone," the Shake and Bake said.

"What?" the clerk asked.

"WIA. Medevac'd. You should forward it."

"Oh," the clerk said, his fingers dancing as he shifted hands and put the letter in a different pocket. The clerk called more names, a roll call of the living and the dead, adding more letters to both pockets. Two packages went unclaimed.

Behind the clerk, the sun was settling toward the vague peaks on the horizon marking Laos. Singer watched it over the clerk's right shoulder. Somewhere amongst those peaks was the A Shau, where he'd been this morning. Closer, he could see stretches of the road that led there. Everything looked different in the sun. A distortion of truth. So many men were gone.

"That's it," the clerk said.

Singer looked at his single letter and then at the clerk, who was bundling up the unclaimed items. Not much after weeks in the field. The New Guy rushed up to the clerk as the rest of the men walked off, those with packages trailing hopeful-looking friends.

"You sure there's nothing else?" the New Guy asked. "There's got to be more."

"Nothing," the clerk said.

"Check again. I've got to have something."

"Sometimes it takes a while for mail to catch up with you."

"Fucking great."

"Hey, it ain't my fault." The clerk hurried away.

"Sure."

Singer held the blue envelope, feeling its thinness, and watched the clerk depart and the New Guy storm off. The Shake and Bake had kept the New Guy away from Singer since the New Guy nearly killed Singer in the first days in the A Shau. Whether to protect Singer or the New Guy, Singer wasn't really sure and didn't care. He was just happy not to have to look after the guy. How long could someone like that last? How many would die with him? It wasn't his concern. He was clean, had his letter, and would spend at least tonight in the relative safety of the firebase.

Some things, like a letter, a shower, or a drink of water had taken on such great importance, and yet so many things just didn't matter anymore. The sun still shone and the base held the heat of the day. Artillery pieces sat quiet in sandbagged pits where shirtless artillery men stacked rounds. Chaotic piles of spent shells were spread outside each pit. Beyond the artillery were the bunkers and the lines of rolled wire that encircled the base.

Singer stood soaking up the sunlight and the security of the sprawling firebase with its many artillery pieces that had been unable to help them where they'd been.

In the distance, the mountains of the A Shau stood solemn and foreboding against a liquid blue sky, offering no hint of the violence they held and all that had happened there. But Singer knew their deception. For a long time he stood with the sun in his face and stared at the mountains. The morning had been shrouded in jungle darkness and marked by digging through battlefield litter for parts of themselves. That he was standing here in the sunlight again, freshly scrubbed, a letter in his hand, had been unimaginable just a day ago. Even now, there was something unreal about it. Though safely out of the A Shau, it was still the A Shau, the dying and killing that dominated his thoughts. The shower had washed the smell of the days of sickness off his body, but the odors and horror of the A Shau remained. Payback would come. He promised all of them that. It wasn't much, but it was all he had to cling to now. Payback would come.

Alone, Singer ambled back toward his bunker on the southeast side of the firebase. He stopped when he saw him. He'd thought he was dead, but there was no mistaking the pudgy figure coming toward him. So many good men were already gone. There was no justice in death's selections. He tried to remember when he'd last seen him. It was the day in the A Shau when the man had sent him back down the same trail after Trip was hit and he and California narrowly escaped. He had told the man it was a bad idea and argued for an alternative plan. But the man had said that the CO wanted to see bodies and he had been insistent that Singer go down the same trail again, ignoring the folly of it or the likely outcome. He'd hoped he would never see the man again. He knew what Trip would do if he were still here.

"Singer."

The voice tore into him as much as the memory and he tightened his grip on the sling of his M16 that hung from his shoulder as Sergeant Milner approached in cleaned fatigues, the trousers with a pressed crease.

"Make sure you shave," Sergeant Milner said.

"I been a little busy lately, Sarge."

"You're not busy now. The men in fourth platoon will look like soldiers."

"Where you been, Sarge? We could have used your help today picking up the CO's body, what was left of it."

"Get a haircut, too, and clean that rifle."

"Use the same trail, Sarge?"

"Get one today or you're on report," Sergeant Milner said, stepping past.

"Right away, Sarge, I damn sure don't want to die with long hair," Singer said. "Fucking pogue." He didn't care if Sergeant Milner heard him. Fuck the man.

Singer crossed the firebase, past bunkers with the antenna array, the sandbagged tents and the smell of burned coffee, past the massive eight-inch guns, to the bunker line below. He ignored the men he passed. At the bunker California was sprawled shirtless on the bunker top, his hands clasped behind his head resting on his helmet. His arms were brown, but his chest was starkly white and his ribs had started to show. He never moved as Singer approached.

"Think you're at the fucking beach?" Singer asked.

"It's the best I can do until I get back to the real thing."

"Don't be fucking off, you'll get us both killed."

"If we aren't dead after that, nothing can kill us."

"Sit up and watch the goddamn perimeter."

California turned toward Singer and pushed himself up slowly. "What's got you so pissed?"

"Fucking Sergeant Milner."

"Just avoid the man, his time will come."

"He told me to get a fucking haircut. We were picking up body parts this morning and the man is worried about a haircut. I never even saw that fucker after he sent us in and Lieutenant Creely got killed."

"I heard he preempted a R and R and got out of there."

"That sounds like the man, but I can't believe they let him go."

"Everyone knows the man is dangerous. Hell, I could see that the first week I was here."

"Yeah, the man's a clerk, probably cut his own orders," Singer said, setting his helmet on top of the bunker and running his hand through his hair.

"Maybe Top decided to get rid of the man," California said.

"Maybe. Too bad he came back."

"Just stay out of his way or he'll have you burning shit and on ambush every day." California lay back down and stared at the sky.

Singer climbed up onto the bunker top. He repositioned his helmet and rested his rifle on it before sitting down cross-legged with the letter in his lap. The sandbag bunker top was uneven and rock hard and Singer shifted, trying to get comfortable. The firebase cast a long shadow across the road and toward the surrounding low hills and he could feel the approach of night. He held the letter to his nose once more, but still could find no trace of perfume that always marked her letters and carried memories of some of their best times together. He looked over self-consciously, but California was gazing at the sky, perhaps trying to imagine the sea.

"Sorry, no mail," Singer said.

"Didn't expect any," California said. "You get a care package?"

"No, just a letter."

"Tough times all around."

Singer worked the envelope open and pulled out the sheet of paper, then looked inside the envelope for more.

"What the fuck is this?"

"What?" California asked, turning away from his imagined sea.

"One goddamn page? That's not a letter."

"It's a page more than I got."

Singer held the page away from his face. Something was wrong. It was the same blue paper, the same flowing script of lines and loops, but the shortage of words and the lack of a lipstick kiss at the bottom of the page that ended all her letters were bad signs. He flipped the page over to find just an expanse of empty blue. No words. No kiss. Nothing.

Before he read the first line, he knew what was coming. Still he plowed through the words. She told him she was so sorry, especially to tell him while he was there, but she couldn't put it off any longer. She hadn't meant for it to happen. A classmate of his—she gave his name as though it would comfort him—had offered to take her out just as friends so she wouldn't have to spend so much time alone, because he knew how difficult that must be. He must know it was hard waiting, being alone. Neither of them meant to fall in love, but they had. She was so sorry. She didn't want to hurt him, but she wanted to be honest with him and tell him. She couldn't write him anymore. It was just too hard for her. She hadn't intended it to happen. She hoped he would be okay.

Fuck. She hoped he would be okay. He flipped the page over again, not believing there wasn't more. Wasn't it enough? Fuck. How could such beautiful script hold such ugly words?

"Well?" California asked, sitting up and drawing his rifle nearer.

"What?" Singer asked.

"What's the girl say?"

"It's a fucking 'Dear John' letter."

"No shit? Welcome back from the A Shau. You're joking, right?"

"Here." Singer extended the letter to California.

"Fuck. Guess I was lucky not to get a letter," California said after reading the letter and handing it back. "That the girl you sending your paychecks to?"

"Yeah."

"You're fucked, man."

"Doesn't matter," Singer said. "What would I do with it here?"

"What about after? You'll never see that again."

"She can keep it. Don't mean shit."

"Just like a bitch to fuck you over like that."

"It's the asshole dating her that pisses me off. Can you believe it's some fucker who knows I'm here? A guy I went to school with, for Christ's sake."

"You know the dude?"

"I know the name. Saw him around, but I never hung out with him. Fuck. I could deal with some anonymous asshole, but somebody who knows I'm here? That's the worst of it. Fucking low-life bastard."

"A guy like that is lower than whale shit."

"He's probably hanging around on some chickenshit deferment."

"Fuck, isn't everybody except us? We should take care of that guy."

"He's a dead man. Fucker won't know what hit him."

"Shit, I'd help you with that if you buy the beer."

"More beer than you can drink. We'll do it together, then."

"Fuck him," California said, picking up his M16 and firing into the wire.

"Jesus, are you fucking nuts?"

California just grinned.

Then Singer started laughing and they were both laughing and the sun hung in the sky and the shadow of the hill reached east toward the river. No one came to investigate, as though occasional fire on the perimeter was a normal thing.

"You are nuts," Singer said, holding the letter to his lighter's flame.

"This place is an asylum," California said. "And we're the fucking inmates."

The letter flamed and Singer turned it in his hand, watching the flame climb up the blue paper, a black curl chasing the flame. He dropped it on to the sandbags and the last of it turned black and fell apart as the flame went out. The ash lay there in the stillness of the evening air and Singer looked at it, thinking how little it meant to him. What did it matter? The letter? The money? None of it mattered anymore.

When had he stopped loving her, stopped caring? Her letters were a comfort and he loved the brownies she sent, though never as much as Rhymes. But if he was honest about it, she was from a different world, one he barely remembered and one he wasn't sure he could ever return to.

He stopped loving her a long time ago. Maybe after May fifth, when he had stopped loving himself.

There was so little left to love anymore. He had loved some of the guys around him, but they were gone now. He loved his rifle. Beyond that, there was no love. Maybe he had to let go of love to do these things. He picked up the ash, crumbled it in his hand, and threw it to the wind.

The night settled slowly and quietly over them. The landscape became dark and featureless, merging with the sky so that it was difficult to tell where one ended and the other began. It was a different darkness than the jungle. Less smothering. Less frightening. Below to the south was the road that lead out from Hue and the sea, passed Firebase Boyd and then Birmingham, passed the ambush site of weeks ago on to the A Shau. A dirt ribbon offering illusions of civilization and security. Singer sat adrift, somewhere along the road between where he'd come from and where he'd been. He had begun to believe that once you follow the road west you could never go back. Above, the sky was clear and unobstructed and Singer leaned his head back in disbelief that he wasn't still entombed by a jungle canopy. He had forgotten what it was like to see a star-filled sky, the wonder of it, and he imagined what Rhymes might have said or how Trip would have ridiculed them both.

California put a cigarette in his mouth and covered his head with his shirt to light it, then cast the shirt aside and cupped the cigarette in both hands. Singer pulled his web gear next to him and stared out at the darkness.

"I'd kill for a beer," California said.

"Make it a case if you're going to do it."

Far off to the south there were soundless flashes and a stream of red tracers colliding with emerald ones from the opposite direction. A battle of lights with no sounds. Flares burst above the fighting and drifted down on unseen parachutes. Distant, short-lived stars. Singer thought of the A Shau and the floating lights on the hillside and the daily assaults against the base camp. But tomorrow the sun would rise and travel across an unobstructed sky and he would mark another day. California sat beside him, transfixed by the light show or lost in his own thoughts of survival and escape. The lines of scarlet and jade streaked across each other in a flurry of dueling lights. Death made silent and remote.

A new, broken line of crimson poured from above out of the darkness, as if originating from nothing, and streamed into the vague dark shapes that marked the ground and the source of the green tracer rounds. Singer watched the lines of light flashing near the horizon. There was a beauty in it. For a moment he imagined the men locked in a frightening nighttime battle and the life-and-death dramas behind the streams of red and green tracers. Nameless, faceless men like most of those around him now. He was thankful it wasn't him. He felt almost euphoric for the safety of a firebase and at having survived the A Shau. Tonight there was a beauty in the lights.

Long after the last flare had gone out and the source of the tracers was extinguished or departed, he sat holding his rifle, marking the passing of the night, occasionally looking up and being surprised to find the stars still there. When California's turn for watch came, Singer lay down on the bunker top, preferring the open air to the small, hot space inside a bunker. Better to take his chances in the open where he could move and maneuver. Bunkers were too much like graves. Boxes with just one way out, which the enemy could easily target.

On Firebase Boyd, a bunker had been hit in a nighttime attack, partially collapsing, burying the men inside. If he needed cover there was the hole he'd dug and put up a few sandbags around, but he wasn't living like some mole in a fucking death trap. After listening to the story, California shared his aversion to the inside of bunkers, so they spent the night on top, rotating guard and sleep periods every two hours.

Despite his fatigue, Singer slept fitfully. He dreamed he was trapped by enemy fire and trying to crawling back to the guys, who kept moving farther away. Just when he got close and thought he would make it, an NVA jumped up a few feet away, firing an AK at his face. He startled awake, reaching for his rifle, knowing it was too late, before he felt the bunker below him and saw California sitting there and then the stars and realized it was a dream. Unsettled, he lay back down, giving into his exhaustion only to be startled awake again with his own death fresh in his mind.

When Singer's turn for guard finally came again, he sat up, relieved to abandon his efforts to sleep and to escape dreams of his death. The darkness had deepened and the air remained hot and still, oppressive even in the night. The first row of wire was barely visible, and the second and third were lost in the darkness.

The slow, rhythmic breathing of a man deep in sleep came from the prone form beside him. After waking Singer for his shift, California had lain down and curled up on his poncho liner and hadn't moved since. How did he do it? The man was crazy, that was for sure. But with Rhymes, Bear, and now Trip gone, California was all he had.

Singer ran his hand along his rifle and shifted his weight against his fatigue. His eyes were heavy with the effort to see beyond the wire. His mind was weary with the struggle to understand it all. There was no clarity, only the power of his rifle and the proximity of death and his involvement in it all. He didn't know who he was anymore. Maybe he never had. So much had changed in so short a time. He had survived so much and yet had so far to go. Would he ever make it home? Who would he be if he did? So many guys he cared about were gone. It was up to him to give their deaths meaning. So many things were fucked-up. Little was certain, except more would die. So many had died, and for what? None of it had the clarity offered by stateside vision. So much rested on him now.

Behind him came a scream and before he could turn there was a flash of fire and a shockwave passed over him. He hugged the bunker top, scanning the area for movement before a voice behind him yelled, "Fire," and another eight-inch gun boomed and then they were all firing, and he lay there sweating while California slept undisturbed. When the fire mission was over the firebase grew quiet again and he was alone with the night.

He watched the sunrise as though he'd never seen one before, following it as its brilliance crept above the horizon from out beyond where he knew the sea to be, illuminating a landscape as confusing as his thoughts. Around him were the noises of an awaking firebase: conversations of men in morning rituals, barked orders from an officer, shuffling feet, the clang of metal against metal, the hum of a generator. So different from the quiet tension of mornings in the jungle, where noise invited disaster.

"You getting up?" Singer asked.

"Fuck." California stuck his head out from under his poncho liner and squinted, shielding his eyes with his hand. "I'm on vacation today." He pulled the poncho liner back over his head.

"Tell it to the lieutenant. We got a formation in two hours."

"Fuck," California said again, then sat up and uncovered his head. "You can't get any rest in this fucking place. Somebody's always wants you to do something."

"Shit, you slept all night."

"I was dreaming I was at the beach with a blonde with breasts like grapefruits and an ass made for riding."

"I thought you were dead. You didn't even wake up when the big guns fired last night."

"It's a harsh motherfucker to wake up and find you're still in this place. Who wants to?"

"How'd you ever end up here?"

"Passive indifference, man. Passive indifference. And you?"

"I'm not sure anymore."

Singer lit a heat tab and ate a can of heated Cs before retrieving a helmet of water and shaving. He stared at his distorted image on the small piece of mirror and ran his hand over his face. Did he really look like that?

While he waited for formation he sat on the bunker top, his equipment laid out in front of him, and cleaned the rounds in his magazine, methodically emptying and refilling each one. When it was time, a couple of guys came to cover the bunker and he and California strolled slowly to the area near the helicopter pad. Singer was in no hurry to get there.

"How'd you get the name Singer?"

"Same as you. One of the old guys gave it to me my first day with the company. Guy named Shooter, killed the day before you showed up."

"I've never heard you sing."

"Nothing to sing about anymore."

22

It was a small formation, smaller than before. Each time they held one of these, the number of remaining men was fewer. Singer took his place in line with the survivors of fourth platoon. The faces from the days in Hue were absent. A line of boots stood in front of the company formation. Behind each pair of boots was an M16 stuck vertically in the ground by its bayonet, a helmet set on top of the rifle, casting harsh shadows in the hot, morning sun. A grouping for each man killed in the A Shau. Each setting was identical: pair of boots, rifle, and helmet. There were no names, but Singer knew some of them and the circumstances of their deaths.

A chaplain was speaking and a colonel had spoken before him, but Singer heard only the gunfire and felt the weight of the body bags and saw the wounded lying beside a trail. They would have to pay. At the side of the formation, the clerk with the dancing fingers put a battered bugle to his lips. His fingers did a slow waltz across the valves and the mournful wail of "Taps" drifted across the firebase. Everyone stood still and silent. Singer walked back toward his bunker, more angry and resolute than before.

In the afternoon, the Shake and Bake came by the bunker and told Singer that Top wanted to see him at the CP. It had taken longer than Singer had expected, but the accounting he knew was coming had finally arrived. At least the Shake and Bake had told him he could leave his gear at the bunker, which meant he'd be coming back. Singer walked across the firebase to the CP with just his rifle. The sun was high overhead, in the early stages of descent, and a light breeze caused the flag above a central bunker to lift slightly. A couple of shirtless men were throwing a football back and forth near the artillery pits next to the big guns and took no notice of Singer. Their job was the guns. Countless men like Singer rotated on and off the firebase, eventually disappearing forever one way or another.

As Singer neared the CP, he heard loud voices. Before he could enter the sandbagged tent, a gangly lieutenant with a ruck over one shoulder and an M16 in his right hand ducked under the flap, took three steps, then stopped and turned back. Top stood in the doorway.

"This is all your doing," the lieutenant said.

"Sir. You're a lieutenant and I'm just a first sergeant. How could I possibly have you sent to the Cav?"

"I know you're behind these orders. I just gave the man some work details. He still went home okay."

"Your orders to report to another unit came from Brigade headquarters. You can't think that a lowly first sergeant could influence such things?"

Singer, an uncomfortable observer to the exchange, couldn't be sure that Top had winked at him.

"You screwed me over," the lieutenant said and walked away.

"You screwed yourself over. You won't be an XO there. Maybe you'll learn something and do better with the Cav. Sir."

Top watched the lieutenant walk toward the helipad. "New lieutenants," he said, shaking his head. "Singer, you feeling better?"

"I'm fine, Top."

"Good," Top said. "Have you written home lately?"

Singer paused to think.

"When'd you last write your mother?"

"Not sure, Top. A few weeks ago, I guess. Before the ambush."

"Write her today. That's an order," Top said.

"Yes, First Sergeant."

"The company got a Red Cross inquiry while we were in the A Shau. There was a mistake and a letter went to your family saying you were wounded May fifth. With no one able to locate you in the evac system and then the company in the A Shau, well . . . the army sent a correction, but that won't clear up your family's worries. Your mother needs to hear from you. Write her today, okay?"

"Sure, Top. Is that all?"

"No," Top said. "A couple of officers are here investigating Lieutenant Creely's death. I told them you were the one they should talk to. They're waiting for you in the mess tent."

"What should I tell them?"

"Just tell them the truth. No need to dress it up or leave anything out. Let them bury what they don't like."

"Okay, Top." Singer turned to leave.

"One more thing, Singer."

"Yeah, Top?"

"I put you in for a Bronze Star."

"Oh."

"You did good in a tough situation."

"It was screwed up, wasn't it? You hear anything about Trip?"

"He was talking shit when they put him on the dustoff. He'll be okay. There'll be an award ceremony in a couple of days."

"Thanks, Top."

"Don't keep the officers waiting." Top ducked back into the tent.

At the mess tent, Singer found the officers, a captain and a first lieutenant, waiting with notepads and coffee. Singer came to attention and saluted a few steps in front of the table where the officers sat, then waited to be released. The captain told him to sit then asked questions while the lieutenant made notes in black ink on a yellow legal pad. They were trim, fit men with light skin and clean, manicured hands. Their uniforms were starched and pressed, and their manner was formal and precise. The captain had large sweat circles under each arm. Lawyers with the JAG office, or maybe just the general's staff. Other lieutenants had died and no one had asked about them, but Lieutenant Creely would have been the general's son-in-law, which made all the difference.

Singer declined coffee and told them the story just as he recalled it. He told them of the initial contact and then Lieutenant Creely's insistence that they go back in the same way to find bodies. He left nothing out except the RTO's threats and the nature of Doc's death, which didn't really bear on Lieutenant Creely's demise. Everyone buried things. When he told them of how Lieutenant Creely came forward screaming profanities, the lieutenant stopped writing and looked up from his pad and the captain held Singer's eyes, as if judging his truthfulness. The captain asked questions about why Lieutenant Creely had come forward, why he had taken the point, how far Lieutenant Creely had walked, the proximity of the enemy when they fired, whether Lieutenant Creely had died right away, and the efforts to reach him. Singer repeated what he'd seen, adding details to clarify what he'd already reported to the officers. The last question the captain asked was for Singer to speculate on why Lieutenant Creely had done what he did. Singer told them of the rumors about Lieutenant Creely after May fifth, how Top had run the company that day, and how he thought that had precipitated Lieutenant Creely's craziness. The captain listened intently, then thanked Singer for his honesty and dismissed him. The whole time, the lieutenant never spoke. That was it.

Singer headed back to the bunker, figuring most of what he told the officers would be left out of their report and quickly forgotten. Lieutenant Creely's record would be massaged and his service would look good, at least on paper. Few would know the truth. That was true about all of them. Lieutenant Creely would likely receive a posthumous award for valor, restoring his reputation in some quarters as he had hoped, though not exactly the way he'd likely planned. The general and his grieving daughter would have the belief that the lieutenant died a hero and had an award to prove it. True or not, none of it really mattered. So much of the war was a lie. What was one more lie to save a man's reputation and comfort a fiancée and prospective father-in-law?

Back on the bunker top, Singer put his rifle down in the shade of the poncho liner he'd rigged up on a couple of poles with the other end weighted down with sandbags and prepared to sit down. He wanted to see the sun, but he didn't want to sit in it. California, on the other hand, was lounging on the bunker top, shirtless, facing west, leaning back on his arms to catch the retreating afternoon sun.

"Was that about Sergeant Milner making problems?" California asked without turning.

"No, just a couple officers with questions about Lieutenant Creely," Singer said to California's back.

"You tell them that fucker nearly killed us?"

"He saved us. If he hadn't—"

"He nearly got us killed, the crazy fucker. He never intended to save us."

"He's dead. What does it matter?"

"Good riddance, too. It would have been us lying there for days, getting blown to shit, not enough pieces to fill a body bag. Who the fuck would have cared?"

"How do you do it?"

"Do what?"

"Sit in the sun like that?"

"The sun is my god."

After taking off his helmet and shirt, Singer crawled under the poncho liner with the sheets of paper and pen he'd gotten from the captain at the mess tent. The captain had braced himself when Singer had asked permission to ask a question, as though he expected something about Lieutenant Creely or the filing of their report that would be difficult to answer. When Singer just asked for a sheet of paper, the captain visibly relaxed and offered him the entire tablet, which Singer declined, saying he just needed a sheet to write home and that a tablet was excessive weight and would be quickly ruined in his ruck. The captain gave Singer two sheets and insisted he also take his pen, a fancy, silver model, apologizing for not having an envelope. Singer tried to decline the captain's personal pen, telling him he could get a pen at the CP, but the captain insisted and dismissed him.

Sweat dripped from his nose as he sat with his knees pulled up and the captain's pen poised above the paper resting on his helmet. He wiped his hand on his pants leg, trying to dry it enough so he wouldn't ruin the paper. He'd written a couple of lines of "how are you," trying to sound comforting, but now he was stuck. What could he say? Who would understand, even if he told them? Certainly not his mother. What would she think if she knew what he'd done or how he felt? She'd likely be disgusted, as he was in some moments.

How could he hate and fear the fighting yet love something about it at the same time? He hated himself for loving it, but that didn't change the thrill he found in the power of his rifle. At times he thought of nothing but revenge. He feared what he knew he was capable of doing. But none of this was anything he could write about or even speak of. He would wrestle with it alone, afraid to name it.

He stared out from under the poncho liner, past the wire to the land-scape beyond. Still holding the pen, he laid his hand on his rifle. If his mother knew these things, how could even she love him?

He reread what he'd written for a countless time. Barely two lines. What little was there looked fluid, almost beautiful, even if meaningless. He thought of crumpling it up and abandoning the effort. A rifle was an easier tool.

If his father had experienced similar things in his war, he never spoke of them before his death. At least not sober. It was only when his father drank with his friends that sometimes he would talk of the war, but mostly about the years away from home or the long time spent on ships or islands waiting for the next assault or the end. His father hadn't given him any clue what to expect, how to deal with the aftermath, or what to write home to his mother.

In the end, Singer settled for unimaginative lies that he was on a large base and duty was easy, but the movies at the base theater were old and he occasionally saw helicopters and sometimes lights in the distance, but that he never had to leave the safety of the post. If she heard different, it was just a paperwork screw-up, which was a common thing. That was the army. Don't worry. Most days he was just too tired from working in the heat to write. Safe lies that his mother might believe. That she would want to believe. He got a battered envelope from California, which he must have carried in his ruck since he arrived in-country, and dropped the letter up at the CP. He gave the captain's pen to the clerk who would make better use of it. The feel of a rifle gave a comfort that a pen could never offer.

Near dusk California took a walk and returned, grinning, with five warm beers hidden in his pockets.

"I tried to get some ice, but that was too well guarded. It would have been difficult to carry it, anyway," California said.

"I didn't hear any gunfire," Singer said.

"No one died over it, but no one tried to stop me, either."

Singer was glad of that. He wasn't so sure about California, but thought him better a friend than an enemy, though he still didn't trust him at his back. But beers were beers. The man could find things. Just to be safe, they waited until it was dark before they drank the beers, sitting together on the bunker top, waiting for another light show that never materialized.

The days on the firebase were long and boring, especially after events in the A Shau. Going from the adrenaline-filled days of firefights and close escapes to the hours of inactivity with nothing to do but stare at the wire was more difficult and quickly becoming less appealing than it had been in the heat of battle. How many times could you clean your rifle and ammunition? Then there was the harassment about uniforms and haircuts from NCOs and officers who brought their stateside mentality with them and cut no slack to men just in from jungle fighting. It tested Singer's self-control. The biggest challenge was dodging the daily details or the occasional small-unit patrol or nighttime ambush. Something Ghost had made an art form. So far Singer and California had avoided them all, just by luck or maybe some consideration extended by Top or the Shake and Bake. Either way, it didn't matter. A few more days of this boredom and Singer would be volunteering for patrols. Too much time to think was not a good thing. Better to be moving. Better to have your rifle in your hand and be free to use it. Singer felt a person could only sit here so long before it would kill them as sure as an AK bullet, just slower.

No more mail came, no postscripts to the "Dear John" letter. It didn't matter. He thought of her once, a kind of fleeting thought of what she, or they, might be doing. It was the first he had thought of her in days, since her letter, actually, which surprised him. That he didn't care and gave no thought to writing her didn't surprise him at all. He would miss her care packages, but the brownies were less appealing with Rhymes gone.

A few days after the memorial service, Singer stood at attention in a short line of men facing the company. To the side, the general, a small group of officers, and Top stood listening to a lieutenant read the events of each award. After each reading, the general stepped forward, Top and the officers trailing him, and pinned the medal on the recipient's uniform. Ceremonies where awards for valor were presented in the days immediately following a major firefight were as much a post-battle ritual as the memorial services for those killed. After May fifth, Singer had stood in a company formation and listened to Bronze Star awards for Sergeant Edwards for leading fourth platoon's assault against the ambush and for the men who had rooted out the NVA from the spider hole inside the company perimeter at the end of the day. Sergeant Royce, though absent, was awarded a Bronze Star for his efforts to save Sergeant Edwards and for "holding the crater against repeated and determined enemy attacks." Fiction, Singer knew, but he said nothing. Top was recognized with a Silver Star for assuming command and leading the company counterattack and defense. Lieutenant Creely had watched with harshly squinted eyes that formed sharp lines on his face, his fists squeezed tightly at his sides. The ceremony had not been comforting with the events of the ambush so vivid in Singer's mind and the losses still raw, burning in his chest and begging answers. Yet he'd envisioned himself standing in front at some future ceremony, being decorated for valor as a necessary validation. Of what, he couldn't explain.

Today he stood awaiting his award, less certain of what any of it meant, or even of himself. Some days he was able to charge into gunfire without any thought of risk, other days nearly paralyzed by fear, or motivated to fight by things that had nothing to do with bravery.

Lieutenant Creely got his award, a Silver Star for "taking the point in the face of ongoing enemy contact to lead and inspire his men against a superior enemy force." An award for craziness? What did it matter? Singer was alive and wouldn't have to follow the guy again. Give the man anything. No matter the lie.

There was a posthumous Silver Star for Doc, for going "forward to treat Lieutenant Creely, his commanding officer, making repeated attempts to rescue him despite enemy efforts to repel him . . . killed in his third attempt, when the enemy directed overwhelming fire on him." It was mostly true, but had been dressed up for more dramatic reading, as if a man going forward under fire to retrieve another wasn't dramatic enough. A major on the general's staff held the medal and citation that would be sent to Doc's family.

The award for Singer was read and while he recognized the general theme, most of the details were fiction. The number of enemy soldiers Singer supposedly killed was named, but how could anyone know? Even he had no idea. The clerk with the nervous fingers had a knack for elaborate storytelling, which must have pleased commanders. Trip would have sneered at the clerk's ability to write such lively combat stories without ever having seen any combat, while drawing the same combat pay as the men he wrote about. Rhymes would have just smiled, leaving Singer to guess what he was thinking. All bullshit, Bear might have said.

What other fiction did the clerk write? It didn't really matter. None of it changed what Singer did or didn't do. He had his award, even if he wasn't sure anymore what it proved or if it validated anything.

Top stood tall and straight, impeccable uniform, the hint of a smile, looking like the proud father basking in the accomplishments of his sons. If he recognized the fiction that dressed up the awards he gave no hint of it. His valorous awards for his service in Korea might have been the same. Well-written stories of bravery were perhaps a long tradition that made talented citation writers like the clerk valuable men. Courageous acts weren't enough unless they read well.

After Singer's citation was read, Top said something to the general, nodding toward Singer. May fifth or the shoot-up in the base camp? The general gave an affirming nod and something that might pass for a smile came to the general's lips. The platoon's Cherry Lieutenant who tried to stop Singer's shooting in the base camp might have said it was craziness not so different from Lieutenant Creely's. Singer knew it was fear. Raging, searing fear, out of control. Some fled, others raged with their weapons. If firing nonstop in your fear was courageous, let them decorate him for it.

The general pinned on the award and shook his hand and saluted, followed by a short line of officers who did the same. Top was the last and lingered, shaking Singer's hand longer than necessary as though he was going to say something, but then stepped away after saluting smartly. Singer stood in the glare of the overhead sun, beads of sweat rolling down his cheeks, aware that his actions were nothing as dramatic as the citation's words. Much of it he didn't even remember. Had he really gone crazy, firing without stop again? He had refused to leave California and tried to crawl back to help Trip, but it wasn't about bravery. It just wasn't in him to leave someone, and in those moments fear seemed to fade. Brave? He wasn't sure. It was nothing more than many others would have done. No more brave. No less afraid. And what would Lieutenant Creely's RTO have said? Or Rhymes or Bear or Trip? Would they have thought him crazy? Or worse, a fraud, a product of a clerk's lively imagination?

No matter, the Bronze Star for valor was there on his chest and would be part of his record. He was officially brave. No longer a boy. But it didn't really change anything, as he had once thought it might. He was still just eighteen, with months of more A Shaus ahead of him and the prospects of seeing his nineteenth birthday very slim.

Singer waited for the ceremony to be over, barely listening to the other awards, not caring. The dark pools of shadows at everyone's feet had grown smaller and some uniforms were marked with expanding lines of sweat. A helicopter came in and then departed quickly, for a moment drowning out the ceremony. A cloud of red dust drifted across the base. Empty-handed, at the front of the formation, Singer felt exposed and defenseless. He had to get his rifle back in his hands and get off this firebase. Maybe that was the point of such ceremonies.

The general closed things with some generic praise he had probably said a hundred times to a hundred similar formations, then he left with his staff, looking pleased. The formation was dismissed and Singer fled back to the bunker and his rifle. Surviving, he was starting to believe, might be much harder than dying.

California had his shirt off and was up in his position on the bunker top before Singer could climb under the poncho liner next to his ruck.

"I thought this place had beaches," California said.

"You're in the wrong service to see any of them."

"Fuck, I got to see about a transfer."

"I'm sure if you ask they'll make you a beach guard somewhere."

"My talents are wasted in the infantry. Now you, that's another thing." California folded over the page on the newspaper. "We made *Stars and Stripes.*"

"Who did?"

"Says right here, C Company, 2/504 of the 82nd Airborne Division, that's us, right? We killed 219 NVA in a three-week action in the A Shau." California flipped the page and then flipped back. "You see that many bodies?"

"More fiction."

"You'll be relieved to know our casualties were minimal."

"Tell that to the dead guys. Can you scrounge more beer tonight?"

"Anything is possible."

"Except you being a beach guard."

California put the paper aside, leaned back on his ruck, and closed his eyes. "Wake me when the tide comes in."

* * * * *

Singer pulled the trigger hard, burning through another magazine. He had to kill them all before they breached the wire. "Fire! Goddamn it, fire!" A flare burst above the base camp, illuminating NVA bodies tangled in the wire, hanging on the coils, and strewn across the ground. A few had breached the gap, but died just inside it. NVA were still trying to climb over the bodies, but slowed by the piles, they were easy targets. He fired into them without pause, making the mounds of dead men grow, grinning at his progress.

He sat up, blinked to clear his vision and swiped at the sweat that burned his eyes. Everything was quiet, the blackness impenetrable. A hard lump of fear sat in his gut like a bad meal. Was he looking out at the night or looking in? Both were equally dark and scary. He squeezed his eyes shut, then opened them to the same darkness. Beside him he felt for empty magazines, but there were none. He checked his ammo pouches and bandolier and found them full. A soft glow of moonlight suddenly illuminated naked, intact wire beyond the bunker. Not a single NVA body. He held perfectly still, straining to listen for any movement. The only sound was a slow rhythmic breathing from California's curled form beside him. Singer closed his eyes against the starkness of the wire reflected in the moonlight and his relief mixed with disappointment. When he opened his eyes, the darkness had returned. He felt the edge of self-hatred that nothing would relieve.

The dawn brought another morning of dull routine. Singer told California nothing of his dream. Had Rhymes still been there, he might have sought his counsel.

The company stayed on Firebase Bastogne longer than normal as a flood of replacements came in to restore the unit's numbers after losses in the A Shau and the May fifth ambush. Even with replacements, the company was barely at half strength, less than one hundred men. New soldiers arrived by convoy with fresh uniforms and unmarred boots and no sense of the unit's past days or the men who had gone before them. Cherries with young, animated faces, who asked questions about rumors of the company's bad luck and what things were like in the field.

Even worse, they were all Legs. Not a paratrooper among them. There weren't enough jump-qualified soldiers coming in-country, so the army sent what it had. Legs. Fucking Legs. They were no longer a unit of paratroopers. Singer wasn't sure what they were anymore. Some kind of bastard, misfit unit. They still wore the patch, had the name, but the spirit of the unit was destroyed. The spirit of the airborne, of Rhymes, Doc Odum, Bear, Red, and Trip was lost.

Things were so bad that the new CO, who came in with the replacements, had the new guys training on weapons and the whole unit practicing fire-and-maneuver in the hills below Bastogne as if they were all in AIT again. This wasn't Fort Bragg or Fort Sill. This was the fucking Nam. They were supposed to be a fighting unit, not a fucking training outfit. Singer needed to get away from this chickenshit base and back in the field, where they had some hope of killing NVA.

Singer hated the new guys for all of it. Their clean uniforms, their fresh faces, their Leg status, their stupid questions, the training games, and for not knowing Rhymes, Doc Odum, Bear, Red, Trip and the others and for not caring. Mostly for not knowing or caring. Singer avoided them, sitting alone under his poncho liner. He didn't want to hang around new guys, some who weren't really new, but that was how he thought of them. He stopped talking even with California because there were always new guys around. He didn't want to listen to new guys' questions or see the light in their eyes, know their names or faces. He didn't want any more friends.

Sometimes he thought about her, though he tried not to. Fuck her and fuck her asshole boyfriend. He didn't care. They could sit around at the drug store drinking their Cokes and spend their nights at the drive-in. Fuck them. What did they know? They could never understand the Nam or how things were different here or how he was different. Fuck them and their boring little lives. None of it mattered.

He wiped his rifle down, not caring that he'd done it three or four times already today. He'd be ready, even if the unit wasn't. Everything was different now. He had to look after himself. The second-tour guys were gone. There might have been a few who reached the end of their service time and rotated home, but he couldn't name one. Maybe Trip had made it. Only Top stayed, the last remnant of the unit that had come from Fort Bragg. Top would stay until the last of them had made it out or the war was over. Sergeant Milner disappeared, which was the only good thing. Singer heard he went to Saigon to work for a supply unit, to be a clerk again. Others thought he went home. Either way, it was good to be rid of him. The Cherry NCO who took his place couldn't be any worse, though how a staff sergeant had avoided Nam service until now raised questions. No matter, he could take care of himself. And in a pinch, maybe Top would have his back.

With a click, the round seated in the magazine. Singer wiped down another round, then carefully pushed it into the magazine. He was loading more than just rounds. Each round was a measure of payback. He placed the loaded magazine next to him, them took another from his web gear and started the process over again. When the time came, he'd make it count. Next time there wouldn't be a Cherry lieutenant around yelling for him to cease fire. No one could stop him. There would be payback. He was the only one left to do it. No one else remembered or cared.

The night offered solitude, and for that reason alone he'd grown to like it. He sat up on the bunker with his rifle while the others slept and didn't have to talk with anyone. He waited for the NVA to come, but they came only in his sleep, when the killing was easy and endless. That he could no longer remember who he was before sometimes scared him. Only the killing would keep Rhymes and the others alive. Yet he knew in some way it also meant the end of him.

On clear nights he leaned back and looked at the sky, the pinpricks of light so far away, removed from everything, and imagined what it might be like to be up there away from this place, to lose himself in the vastness of the sky. There was no way to get to the stars, just like there was no way back to what he'd been before.

Only his rifle mattered. And the gunfire that would fill the emptiness.

23

June 18-19, 1968
Vietnam

The order for Singer to report to the Cherry Lieutenant at the platoon CP came unexpectedly in the evening, delivered by a Cherry he didn't know. A bad feeling spread from Singer's gut as he strolled toward the CP. When Singer arrived, he found the New Platoon Sergeant, an older, scrawny guy with a weathered kind of toughness and a big moustache that emphasized the smallness of his face, there as well. As soon as he saw the two of them sitting there exchanging conspiratorial looks he knew something was up and braced himself.

Singer hadn't liked the Cherry Lieutenant since he'd stood over him in the A Shau screaming, "Cease fire," without having any sense of the threat. In the days following, in their repeated assault on the base camp, the Cherry Lieutenant was all but absent and Singer never saw him fire his weapon or affect any kind of leadership. Yet since they made it back he'd taken to telling anyone who would listen, especially the Cherries, that "this killing was more fun than sex." Bravado bullshit that Singer figured the guy used to cover his fear and incompetence. The guys he'd seen who were good at it, the guys he wanted with him in a firefight, were the quiet ones. The talkers usually hadn't seen any real action and would cut and run whenever things got hot. Singer wasn't impressed.

The New Platoon Sergeant, Sergeant Milner's replacement, was proving to be little better and equally dangerous in a different kind of way, taking stupid risks, believing he knew what was going on or, like the dead CO, was out to prove something. The guy was a Cherry and a Leg, but he acted like he was some kind of third-tour ranger, strutting around as though he was due admiration and awe. He'd done nothing to earn Singer's trust or respect. Singer doubted the man ever would. Since arriving in the company, the New

Platoon Sergeant was in constant company of the Cherry Lieutenant, the two having formed some weird alliance that seemed to feed their shared illusions. Singer didn't like the look or feel of things.

After Singer sat down, it was the Cherry Lieutenant who spoke, but Singer couldn't help thinking the New Platoon Sergeant was somehow behind it and there were hidden agendas. An ambush loomed somewhere ahead. He could feel it.

"We're—" The Cherry Lieutenant caught himself and started over. "I'm going to make you a squad leader. With all your experience in-country, you should be leading a squad."

There was something insincere about the way the Cherry Lieutenant said it. Mocking, even. The New Platoon Sergeant sat there grinning and playing with his moustache.

"I don't want it, sir," Singer said.

"What do you mean you don't want it?"

"Didn't I tell you," the New Platoon Sergeant said.

"Be quiet," the Cherry Lieutenant said, turning quickly back to Singer.

"I don't want it. I don't want to lead a squad."

"It's not about what you want. This is the Army. This is not your choice."

"Sir, I respectfully decline any appointment to a leadership position. I am fine just carrying my M16," Singer said, patting the rifle on his lap.

"You think your medal gives you some kind of special status?"

"No, sir, but I believe I'm most effective where I am."

"You're a lone wolf and you're dangerous. I won't have that in my platoon. You'll do what you're told. You'll fire when I say to fire and you'll cease fire when I tell you to. If I want you to lead a squad, you'll damn well lead a squad."

"If I wanted to lead, I would have gone to OCS."

"You couldn't make it in OCS, Singer."

"Anyone can make it through OCS, sir. It's making it here that's the test."

The New Platoon Sergeant leaned in toward the Cherry Lieutenant. "If he doesn't want a squad, we should send him out alone."

"How has an E-7 avoided Nam duty until now?" Singer asked, glaring at the New Platoon Sergeant.

"You think a few months in Nam and a medal make you something special, don't you, Singer," the New Platoon Sergeant said, pulling at his moustache. He turned toward the lieutenant. "Send the fucker out alone and see how he likes that."

The Cherry Lieutenant was silent.

Singer smiled. The New Platoon Sergeant probably thought his moustache made him look tough, but it only made him look ridiculous. There might have been a time when Singer would have been intimidated, but not anymore. He had killed men and had men nearly kill him, countless times. What was there to be afraid of anymore? The platoon sergeant was a Leg and a Cherry. A phony. His rank and age meant nothing to Singer.

"I've killed better men than you," Singer said, moving his hand to his rifle and smiling again.

The New Platoon Sergeant laughed, a small, strangled laugh from high in his throat. "You're crazy."

"You have to be crazy to charge an ambush. I've been nose to nose with NVA more times than I can count and I'm here and they're not. So you do what you want," Singer said, "but I'll refuse any promotion or any squad leader position. I'll go out alone before I'll sit back and send men to their deaths." Singer stood up. "Are we done, sir?"

"No, we're not done. You'll do what I tell you," the Cherry Lieutenant said. "Next time I order you to cease fire, you'll cease, or you'll be getting a court-martial instead of a medal."

"Airborne, sir." Singer gave a mocking salute then quickly turned and walked out, not waiting for anything else to be said or to be formally released. They were done as far as he was concerned. As he walked away, he heard the New Platoon Sergeant's voice.

"We need to get rid of that guy."

Singer smiled to himself. Let them try.

On the way back to his position, he wondered what the repercussions might be. If the guys were here things would be okay, but he reminded himself that with Trip gone now, no one had his back anymore and he had to be careful. Maybe California would back him if he got in a jam, and the Shake and Bake seemed solid, but he doubted either would stand with him if it came to that. Top was still here, though he seemed deflated by the ambush and the A Shau or the changes in the company, or perhaps by both, and less willing to take on the command structure. There wasn't anyone he could count on for sure. Still, he didn't regret it. He was tired of the inept leaders and stupid orders. They were the ones who got people needlessly killed. He wanted them to let him do what he was trained to do and leave him alone.

The issues with the Cherry Lieutenant seem to have roots in the events in the A Shau. For the New Platoon Sergeant as well, even though he wasn't there. Fuck them. He'd only done what the situations required. Next time he'd do the same. He hadn't asked for any medal. If they wanted a medal so badly let them get one the way Lieutenant Creely had, posthumously. In the A Shau, the NVA had quickly eliminated Singer's problems with Lieutenant Creely's RTO. Maybe they would solve this situation, too. The way things had been going, there was a good chance they would.

The day after his meeting with the Cherry Lieutenant and the New Platoon Sergeant was quiet, with no mention of the conversation. Singer stayed at his position and didn't see either of them. No word came down and he wasn't given a squad. That night with California on watch he lay down on the bunker top, thinking it might all blow over.

"Singer," the Shake and Bake whispered.

Before Singer opened his eyes he closed his hand on his M16. In the blackness he could barely make out the face of the Shake and Bake, who leaned in so close he could smell his sour breath.

"Get up. Our squad's been ordered out on ambush."

"Now? All the ambushes went out hours ago."

"We move out in five minutes."

"That's crazy. It's too dark to be moving around in the middle of the night, especially with a bunch of Cherries." He was sitting up and fully awake. Beside him, he could sense California straining to hear. "Is there any real intel or is this something hatched over late-night beers?"

"I was just given the location and told to be off the firebase in five minutes."

"Do you know the site?"

"It's in a new area southeast of here."

"Fuck, this is insane. Without a daytime recon we won't have a clue where to set up. Even if we can find it, trying to set an ambush without knowing terrain is just asking for trouble."

"We've got our orders."

"I can guess whose harebrained idea this was." He expected they might come after him, but he never thought the whole squad would have to pay.

"You know the chain of command. Let's get going."

I'll take the point, then," Singer said as he stood and strapped on his web gear.

"No. I want you in the middle."

"You can't put a Cherry on point. I've got the most experience. And we need someone dependable on drag."

"California can handle drag. In the middle you can keep an eye on the Cherries so they don't get lost or accidently shoot each other."

"But the point—"

"I'll take the point myself. You and California had enough of that lately. Besides, if we get hit I want you to lead the counterattack or the retreat."

"Going out so late, there's a good chance of that. We should just lay up outside the wire."

"Just keep the Cherries together."

Singer had California help him gather up the Cherries. The blanket of clouds that had hung dark and threatening throughout the day closed off any moon or starlight, producing a black, featureless night that would require physical contact to stay together. Even with experienced men this would be a tough mission, but with four Cherries and the New Guy who had nearly shot him in the A Shau, they'd be lucky if they didn't end up lost or dead. Groping along in the blackness in the middle of the night, there was a high risk they'd be ambushed by NVA who were lying in wait for hours already for just such an opportunity.

Before they left the firebase, he tried to impress this likelihood upon the Cherries. While they were standing just inside the wire, so close Cherries' shoulders pressed on him from both sides, he told them this was a serious situation in which any fuck-up could cost them their lives.

"If any of you make the slightest noise, cough, sneeze, or fart, I'll tie you up and leave you for the NVA."

He felt the men beside him stiffen.

California leaned in, nodding.

The Cherries looked at him like he was crazy, but Singer could see that they knew he was deadly serious. He wasn't going to have some stupid Cherry get him killed after all he'd survived already.

"Stay close and quiet," the Shake and Bake said, before disappearing in the night to take the lead.

Their eight-man squad began to worm forward. The knot in Singer's stomach was starting to burn. He hurriedly checked his grenades again, then slipped through the wire, groping blindly to stay in touch with the man in front of him. Stuck now in the center between two Cherries, Singer wished he'd insisted on point or drag. Either place he wouldn't have felt so trapped.

Somewhere just a few paces ahead, lost in the darkness, the Shake and Bake was blindly guiding their tightly packed group toward an objective they'd never even seen before. Half of the squad were Cherries with less than three weeks in country. The burning in Singer's stomach, which had climbed into the back of his throat, already told him it was going to be a bad night.

He felt his way along, stepping softly, reading the terrain with his feet, concentrating on being quiet and not stumbling. The Cherry behind him touched his back, then held on to his web gear. Three men back, California had the rear and the responsibility to see that no one got left behind and that they didn't get hit from the rear. Far from ideal, but that's the way they set it up. The Shake and Bake up front, California in the back and Singer in the center with Cherries and the New Guy with the radio sandwiched in between.

Near the bottom of the slope, Singer risked a quick look up, but couldn't see a single star. He quickly returned his focus to the Cherry's back, barely a foot in front of him. He stepped carefully so as not to entangle their feet or to be tripped by the Cherry behind him. If they could make it to the position, they'd be okay. That would be the tough part. Once they got set up, things would be okay. Hell, if things went well, he might even kill some NVA tonight. He brightened at the thought.

Below the firebase they moved east across rolling terrain, through broken jungle and grassy fields, avoiding the road and its promise of an ambush. Slow, agonizing meters. They clawed through the darkness, Singer raw with the tension of nighttime vulnerability and the uncertainty of reliance on Cherries. When they cut a trail that was more than just a foot path, they held up for some minutes before turning south down the trail that Singer figured would lead them to the river, if he had his directions straight. On the trail their chances of being ambushed jumped immeasurably. Singer's muscles tightened in his back and arms and he hoped the darkness would continue to hide the squad. The Cherries, if anything, seemed to relax on the open, even ground of the trail, oblivious to the increased danger. Behind him, the Cherry removed his hand from his back and Singer felt a weight fall away.

How many of them would make it? He chased the thought from his mind. It wasn't his squad or his mission. It was the Shake and Bake's to lead and bear. The men around him weren't his to carry and never would be. He didn't know them and didn't want to. It was as if he patrolled alone. In a sense, he did.

The Cherry Lieutenant and New Platoon Sergeant tried to put the weight on his shoulders, make him responsible for more men's lives, but he refused it. That was what this late ambush was all about.

This last-minute, midnight ambush was their idea of revenge. If he'd known they were going to make the whole squad pay, he would have agreed to go out on his own. That would have made them happy. They had probably wanted to send him out alone, but were smart enough to know they could never get away with that. It helped that they viewed him as crazy and perhaps were even afraid of him. If they were worried about their backs, they wouldn't do shit. Fuck them. A late-night ambush was nothing. Fuck it. Even if it was a fucked-up mission, it was still good to be off the firebase with his rifle in his hands.

Though they must be close to where they would set up, the knot in his gut had not gone away. Muscles tense, he took another small, deliberate step, envisioning the onslaught of fire that the next step would bring. Survive the first burst, then bring payback. He slipped his trigger finger inside the trigger guard.

Up ahead Singer heard the soft gurgle of water flowing over rocks, but he couldn't gauge the distance. In front of him, the Cherry stopped, and Singer held up. The Cherry behind him touched his back and they all stood there in the darkness in the center of the trail, unsure of what lay beyond the blackness on either side. Seconds ticked painfully past. Beads of sweats slipped off Singer's forehead and ran into his eyes, but he kept both hands on his weapon. There was the sound of rapid, shallow breaths and the soft swirling of water, like strokes of paddles. The Shake and Bake slipped up beside Singer as if materializing out of nowhere, his black face lost in the darkness except for the white orbs of his eyes.

"Set up here on the left," the Shake and Bake said. "I'll be across, next to the river."

"We should stay together."

"This is the way they wanted it," the Shake and Bake said, then disappeared as silently as he'd materialized.

Singer didn't need to ask who "they" were.

The Cherry in front of Singer shuffled ahead and Singer let him go, listening to the faint crunch of ghost-like footsteps long after the vague image of the man vanished. He felt the urgent touch of the Cherry behind him, who kept his hand there at the center of his back. Singer waited until the sounds of footsteps were lost in the sounds of flowing water and he was sure they were alone. So this was it. They would have him directing men one way or another. When the shit happened he'd probably end up yelling directions to someone anyway. It was just the formal responsibility he didn't want.

He turned, and with his hand in front of the Cherry's face, he pointed, then waited for him to turn and tell the Cherry behind him and then for California to get the word. He moved left toward the trail edge, the Cherry's hand on his back. The trail was wider than he first thought. It would easily accommodate tanks or trucks and looked to be a major river-crossing point, more like a road than a trail. He wondered why they'd never seen or used it before, except that before this they had always gone west. At the trail edge, he discovered a high berm, but in the darkness he couldn't tell what lay beyond it. He imagined the brush and trees that in the blackness merged with the sky. They would have to feel their way into a decent site from which to cover the trail. If they moved more than a few feet away they would be unable to make out even the vaguest outline of the trail, so they would need to stay close. The Cherry stood motionless behind him and he could sense the other Cherry and California, knowing they were waiting for him to get them into cover. He hoped California was watching their backs.

Singer took a deep breath and climbed up over the berm. The ground dropped away out from under him and he felt himself falling and flailed for a hand hold. Then someone had his arm and was pulling him up, dragging him back over the berm. When their faces were close he saw California grinning. Slowly he gained his feet on the trail again and took his arm from California's grip.

"Fuck," Singer said, then held his rifle up in front of his face as if to confirm he still had it.

The two Cherries had moved in close around him and while he couldn't make out their faces, he could feel their fear.

"Cover the trail," Singer said, and waited for them to turn. "We're on the edge of a fucking cliff."

"That don't make sense with the river up ahead," California said from the darkness.

"None of this makes sense. Hold my rifle." Singer held his rifle out and once California took it, he turned back toward the berm.

They couldn't stay out on the trail. It was only the impenetrable gloom that had hid them this long. But that wouldn't help if an enemy patrol came along while they were still standing on the trail. This time he lowered himself over the berm more carefully, gripping the top with both hands, lowering his legs until his feet dangled free below him without touching ground. How far below the bottom might be, he had no idea. He lay against the sloping wall, but it wasn't enough to hold him, so he searched blindly for a foothold. He dug his feet into the wall, bracing them, then let his hands go one at a time and found he could hold himself in position without much effort. It was far from ideal, but they'd have cover and would be able to fire-up anyone who came down the trail.

"California?"

"Yeah?" California leaned his head over the top of the berm.

"Hand me my rifle, then have the Cherries slide in on each side of me."

It took a while, but eventually they were all settled, hanging on the slope, listening for any movement on the trail that was hidden in blackness. Singer could see nothing beyond the top of the berm. The situation made it impossible to put out a claymore, so they'd use grenades and rifles to take out anyone who came along. They set up sleeping shifts with California and one

Cherry watching while Singer and the other Cherry slept. They would switch every hour to make sure those on watch stayed alert. Once he settled in, Singer found it wasn't that uncomfortable and felt himself drifting off, cradled by the darkness and lulled by the sound of flowing water.

The shaking raised him from a light sleep and he opened his eyes without moving to find the Cherry's hand on his shoulder and his face close, his wide eyes darting wildly about. Singer started to lift his head to peer at the trail, but then he heard it behind him even before the Cherry gestured. The faint patting of feet. The scratching of clothing and equipment passing through brush. An enemy column. Fuck. Not on the trail, but behind them. Singer's heart quickened and his mouth became a desert. They lay on the slope fully exposed, their backs to the enemy. Only the darkness was keeping them alive. It was impossible to tell how many enemy soldiers there were or how they were armed, but as vulnerable as they were, stretched out against the slope facing the wrong way, even one enemy soldier put them in grave danger. They had to move quickly and silently.

Singer woke the Cherry on the other side of him, pressing his face close and holding his finger to his lips. He could see the confusion in the Cherry's face and his eyes widen as he heard the noise. The soft footfalls behind them came in a slow, uneven rhythm, stopping and starting as though they were moving with great caution or pausing to pass some obstacle. He signaled both Cherries that they would climb over the slope together and waited for the Cherry to signal California. A metallic click, like the closing of a rifle bolt, froze them just as they started to move and they lay there with their backs to the enemy, Singer holding his breath, hoping the others would do the same and that the blackness would continue to hide them. A Cherry started to turn, but Singer put his hand on his shoulder and held him still. The footsteps and whisper of movement continued and no fire came. Singer started pulling himself up as quietly as possible. The others immediately joined and finally the four of them slid over the edge, back onto the open trail. Both Cherries tucked in closer, so he could feel their bodies next to him. Singer had only the slightest relief at having the berm between them and the enemy, knowing they were exposed in another way and that he had no idea of the landscape or how it connected with the trail they were on. If an enemy element came down the trail they'd be pinned in the open between the two groups with nowhere to go. They hunkered against the berm, their backs exposed to the trail. Singer peered into the darkness in a hopeless effort to see beyond the slope while he strained to identify every sound. Their move back over the berm had been surprisingly quiet, but not entirely without noise. The footsteps stopped. There was only the gentle flow of water.

"Maybe an animal?" a Cherry said.

"Shut the fuck up," Singer whispered and again held his finger before his lips, his face inches away. He wanted to put the point of his knife to the Cherry's throat. The Cherry, perhaps reading his thoughts, turned away and shrunk back into the blackness.

An animal, Singer knew, would have bolted when it heard them and there would have been the sounds of the animal crashing through brush and the splashing of water if it fled across the river. He had experienced that numerous times back home when he made the wrong move on a stalk or surprised an animal he hadn't known was there. An animal would always flee. Only men would stop and listen. Singer could feel the enemy motionless before him, hidden in the darkness, trying to identify the source of the noise he, California, and the two Cherries made sliding over the berm. Both groups were doing the same thing. Waiting. Listening. But Singer knew he had the advantage. He knew they were there. He lay motionless, sweating and struggling to decipher any sound apart from the gurgle of the river. The enemy would move eventually, and then he'd have them. Right now, complete silence was their best weapon. The enemy didn't know what or where they were or that they themselves had been made.

While he focused on the enemy in front and below him, he still worried about their backs and the wide trail behind them, so he had the Cherry on his left face that direction with his back to the berm, even though seeing anyone before they were on top of them was hopeless. If a patrol came down the trail now it would be big trouble, and he wasn't sure what he'd do. He hoped he wouldn't have to confront that dilemma.

In the ideal ambush they knew the lay of the land, the likely approaches and escape routes, and then determined the size of the enemy patrol and engaged elements small enough to completely destroy. With enemy elements too large to overwhelm, they held their breaths and let them pass. This was far from the ideal ambush and there was no telling how large the group was, but the thought of simply hunkering down and letting them pass never occurred to Singer. They would kill as many as they could and then get the hell out of there.

The killing was close, he could feel it. He just needed them to move again so he could key in on them and make the most of the first moments. If they didn't get them all in the first flurry, some would inevitably recover from the initial shock of the attack and forge some kind of defense or even a counterattack. His heart raced and his breaths came in rapid pants, and he tried to slow them to be able to do this right. Sweat ran down his face and his chest pushed against the berm with each inhale. He held his rifle tense and ready, though he would primarily use grenades while the others fired. He'd already prepared, taking four grenades from his web gear and getting one from each of the guys so seven grenades lay on the ground in front of him ready to throw. As soon as they'd crawled over the berm he'd leaned his head to one side and then the other and whispered to them that when he threw the first grenade, they should each throw a grenade then use their M16s and keep firing until he told them to stop. Overwhelming firepower was what they needed, or at least the illusion of it. California would understand this, but he wasn't at all sure about the Cherries. It was difficult conveying information, and he'd wished he'd put California next to him. He indicated the slope and the drop in front of them to each of the Cherries and that they'd need to point their rifles down over the berm into the dropoff. He hoped they both understood it. Now they only had to wait.

Waiting was always the hardest part. On his right he could feel the Cherry still as a dead man and had to resist the urge to check that he was alive. The strain of trying to hear the slightest noise was exhausting and he could feel his strength seeping away. The tension was taking a toll. So much time had passed that he was starting to doubt what he thought he had heard before. Maybe it had been an animal. Or maybe his imagination had twisted a night noise into the movement of enemy. Hadn't that been what he wanted?

He started to exhale then stopped suddenly halfway, holding his breath. There it was. Irregular, faint, almost inaudible. They were moving again. He focused all his energy and the sound amplified in his mind. The soft crushing of forest litter under foot, the pause in the same place where he envisioned each man stepped around brush or over a fallen log, the swish of leaves against cloth. He pinpointed it, measuring its width, estimating the distance. He was in an elevated deer stand again, hearing the footsteps of a buck coming down a trail in dim forest light, sighting down the barrel of his rifle, estimating the range, waiting for the deer to materialize, all his thoughts focused on the kill, knowing he would make the shot, that the buck would die. He felt the same certainty now. The same controlled excitement at the prospect of the kill. He thought of Rhymes, Stick, Red, Doc Odum, Trip, and his promise to Bear, and the enemy below him.

Extending his arm, he touched the Cherry on his left, who turned back soundlessly to face the berm. He had the enemy's line of movement marked and he laid his rifle down and pulled the pin on a grenade, squeezing it to hold the arming handle tight to the grenade until he threw it. He sensed the Cherries on either side of him moving to pull grenades. A smile crossed his face as he focused on the closest sound, not far at all, and he lobbed the grenade over the berm and immediately picked up the second and pulled the pin as the first exploded. He threw the second grenade farther out as three more grenades exploded in quick sequence, almost as one. Bright fireballs. Crashing brush. Then California was firing and the Cherries joined in, the flashes of the muzzles blinding in the darkness. One after another, Singer hurriedly threw grenades, varying their position, trying to catch a line of retreat. Explosions flashed across their front. Just to his left, against the slope, came the explosion of an incoming grenade. The berm shielded them. He heard a second grenade thud just below the top of the berm and then a moment later the explosion below them. AK fire from a single source passed just over their heads. Singer heard the crack of a close round and ducked too late had the round been on. For a moment only the AK was firing.

"Kill that fucker!" Singer said and heard the noise on the wall directly below them just before a second AK opened up, shooting straight up the wall.

He pulled the last of two grenades from his web gear and dropped them over the wall. After the explosions he held his M16 out and fired straight down until the magazine was empty.

Both AKs went silent, and then only California and he were firing.

On impulse he turned quickly and sprayed two magazines of rounds up the wide trail behind them. The trail was black and quiet, a dark void. Still breathing heavily, he held his fire and tried to see into the blackness of the trail that ran behind them, feeling the edge of fear just begin to creep in and replace the exhilaration. California stopped firing, too, and the eerie post-battle quiet descended. A mix of excitement and sadness settled over Singer, the same as with every deer he'd ever killed. He pushed it away, working to stay focused on the threat that remained. From the east, he heard distant loud sloshing of water that might have been anything and turned back to face the berm, trying to determine if it was moving toward them or away. Much closer below him came a low, muffled moan, and he emptied a magazine at the sound. The sound and feel of his rifle invigorating.

"We got to get out of here," Singer said.

The Cherry on his right started to stand.

"Stay down. California?" Singer reached across the Cherry on his left. "California?" The Cherry between him and California lay unmoving with his face against the berm.

"Yeah," California said.

Singer pushed on the Cherry's shoulder and rolled him over. He saw the dark flow that started just below his helmet and spread down his face in a wide rivulet. Vacant eyes that registered no hint of surprise stared out at the darkness. Singer felt at the hole where the bullet had entered.

"Fuck," Singer said.

"Is he dead?" the other Cherry asked.

"California?"

"Yeah, I'm right here."

Singer looked up to see California leaning in on the other side of the body. "I've got to find the Shake and Bake and get us out of here." Singer wiped the blood off his hand onto his pants leg and gripped his rifle. "Watch the trail. Have the Cherry watch over the berm. Don't get jumpy and shoot me coming back."

"Be quick. I don't want to sit out here too long on this fucking trail with my dick in my hand."

Singer was already gone. He ran across the trail to the far side and then toward the river in a running crouch, uncertain where the other position was exactly. He cursed his lack of a radio and the split positions as he ran. Things were fucked up and they needed to get out of here. He had to find the Shake and Bake's position fast. After the shooting, everyone would be jumpy, and he hoped the Shake and Bake could control the New Guy and the Cherries. He flashed back on the New Guy's rifle in his face and rounds exploding over his head.

"Don't shoot," Singer said, still uncertain where they were set up. "Coming in, don't shoot."

"Hold your fire." The Shake and Bake's voice. "Over here."

"Don't shoot, coming in." Singer moved toward the voice, more cautiously now, slowing when he left the trail. "Don't shoot. Don't shoot."

"Over here."

Singer dropped in beside the voice hidden in tall brush on level ground. The river had to be close, as the sound of water flowing over rocks was much louder here. It was disconcerting how it masked other sounds. Singer tried to see the river or the trail, but the darkness remained impenetrable. His feet were against a man, but he couldn't see him, only feel that he was there. His chest was heaving and he struggled to catch his breath to speak. The run had been farther than he'd imagined, the positions too far apart in the darkness. He was thinking about California and the Cherry who he left at the berm.

The Shake and Bake shifted over tight against him. "What happened?"

"We fired-up a patrol behind us, below the trail." Singer gulped air. "Our position's blown, we got to get out of here."

"How many?"

"Not sure, a couple squads, maybe a platoon or more. We killed some, but some got away and there could be more coming. It's fucked-up over there, drops off steeply and you can't tell shit. We got one KIA. It's really fucked up."

"Who?"

"I don't know his name, one of the Cherries."

"Shit. The others okay?"

"Yeah, but we're sitting with our asses on the trail with no cover. We're fucked if more of them come down the trail. We need to move now."

"Okay, hold on a sec." The Shake and Bake relayed the information on the radio. He listened, giving terse acknowledgements before signing off.

"The lieutenant wants you to search for bodies."

"You're kidding me, right? We should be moving already. We got an exposed position, an enemy patrol somewhere around, and one KIA already. Let's get the hell out of here."

"See what you got for bodies first."

"Fuck. It's not enough to kill them, we got to count them, too. Let the goddamn lieutenant come down here and count them."

"Just send someone out and get a count."

"Yeah, right. You can't see your hand in front of your face and we're supposed to find bodies. "

Singer pushed himself up and in a step was back alone in the darkness. He ran a few careful steps, struggling to stay oriented, and was relieved to feel the trail that he could follow back north toward the guys. The Shake and Bake had his orders. There was no point in arguing, but none of them knew how screwed-up the position was, with a slope that even if they got down it okay, they might not be able to get back up. Even if they knew, none of them would care. It was all about the body counts.

In this disorienting blackness a body search was madness, even on level ground. He wasn't sending someone out to get lost or killed just so someone else could put numbers in a daily report and advance their career or make some fat-assed general happy. In the end someone would make up their own numbers, anyway. No one seemed concerned that they were sitting here, eight guys—seven now—exposed without a decent defensive position and an enemy patrol wandering around. Fuck counting the bodies. They could do it in the daylight when they could see what they were dealing with. Right now he needed to get them out of here. He had been stupid to think the Shake and Bake would immediately follow him back to pick up California, the Cherry, and the KIA and they would retire to the firebase, their work done. He should have moved them before looking for the Shake and Bake. What chance would two guys have if the NVA attacked? He figured he knew about where California and the Cherry were and that he was halfway there, but he was moving blindly, using the trail edge for orientation. He could kill the fucking Cherry Lieutenant whose order it was to split up the position and the weasel platoon sergeant who was likely behind it all. He stopped and knelt and listened. Only the murmur of the river. Still he couldn't help feeling they weren't alone.

"Hey," Singer said softly, waiting. "Hey."

"Here." California's voice was farther away and not as far to the right as he'd estimated.

"Coming in, coming in," Singer said as he crouched and ran hard toward the voice.

There was a *whump* of impact when Singer bowled into California after tripping over the Cherry's body. Their rifles clattered together and California fell backwards with Singer on top of him. Singer rolled over and lay there, waiting for what the noise would bring, but there was no enemy response.

"Jesus, what took you so long?" California asked.

"Why didn't you warn me?" Singer asked, pushing himself up away from the body. "Anything move out there?"

"How would I know?" California asked, sitting up. "I can't see shit. Let's get out of here before they come back. Where are the others? We need help carrying him."

"Are we leaving?" the Cherry asked.

"They're holding their position. The Cherry Lieutenant wants a body search."

"Fuck him. I'm not going out there. Send the Cherry," California said.

"What?" the Cherry asked.

"Don't worry. I already did it," Singer said.

"Really?" the Cherry asked with an audible release of breath.

"It's done," Singer said.

"Right, right, he made the search already," California said. "Now let's get out of here."

"Jesus, you should have told us. I could have killed you," the Cherry said.

"There wasn't any chance of that," California said.

Singer bent down, groped for the dead Cherry's rifle, and slung it over his shoulder. He took hold of the dead man under one arm.

"Grab him," Singer said.

When California picked up the other side, the Cherry's head flopped and his helmet fell off, hitting the ground with a dull *thump* that caused a moment's pause.

"Bring his helmet." Singer said. He and California fast-shuffled across the trail, dragging the Cherry's body. They worked their way back into the vegetation on the other side of the wide trail, stopping once when the dead man's feet became tangled in brush and a second time to lug the body over a downed limb.

"We should be okay here," Singer said, lowering the dead man's head and shoulders.

California dropped his side heavily. "Now what?"

"We need to wait a while. It won't look right if I report too quickly. We got decent cover and we're far enough back that a patrol could go down the trail and never see us."

"Shit, I can't see you from here."

"Where's the Cherry?"

"He was right behind us."

"Fuck." Singer listened, but there was nothing, just the constant flow of the river and the suffocating darkness. Could things get any worse? "Hey?" Singer said. "Hey?" Slightly louder, when there was no response. "Fuck, I'm going to kill that fucking Cherry Lieutenant and New Platoon Sergeant."

"You want all the fun," California said.

"Stay here. Don't fucking move. One lost guy is enough."

"Where am I going to go on my own, dragging a dead guy?"

Singer started carefully back down their drag trail, surprised then worried at how easy it was to follow. He moved slowly and quietly, stopping frequently to listen. He could sense a looming disaster. If the Cherry wandered south, the other ambush position would probably kill him. Going any other way, the Cherry risked wandering into the enemy. Singer took a deep breath. His best hope was that the Cherry would sit tight wherever he was. Even if he did, there was still the danger that the Cherry would fire on Singer or that Singer might shoot the Cherry before they could ID each other. Calling out to locate each other, the enemy might kill them both. He didn't like the odds and shuddered at the prospects. The advantage of being able to just fire at the slightest sound was lost now. Even with an enemy patrol in the area, he'd have to restrain himself and ID any target. That hesitation could cost him his life.

He cursed the Cherry and the darkness, the Cherry Lieutenant, the New Platoon Sergeant, the Shake and Bake, and everyone else he thought responsible for his predicament. He cursed Rhymes, Bear, Doc Odum, Trip, and even her for leaving him. Mostly he cursed the NVA and vowed again to kill them all. He felt the power and the release his M16 had offered and would offer again and took another step, ready for anything. At the trail's edge, he stopped and knelt a long time. The night was like a black cloak, isolating and disorientating. If the Cherry was out there, he couldn't hear him. It was too dangerous to be calling out in the darkness with the enemy patrol nearby. His best chance was to hear the Cherry. The thought of returning and hunkering down with California and looking for the Cherry in the morning was appealing, and he nearly gave in to it.

Eventually he crept north, away from the other ambush position, staying next to the trail edge, counting his steps. He would stop at fifty, cross over, then come fifty back and cross back, which should put him back at the drag trail into the spot where he left California with the body. A systematic block search was the best he could do. If he found nothing, then he'd have to go back and report the Cherry missing and they could get flares and maybe a reaction force to help search. He hoped it wouldn't come to that, but it looked like it might.

Each step carried the dread that the enemy or the Cherry would hear him and fire without warning. Right now the Cherry, lost and frightened, ready to fire at anything, was probably a greater threat than the NVA. He set his foot down in stages, slowly adding his weight, then listened before taking the next step. He hoped he wouldn't hear distant AK fire or M16 fire from the other position, which would mean he didn't need to search anymore. They would have to carry in two bodies. While listening after the thirty-seventh step, he heard it. Scratching in the trail. Shuffling feet. He didn't like doing it, but he had to risk it.

"Hey?" he said and immediately took three steps back to change his position in case they fired at his voice. There was no response and the scuffing sound continued.

He purposely fired high, a short burst that would provoke a response. Then he quickly changed positions, going prone next to the trail, ready to fire again.

"It's me! It's me!" the Cherry said. "Don't shoot, it's me!"

"Jesus," Singer said and wiped his face with his hand.

Singer talked the Cherry to him, a slow process. Though certain it was the Cherry, he remained ready to fire and didn't let off until the Cherry was next to him and he was sure they were alone.

"What the fuck are you doing? Are you trying to get killed?" Singer asked.

"I couldn't find the helmet, then you were gone."

"Couldn't you hear us and follow?"

"I could hear something, but I wasn't sure it was you or—"

"Jesus Christ, how'd you get down here?"

"I don't know. I didn't know what to do."

"Okay, okay, we got to get out of here. Hang on to my belt. Don't let go."

Singer counted thirty-four steps heading south, the Cherry holding tight to his back, found the drag trail, then worked his way back to California, calling softly until he was beside him.

"Get that rifle out of my face." Singer pushed the muzzle of California's rifle aside.

"Can't be too careful with so many gooks around," California said. "You found the lost sheep?"

"Yeah, let's try to stay together now. We've been damn lucky so far."

"Not him."

"Yeah, well . . ." Singer didn't know what else to say.

"Why's it always the big guys who get killed? I'd like to carry a light guy for once," California said.

"I got to go report back to the Shake and Bake and see if we can finally get our asses out of here."

"About time. This whole night's been a circle jerk. I'm tired of this waiting alone shit."

"You got the Cherry."

"Great. If he doesn't wander off again," California said.

"I didn't wander off," the Cherry said. "You guys left me."

"I voted not to look for you. Keep up or die."

"Okay, enough. If anyone asks, you both know I did the body search already, right?" Singer asked.

"Right, you're covered," California said.

"Why would anyone ask?" the Cherry asked.

"Jesus," California said.

"Just confirm I did it and you don't need to mention your being lost."

"Well, you did do it, didn't you?" the Cherry asked.

"You want to do another by yourself?" Singer asked.

"No, no, I know you did it already, I was just—"

"California, keep an eye on the Cherry and remember I'm out there."

"Which one, the dead one or the live one?"

"Both. Stay alert. I'll be back as quick as I can."

"You keep saying that. If you're not back soon, maybe we'll head in by ourselves," California said.

"Just stay put. We'll be out of here soon enough."

"Not soon enough for me," California said.

Singer worked his way back to the second ambush position vowing to never let anyone separate the positions again, no matter who ordered it. This was beyond crazy. It would be easier if it weren't so fucking black, but it had undoubtedly saved them when they were lying on the slope with their backs to the enemy. He'd only seen such impenetrable blackness a couple times in his life, and on those other occasions he'd been able to use a light. This was like nothing he'd ever done before. He was relieved when he heard the Shake and Bake's voice and finally slid in beside him without the New Guy or the Cherries firing him up.

"This is fucking nuts." Singer said.

Nearby, the river flowed with a constant low murmur like a garbled conversation.

"What took you so long?" the Shake and Bake asked.

"I'm getting tired of that question. It's fucking dark out there and tough to move around."

"What you'd find?"

He considered making up a number. Eight would sound good. Twelve would sound better. Who would go out to check? If they weren't there in the morning, who was to say they weren't there now? "Nothing, they took their dead and wounded with them," Singer said.

"You sure you hit some?"

"We killed some, but the bodies aren't there." Maybe they'd find some in the morning, but it didn't matter.

"What was that M16 fire a while ago?"

"I heard something, but not sure what it was. You ready to go?"

"We've been ordered to stay," the Shake and Bake said.

"What?"

"They want us to hold these positions."

"Are they crazy? Our positions have—"

"If we weren't hit right away, the lieutenant figures we won't be hit and the company is coming this way in the morning. They don't want any NVA setting up here to hit the company."

"The lieutenant is nuts. If the NVA want, they can set up the other side of the river. We're accomplishing nothing here."

"Our orders are to hold here."

"Well, I am not keeping the same position we fired from just waiting for them to come back and hit us. It's stupid. I've already moved the men across the trail. We're north of you now on the same side. Make sure everyone knows. I don't want to be carrying in any more bodies."

"Just hold tight. A few more hours it will be light."

"A lot can happen out here in a few hours. This is fucking bullshit. We killed them and now we should get out of here."

The Shake and Bake didn't answer. Their talking was done.

Singer moved back, feeling his way in the darkness for what he hoped would be the last time. He didn't know how many times he could run around in the dark before getting shot by an NVA or one of the nervous Cherries, but he figured he'd already used up more than his share of luck and didn't want to have to push it any farther. California wasn't happy when Singer told them they were staying and made more threats toward the lieutenant and the platoon sergeant. Singer shared California's anger but didn't comment.

"What do we do now?" the Cherry asked.

"Like before, we wait and listen. If anyone comes by, we kill them. When it gets light, we'll go in or the company will come out," Singer said.

"Too bad the Cherry Lieutenant ain't coming out tonight," California said.

"Yeah, him and that fucking New Platoon Sergeant," Singer said.

After that the three of them lay there in silence in a tight circle, isolated by the darkness despite their physical contact. There was no need for a guard rotation. With enemy patrols in the area, none of them would sleep. Singer could feel the quiet tension radiating from each of them. The minutes were dragged out by the darkness and the dire possibilities the night still held. Singer felt alone in his wait for the enemy, yet he had to worry about California and the Cherry. Despite his effort to avoid it here he was again, responsible for others.

Singer put his head down and briefly closed his eyes. Open or closed, it was hard to tell the difference. When he lifted them, he could see nothing on the trail. The Cherry's leg pushed tighter against his own. He could hear the Cherry's slightly nasal breathing. On the other side of the Cherry, California was invisible, but Singer knew he'd stay alert. He reached over and patted the dead Cherry's body, then let his hand linger there a while. They were both beyond comforting anymore.

The patrol had started so long ago Singer could barely remember its beginning. If they got hit now he didn't know what their chances would be, seven men alone in the dark, three Cherries and the New Guy spread out in two positions that didn't really support each other. And a body to carry if they had to move. The firebase wasn't that far away, but on this kind of night it would take a reaction force a long time to get to them, if they even sent one. It didn't matter. Against a large enemy force, they would all be dead before help arrived. He wasn't counting on any help. He'd have to do it on his own. One dead was all he intended to allow tonight.

The flowing water gurgled softly. While he listened for the sound of footsteps that would mean the killing and the dying wasn't over, his anger festered and he plotted his revenge.

24

June–July 1968
Vietnam

The dawn sulked across the landscape in diminishing shades of gray that held no promise of sunlight. A low blanket of clouds hung menacingly across the sky, and leaves hung deathly still in the breathless air. The soft murmur of the river was the only sound. They'd made it through the predawn hours without any further enemy contact, but even with the growing light, Singer remained on edge and continued to listen and search without turning his head, as he'd practiced in the woods around home. He knew even slight movement could give away his position, which at home might mean a year without venison and here could bring death. The enemy might be waiting for dawn, thinking they'd relax or sleep. He wouldn't relax until they safely joined up with the company.

"You awake?" he asked.

"Yeah," California answered as he had each time Singer checked, which was often.

"Yeah," the Cherry said more softly.

"Stay alert," Singer said so softly that he wasn't sure they heard him.

He mentally fingered his only grenade, which he'd taken from the dead Cherry, measured the movement it would take to pull and throw it and then once more in his mind counted the magazines that remained in his ammo pouches and the bandolier that hung across his chest.

The umbrella of grayness made it impossible to measure the passage of time, but it wasn't long before the Shake and Bake came up the trail with the New Guy and the two Cherries from his position next to the river. Singer stayed at his night position with California, the surviving Cherry, and the body, watching them approach, unsure what was happening. Fatigue was evident in the slump of their shoulders and the slack position in which they carried their rifles. The Shake and Bake stopped near the dead Cherry's helmet, which still lay on the trail where it had fallen hours before. The New Guy and two Cherries stared at the helmet, then looked about uneasily.

"We're going in," the Shake and Bake said.

Singer stood up stiffly. It had been hours since he moved, and he was uncertain if he would have been able to run had he needed to. Everything looked different in the subdued daylight. The river and the mountains behind it looked almost serene. But heavy clouds set a somber mood. The acrid residue of fear hung in Singer's mouth, and his anger at another senseless loss had yet to fade.

"I thought the company was coming out."

California and the surviving Cherry stood up just behind Singer.

"We've been ordered back to the firebase," the Shake and Bake said.

"They never were coming, were they? We stayed out here for fucking nothing. The fucking Cherry Lieutenant thinks this is a fucking game."

"We're heading in," the Shake and Bake said, looking at his watch.

"Most of us, anyway," Singer said. "Are they sending an evac for the KIA?"

"Not sure they can fly today." The Shake and Bake looked up at the sky as if considering something besides the flight of helicopters. "Anyway," he said, looking back at Singer, "we've been ordered to walk in."

"We should leave him and let the Cherry Lieutenant come get him," California said. "I'm tired of carrying bodies."

"Fuck them. Their time will come," Singer said.

"It's coming," California said, and he and Singer exchanged a look.

Singer slipped the strap of his M16 over his shoulder, bent down and grabbed the dead Cherry's feet and waited for California and the other Cherry to each take an arm. The body seemed heavier this morning than last night, when he'd been wired with adrenaline. He pivoted in place so California and the Cherry could lead and carry the dead Cherry headfirst. They moved out to the trail and fell in with the others, laying the dead Cherry down on the ground while they waited to get going. The two Cherries with the Shake and Bake stared at the dead man, the first dead GI they'd seen. The New Guy looked away. Singer wished they had a body bag.

The Shake and Bake came over. "Carlson," he said. "Terry Carlson."

Singer closed his mind to it and let the name drift away in the dead air.

The Shake and Bake knelt and pulled up at the chain that held the man's dog tags, bending down to read them as if to confirm he was right. He left them hanging round the Cherry's neck, and when he stood, Singer saw a sadness in his eyes he'd seen before in the A Shau.

"Okay let's get going." The Shake and Bake looked at the two Cherries with him. "Take his legs."

"No, I got him," Singer said, moving back to stand at the dead Cherry's feet.

The two Cherries glanced at the Shake and Bake, who merely shrugged.

"Okay. You take the point, you bring up the rear," the Shake and Bake said to the two Cherries. "Take it slow, just follow the road. It's only a short ways back. Even though we're close, it's still dangerous, so be careful. Everyone, stay alert." He looked at the second Cherry. "Your job is to watch our backs, which means you spend most of your time looking behind us."

"I know, Sarge," the second Cherry said.

"Pick up the helmet," Singer said.

"I got it," the Shake and Bake said. "Move out."

The Cherry on point started out uncertainly and the others followed, with Singer, California, and the surviving Cherry carrying the body as they had before.

As they moved passed the berm, Singer stared at it and the tangle of brushtops and tree trunks just beyond it, which gave no indication of how far down it was to solid ground. He dismissed the urge to drop the body and peer down over the berm. What a fucking place for an ambush position. They'd have never set up there had they seen it before in daylight. Scenes of clinging to the slope in pitch darkness, their narrow escape back to this side of the berm, and the brief firefight flashed through his mind.

"Hold up a minute," he said, then stood there oblivious to the fact the others in front of them kept moving.

He saw the markings on the berm where they'd crawled back and forth over the top, the impressions where they'd lain, and the scattered M16 shell casings. But it was the dark stain near the top of the berm and the rivulets that ran from it to the small pool at the bottom that held his attention. He saw the Cherry's head against the berm as if bowed to say a prayer and the bullet hole in the Cherry's forehead. He felt wetness on his fingers and then Stick's chalky, ghost-like face and the wet stain beside it.

California and the Cherry who held the dead man's arms kept looking back at Singer, but he was oblivious to their stares.

"Shouldn't we be moving?" the Cherry on drag finally asked, watching the first group, who were already fifty meters away.

Singer didn't answer.

"Hey, come on. We need to get out of here," California said. "This guy's heavy."

Singer tore his gaze from the spot where the Cherry had died and looked at the voice.

"You okay?" California asked.

"Yeah, fine. Let's go."

As they moved, Singer stared straight ahead up the road to avoid looking down at the dead Cherry's face. Too many men were in line already waiting for him to avenge their deaths. He was determined not to add any more. Up ahead with the Cherry on point, the Shake and Bake and the New Guy stood waiting.

"Is there a problem?" the Shake and Bake asked when everyone had caught up.

"No problem," Singer said.

"If you need to stop or switch off, say something," the Shake and Bake said. "Let's stay together."

"Just like last night, right?"

"We had orders."

"There are orders and then there's what you need to do to survive and to protect your men. I thought you learned that by now."

Singer saw California looking back at him and figured they were both thinking of the A Shau, when Singer refused an order to pull back and leave California pinned down and on his own.

"Try to keep up." The Shake and Bake turned and motioned to the Cherry on point to get moving.

"Right," Singer said.

They trudged back along the trail to where it met the road, then turned west and followed the road for almost two klicks until they were at the foot of the hill the firebase occupied. There they turned off and climbed the spur that the convoys used for overland resupply to the firebase. The gloom hung over the morning threatening rain. Singer's arms ached, but he wouldn't give up the job of carrying the dead Cherry. Twice he had to stop to rest or regain his grip, but still he refused help. The Shake and Bake had again tried to have the two Cherries relieve Singer, but didn't force the issue, standing by patiently each time Singer stopped. Just before the gated entrance to the firebase, Singer stopped again and set the Cherry's legs in the red dust of the road. He took his rifle off his shoulder and handed it to California.

"Help me with him."

Singer bent down and grabbed the dead Cherry's shirt and right arm and pulled him up and threw the body over his shoulder, then stood, bearing up under the weight.

"What are you doing?" California asked.

But Singer was already walking toward the gate. The guards stood motionless as the seven men entered. Then they dragged the concertina wire gate shut. Men looked up. Some stood to watch the procession. A medic ran forward.

"I'll take him," the medic said.

"Get out of my way." Singer pushed past and marched across the perimeter.

California, the Shake and Bake, the New Guy still carrying the radio, and the three Cherries trailed behind.

"Where's the Cherry Lieutenant?" Singer stopped and looked around when he reached his company's area.

"Let me take him to the first aid station," the Shake and Bake said.

"Where's the Cherry Lieutenant?" Then he saw him and advanced toward him.

"Let it go," California said. "I'll find us some beer." He hurried to catch up.

At the last minute, the Cherry Lieutenant looked up and stood to face Singer. The New Platoon Sergeant stood hesitantly and backed away.

Singer marched up to the Cherry Lieutenant and laid the Cherry's body heavily, so close that the Cherry Lieutenant had to take a step back to avoid being hit by the body.

"What the fuck do you think you're doing?" the Cherry Lieutenant asked. "Take that man to the first aid station."

"He's dead. You did this," Singer said. pointing his finger in the Cherry Lieutenant's face. "This is your fault, your responsibility."

The Cherry Lieutenant's hand settled on his sidearm. "You were out there. It looks more like—"

"You killed this man, you and your stupid ambush." Singer realized his hands were empty and recalled giving his rifle to California.

"Dead are a cost of business."

"He didn't have to die except for your fucked-up orders."

"How many did you get?"

"What?"

"Did you kill any NVA?"

"Your stupidity got this man killed and might have gotten us all killed."

"Did you kill more than you lost?"

"This isn't a fucking game."

"It is. Haven't you figured that out yet?" The Cherry Lieutenant grinned, showing perfect teeth.

"The man's dead. We'll see if you're still smiling when your time comes."

"Are you threatening me?"

"Men like you never last." Singer turned away and grabbed his rifle back from California, who was just a few steps away.

"You better learn to keep your mouth shut and follow orders or you'll finish your tour in LBJ," the Cherry Lieutenant said.

Singer stopped and started to turn back, but California grabbed his shoulder.

"It ain't worth going to jail for," California said. "There's too many people watching."

Singer pushed his way through the group that had gathered and saw the New Captain with Top beside him, standing a ways off, watching the scene. Close enough to have heard everything. This time he'd done it and would surely pay for his insubordination. Maybe Top could get away with challenging officers, but Singer was in trouble.

"Let the gooks get him," California said, back at the bunker after the first beer. "He won't last long."

"If he doesn't get us killed first."

"You need another beer," California said, holding one out to Singer.

But the beers didn't dull his sense of dread or mollify his anger. Something bad was coming. Even the sun was hiding.

When Top came by in late afternoon, Singer was sure the ax was about to fall, that he was looking at an Article 15 or even worse. But Top only asked him what had happened. Singer told him all of it—the late ambush, the order to split the squad, the screwed-up terrain, the order to stay out after contact. He even told him of the earlier confrontation with the Cherry Lieutenant and New Platoon Sergeant and their issues from the A Shau and award ceremony. If Top was surprised by any of it, he didn't let on. His face remained stoic as he asked questions, nodding at the responses. But Top's eyes narrowed and lines around his eyes deepened as he listened.

"Okay," Top finally said. "Stay out of the lieutenant's way and don't go off halfcocked again."

"But I—"

"If there's a problem, see me first." Top looked back and forth between Singer and California. "Don't do anything stupid, either of you."

"Right, Top," Singer said.

California nodded, but looked to be suppressing a grin. Maybe it was just too many beers.

Top started to leave, then turned back. "Bravo Company found two bodies at your ambush site, and two fresh graves across the river."

"Thanks, Top."

After talking with Top, Singer laid low and kept quiet, waiting for what would come. He watched his back more carefully and avoided the Cherry Lieutenant and New Platoon Sergeant. But California was less cautious, openly threatening to solve the problem, especially after a few beers, when he didn't seem to care who heard him. Whether Top intervened or the New Captain reined in the Cherry Lieutenant or the Cherry Lieutenant heard loose talk and realized the danger, an uneasy truce developed.

In the days following the ambush, the Cherry Lieutenant, as well as the New Platoon Sergeant, gave Singer a wide berth. Singer was given only the usual assignments, with any orders always coming through the Shake and Bake. There was no more direct contact with Singer or talk of giving him a squad. There were no more last-minute, late-night ambushes or split-squad positions. When listening posts were assigned, they went to other squads. If anything, Singer and even the squad seemed to be catching a break. Someone or something had warned off the Cherry Lieutenant. Still, Singer felt the underlying tension and a sense that a fuse was burning.

Weeks passed without a run-in, but Singer didn't expect it to stay quiet forever. He remained on his guard.

* * * * *

Rivulets of sweat rolled down Singer's face and bare arms, and his soaked fatigues clung to his flesh. He squinted against the brightness, happy to be free of the jungle, even if only for a day. The company was patrolling southeast of the firebase across rolling grassland, with a scorching sun suspended in a cloudless sky. They were following a weak trail that drifted from one hilltop to the next, but in the open grassland, even on a trail, the danger of being ambushed was small. The openness diffused the dread and the tension Singer carried. Grasslands offered distance and a reaction time different from jungle trails, where when trouble came it was on top of you before you ever knew it was there. From his position on a high mound near the rear of their formation, he could see the men of the company snaked out ahead of him, a rare perspective the jungle never offered. He lingered for a moment, enjoying the prominence of his position and the oven-like breeze that caused the grass to sway. He turned his face upward to the sun and studied it as though seeing it for the first time. Or maybe the last and was trying to hold an image of it. Below him the line of men, laden with rucks and weapons, meandered toward the horizon, disappearing in swales and reappearing on the next hilltop looking smaller and more obscure, until it became impossible to make out the next man in the line.

On the plateau, a hundred meters below his position, he watched a man stop and study the ground before backing up a careful step and going around. The man turned and looked at the man behind him and pointed at the ground. If words were passed, Singer couldn't tell. Then the next man did the same, sidestepping the spot, hesitating, turning as he pointed, and saying something as the first man may have done. Likely every man since the point man had done the same, but Singer had been gazing at the most distant figures and then the sun. Now the scene captivated him, though he'd seen and done the same thing countless times before, carefully moving past all nature of booby traps, making sure the man who followed had it marked. The next man approaching it was obviously the platoon leader, marked by a trailing RTO just two steps behind with a handset to his ear, an antenna waving invitingly with each step. First platoon, Singer guessed, though he didn't know the men. The lieutenant stopped, his gaze held to the ground. The RTO extended the handset toward the lieutenant, but the lieutenant was already bending over, stretching a hand out toward the earth. Then they both disappeared in a cloud of smoke and dirt. Within the roar, Singer was sure he heard the bodies absorbing the explosion, an instant of muffled sound before the noise spread out from the hill across their ranks, each of them rocked by it, taking it in, impacted in some immeasurable way.

The explosion put Singer on the ground with contact-reflex to which only the newest Cherries were immune. Quickly he had his head up, peering through the grass, his rifle ready. The smoky residue of the explosion was already drifting off, dissipating in the breeze. Men were shouting and a medic, with his first-aid pack, sprinted back toward the spot where the two men had stood. From his angle above them, Singer could see the two twisted forms where they'd been tossed by the force of the blast. Neither moved or showed any signs of life. Had he not known they were men, he might not have guessed. Ten meters back another man sat, helmet off, clutching his left arm in front of him and staring at a bloody, mangled hand. Ahead of the blast, maybe six meters, a man sprawled facedown, arms spread, hands empty, his right leg pushing back and forth in a slow, repetitive movement as if with the one leg the man was trying to crawl away. Only the leg moved. The medic ran past to the two forms nearest the blast, spending only a moment before moving back to the sprawled man with the active leg, where one man already worked to remove the man's shattered ruck while another examined the unmoving leg. Someone came forward and knelt beside the man with the mangled hand.

As this went on, crouched men ran along the line, organizing a defense. Singer looked out over the grassy slopes to his left and right, watching the grass swirl, stirred by the breeze or an army crawling in it. He imagined men rising from the earth, assaulting their line, and he welcomed the prospect rather than feared it. He ached to fire. Four men were down, two certainly dead, and maybe the third man would die. He didn't know them, but still he wanted a chance. But it was only the breeze that stirred the grass. No attack came. Singer's M16 was silent, as were all their guns. There were no NVA. No one to absorb their anger. Just the explosion and four casualties.

When no attack followed the explosion, the tension flagged, leaving a residue of unspent anger. Men rose slowly and stood restlessly, waiting.

California edged up closer to Singer. "Want one?"

Singer looked at the cigarette and shook his head, then turned back to the scene below him.

"Too bad," California said, watching as the bodies were rolled into ponchos.

"Shit, he tried to pick up the fucking booby trap." The scene replayed through Singer's mind. "What the hell could he have been thinking?"

"I mean too bad it wasn't a different lieutenant."

"Yeah, too bad," Singer said.

"Some days there's just no luck." California blew out a long stream of smoke. "His time is coming, I can feel it."

A helicopter came in from the west unchallenged and the bodies of the lieutenant and RTO were loaded next to the unconscious form of the man whose leg no longer moved. The fourth man walked to the chopper clutching his heavily bandaged hand to his chest and climbed on board with the help of others. Remnants of rucks and weapons were quickly loaded, and the men hurriedly backed away. The chopper engine revved and the bird lifted off, wind buffeting men and flattening the grass, before gaining altitude and swinging back west. Singer watched the bird climb and speed away, its rotors slapping air in a haunting rhythm. The sound caused a tingle through his body, as it did each time he heard it. Desire and dread. He turned away, thankful that it had been others again and not him, though he would never express that gratitude out loud. The sound of the rotors faded and was replaced with a silence heavy with frustration and despair. Singer opened the chamber of his rifle, checked the round, then reseated the bolt and fingered the grenades that hung from his belt and web gear. Before the bird was even out of sight, a distant dot in an otherwise unmarked sky, the company started off again, continuing on as though nothing had happened. The grass stirred in the breeze as before and the sun still shone, but the day was different in some indiscernible way than only moments before. Maybe they all were.

Singer followed the trail down through a swale and up again past the shallow crater and the matted grass still wet with blood. After wiping his mouth with the back of his hand, he squeezed his rifle and squinted against the harsh brightness of the day, glancing left and then right at green slopes and adjacent hills that looked deceptively innocent. He wasn't fooled.

Five days later, without having found any NVA, helicopters picked them up from the grasslands not far from where the booby trap killed the lieutenant and RTO and dumped them out in a jungle clearing on a nameless mountain between Hue and Laos. Their insertion was unopposed. After leaving the LZ, they slipped into the jungle to begin more days of struggling up mountains in jungle dimness, searching for the NVA.

The column stopped moving, which had been the pattern during the steep, late-afternoon climb.

"Jesus, not again," Singer said.

A few meters above him, California stood silently, his mouth hanging open, sweat running down his face. California either hadn't heard him or was too tired to comment. Before, California would have always had a smart remark, but in the last month he'd grown more quiet, sullen, really. Maybe it was just a reaction to Singer's own brooding. In the weeks since the A Shau, he'd been increasingly less interested in talking to California or anyone else. What was the point? He said what was needed to do the job. That was enough.

He was tired. Shit, they were all exhausted the way they'd been pushing, moving all day with full gear. If there was any point in it, no one was letting him in on it. Sometimes Singer wished they could just dig in and wait and let the NVA come to them instead of the relentless patrolling, climbing, and struggles against the jungle vegetation. If he never saw another mountain again, he'd be happy. When he got out of here, he'd spend his days in the desert, where the sun was always shining and most of the vegetation was little higher than a person's knees. Sometimes these days he imagined he might make it. He already made it longer than he expected and outlived so many others, many better soldiers than himself. Another month and he would be halfway through his tour. Four more months and he would be nineteen. Four more months. An eternity when a few minutes under fire could be a lifetime to survive. Still, some days, the quiet ones, he allowed himself to think he just might live long enough to be nineteen. Nineteen. He felt so much older than that already.

With some effort balancing on the slope he turned to face left, bracing his feet to keep from slipping back onto the man below him, and leaned forward, shifting the weight of his ruck onto his back and giving his sore shoulders a rest. He didn't look at the man who he knew was below him, one of the Cherries who had survived the last month but still remained a faceless, nameless body beside him. He didn't need to know him to fight next to him. He knew how the Cherry reacted under fire. That was enough. Sooner rather than later, one or the other of them would be gone, either killed or wounded. More nameless Cherries in clean fatigues with oiled rifles and fresh, youthful faces would step off helicopters to replace them and start their own death lottery. What was the point?

Singer pulled the operating rod back and looked just to be sure he had a live round chambered, though he'd checked it last time they stopped not ten minutes ago. He reached back and lifted the bottom of his ruck to gain a moment of relief. The ache in his shoulders was spreading to his back. His whole body hurt, and he thought about being able to drop this weight and lie down or at least sit for a while. Maybe he could get some aspirin or Darvon from Doc when they finally dug in. A beer would be better, but here there was no hope of that. The company had been moving since dawn with full rucks, much of it uphill, the last hour the most brutal as they seemed to be going straight up as they headed for what promised to be their night camp. The canopy was thinner now on the steep slope and from the amount of diffused light, Singer guessed they had another hour of daylight left. He took a drink of warm water, swishing it in his mouth before swallowing, leaving his mouth moist but his thirst unsatisfied. A week of patrolling in full gear and they'd done nothing but wear themselves out. It had been a couple of weeks since they'd killed any NVA, and Singer was starting to wonder when he'd get a chance again.

He still dreamt of easy, limitless killing, when he would kill enough NVA to fill the hole left by the deaths of Rhymes and the others and quiet the relentless rage that ate at him. An endless line of NVA moving along a trail who would make no effort to fight or hide as he dropped their comrades beside them. It was the only hope for comfort. But any killing had come with costs, adding to his rage. The emptiness only grew, as did his self-loathing. Sometimes he saw himself sinking down into a dark underworld of evil. He felt powerless to stop it.

It was his job to make them pay. He was the only one left, the only one who remembered. He wondered if Rhymes, Doc Odum, Bear, or Trip had felt the same way during their first tours and if that had made it any easier coming back. If they had, they'd never spoke of it or given any indication. They'd seemed more motivated by survival than revenge. But who of them would admit to such things? It was difficult enough to acknowledge it even to himself.

Singer wiped his palm along his brow, trying to clear the sweat away from his eyes. But he only managed to irritate his eyes more. He bounced his ruck once more, shifting the weight without relief. His fatigues, wet with sweat, were plastered to his back. With the company stopped and strung out on the slope, he stood waiting with no promise of moving again. This far back in the column it was impossible to know what was causing the repeated holdups. It could be signs of the enemy that had the point moving cautiously or it might just be difficult stretches in the climb.

He looked upslope but was unable to determine how much farther it was to the top. Beyond California, the slope was a dark tangle of rocks and trees, formless shapes merging into blackness. Somewhere ahead of California were the Cherry Lieutenant and the New Platoon Sergeant. He wasn't sure where and didn't care, just as long as they stayed away from him. But he was happier when they were in front of him. He didn't trust their leadership and he sure didn't trust them behind him. It was hard to always have to watch his back while still worrying about what was up ahead.

A month later, he was still pissed about the late-night ambush, which he was sure the Cherry Lieutenant had ordered with the New Platoon Sergeant's urgings.

So much had changed from the early days, when he was surrounded by guys from Bragg on their second tours and confidently led by Sergeant Edwards, who would never needlessly endanger any of them. His only worry then had been the enemy, whom he really didn't understand. Few, if any of them, did. He had been innocent and naïve then, younger and less angry.

Now he was angry all the time. Angry at the deaths, the stupidity of it all, and at incompetent leaders who saw their men as pawns toward obtaining body counts and their next promotion. Angry at the things he'd done and at the knowledge that he would do more. How different might it be for the NVA? They were probably angry and frustrated, too. Sometimes it seemed like none of it mattered. They fought and died over a piece of ground only to abandon it the next day. Hadn't they just walked away from the A Shau? It made no difference which of them died. What did either's death gain? The war would go on regardless. There would always be politicians and generals to manage the wars and young men to fight them. Maybe they were all just pawns.

Christ, he was making himself crazy. He had to stop chewing on things. He switched his foot position, shifting his weight, and leaning to put the weight of his ruck on one shoulder. If they didn't start moving and get to the top soon, he was going to sit down right here. He had to sit down and get this fucking ruck off his back. He glanced upward and again tried to see where the slope might end, but the top was no more visible than it was before. God, he was tired. The days of patrolling, struggling against the terrain and vegetation that impeded every step, the need to be always alert, the nights of sleep deprivation, and the constant tension were taking a toll. Tomorrow would bring more of the same. And the day after that, and the day after that. Tired men made mistakes. Singer checked the chamber of his rifle again.

Finally, they were climbing again. Dusk was gaining on them, and they would be rushed to dig in and put out defenses once they reached the top. Singer carefully placed his foot, then pushed or pulled himself up another meter with agonizing effort, sometimes freeing a hand from his rifle to grab a tree to assist him. It was a brutal climb at the end of the day that sucked away the soldiers' last bit of strength and challenged a person's will to go on. In just a few steps, Singer was struggling for each breath again. It was as if the whole jungle was sucking away the air, threatening to suffocate him.

How much farther could it be? Above him, California slipped, thrust a leg back to stop his slide, and teetered there motionless, his final direction uncertain.

"Keep moving. It's just a few more meters to the top," a resonant voice with a command presence called from the shadows beyond California.

California dug the toes of his boots in and crawled forward, using one hand for balance before finally gaining his feet. As Singer moved up, struggling through the same stretch, he saw the man beside the trail with his RTO a few steps behind him. The New Captain was a mystery though he had been leading the company for a few weeks, showing up in the wake of the company's fight in the A Shau and Lieutenant Creely's death. No rumors swirled around him as they did with Lieutenant Creely, but then, he wasn't dating the general's daughter. A 173rd Airborne Brigade combat patch, which reminded Singer of Rhymes, was the only clue to his past. The New Captain was old, maybe twenty-eight; an old man in an army of nineteen-year-olds. Despite his age and the difficult climb, the man showed no signs of weariness. While his fatigue shirt was blotched with sweat, he stood unbent on pillar-like legs and his breath was even and unhurried. He had the build of a power linebacker and Singer could imagine him a football star in his college years. The New Captain watched the line of men crawl their way up the mountain, gazing down the slope repeatedly as if waiting to be certain the last man would make it. When Singer came up alongside the New Captain he expected the man might say something, but the New Captain watched Singer pass, unsmiling and wordless. If the New Captain recognized Singer from his run-in with the Cherry Lieutenant or the award ceremony after the A Shau, he gave no sign. Singer was both relieved and disappointed.

"You're almost there now," the New Captain said to someone behind Singer after Singer had moved by. "Keep—"

Boom!

A huge explosion above Singer drowned out the New Captain's words and had Singer on the ground, clinging to the slope. His mind raced to grasp what was happening. More rounds whistled overhead. There was no mistaking the sound.

"Incoming!" someone yelled.

Three thunderous explosions came in quick succession, and Singer could feel the earth below him shudder. He pressed himself tighter against the ground.

The New Captain was screaming, "Cease fire, you morons! Get that artillery out of my ass!"

Frantic screams for a medic came from somewhere upslope.

The earth shook with two more booming explosions, on the side slope now, that seemed to heat the air, then suck it away. Shards of metal ripped through the vegetation, shredding limbs and slamming into trunks with sickening thuds.

"We're being killed by our own artillery," someone yelled.

Singer tried to bury himself inside the earth.

"Medic! Medic!"

Ghostly screams sounding somewhere between desperation and despair rained down the slope.

"I'm on the right hill. Goddamn it, you're shelling my NDP. Cease fire, for Christ's sake!" the New Captain screamed into the handset.

Another round exploded and then the air was still. Singer held his breath and listened for the whistling of the next rounds, unable to do anything but wait and trust his fate to chance.

The New Captain shoved the handset at his RTO and ran upslope past Singer and out of sight. Singer hung there in place, waiting. No one moved. There was nowhere to go, no escape. Indistinct voices above him, some angry, drowned each other out. Then the sound of chopping, machetes hacking wood.

"Fuck," California said, "whose side are those fuckers on?"

"Were those ours?" the Cherry below Singer asked.

"One-seventy-fives out of Bastogne." Singer rolled over and sat up.

"Just another day in the Nam," California said.

"Why are they shelling us?" the Cherry asked.

"Routine H and I. Someone's fuck-up," Singer said, then looked up at California. "Maybe they figured out you were stealing their beer."

"Fuck, I only took a few cans, nothing to get so pissed about."

"You think it's over?" the Cherry asked, staying prone.

"I figure they owe us a few cases now," California said.

"It's never over," Singer said. "Never."

Singer heard the helicopters hovering, but couldn't see them. The sounds of a Cobra roared and ebbed as it circled the hill. There was no enemy fire and the birds came and left unmolested, but Singer knew the enemy was watching, biding their time. Singer scanned the ammo and grenades that hung on his body. He was waiting.

A gecko called off to Singer's left. "Fuck youuuu." Another answered from below in the valley. "Fuck youuuu. Fuck youuuu."

"Fuck you, too," Singer said.

The last of three birds was already away and it was nearly completely dark by the time Singer reached the top. The canopy was broken where the casualties were extracted and light of a nearly full moon filtered down, illuminating a small section of their NDP as if a spotlight was being shined on them. Shadows moved at the edge of the light. The Shake and Bake gave him his position with the Cherry in thick brush and trees on the edge of a gradual drop, instructing them unnecessarily to dig in. California would be one hole over with another Cherry. Rumor was that five men were killed from the group that had just gotten to the top. Had the company been a little quicker getting up the mountain, there would have been a lot more of them killed. Singer was thankful for the delays he'd earlier cursed.

Despite the difficulty of digging amidst the roots, Singer dug in deeper than usual, pushing the Cherry to dig more each time he stopped. After setting out a claymore, Singer laid out four grenades on the lip of the hole next to the claymore trigger. He checked the chamber and magazine on his M16, then sat back wearily, nearly spent, and ate a can of cold franks and beans, too tired to heat it. The Cherry ate in silence after Singer ignored his attempts at conversation. The shifting moonlight cast eerie shadows through the vegetation, creating the sense of movement. Behind him, Singer could still hear the sounds of men settling in or an ambush heading out. A muffled voice. A bolt being closed. The rustle of a pack. A soft cough. The metallic scrape of magazines. The snap of a round being seated. Singer took a drink, wiped at his teeth with his finger, and drank again before returning the canteen to his pack.

"You got first watch," Singer said. "Wake me if you hear anything or if you even think you hear anything." Singer moved his web gear next to his pack, making sure he could get at his ammo pouches easily. "Don't fall asleep. If you can't stay awake, wake me, and we'll sit up together."

"Okay," the Cherry said.

"And don't blow the claymore unless you're sure we're being attacked. We only got the one, we want to make it count."

"Got it."

"You got a shotgun round in that thing?" Singer pointed toward the Cherry's M79. "HE rounds aren't worth a shit in here."

The Cherry broke the weapon open, silently exchanged rounds, then snapped it shut again.

"Set a couple shotgun rounds out so you're ready."

The Cherry dug in his bag of rounds and set three out next to him.

Singer saw Rhymes with the expended round in his chamber and no chance to reload, dying with the odd smile on his face.

"I'm okay," the Cherry said. "I've done this before."

Singer looked up, trying not to focus on the Cherry's face, but he couldn't help but see that the man's eyes still held some life. "Right." Singer took off his watch and handed it to the Cherry. "Wake me if there's anything strange."

He bunched up his poncho liner for a pillow, pulled a bandolier of ammo close, hugged his M16, and fell asleep.

"Medic! Medic!"

Singer sat up, startled from his sleep by the calls for help. The Cherry glanced at Singer, then turned back toward the darkness that shrouded the front of their position, looking unalarmed. The screams had been vaguely familiar and Singer strained his memory while he listened, waiting for the man to call again. Minutes passed. The only sound was the soft hum of insects.

"Did you hear anything?"

"Nothing. Everything's quiet," the Cherry said, sounding bored.

Singer felt his chest for wetness, but his fingers were dry despite the real sense that he'd been shot. He struggled for each breath, not convinced he wasn't hit. The night was strangely still and dark, with none of the moonlight he remembered from before he fell asleep.

"Nothing? You sure?"

"No . . . yeah, I mean, it's been like this. Quiet."

He heard the screams for help again, but this time he knew they were in his mind. He recognized the voice. A coolness swept up his back and goosebumps rose on his arms.

25

August 1968
Vietnam

Singer knelt to examine the body. The air was already foul with the stench, and he tried to hold his breath as he looked at the man's uniform, quickly feeling the pockets, anxious to finish. He'd left the worst body for last, moving quickly through the chore of checking the others, barely noting the injuries or even that they were men. But this one was different. The man's legs were gone, his body ending mid-thigh in ragged bone and shredded flesh. Singer looked around the NVA's body now, but saw nothing of the man's legs or feet. They were simply gone. The blast from the claymore ripped them away, tore open the man's bowels, and punctured his chest and arms. Somehow only the man's face was undamaged. He had a broad nose, small dark eyes clouded in death, and thick lips that would have been attractive on a woman. The boyish face was turned to the side, as though trying to look away in the last terrible second.

His legs wobbled when he stood and he felt lightness in his head, as if he'd risen too quickly. The wreckage of bodies lay around him. Some had nearly gotten past, shot and tumbling forward, carried by their momentum, falling at the very edge of the hole he and California fought from.

He closed his eyes, bowed his head, and drew the back of his hand across his forehead. Nothing had changed when he opened them.

So much of it blurred together in the aftermath. Men charging at them with seemingly little regard for their own lives, the rapid crack of AKs, grenades exploding, machine gun fire, the whoosh of RPGs, the flashes of light, and the figures caught and frozen in the moment. And the sound of his M16 and California's beside him. Frenzied chaos. Yet he saw each target clearly, almost in slow motion, and he swung on each steadily until there were no more.

In the immediate aftermath, he was so excited and alive he had to restrain himself from cheering. He was certain he'd smiled. But as the smoke of battle drifted off and flies gathered to the carnage, he was no longer sure of where the evil lay in what had happened.

The payback that he'd wanted for so long was strewn all around him. Yet it hadn't brought any of the guys back. If anything, they seemed more distant than ever. Despite the number of enemy dead, he felt none of the satisfaction he'd expected. Instead, as he stood among the ruined forms of men, he felt a sadness nearly akin to regret. Recalling his desires and his excitement within the battle gave rise to a new feeling that couldn't be anything but shame.

He moved away, leaned over beside a large tree, and retched. He straightened up and wiped at his mouth, then looked around sheepishly, hoping no one saw or heard him. California was gone, already medevac'd along with the others. All around the perimeter they were counting and examining bodies from the previous night's attack, when the company defenses were breached and they were nearly overrun. With California medevac'd, he was left by himself to check the scene in front of their fighting hole. He wiped at his eyes and felt the first of the tears that he knew weren't for the dead around him, for California, or for any of the others.

The tears led to soft sobs that he gave up trying to restrain. He cried for all that he had done, for what he'd become, and for his belief in lies. That there was glory in killing and that you could kill without inflicting self-harm were two of the biggest lies. What had brought him to this end? How had he slipped so far from goodness?

He heard another helicopter settle into the LZ that had been cut to evacuate the dead and wounded. More senior officers coming in to survey the scene. There had been a parade of them already, walking the area with the New Captain, their photographers in tow, taking pictures of each other with captured weapons. Posing together like alumni chums after a homecoming game victory. The company's overnight fight—or maybe their unexpected survival—was big news.

None of it meant anything to Singer. Survival, yeah, that meant something. It meant everything. But the stream of officers and photographers meant nothing. They were no better than the scavengers already gathering to clean the bones of the enemy dead that would be left behind where they'd died.

California was gone, but the memory and questions remained. Last night, California had been crazy. In the early stages of the attack he had fought like a wild man, throwing grenades and firing his rifle. Laughing even. Singer was sure that he'd heard him laugh during the fighting. Then, when the company perimeter was breached and the fighting was closer behind them, he'd left.

"I've been saving these," California said, pulling out two grenades.

The battle at their position had diminished after they'd blown the claymore and never regained any of its initial fury, instead shifting left around the perimeter. Now there were explosions and gunfire behind them, clearly inside the company's defenses.

"You got this," California said.

A question or a statement?

Before Singer could seek clarification, California shoved the two grenades into his pockets and grabbed a nearly empty bandolier and, still carrying his rifle, crawled out the back of the foxhole.

"Goddamn it, stay here," Singer said.

An explosion silhouetted California, already up and running in a crouch, before Singer quickly turned back to continue firing to the front. The muzzle flash of an AK. A figure rose, started right, illuminated in a blast, and Singer fired and the figure fell. He shifted his fire without pause into the shadows.

A thunderous series of blasts and Singer buried his face as the ground shuddered with the close impacts. Artillery rounds were exploding, closing in around the hilltop. The FO must still be alive, Singer figured, or maybe it was Top. Somebody had done a hell of a job walking the artillery in to the outside edges of the perimeter. The only safe place on the hill from the exploding artillery was inside the small circle of Charlie Company's foxholes. The artillery was saving them. Singer could almost forgive those guys for the accident last month.

He lifted his face, staying low, his firing more controlled, short bursts as he worked toward the end of his ammo. Fighting inside the perimeter behind him died down to just a few scattered explosions and isolated gunfire as the last intruders were routed out. Sporadic M16 and M60 fire came from around the perimeter, mixed with only occasional AK fire. Artillery rounds slacked and shifted out from the hill, trailing off down toward the valley on what Singer knew would be likely escape routes. The NVA looked to be mostly dead or retreating. Only a few hardcore soldiers or drugged troops were still continuing the fight.

It was then, near the end, that California came crawling back, dragging more ammo and a useless left arm. He dropped the ammo that he carried, along with his rifle in his right hand, and slid awkwardly into the foxhole.

"Did you miss me?"

"You're an asshole. Don't ever leave like that again or I'll shoot you."

"I had things to do." California grinned. "Besides, I was saving your ass."

"What the hell do you mean?"

"You'll see. I brought you more ammo, didn't I?"

Singer looked at California's left arm. The forearm swung freely from a shattered elbow, the hand was pale, and the fingers slightly curled.

"You're hit."

"I can't feel a thing." California lifted his arm and his forearm dangled at ninety degrees, swinging slightly, his fingers without movement.

"I'm going home." California fired his M16. "Going home, motherfuckers."

"Damn it, sit down and let me look at it."

Singer put a field dressing clumsily on the elbow, but without a decent splint and more wrap, he was unable to stabilize the arm. Later the medic rewrapped it and California sat among the more severely wounded, waiting his turn to get out.

"See you in the world," Singer had said after he walked with California to the CP, where they were gathering the wounded.

"Yeah, the world. I'll save some for you," California said.

One man over from California, the Cherry Lieutenant lay without a shirt, his chest and stomach heavily bandaged and his eyes closed.

California looked over at him. "More fun than sex, eh, sir?"

The Cherry Lieutenant's eyes stayed closed and he remained motionless, his breathing shallow.

The New Platoon Sergeant with his handlebar mustache lay among the dead.

* * * * *

Alone now at his foxhole, Singer tried to ignore the enemy dead scattered nearby, wishing he had dragged the closest ones away from the hole and out of sight. There was no ignoring them. It was difficult to make sense of it all or understand what any of it meant, except that he was alive. Somehow he had survived again, unscathed when so many around him were dead or wounded.

Other things were troubling, as well. California's disappearance during the battle. The New Platoon Sergeant's death. The Cherry Lieutenant wounded and appearing near death. With California wounded and leaving, maybe none of it mattered. Questions hung over the events that he didn't want to ask. Things he didn't want to know.

His gaze kept returning to the bodies. So much death. He couldn't deny his hand in it or the things he felt. How could battle be so alluring and the consequences so repelling?

He waited to head out, anxious to get away from this place and to leave the dead to the jungle. Payback. It was never as he envisioned it. Just another lie or self-delusion. At the CP, there was no sign yet that they were leaving soon. Eventually they would saddle up and leave the hilltop, as if it never mattered. He doubted it would be as easy to leave the killing. It was the only time he ever felt alive.

A light drizzle started, fighting its way through the sheltering canopy. At first there were just a few dark spots on the soil and the odd drop hanging on the leaves. Then it came in torrents, filling the air, pounding the earth, washing away the blood and offal. The world blurred and colors faded. Would it wash away his guilt? Singer put his head back, closed his eyes, opened his mouth, and held out his empty hands, palms up, letting the rains drench him.

In the days that followed, Singer repeatedly touched his chest, looking at his fingers each time still expecting to see blood, certain he'd been hit. But there was nothing except the sense of the rounds' impacts and the ache of the wounds. The voice kept calling, "Medic, I'm hit, medic." Now he heard it in his waking hours as well as in his sleep. Pleadings in his own voice from some distant place within him.

Maybe he always knew whose voice he was hearing but had been afraid to admit it. He understood clearly that it was a remnant of himself, of whatever was left of him that was decent, begging to be saved.

Still his anger festered and with it came the desire for more chances, more killing, even when he knew it would bring nothing except his own death. Or maybe it was already too late and everything he was before was dead already. Maybe being dead was better than this place somewhere in between.

His headaches now were nearly constant. He started consuming aspirin that brought only intermittent relief.

"I just gave you some. What'd you do with them?" the medic asked.

"I need more."

"You shouldn't take so many. This is the last I can give you."

Singer looked at the few tablets in his hand. "It's not enough."

"That's all there is."

"Fuck," Singer said.

With the medic reluctant to supply them he started getting aspirin from anywhere he could, even sending the Cherry to the medic for some and stealing more from the aid station when they were at the firebase. But the headaches and the voice persisted, as did the sense that he was bleeding.

Relief was nowhere to be found. Through it all, they kept patrolling, searching for the enemy and another fight. Oddly, this time when they returned to the jungle, Singer didn't mind the darkness and the isolation. It was as though the light of day exposed all the harsh ugliness of war and of himself in ways he could no longer bear to see.

Still he continued to hoard grenades and reload magazines, awaiting the next firefight, promising he'd be ready. Knowing afterward he'd hate himself more than he did already.

Maybe this was why men stood up in battles and invited their own deaths.

He would have to decide soon if he was brave enough to bring an end to it and save himself.

26

September 28, 1968
Vietnam

The battle was finally over. The end came unexpectedly, without drama or any precipitating event. Something in the accumulation of things had ultimately tipped the balance, and Singer knew in that moment that everything was finished. He was going to end the killing. Military authorities would court-martial him and put him in a military prison, but still he was determined to do it.

Though he was about to dramatically change the course of his life, he felt unusually calm. In the final hours, after weeks of agony, the choice had come easy, and he moved now with the same conviction as he had in battle to the cries of the wounded, knowing he had to help. This time it was even more personal and there was no one else that could do it. He picked up his rifle but left his ruck, though he doubted he'd be coming back, and went in search of the platoon leader.

The darkness of early evening that masked the bunker line and the distant hills made what he was about to do easier. The courage he felt might be lost in the stark light of day and under the eyes of the men of the company and the others on the firebase.

In late afternoon they'd come back to the firebase for a couple days on the bunker line, after nearly three weeks in the jungle with sporadic firefights. There'd been nothing unusual about the operation or the fighting that might have changed things. While in the mountains, they'd found another jungle camp, smaller and less elaborate than in the A Shau. This time they had the air support that had been strangely absent then. The enemy offered only light resistance, quickly fleeing in the face of jet fighters and gunships, abandoning a cache of new weapons that had the men celebrating and some of the officers looking nearly giddy with the find. They chased the enemy in the mountains through the pursuing days, with brief running gun battles that never grew into anything big. There were casualties and medevacs, but far fewer than in earlier months, and none of them from friendly fire.

The New Lieutenant, who joined fourth platoon just as the operation began, relegating the Shake and Bake to platoon sergeant, was gruff and humorless but demonstrated some field and command skills, directing the men in a more competent manner than the parade of lieutenants before him. Measured in his risk-taking, fair with his assignments, and leading from up front, sharing the danger, he'd gained some acceptance by the beginning of the third week in the field. They came back to the firebase with the platoon mostly intact. It had all been much the same as all the other field operations and fighting. Yet by the time they reached the firebase, Singer knew everything had changed.

To do what he intended, Singer needed to see the New Lieutenant first. Despite the New Lieutenant's steady first days afield, Singer still wasn't sure about him or what to expect when he faced him, but there was no avoiding it.

Now was the time to do it. They wouldn't stay on the firebase for more than a few days. When they headed out again, it would be too late. Doing it in the field would complicate everything and perhaps even change the outcome.

From his pocket, Singer pulled out the gold tooth he had taken from the NVA body in the aftermath of the May fifth battle when he, Trip, and the New Guy searched the ambush site. He held it in his hand, noticing how it glinted in the moonlight as it had in the peculiar ray of light that penetrated the jungle on the day he collected it. May fifth. That was when it all started, wasn't it?

No, it was long before May fifth that he started down the path to becoming what he now knew he was, but tried so long to deny. There were things that led him to this point long before he ever killed the first man. Through weeks of basic training, he'd march to the cadence song refrain, "I want to go to Vietnam. I want to kill some Viet Cong," until he almost believed it. At the rifle range, he fired his M16 again and again at human silhouettes until the shape came to signify nothing more than a target to be struck down with dead-on shots. He ran through the bayonet course, thrusting his bayonet into life-sized dummies, screaming, "The spirit of the bayonet fighter is to kill," learning the mantra of the bayonet fighter along with the killing thrusts of the long, heavy blade. "The spirit of the bayonet fighter is to kill." He said the words with none of the enthusiasm now that he yelled them then. Now there was something sad and sinister about them.

Even years before his military training, the potential for what he had become was likely set in the games of his youth: in the wars he played out with miniature soldiers and tanks on the living room floor, hiding the tanks under the sofa, from where they made their surprise attacks; in the games of cowboys and Indians in the woods that stretched behind the house, when he wielded his plastic pistol and toy rifle with boundless enthusiasm, mowing down friends with imaginary fire; in the board games of attack and conquer he'd played with friends when they were older, gathered around the board's map, each of them leaning in, intent on victory; in the days spent stalking deer, honing his skills, celebrating his kills, savoring the status they brought him; in the . . .

All of it had served to bring him to this point. Where it actually started didn't matter. He had to stop it now before it was too late, if it wasn't already. This was where it would end.

He'd come to the war with the excitement and apprehension of a young man on the edge of discovery, full of idealism and naïvety, still believing in the glory of war. That had all been exploded in the May fifth ambush that was nothing like the imaginary games of youth. From there, the killing followed a progression he would have never believed possible. Even now, it was hard to understand how it happened. The early killings came without forethought or design in the heat of the first battles out of a desire to survive. But in the rage that followed he wished and prepared for it, waiting to even the score. When finding it still left him empty and vengeful, he sought more, even as he felt himself slipping away. The harder he tried to keep dead friends alive through the killing, the more he lost himself. It took a long time to understand this. He felt himself drowning, sinking into the depths of darkness from which it would be impossible to return once he reached a place where the light on the surface was no longer visible. It was when the power and excitement of the killing became the sole compelling force drawing him in that he knew he was near that point.

The closer he came to being completely lost, the stronger his self-awareness grew, along with his headaches and the petitioning cries that only he could hear. The person he was before was nearly dead. He had become something he couldn't bear to consider. He wasn't sure if any remnant of his former self remained, but he was certain if he didn't stop the killing now there would be no hope.

"Something wrong?"

Singer quickly closed his hand around the tooth and looked up to see the Shake and Bake, eyes dark despite the moonlight, the shine gone. "No. Fine. Everything's fine. I just need to see the lieutenant."

"What do you need?"

"I got to talk with him about something."

"I'll pass it on."

"It's personal."

"Be quick, then, and get back to your position."

"Right."

After the Shake and Bake left, Singer returned the tooth to his pocket. He looked up at the moon and a scattering of stars. How long would it be before he would stand outside and see the sky again? He found the New Lieutenant near the platoon CP.

Helmetless, a crew-cut of muddy-brown hair emphasized the New Lieutenant's blocky features. His ears showed the kind of damage seen in wrestlers. One on one, he'd be a formidable foe.

"Sir, I need to talk with you," Singer said after saluting, which he wouldn't have done in the field, but it seemed important now.

"What do you want?"

"I am done, sir." There it was. He'd said it.

"Done with what?"

"I won't do it anymore. I'm done. I won't kill anymore." Singer held out his M16 and ammo bandolier.

The New Lieutenant took a step closer, ignoring the rifle. "Singer, is it?"

"Yes, sir."

"Are you trying to be funny?"

"No, sir."

"Get back to your post right now," the New Lieutenant said. "This is a war. You are in the army. Quitting isn't an option."

Singer didn't move. "I won't do it anymore."

"How old are you, Singer?"

"Eighteen, sir."

"How long have you been here?"

"Seven months, sir, I came over with the Brigade."

"Seven months, Christ, and you want to quit now? Quitting in a war zone, do you know what will happen to you?"

"It doesn't matter, sir."

"They'll court-martial your ass and then hang you for refusing to fight. They'll lock you up and throw away the fucking key. Your life will be over. I'll see that that happens. Is that what you want?"

"I won't kill anymore, sir."

"Then you belong in jail. There's no place for you here. I don't want you in my platoon. Give me your rifle."

Singer handed over his M16.

He stood there, aware of his empty hands and of a new aloneness beyond anything he'd ever felt. For the first time in months, he was without his rifle. Could he be done with killing just like that?

"Wait here," the New Lieutenant said. "The CO will deal with you."

27

September 29, 1968
Vietnam

The Huey lifted off without urgency and climbed lazily before heading east, following the river toward Hue with its lone passenger. The door gunners sat back, holding on casually to their guns. This was a simple transport mission. They flew above any possible enemy fire.

Hot air buffeted Singer as he leaned out of the Huey and strained to look back at the firebase with its bunkers, tents, and artillery pieces. At first, he could see men moving about and sitting on bunkers guarding the perimeter. He could identify Charlie Company's positions, where he'd been yesterday until he irreversibly changed things. As the helicopter flew east, the men of Charlie Company grew smaller until they weren't visible anymore and all Singer could see was the bare, reddish-brown mountaintop that marked the base that had been a sanctuary between missions for so many months. He knew he was seeing it for the last time.

He looked out at the mountains beyond the base, deep-green summits of nearly impenetrable jungle fading into vague, dark peaks on the horizon, and considered all that had happened there and how it had changed him in so many ways, changed his very view of himself and even of humanity, and yet the mountains and jungle stood as always and armies went on fighting, men killing and dying to an uncertain end. The thin, pale strip of road came from the east and ran past the base, disappearing in the mountains, ending somewhere near the A Shau. A line of connection with where he had come from and who he had been, and where he had gone and what he had become. The May fifth ambush site along the road lay quiet and barely distinguishable from the surrounding terrain. So much had ended there, yet from the air it seemed so inconsequential.

The scenes flowed through his mind like the changing landscape that streamed by below. Details, names, and battles, lost to him after the carnage in August, when he climbed through the NVA bodies in front of his position. The pounding rotors chopped up memories, casting them throughout a torn landscape.

He slid his hand into his pocket and touched the gold tooth. Rolled it between his fingers, feeling its smoothness. In his pocket he still carried the photo, the face of the enemy he didn't have to look at to see.

Below him, the river flowed from this ground toward the sea without a hint of the blood that was spilled along its banks. But he knew it held the memory as certainly as he did.

He was like the river that ran through this land, seeping into the soil as it passed, leaving part of itself behind while it flowed on, carrying part of the earth, of this place, wherever it went. Blood and water. River and memory inseparable.

The Huey bore east carrying Singer away, leaving the mountains and jungles further behind. But even as these places faded in the distance, he could feel them tugging at him, holding him, pulling him back. Was it possible to ever really leave?

The rotors slapped the air, and he felt the fear and exhilaration of another air assault. He clutched his weapon toward him and for a moment was confused by why he was alone and where all his ammo was.

The rotor's sound was the same regardless of the mission. But the emotions they stirred varied. There had been times when the sound had brought hope, coming to whisk him away out the hands of death that clutched at his feet, pulling him down. Fear or relief, depending on direction. Like so many things. But now there was something melancholy about the music of the rotors. He was leaving so many things behind.

Courage or cowardice? The question sat there waiting for an answer he couldn't provide. He had seen the thin line between the two on the battlefield and how they could be part of the same person on the same day. Today he was unable to make such judgment about what he'd done. But it didn't seem anything like courage.

He looked at his gear piled on the floor of the Huey. His web gear was nearly empty, much lighter than what he'd carried through the months. The grenades were gone and he'd given up all but one of his forty magazines of M16 ammo. The M16 he'd surrendered had been returned to him. Unloaded, he held it on his lap. He'd promised the New Captain he'd continue to carry it, even though he never intended to use it again.

He shifted back on the seat and stared ahead without seeing where he was going, still seeing where he had been.

Things had gone okay with the New Captain. It wasn't the disaster it might have been, with the New Captain sending him away under armed guard to await court-martial. Instead, he was riding a helicopter unescorted to a rear base. It was Top who had interceded to see things went that way. Singer hadn't anticipated that, but he wasn't surprised by it either. Top was always there tirelessly trying to save them. He didn't want to think about how things would have been different if the New Lieutenant, intent on making an example of him, had gotten to the New Captain without running into Top first. He knew Top had saved him.

It was Top who came and retrieved him from where he waited at the platoon CP, mulling over the likely outcomes of his decision. Top carried Singer's M16, which he'd collected from the New Lieutenant.

"Come with me," Top said.

When they were alone in the darkness, Top stopped and turned toward Singer. "Okay, tell me what's going on."

Singer explained as best he could the transitions from the earliest battles and the things he'd been feeling, his fear that he was losing himself and becoming something he didn't like and didn't want to be, and how he'd decided he wouldn't do it anymore. Would Top understand any of it? He watched Top's face for some hint of what he might be thinking, but Top's expression gave no clue. When Singer finished he braced himself for the harsh judgments and condemnation that would follow.

"Let's go see the captain," Top said and started walking again.

Nothing else was said until they reached the company CP bunker and Top told Singer to wait outside. Again Singer stood alone in the darkness, uncertain of what would happen, not unlike the moments spent lying in the dark on ambush wondering if the enemy would come, how many, and whether he would survive. The minutes dragged by, now as then, until it seemed a half hour had passed before Top called Singer in.

Singer stepped down and pushed through a dark-out curtain to find the New Captain standing next to a long table that held banks of radios and piles of maps, a dim bulb burning overhead. A Spec 5 was talking on a radio and then laid the handset down and wrote something on the short stack of papers in front of him.

When the New Captain looked up, Singer saluted, then stood before the New Captain at attention.

"At ease," the New Captain said and led Singer over to a corner with a smaller table and crudely fashioned chairs. The New Captain sat down, pushing aside a flashlight and the papers under it.

"Sit down," the New Captain said.

Singer sat down on one of the chairs opposite the New Captain. Top, instead of leaving, as Singer expected, sat down on a chair beside Singer. The New Captain dwarfed the table and when he leaned forward and rested his thick forearms on it, Singer thought it might collapse. The New Captain's hands were in loose fists and a gold band glistened on his left hand. On his right he wore a ring similar to the one Singer had seen on Lieutenant Creely.

"Top says you are a good soldier."

Singer looked up at the New Captain's face, uncertain what to say. When Singer didn't respond, the New Captain continued.

"You've been in the field since you came over with the Brigade?"

"Yes, sir."

"You were awarded a Bronze Star for valor?"

"Yes, sir."

"But now you say you won't fight anymore."

"Yes, sir," Singer said, and went on to try to explain, as he had with Top.

The New Captain listened, at one point nodding and at another pursing his lips. When Singer finished, the New Captain was quiet for a long moment. He picked up a paper from the table and glanced at it briefly, then set it aside before he spoke again.

"I want to make sure I understand correctly that this is a private thing, based on your personal convictions."

"Yes, sir, that's correct," Singer said.

"There's no group that's been discussing these things?"

"No, sir."

"This is not about religion, then?"

"No, sir."

"You are alone in this and you came to this decision by yourself?"

"I haven't talked about this with anyone until I went to see the lieutenant tonight." Singer felt sweat roll down his arms and wetness on his face, but kept his hands still.

The New Captain glanced over at Top and some unspoken thought seemed to pass between them. The New Captain's shoulders dropped and some tension he'd been holding appeared to seep away.

"How old are you?" the New Captain asked, looking back at Singer.

"Eighteen, sir."

The New Captain was quiet again. He lifted his forearms, resting his elbows on the table, and brought his hands together and began spinning the gold band as though that helped him think. Then he pushed back from the table and set his hands on his lap.

"Okay. I'm sending you to Camp Eagle, where you'll finish out your tour with the company support elements. It will show as a normal reassignment. I'm giving you back your M16. I expect you to continue to carry it so as not to draw attention to yourself. No one will know about this except me, Top, and you." The New Captain sighed and looked over at Top. "That sound okay to you?"

"Yes, sir," Top said.

"This will be best for the unit and give this man the chance you say he deserves."

"It's a good plan, sir," Top said.

The New Captain turned back to Singer and leaned forward across the small table. His face tightened and his eyes narrowed. Singer felt the heat of the New Captain's glare and struggled not to look away.

"You'll carry your M16 and keep these things to yourself, including what we've discussed here tonight," the New Captain said. "I don't want any reports of a problem."

Singer nodded to fill the silence the New Captain left hanging uncomfortably in the air.

"Top has said good things about you and I don't expect any problems. But I want you to understand if I have even the smallest problem there will be different and far more serious consequences. Is that understood, Specialist Miller?"

"Yes, sir. Thank you, sir." Singer pushed the word out across his dry tongue.

"Don't thank me, thank Top. He's the one who convinced me this was the best way to handle this. He even said we owed you this. I don't think we owe you, but I understand you have fought with distinction, and I think this is fair."

That was it. The New Captain stood and Singer saluted and then was outside the bunker facing a different world.

Top met Singer at the helipad at first light and stood with him until the bird throttled up.

"Thanks, Top."

"I never met anyone like you, fighting as you did . . ." Top shook his head. "I don't understand you, Singer."

"I'm not sure I really understand, either." Singer saluted. "Airborne."

Top snapped his heels together and brought his hand up smartly. "All the way."

Then they both smiled and Top reached out his hand. Singer took it and felt Top's strong fingers close around his, and he wished Top was coming, too. He was on the chopper, looking down at Top for the last time. Top held out his fist in a thumbs-up gesture and Singer returned it, watching Top standing there getting smaller, looking like a lone figure on a mountaintop, a statue to some gallant, historic figure. He couldn't help wondering if Top would make it. But he knew he would never know.

Glossary

175s–Artillery, the number referring to the gun's caliber in millimeters.

Airborne–Parachute-qualified soldiers and units. Part of the salute between paratroopers.

AIT–Advanced individual training.

AO–Area of operation.

APC–Armored personnel carrier.

Article 15–Non-judicial military punishment.

ARVN–Army of the Republic of Vietnam, soldiers of South Vietnam.

Bandolier–Ammunition belt usually slung over a shoulder.

Bird–A general reference to a plane or helicopter.

Cav–Reference to the 1st Cavalry Division, an airmobile unit that made extensive use of helicopters for troop deployments.

Charlie–A general term for the enemy.

Cherry–A new guy with no combat experience.

Chopper–A general reference for helicopters.

Claymore–An anti-personnel mine, command-detonated and directional.

CO–Commanding officer.

Cobra–An AH-1 helicopter gunship with rockets and miniguns.

Cold LZ–Landing zone without enemy opposition.

Concertina–Coiled barbed wire used to ring firebases.

CP–Command post.

Cs, C-rations–Canned rations issued to field troops in Vietnam.

DEROS–Date eligible for return from overseas.

Dink–A derogatory term for the enemy, sometimes applied to native people.

Doc–Term for army medics.

Duce-and-a-half–A two-and-a-half-ton class army cargo truck.

Dustoff–Medical evacuation helicopter.

ETS–Expiration term of service, the date a soldier is discharged from active duty.

Firebase, FB–A semi-permanent position with bunkers, wire, and artillery support.

FO–Forward observer, an artillery officer who patrolled with field units to call in artillery.

Gook-A derogatory term for the enemy, sometimes applied to native people.

Grunt-An infantryman.

H and I-Harassment and interdiction artillery fire.

Huey-UH-1 helicopter used to shuttle troops, evacuate wounded, and bring in supplies.

JAG-Judge advocate general.

KIA-Killed in action.

Klicks-Kilometers, approximately 1.7 miles.

LAWs-Light anti-tank weapon

LBJ-Long Bien Jail, a U.S. military prison in Vietnam.

Leg-Derisive term for non-paratroopers.

LRRP-Long-range reconnaissance patrols that carried freeze-dried rations.

LZ-Landing zone.

M60-A belt-fed machine gun weighing twenty-three pounds, using 7.62 millimeter ammo in 100-round belts.

MACV-Military Assistance Command Vietnam.

NCO-Non-commissioned officer, sergeants of any rank.

NDP-Night defensive position.

NVA-North Vietnamese Army; soldiers with the North were called NVA.

OCS-Officer candidate school.

Pogue-Derogatory term for rear-area or noncombat troops.

Point-First man on a patrol.

Poncho liner-Light-weight nylon, camouflaged blanket used for shade or warmth.

PRC25-Portable radio for two-way communications, called the "prick 25."

Quad-50-Four fifty-caliber machine guns mounted together.

R and R-Rest and relaxation.

REMF-Derogatory term for rear-area or noncombat troops.

RPG-Rocket-propelled grenade.

RTO-Radio telephone operator, man who carried the PRC25 communications radio on patrols.

Rucksack, ruck-Military frame pack.

Shake and Bake-A person awarded NCO rank from a school rather than field time.

Short–To have little time left in a one-year tour of duty.

Short-timer–A person with little time left in their Vietnam tour.

Slack, slackman–The second man in a patrol, walking behind the point man.

Specialist Fourth Class–Military rank E4/SP4 awarded after Private First Class, one rank below an E5 sergeant, equivalent in pay grade to a corporal.

Top–A First Sergeant, the highest-ranking NCO in company-sized units.

VC–Viet Cong, fighters in the South aligned with the North.

WIA–Wounded in action.

Web gear–Belt and shoulder harness that supported ammo, canteen, and first aid pouches.

XO–Executive officer, the officer in charge of a unit's administrative responsibilities.

Acknowledgements

In 2003, I moved back to Hue, Vietnam, to be closer to my past and to the guys who didn't make it. There I began writing down the first words that would become *Perfume River Nights*. It took more than twelve years before it was completed and would become a book. But the story is one I've carried since I was an infantryman in Vietnam in 1968.

Like with any project that takes years to complete, many people helped me to various degrees with the telling of *Perfume River Nights*. Some of them unknowingly. Unfortunately, I can only acknowledge a few of them here.

Most prominently, I want to recognize the soldiers who fought in Vietnam. Their unheralded courage and struggles to protect each other and prove themselves in the most difficult of circumstances, which cost so many their lives, gave me the idea for this story.

Additionally, I extend my deepest thanks to:

Corinne Dwyer, Anne Rasset, and Curtis Weinrich of North Star Press, for giving this story life as a book.

Mary Logue, editor, poet, and author, for her editing that helped me refine the story. Her support and advocacy was instrumental in my perseverance and publication of the story.

My daughters, Jennie Bosl and Melissa Thiebaut, for loving and sustaining me regardless of whether the story they knew I carried would ever be a book.

Walailux Sringam, for providing me companionship and encouragement during my years of editing this story.

Dr. Ernest Boswell, for making it possible for me to be here and to write. He was a constant supporter of me and the story. Our conversations about Vietnam and his questions about *Perfume River Nights* helped me advance the story and continue the effort to tell it.

Fred Bengston; Lisa Edelbrock; Harry Larson; Ann Marie Biermaier, OSB; Mike Sweeney; and Stefanie Weisgram, OSB; who enthusiastically read and commented on the lengthy manuscript. Their excitement for the story buoyed me during times of doubt.

John Buck, for composing the reading guide questions that add to the value of the book as a starting point for discussions on the difficult topics of war, ethics, courage, and violence. His excitement for the story and conversations about life were immeasurably helpful.

The Sisters of the Order of Saint Benedict affiliated with Studium, especially Studium Director Ann Marie Biermaier, OSB, and Assistant Director Theresa Schumacher, OSB, for providing me a place to live and write upon my return from Asia. The sisters' kindness and hospitality eased a difficult transition and provided a supportive atmosphere in which to write.

Barry Pomeroy, professor and author, whom I met by chance in Krabi, Thailand. Even though he was on vacation, he offered to meet with me to review my writing and discuss *Perfume River Nights*. His encouraging words and belief that I could do it stayed with me through the difficult years of writing and editing.

Author Judy Healy, for her interest in *Perfume River Nights* and for referring me to editor Mary Logue.

Natalie Goldberg, who unknowingly saved *Perfume River Nights* through her books *Writing Down the Bones* and *Wild Mind*, which I discovered in a small bookshop of used titles in Northeastern Thailand at a time when I was close to abandoning and discarding the manuscript.

Le Quynh Anh in Hanoi and Pham Thi Yen Nhi in Hue, for their years of friendship, support for my writing, and help with Vietnamese.

Danny Bowes, for adapting the cover photo to suit my wishes and for the English-American summits we held in Hanoi, Bangkok, and Chiang Mai that were a comfort during the troubling news of wars.

Jerry Fangel and John Hurt, Vietnam combat veterans, for helping me recall or verify a military post, piece of equipment, or procedure. Any error in this regard, though, is entirely my own.

My uncle, Dick Maley, a Korean War veteran, Don Miller and Bob Harringer, World War II veterans, for the stories, letters, and adventures they shared with me. Their company and correspondence were both a comfort and inspiration. Don's advice before I left for Vietnam to "never get up in the same place you go down" stayed with me throughout my combat tour and the intervening years.

Family members, friends, and acquaintances in the States and Asia, including the Caribou crowd, the Paramount Painting Group, and the Hue Coffee Group for offering stories, counsel, and encouragement through the years. Though far too numerous to mention, all added some valuable piece toward the completion of *Perfume River Nights*.

Reading Guide Questions and
Topics for Discussion

1) During the Vietnam War, one combat tour was the rule. But in the story, 82nd Airborne combat veterans, some with just weeks left in the army, are sent back to Vietnam. How do soldiers of Singer's fourth platoon deal with this? How did the circumstance of their return influence their actions in Vietnam?

2) At Fort Bragg, Singer is the new guy in a platoon of combat veterans. In Vietnam, Singer eventually becomes the veteran dealing with new guys, or Cherries. How and why did the relationships between combat veterans and Cherries differ in each situation?

3) During Singer's months in Vietnam, his bond with some of the men deepens to what he later refers to as love. Whom does Singer love and why? Discuss the formation and dynamics of the special relationships that form in combat as represented in the novel.

4) Early in his tour, Singer looked forward to combat, declaring, ". . . I came to fight. I mean, that is what we are here for, isn't it?" Bear replies, "This ain't your war. It sure the fuck ain't my war." Why do you think Singer holds this view? Why does Bear think it isn't his or Singer's war? Does Singer come to share Bear's viewpoint?

5) On guard duty at night on the island on the Perfume River in Hue, Trip hears movement and fires his M16. The report the next morning that a body was found, but no weapon, brings a reprimand from Sergeant Milner. Shooter, however, congratulates Trip and Bear uncharacteristically defends Trip, saying, ". . . this is the Nam. There are no rules." What does this scene reveal about each man? What does it say about war? Discuss the need of soldiers to make split-second decisions to shoot or not and the impacts of such decisions.

6) While filling canteens in a stream, Singer encounters the NVA soldier with the gold tooth but fails to kill him. Why does he let an enemy soldier escape and what are the consequences?

7) A day after the May fifth battle, Singer finds the man with the gold tooth dead in front of his fighting position in the crater. He "vows an end of mercy" before smashing the dead man's face and taking the gold tooth. Discuss the significance of this act and the meaning of the tooth to Singer. What spiritual aspects does Singer see in this encounter? How might others inside and outside the military view this act?

8) The fierce combat at the crater where Singer is nearly killed and other squad members die is a pivotal episode for Singer. Discuss the changes Singer experiences throughout his time at the crater. At some point, Singer loses his terror and fights more ferociously, finding something "primeval and sustaining . . . that felt good." Discuss this "primeval" response. How was Singer different in the months after this?

9) In the A Shau Valley battle, Singer disobeys an order to "Cease fire" and on another day to "Pull back." Weeks later on a night ambush he disobeys an order to search for bodies. Discuss why Singer disobeys these orders and whether he was justified. Were these acts of disobedience a precursor to Singer's final act? Discuss the roles and impacts of discipline and disobedience in the military. When is it important to disobey orders?

10) Singer's relationships change through his months in Vietnam. He stops wanting to know platoonmates' names and faces. He's less interested in their conversations. His interactions with NCOs and officers are more contentious. He dismisses a "Dear John" letter and even stops writing home. Discuss these changes and possible causes.

11) One of Singer's struggles is with the harm he's doing to himself and a compelling need to extract revenge, which he sees as keeping his dead friends

and himself alive. After the May fifth battle, he finds a power in his rifle and only feels alive when he's firing. But he also finds he's losing himself and doesn't know himself anymore. Discuss this struggle, how it manifests itself and whether it was ultimately resolved.

12) In the last battle scene, California seemingly abandons Singer and moves toward the interior of the perimeter. When he returns, wounded, he tells Singer he was saving him. Only after Singer finds his nemeses the New Platoon Sergeant dead and the Cherry Lieutenant dying does he suspect what California did to save him. Discuss California's acts, the reasons, and implications.

13) Near the end of the story, a sobbing Singer reflects "That there is glory in killing and that you can kill without inflicting self-harm are two of the biggest lies." How does Singer reach this conclusion? What is the truth in it?

14) Why after months of combat and an award for valor does Singer refuse to fight anymore? How would you judge Singer's actions? What do you think of how the New Lieutenant, Top, and the New Captain deal with Singer's refusal?

15) Striving for courage is one of the story's themes. How does each character view courage? Discuss the incidents of courage and instances absent of courage. Does surviving or dying in an act determine whether it was courageous or reckless? What role does the group play in creating expectations and eliciting behaviors?